THE REYKJAVIK ASSIGNMENT

ALSO BY ADAM LEBOR

The Yael Azoulay series:

The Washington Stratagem

The Geneva Option

The Istanbul Exchange (short story)

The Budapest Protocol

THE REYKJAVIK ASSIGNMENT

A YAEL AZOULAY NOVEL

ADAM LEBOR

HARPER

NEW YORK • LONDON • TORONTO • SYDNEY

HARPER

HarperCollins books may be purchased for educational, business, or sales promotional use. For information please email the Special Markets Department at SPsales@harpercollins.com.

FIRST EDITION

Designed by Lucy Albanese

Library of Congress Cataloging-in-Publication Data has been applied for.

ISBN 978-0-06-233003-1 (pbk.)

16 17 18 19 20 RRD 10 9 8 7 6 5 4 3 2 1

For Róbert and Zsuzsa Ligeti, who welcomed me

At Yael's feet he sank,
—he fell; there he lay.

THE SONG OF DEBORAH

JUDGES 5: 27

PROLOGUE

Northern Syria

He dreams of death.

The pistol's muzzle, warm and heavy against the back of his neck.

The sweet reek of cordite.

A millisecond of agony.

Oblivion.

The blindfold was ripped from his head.

Rifaat al-Bosni sat up slowly, opened his eyes, squinting against the glare of the midday sun.

A boot smashed into his ribs.

He toppled over, bolts of pain shooting down his side, fought to breathe, scrabbled in the dirt, finally righted himself.

The *khamsin* was a yellow fury. The light blinded. The wind howled. The air was thick with sand, so hot it was barely breathable, slashing at the exposed skin of his face.

His shoulders were on fire, his legs numb, his wrists bleeding from the plastic cuffs that held his hands behind his back. He had not eaten for two days, had drunk only a cup of brackish water that morning. Cold sweat, peppered with grit, sprouted across his face. He closed his eyes for a moment.

The boot pushed hard against his chest.

"Get up, *kuffar.*"

He knew that voice. Younis spoke with the flat vowels of Manchester, a city in northern England. His face and neck were wrapped in a black and white keffiyeh. Only his eyes were visible, dark and gleaming.

Al-Bosni swallowed, coughed; even the interior of his mouth was coated with sand. "I am not a kuffar. I am a believer. Just not in your God."

Younis laughed. "This is not a theology class." He kicked al-Bosni in the thigh. "Get up."

Al-Bosni struggled to his feet, then his legs collapsed. He sprawled in the dirt, daggers stabbing his thighs and calf muscles as the blood returned. He lay on his side, pulled his knees back and forth. The daggers became pins and needles.

Younis kicked him again. "What the fuck are you doing? Exercising? You have five seconds."

Al-Bosni ignored the blow and stood again, carefully. His legs wobbled but stayed upright. The wind was so strong against his back, it helped him stand. He blinked, coughed again, and looked around. A giant black banner inscribed with white Arabic script, *There is no God but Allah and Muhammad is his prophet,* flapped back and forth in the wind. The *rayah.*

Reached by a single dirt track through the arid scrubland, the settlement was spread over two sides of a narrow inlet of the Euphrates. Huts huddled together a few yards from the river's edge, but the fishermen and their families were long gone. There was no shop, not even a mosque.

Al-Bosni had been taken prisoner two weeks ago, in Aleppo. The Islamists now controlled hundreds of square miles of territory, from this hamlet with no name to the outskirts of Baghdad. Much of the border between Iraq and Syria no longer existed. A caliphate—an empire of Islam—had been declared, and its brutality was unrivaled. Scenes of torture, executions, and beheadings continuously streamed on social media. Every few days American air strikes pounded the Islamists' positions, but the leaders kept relocating to small settlements like this one. Al-Bosni had been fighting with what remained of the Free Syrian Army, of moderate Muslims and secular nationalists. Unlike many of his comrades, he was still alive. On either side of the rayah a line of severed heads stared back at him, each mounted on a pole.

A mile or so away, out on a tiny peninsula, a different flag flew: the red banner of Turkey. The Tomb of Suleyman Shah, the father of Suleyman the Magnificent, was a tiny enclave of Turkish territory deep inside what used to be Syria. A road led from the mainland to the peninsula, where the gray stone mausoleum stood in the middle of a verdant, manicured lawn surrounded by a high fence. A small barracks housed a garrison of Turkish soldiers. Amid the swirl of alliances, betrayals, and counterbetrayals, somehow the tomb and its surrounds had survived the war untouched.

Al-Bosni glanced at the water. The Euphrates was swollen by spring floods, a fast-flowing palette of brown and green. A tree branch bobbed in the current, rebounded off the muddy bank, was sucked out into the great expanse of water. What bliss it would be to dive in and be carried away by the current, to float down into Iraq, be spat out into the Persian Gulf.

A blow to his back sent him reeling. He staggered, unable to use his arms to balance. Younis's hand caught his shoulder, turned al-Bosni to the right.

Younis was famous on the Internet. He used prisoners for target practice. Ideally Shia Muslims, but those of any faith would suffice. Each time Facebook took down Younis's page, or Twitter shut down his feed, it reappeared a few hours later, the name slightly altered, with even more followers.

Younis pushed al-Bosni toward a mechanical digger that stood near the riverbank, its engine idling. A few yards away black clouds of flies buzzed around a long, deep trench. A jihadist waited by the edge, his face wrapped in a black keffiyeh, a full-sized television camera on his shoulder, filming four fighters as they readied their weapons.

Al-Bosni and Younis stopped near the digger. A long column of blindfolded men, perhaps a hundred in all, waited there, each with his hands on the shoulders of the man in front. Al-Bosni glanced into the trench. Amid the bodies there were flashes of color: white sports shoes, a green T-shirt, a blue jacket.

The first prisoner was led forward. Al-Bosni watched the elderly man shuffle along, shaking and murmuring, worry beads taut in his hands. He stood on the edge of the trench, a dark patch spreading over the crotch of his tattered beige trousers.

The firing squad took aim. The moment he had been captured al-Bosni knew he was a dead man. This, at least, would be quick.

The leader of the firing squad looked at the cameraman. He peered through the viewfinder, then glanced at the gunman and nodded. Shots echoed over the water. The old man jerked sideways, tumbled forward, still holding his worry beads.

Younis jabbed his AK-47 into al-Bosni's back. "Not yet. Schoolhouse."

He pushed al-Bosni toward a single-story building. The walls, once painted white, were now a dirty gray. The windows were covered with black cloth. Two jihadists sat outside on either side of the door, their assault rifles resting on their legs. Banana clips of ammunition were piled up on a small chair nearby. The lid of a long wooden box lay open, showing a stack of Kalashnikov assault rifles, still shiny with grease. Somewhere a generator sputtered, spewing petrol fumes.

The fighters looked at al-Bosni with curiosity. Both were Americans. Al-Bosni had heard them talking in a Florida twang.

He walked into the room. The desks and chairs had been shunted to the side. Another black rayah was draped against the back wall. Two large standing halogen lamps stood in either corner. A fighter stood behind a video camera mounted on a tripod, making tiny adjustments to the controls. Bottles of Turkish mineral water stood on a small table nearby. A long, curved scimitar lay on a chair in front of the camera.

An older man with close-cropped hair leaned against the wall, watching as he methodically ate an apple down to the core. Al-Bosni had never seen him before at the camp. He was in his midsixties, tanned and fit-looking, wearing a light brown North Face jacket and Timberland desert boots.

Al-Bosni looked at the chair, the scimitar, the cameraman.

Not like this.

He forced himself to control his fear. A plan began to form in his mind.

"Water," he pleaded.

Younis slung his weapon over his shoulder, took a bottle, twisted it open, and tipped it over al-Bosni's head.

Al-Bosni leaned back, trying to send a trickle of water into his mouth. His right foot flew up between Younis's legs. The blow was, at most, half strength. But it connected.

Younis grunted, in both pain and amazement. Al-Bosni flicked his foot forward again and swiftly kicked Younis in the groin, harder this time. Younis's face twisted and he lurched backward, his gun clattering to the floor.

Al-Bosni sprinted for the door. He would not make it out of the camp. And even if he did there was nowhere to run. But he would die on his feet, in his own clothes, not in an orange jumpsuit, sedated and dragged before a camera.

The fighters outside the entrance jumped up and spun around to block the door, their assault rifles pointing straight at al-Bosni. He stood still and closed his eyes. Water trickled down his head, along his nose.

The stream flows clear and bright in the morning sunshine. His finger rests against the trigger of the hunting rifle. His father lies next to him, his breathing steady and slow as he points across the water.

He tensed, focusing hard on the memory.

What felt like a sledgehammer hit him in the side. He flipped around, landed on his back, felt the weight of his body pressing down on his arms and cuffed wrists.

The deer raises its head. The air smells of spring. The sound of the shot thunders through the trees. The deer crumples. Pride fills his father's face.

Al-Bosni opened his eyes.

Younis stood above him, the butt of his gun raised like a hammer. He whirled the weapon around, held it against his shoulder, and aimed at Al-Bosni's head.

Al-Bosni smiled, nodded. "Do it."

Tata, I'm coming.

The visitor took a last bite of the apple, flicked the core away with his thumb, and stepped forward. He placed his hand under the barrel of Younis's gun and lifted it upward. Younis's face was a mask of fury. But he did not resist.

The visitor leaned over al-Bosni, helped him to stand, opened a bottle of water, and handed it to him. He took out a pocketknife and sliced through the plastic handcuffs. Al-

Bosni clenched and unclenched his fists, feeling the blood returning to his fingers. His right leg shook uncontrollably. Then the visitor took out a small, light blue booklet the size of a passport from his jacket pocket. He looked at al-Bosni, then down at the identification page.

"Rifaat al-Bosni. Is that your real name?" he asked, his voice curious.

Al-Bosni gulped the water too fast, coughed, violent spasms that convulsed his body. He was angry and scared, relieved and, yes, disappointed all at once. "Does it matter? Who are you?"

"I ask the questions. How did you obtain a UN *laissez-passer*?"

Al-Bosni stared at the visitor, his leg slowly stilling. The man's eyes were hypnotic: one pale blue, the other dark brown. His manner was casual but there was steel underneath.

Al-Bosni replied, "I work for the UN. I am an aid worker."

"Meaning?"

"I help people."

The visitor flicked through the pages of the laissez-passer, looking at the entry and exit stamps. "People in Kosovo, Chechnya, Afghanistan, Iraq . . ."

"I serve where I am needed."

The visitor smiled. "Rifaat al-Bosni. A Muslim with light blue eyes. An aid worker who commands soldiers in battle. Who can plan an ambush, hit a target a kilometer away."

Al-Bosni paused before he answered, drank some more

water, slowly this time. He thought for a moment before he spoke. Who was this man? He spoke mid-Atlantic English, but there was the faint hint of another accent underneath, a staccato rhythm that had not quite been eradicated.

Al-Bosni said, "Sometimes a gun is the best form of aid."

The visitor smiled. "Yes. Sometimes it is." He walked closer to al-Bosni, glancing at the photograph page of the laissez-passer and then staring at his face. He nodded, as if satisfied, and slipped the document back into his pocket. "Armin Kapitanovic, please come with me."

PART ONE

NEW YORK

1

Yael Azoulay kicked off her red wedge sandals and braced her bare feet against the grubby black PVC covering the taxi's partition, her back and shoulders pushing hard into the bench seat. Two anchors in a news studio talked on the tiny television screen mounted on the dividing wall, a ticker relaying the day's closing share prices underneath.

"Now," she said, her voice urgent.

The driver looked right, left, ahead, checked the mirror, and looked ahead again. He touched the brakes, then yanked the steering wheel hard to the left while the car was still moving. The taxi lurched down and to the side with tires screeching, barely missed a blue Honda with a startled young woman at the wheel, then righted itself and sped off in the opposite direction.

Yael dropped her legs down and turned around, steadying herself with one hand on the seat. She picked up her phone, held it against the rear windshield for several seconds as the taxi headed downtown along Riverside Drive, then dropped the handset into her purse. It was six thirty on a pleasant late April evening in Manhattan. The redbrick apartment blocks glowed in the light. A cool breeze blew in from the Hudson, gently rippling through trees that were thick and green with spring. Joggers trotted through Riverside Park, young mothers chatted, their children in strollers, sticky fingers waving.

Yael glanced at her apartment building, a cord of tension inside her. Michael the doorman was still standing under the cream and blue awning on the corner of Riverside Drive and West Eighty-First, with the bottle of wine in his hand. He had stopped waving, looking puzzled, as Yael's taxi sped off.

The black SUV with tinted windows was still a hundred yards behind her, but now it was facing the wrong way. Yael watched the car slow down and start to turn. It was almost halfway around, its thick hood poking into the other side of the road, when a white cement mixer truck appeared behind it. The truck lumbered around the SUV, determined not to give way, then, prevented from going any farther by the heavy traffic, stopped just in front of it. The SUV was now stuck in the middle of the road, triggering a cacophony of car horns.

Yael's taxi driver, a tall Sikh wearing a purple turban and a Bluetooth earpiece, smiled appreciatively at the chaos behind him, then looked at Yael in the mirror. "Where to now, lady?"

Yael thought quickly. They were heading south. She had a minute or two before the cement mixer inched forward, allowing the SUV to finish its turn. Riverside Drive ran along the western edge of northern Manhattan, parallel with the Hudson River. The taxi driver could pick up the Henry Hudson Parkway at West Seventy-Ninth to get her downtown, away from the SUV. That would be the fastest, simplest route, but she would be stuck on a six-lane freeway with limited opportunities for diversions or escape. And the SUV was faster than the taxi and would soon catch up.

Yael turned around and leaned forward as she spoke to the driver. "That was great. You did really well. Take a left at Seventy-Ninth, then turn onto Broadway. Head downtown."

He smiled at the praise. "Thank you, madame."

The driver had talked nonstop in Hindi into his Bluetooth since she had gotten in the car—until she'd handed him a fifty-dollar bill and explained what she wanted him to do when she gave the word. That had been fifty dollars well spent. But her next idea was more complicated.

She looked at the driver's nameplate, encased in Perspex on the top right-hand corner of the partition. "*Aap kahaan se hain*, where are you from, Gurdeep?"

He looked at her in surprise. "Delhi. You speak Hindi?"

"A few words," she said, switching back to English. "You have friends nearby? Other drivers?" New York taxi drivers, almost all of whom were immigrants, usually had numerous friends somewhere nearby. Manhattan was surprisingly small, at least compared to London or Paris.

The taxi driver nodded. "Sure. My cousin is a developer. He made an app so we can keep in touch." He pointed at the dashboard GPS and the half-dozen brightly lit cursors moving slowly across its screen, two bunched up together. "My brother, two blocks away on Amsterdam at Eighty-First, he also has a Ford Crown Victoria, most excellent car," he said, slapping the dashboard. "My other cousin, very nearby at West End and Seventy-Ninth. He has a Mitsubishi minivan." He shook his head and pulled a face. "Not so good. Slow."

Yael glanced at the television. The news anchors were gone, replaced by a shot of the White House. Part of her brain registered the news ticker: *Terrorist scare in downtown D.C., car-bomb found at parking lot near White House . . . President Freshwater pledges Reykjavik trip will still go ahead.* But the rest of her was totally focused on her next move. It was a gamble, but she had no choice.

"Gurdeep," she asked, her eyes on his in the mirror. "Are you a gentleman?"

He looked back at her. "Of course, madame."

Yael flicked back her auburn hair and gave him her most winning smile. "I am in trouble. I need your help."

"More U-turns?" he replied, his thin face intrigued.

Yael leaned forward. "Something like that." She explained what she wanted Gurdeep and his cousins to do.

He glanced at her in the mirror. "But that is illegal, madame. We could lose our licenses."

"You won't," said Yael. She continued talking.

Gurdeep stared at her in the mirror, assessing her and her request. He paused for a few seconds before he replied. "You can guarantee that?"

Yael nodded emphatically. "Absolutely."

Michael Ortega stared at Yael's taxi as it turned around, corrected its skid and sped off down Riverside Drive.

He walked back inside the apartment building's lobby, the wine still in his hand, concentrating fiercely on a short series of letters and numbers.

Enrico Vasquez, his shift coworker, looked at the bottle and raised his eyebrows. Vasquez was Mexican, in his late fifties, portly and taciturn. Ortega was half his age, brawny, with dark blond hair and a soft Southern California accent.

"Changed her mind, I guess," said Ortega.

A taxi pulled up by the building's entrance. An elderly lady, laden down with Bloomingdales bags, got out. Vasquez nodded at Ortega and stepped onto the pavement to help her.

Ortega stopped at the doormen's desk, put the wine down, and grabbed a pen and a sheet of note paper. He quickly scribbled "EXW 2575, black SUV, spider crack in left-side rear brake light," folded the paper, and stuffed it into the back pocket of his uniform. He glanced at the vestibule that led from the entrance into the main lobby. Vasquez was busy chatting with Mrs. Rosenberg, a wealthy widow who lived in a large apartment on her own and gave substantial tips each Christmas, as he carried her shopping toward the elevator.

Ortega grabbed the wine and walked through to the back of the lobby. There was a fridge in the doormen's locker room, where he placed the bottle. He walked back to the lobby and sat down at the long wooden desk, once again wondering at the turn-around in his fortunes. He strongly suspected that his good luck—if luck it was—was somehow linked to what he had just witnessed. The SUV certainly looked familiar. A car like that had brought him into Manhattan from LaGuardia airport. He would give Yael the wine back when she came home. He looked forward to the encounter, no matter how brief. Maybe he would tell her the license plate number as well. He knew an evasive maneuver when he saw one.

As Yael's taxi sped toward West End Avenue, a sharp snap resounded across an enormous office that overlooked K Street in Washington, DC.

Clarence Clairborne looked down at his desk. Two cracks had appeared in the phone: one across the back of the handset he had just slammed down, the other fracturing the cradle. He reached to buzz his secretary, then thought better of it. Instead he continued to watch the four New York traffic camera feeds on his outsized computer monitor.

Moron.

What was the SUV driver thinking? And why were they using this car?

Clairborne had specified at least three vehicles, all unobtrusive: well-used Fords or Chryslers in bland colors, with a team communicating by radio. But no, they tailed a highly security-conscious target in a single car that looked like it had just driven out of a rap video. Of course she had spotted it. A blind cat in a dark cellar would have spotted it. On the screen the SUV was still stationary, stuck behind the cement mixer, in the middle of its 180-degree turn.

The chairman and CEO of the Prometheus Group closed his eyes for several seconds, then picked up the Montecristo Reserva smoldering in an ashtray by his keyboard and drew deeply. He closed his eyes for a moment, relishing the fragrant smoke. Nobody made cigars like the Cubans. The fact that he was committing a criminal offense by smoking them made them taste even better. He slowly exhaled, opened his eyes, and peered at the computer screen again, willing the traffic to move.

The cement mixer had moved forward a few feet. The SUV was slowly completing the turn.

Clairborne shook his head and inhaled again on his cigar. The smoke caught in his throat and he coughed loudly. Why couldn't they organize a simple tail? A better question was, why couldn't he? He had insisted on getting involved, had specified how the operation would be run, but somehow it had all fallen apart. First they use the wrong type of vehicle, and only one of them, and then that one gets stuck in traffic. Step this way, ladies and gentlemen, to see one of the richest and most powerful men in the world get royally fucked by a cement mixer.

The black SUV slowly finished its turn, headed down Riverside Drive, and turned right onto West Eightieth. Finally, the idiot was heading in the right direction.

At least New York's Domain Awareness System was working. The DAS took feeds from thousands of police and privately owned CCTV cameras across the five boroughs and funneled them into a central channel for the New York Police Department. Manhattan's grid system of numbered horizontal streets and wide, vertical avenues made the city easy to divide into zones and therefore ideal for CCTV surveillance. Clairborne had lobbied hard for the technology, persuading city officials that in the post 9/11 world such a system was not a luxury but a necessity, one best supplied by the Prometheus Group's clients and business partners. A Caribbean cruise for the developer and his girlfriend, together with a large brown envelope thick with hundred-dollar bills, had ensured that Clairborne's computer had access to the NYPD system.

The top two sections of his screen showed the feeds from the cameras on the corner of Riverside Drive: the top right side showed the traffic flowing uptown, the left side downtown. The bottom two sections showed the nearby cross streets that ran east to west across Manhattan, from West Seventy-Sixth to West Eighty-Second. If any of his personal drivers had executed a U-turn like that of Yael's taxi driver they would soon be looking for a new job, but it had worked. Clairborne watched her taxi turn left and head up West Eightieth.

He pressed a series of buttons on his keyboard. The cameras showed West End, the next avenue to the east, then Broadway. Both were jammed with traffic. Clairborne was as intrigued as he was angry. Why was she headed into the evening commuter snarl-up? Why didn't she just take the Henry Hudson Parkway and head downtown as fast as possible? And where would she go next, uptown or downtown? Or would she cut across the Upper West Side until she reached Central Park and disappear on foot?

Clairborne put his cigar down in an outsized ceramic ashtray emblazoned with a picture of the White House, a souvenir for presidential dinner guests. The tobacco had soothed him for a few seconds, but now he felt even more agitated. Especially as he was getting involved in what should be a minor operational matter—not a good use of his time when he had one of the most powerful companies in

America to run, a barrel-load of lost contracts to win back, and more. Except nothing was minor if Yael Azoulay was involved. That much he had learned.

Clairborne's fingers moved again across the keyboard. The avenues vanished from his computer screen, replaced by the cross streets. Her taxi had moved a block, but was now stationary behind a red light on the corner of West Eightieth and West End Avenue. The SUV had caught up after the U-turn, now just three cars back. The light on West End Avenue changed to green. Clairborne could see the traffic start to pull away down the avenue, flowing right and left. The taxi could go no farther.

Clairborne rested his hand on his capacious stomach. Finally. Everything was under control. They had her.

2

Very few people had been kind to Michael Ortega in his twenty-seven years. He had grown up in a children's home in a rough part of Oakland, California, abandoned by his mother, a prostitute who had died of a heroin overdose when he was ten. He had never known his father, assumed he was one of her johns. The staff at the home had been dedicated, but overworked and underfunded, and he soon learned to look out for himself. He was quick with his fists and feet and street-smart, and also intelligent. His teachers saw his potential and encouraged him to apply for university scholarships.

Ortega had won a scholarship to UCLA to study English literature, but a week before he was due to move to Los Angeles, he changed his mind. Scared that he would be an outsider because of his childhood in an orphanage, and lack of a family, he enrolled in the Marines. After two tours in Iraq and one in Afghanistan, he came home, another recruit to the legion of militarized young men with a skill-set not especially useful for civilian life. In his case, it was static surveillance from a concealed hide and long-distance photography. Ortega had returned to Oakland, tried and failed to get work as a photographer, drifted through a series of jobs as a waiter, bouncer, and security guard at a mall. Until the arrival, about two months ago, of his mystery benefactor. His initial assignment was a little strange: he was to move to Manhattan and pretend to be homeless, instructed to live in the lower level of the Soldiers' and Sailors' Monument on the edge of Riverside Drive by the corner of West Ninetieth. All he had to do was report on Yael Azoulay when she went for her morning run, and take photographs.

After Fallujah and Kandahar, it was no hardship to sleep out in the memorial. He was protected from the weather and supplies of food arrived regularly. Sure, he felt a little creepy, but his contact had indicated that this was US government business. They needed to keep an eye on Yael because of her high-level access at the UN. He was a soldier, he told himself; he knew how to follow orders and nobody seemed to be getting hurt. He was certainly getting richer. His benefactor's identity remained unknown, but each month $5,000 was paid into a numbered bank account at Bank Bernard et Fils in Geneva. He had checked out the Swiss bank, even spoken to the manager. The account existed and was under his control, the manager had said. Ortega then ordered some of the money to be wired to his usual account at Wells Fargo. It arrived safely. It was real.

Ortega tapped the wooden desk in the lobby. So was this. The apartment block was certainly the most stylish place he had ever worked. The cream walls still had their original art deco lamps and fittings. The floor was black and gray marble. The polished brass handrails shone like gold. Brown leather sofas and enormous Persian rugs added to the comfortable feel. The pay was reasonable, the work was not stressful, and most of the tenants were pleasant and courteous. He even had accommodations—a small studio that looked out onto the courtyard. It was hot and noisy when the building's air-conditioning was running, but it was free.

But there was a price to be paid—specifically in the shape of the short, fat man with a red face who called himself Mr. Smith, who was now walking through the front door of the lobby. For the third time this week. Ortega's stomach clenched as he watched Vasquez ask the fat man if he could help. Smith pointed at Ortega. Vasquez looked at Ortega, then back at Smith.

"It's OK, Enrico," said Ortega. "Can you give me a couple of minutes? It's personal."

Vasquez frowned. The rules stipulated at least two doormen on duty at all times. "Make it quick."

The visitor did not speak, but he didn't need to. Ortega stood up and followed him out of the building. They crossed Riverside Drive and walked into the park.

Clairborne picked up the glass of bourbon that sat by his keyboard, his eyes still fixed on his computer monitor. The drink was specially blended for him by a boutique distillery he owned in Alabama. He grimaced slightly as he swallowed. They needed to adjust the mix. It was too sweet, cloying on his palate. Or maybe the third generous serving of the early evening never tasted as good as the first.

He was just about to take another sip anyway when

Yael's taxi lurched forward and ran the red light. Clairborne's grip steadily tightened on the glass. Delicate crystal from Bohemia, the oversized tumbler was part of a set gifted by a Czech arms dealer in the early 1990s. The collapse of Communism had flooded the market with Soviet weapons. The dealer had sold off a division's worth of AK-47s to a Prometheus Group subsidiary. The guns had promptly been shipped to Sierra Leone.

Yael's cab raced across West End Avenue, weaving around the traffic coming from both directions, swerved sharply, and raced up West Eightieth toward Broadway.

Clairborne watched, squeezing the glass even harder. "Fuck-a-duck," he exclaimed.

The taxi turned right onto Broadway, easily made the next light, and slid into the early evening traffic heading downtown. The SUV was still trapped a block away, behind a brown Ford station wagon and a pizza delivery van, not moving.

Clairborne heard a crack. His thumb was suddenly pressing against his index finger. He looked down for a moment, turned his palm ninety degrees. Two large curved pieces of glass sat in its center, together with a small pool of bourbon. The bottom of the tumbler had fallen onto his desk, which was now drenched with golden liquid, filling the air with a sweet alcoholic stink. Then the pain hit. He gasped as he stared at his hand. It felt as though it had been dipped in acid. He carefully moved over his desk and tipped the two glass fragments into the nearby trash can, a sticky brown mix of blood and bourbon dripping off his palm.

Clairborne grabbed a bottle of seltzer from the bar trolley with his left hand, held his right hand over the trash can. He upended the seltzer bottle, wincing as the bubbles fizzed against the wound. He stared at his palm. There were no more pieces of glass, but blood was welling up. It needed to be dressed. He glanced at the damaged phone on his desk. He picked up the handset. Silence.

He pressed the button several times. A soft hissing. The line was dead. He could shout for Samantha, his superefficient personal assistant who would immediately clean the wound, clear his desk, and remove the mess. And she would give him one of her looks, ever more frequent, that said, *You are losing it, Mr. Clairborne, and if you carry on like this, you will lose your office, your company, and everything that goes with it.* And she was right.

Instead he rummaged in his desk until he found a Band-Aid and a heavy monogrammed white cotton handkerchief. He padded his palm dry, put the Band-Aid onto the gash, wiped up the remaining bourbon with the handkerchief, picked up the base of the tumbler from his desk, and dropped it into the trash can. He sat back for a few seconds with his eyes closed, trying to ignore the searing pain in his hand.

He opened his eyes and glanced at the monitor. The black SUV was still stuck at the corner of West Eightieth and West End Avenue. Meanwhile Yael's taxi was making swift progress downtown a block east on Broadway, zipping past the Seventy-Second Street subway stop, catching one green light after another.

Clairborne slid his BlackBerry across his desk with his left hand. He put it on speaker, then punched in a series of numbers. It rang once before it was answered.

"She's on Broadway, heading downtown, just past Seventy-Second Street subway. Center lane," he snapped.

"I'm on it," a male voice said.

"You had better be," said Clairborne, and hung up.

The SUV finally turned onto Broadway. Eight lanes wide—four lanes uptown, four lanes downtown—the avenue was divided by pedestrian islands in the middle. The first lane was clogged with parked cars and trucks making deliveries to the shops and cafes. The SUV was heading downtown in the second lane. The taxi was four blocks ahead, back in the SUV's line of sight.

Then two more taxis appeared in the third lane, to the left of the SUV: A Mitsubishi minivan and, immediately behind it, a Ford Crown Victoria. Boxed in to the right by the parked traffic, the SUV signalled left, trying to nudge its way out. But the Crown Victoria kept parallel with the SUV, its bumper slightly ahead.

A space opened in front of the SUV. The Mitsubishi darted in front, forcing its way in with inches to spare. Clairborne hunched forward, slowly shaking his head. He glanced at the top right hand of the screen. Now Yael's taxi was speeding southward on the Henry Hudson Parkway, already in the mid-Fifties. The SUV was still stuck between the Mitsubishi and the Ford at West Sixty-Seventh. Broadway cut down through Manhattan diagonally as well as vertically, and the boxed-in SUV was already three avenues away from Henry Hudson Parkway, heading into the maze of midtown. There was no chance it would catch up.

He picked up his cigar. The bourbon had splashed into the ashtray and the cigar had gone out. He grabbed a heavy gold lighter and held the flame to the cigar tip; it smoldered and a thin tendril of smoke appeared. Clairborne put the cigar to his mouth and drew hard. The glowing tip sputtered, hissed, and died. He stared at it in disgust, then jammed the entire cigar into the ashtray. It bent sideways. He threw it across the room and exhaled loudly, pulling a face as he got a good whiff of the bourbon on his breath, then leaned back in his $5,000 executive chair, which had a carbon-fiber frame and an inbuilt computer that automatically adjusted to his posture. He waited for the kid leather cushions to slide into the programmed position, the arms to rise slightly.

Nothing happened. Clairborne pressed the buttons on the right arm control panel. His hand came away wet and smelling of bourbon. He pressed the buttons again. The green light faded, then went out. He reached behind and pushed the chair back away from him, but it did not move. He pushed again, as hard as he could, and there was a loud popping sound. Pain lanced his gashed palm. The chair back came loose in its holding but remained standing straight. A crimson blob was slowly forming underneath the Band-Aid. He stood up, grabbed another handkerchief from his drawer, wrapped it around his palm, gritted his teeth, and punched the chair back as hard as he could.

Clarence Clairborne was not the only person watching Yael. A couple of blocks from the UN headquarters, Eli Harrari sat back in his windowless, soundproof office, a can of Diet Coke in his right hand. Lean, gray-eyed, with a shaven head, he was a good deal calmer than Clairborne.

Like Clairborne, Harrari was breaking the law by hacking into the NYPD network, but he was unconcerned. Diplomatic immunity, and the close relations between his home country and the United States, would ensure any fuss would soon evaporate in the unlikely event that the authorities discovered what his employers were doing. He smiled and took a long drink of the Diet Coke as he glanced at Yael's taxi speeding southward on the Henry Hudson Parkway, somewhere in the mid-Thirties, heading toward Chelsea. He crushed the can and threw it in the trash, nodding approvingly. She was still the best.

3

Yael told Gurdeep to let her out by Tompkins Square Park, on the corner of Avenue A and East Eighth in the East Village. For a small green space in a gritty part of southern Manhattan, the park boasted an imposing entrance: Two rows of redbrick colonnades stood under a cream stone roof. Small enclosures of trees and shrubs, their branches dense with spring greenery, were boxed in behind black mesh fences.

She walked through the middle colonnade and down a tiled path of gray stone that opened onto manicured gardens. Step one: Let the adrenalin burn out. Step two: Center herself. Step three: Switch back to date mode. But before that, step 1a: Conduct anti-surveillance drills to check that she was clean. Following her instructions Gurdeep had taken a long and complicated route, cutting through the backstreets of Little Italy and Chinatown then up into the Lower East Side; doubling back, reversing, even driving the wrong way down a one-way street to flush out any tails. Yael had watched intently all the way but saw no sign of the black SUV; no repeat sightings of any other vehicles; no cars hanging back at a steady, regular distance; no telltale glances from other drivers before they spoke into their phones on speaker. She was confident she was clean. Nobody knew that she was coming here. But still, step 1a.

Yael continued down the path toward a large circular lawn surrounded by a low black metal railing. There the path split in two directions, each snaking around the lush grass. She stopped, hesitated for a moment as if she was lost, then opened her purse and took out a paper handkerchief. It fluttered to the ground. She dropped down to pick it up and glanced behind her, swiftly taking in the scene.

A homeless man shuffled by the washroom near the entrance, a ragged coat hanging off his thin frame, and over to his possessions bundled up in plastic bags along the fence. Three teenage boys laughed and joked as one tried to kickflip a skateboard through 360 degrees while still riding it. He almost made it, then flew off and landed on his backside, triggering hoots of derision. The boys and the homeless man had all been there when she arrived.

Satisfied with what she saw, Yael walked right until she came to a long, curved row of benches and sat down in the end seat. Her vantage point gave her a commanding view of the open area in front of the benches, the playground to her right, and the paths on either side. But still, a voice in her head—ever louder—told her that she should call Joe-Don, her bodyguard, to explain what had happened and ask him to check her apartment was secure. Someone had been following her, and someone had been directing the SUV. She ignored it. If she called Joe-Don, he would demand that she immediately head somewhere safe. And when she didn't, he would use the GPS in her mobile phone to come and find her.

Switching her phone off was not an option. Yael had promised to remain contactable twenty-four hours a day—especially after Geneva, and doubly especially after Istanbul. Just ten days ago the Turkish city had hosted the most ambitious diplomatic gathering in history. Driven in part by the rise of the Islamists, world leaders from around the globe, including Renee Freshwater, the American president, had gathered in an attempt to settle the Israel/Palestine conflict and the crises in Syria and Egypt. The summit had ended in chaos after an American diplomat at the country's UN mission had poisoned Freshwater, who had almost died. She was only saved at the last moment, after Yael persuaded the diplomat, whom she had considered a friend, to give up the antidote.

Yael had been home from Istanbul for nine days, and she sensed she was being watched. Faces glimpsed twice on the streets near her apartment; a stranger glancing at her too often; a newspaper raised on the subway when she looked up and down the car, shielding its reader: the signs were subtle, but real. And to be expected after her recent confrontation with the man who sat at the apex of America's military-industrial complex. Accusing the Prometheus Group chairman and CEO of funneling millions of dollars to a front company owned by Iran's Revolutionary Guard had consequences. Even if she presented the evidence to him personally, in private. Perhaps especially so.

Clarence Clairborne, she was sure, was somehow connected to the diplomat's attempt to kill President Freshwater. *Cui bono?*—Who benefits?—was still the best, and most important question. The death of the US president would mean the end of her policy of rapprochement with Iran, and the pressure on the Israelis to make peace with the Palestinians. It would boost the hard-liners in both Tehran and Tel Aviv and destabilize the entire Middle East. But where the Prometheus Group was concerned, chaos was good for business.

The SUV was connected to everything that happened, of that she was sure. Yael took out her phone and pulled up the video she had made in the taxi. The frame shook from the vibration of the car and the sudden acceleration, but the black vehicle was clear enough. The front license plate was visible: EXW 2575.

She closed the video and scrolled through the home screens until she came to the HomeZone app. Numerous apps existed to allow homeowners to check in on their residence while they were somewhere else. But this was a version encrypted to NSA standards. Any unauthorized movement would automatically trigger an alarm on her handset, Joe-Don's phone, and at the central control room of the United Nations Department of Safety and Security at the New York headquarters. She flicked through six CCTV feeds that filled her screen, checked the network of pressure pads inside the apartment. There were no intruders and no alert messages. However, she did not put all her faith in technology. Tiny scraps of scrunched-up brown paper, the same color as the parquet flooring, were jammed into the apartment's front door and would fall if someone opened it. The edge of each was aligned against a mark on the door frame that was only visible under ultraviolet light, so even if an intruder noticed them it would be near-impossible for him to put them back in the same place.

She shut down the phone. She was not going to call Joe-Don. She was safe here. But the SUV still worried her. Why use such a high-profile vehicle for a mobile surveillance operation? It didn't make sense. Unless whoever deployed the car *wanted* Yael to know she was under surveillance. Either way, Gurdeep and his cousins had come through, in an impressive display of coordinated driving that was well worth the extra $300: $100 for each of them.

The sun was slowly setting, the air slowly cooling. She sat back on the bench, enjoying the calm of the park. A brother and sister ran past, perhaps six or seven years old, playing tag, laughing out loud. A tall black man in jeans and a tuxedo jacket stood on the other side of the open area, blowing giant soap bubbles, Miles Davis playing on his boom box. The iridescent bubbles swelled larger and larger before floating off, carried away by the spring breeze.

Yael closed her eyes, breathed slowly through her nose. Her nervous energy slowly dissipated, only to be replaced by a different kind of jitteriness, a type she had not felt for a long time. Sami Boustani's apartment, on East Ninth, was just a few minutes' walk away. She had spent two hours getting ready, time that was *not* going to waste.

Clairborne wriggled in his seat, trying without success to get comfortable. His palm throbbed, the back of his chair rattled but would not recline. He was a big man, from his size twelve shoes to his bearlike shoulders, a remnant of his time on the University of Alabama football team. He had earned his nickname of "the Bull." But appearances could be deceptive. His booming voice, southern accent, and good ol' boy, steak-chewing, bourbon-guzzling persona were a useful cover for a keen, calculating intelligence that had caught more than one adversary by surprise.

The doors of the Pentagon, the CIA, the Treasury, the Department of Defense, every government department was open to Clairborne whenever he chose. There were just four photographs on the wall of his office, each the size of a sheet of printer paper and discreetly lit. Three showed him with former presidents of the United States. In each one he had his arm around the then leader of the free world. The fourth, mounted separately to the side, showed Clairborne shaking hands with Eugene Packard, America's most popular television evangelist.

But Prometheus was more than just another lobbying firm. It was also a private equity company, specializing in Africa, Asia, and the Middle East. It could rip open virgin rainforest, tear a new strip mine, bring down a recalcitrant government, and reap the benefits with no fear of consequences. Its new social media division could ignite revolutions to order, bringing thousands into the streets on one day to demand freedom and reform, call for a security crackdown on the next. Clients who worried about a vengeful population, or former business partners with a grudge, could rely on a division that provided corporate security and guaranteed anonymity. A seven-figure annual retainer to a New York PR company on Fifth Avenue had helped keep the firm out of both the news and business sections of the newspapers. Until now.

That girl.

They had planned for years, spent tens of millions of dollars, to save America and the free world by ridding the country of its most dangerous president in history, in the process making the Prometheus Group the most powerful corporation in the world. How could one woman, almost half his age, wreck everything?

It was a total clusterfuck. That squaw Renee Freshwater was still sitting in the White House. He had lost contracts worth hundreds of millions of dollars. The *New York Times* had somehow got hold of his e-mails with Caroline Masters, the former UN deputy secretary-general. Masters was the hinge on which everything had turned, the driving force behind the UN policy of outsourcing to Prometheus—first security, and then peacekeeping operations. But no sooner had she got her feet behind Fareed Hussein's desk than she had resigned in disgrace after the fiasco of the Istanbul Summit.

Everything had gone wrong because of Yael Azoulay. She was 230 miles away—and still fomenting chaos all around him. He couldn't organize a proper tail on her car. The chair back rattled as he shifted in his seat. The red stain around the dressing on his palm was getting bigger. He couldn't even smoke a cigar or drink his bourbon. And the visitor was coming in an hour.

The phone on his desk trilled. The number showed as *99. The last person he wanted to talk to, but he didn't have a choice. He hesitated for a moment, closed his eyes, then lifted the handset.

"M—" he started to say.

"No names," said a male voice.

"Sorry. Of course." What was he thinking? The line was secure, an encrypted satellite phone, but even the rawest recruit knew that nobody used real names while talking on a phone.

The voice was clipped and angry. "One car. And highly visible. What were you thinking?"

Clairborne bristled. "I ordered three to be deployed. With a team of drivers."

"Where were they? Starbucks?"

"I don't know. I will find out."

"Should I come to Manhattan and organize this myself?"

"I know, I'm sorry," said Clairborne. "They will be disciplined."

"Sorry does not advance our objectives." The man paused for several moments. Clairborne could hear static echoing down the line. "Still, that was a neat trick with the taxis."

"Sure. Meanwhile, what do you want me to do with her?"

"Just watch. We are inside her apartment?"

"We will be."

"When?"

Clairborne glanced at his Rolex Submariner. "In about ten minutes."

"I can be sure of that?"

"Sure as a cat can climb a tree."

The line went dead.

He pressed a button on his phone cradle, then jabbed the

adjacent one. The voices squealed for several seconds until he lifted his finger.

." . . a neat trick with the taxis," the man's voice said. And it had been, even Clairborne had to admit.

But in his words was something more than just one operative admiring another's technical skills. There was an undercurrent there, almost of admiration. Clairborne played the recording again. It was greater than admiration. It was pride.

4

Yael took out a makeup compact from her bag and flipped open the mirror. She contemplated what she saw: auburn hair loose to her shoulders, light blush, red lipstick, and moderately thick mascara that emphasized her green eyes. A cropped leather motorcycle jacket. Her new dress—black, short enough—fitted perfectly. Red shoes to stir up the mix, and to match her lipstick. It was a vampier look than she usually adopted, but why not?

This would be her third date with Sami. They had been to an exhibition at the Museum of Modern Art, and had dinner together at a Korean restaurant in midtown. He was witty and extremely intelligent company. Even his dress sense had lately improved from his habitual outfit of Gap shirt over a T-shirt and slouchy jeans. Yael suspected—no, she knew—that was partly because he was smartening himself up for her. As she had dressed up for him.

She snapped the compact closed and slipped it back into her purse. To be more accurate, this would be their second attempt at a third date. The first, a few days before the Istanbul summit, had ended in disaster. Yael had spent all day shopping, cooking dinner and tidying up her apartment. Sami was due over at 7:30 p.m. By eight o'clock he had still not turned up. Yael had switched on the television to see him on Al-Jazeera with Najwa al-Sameera, the network's UN correspondent. The two journalists were discussing a video clip of Yael, dressed as an escort, at the Millennium Hotel, a few block from the UN. Sami had got his dinner the following morning—spread all over his office. After a while her anger abated and she rationalized Sami's actions. He was a journalist, covering the UN. They were not together, had not even kissed. He had no choice but to stand her up. So Yael told herself and she forgave him, more or less. The remnants of her anger even added a little extra spice to their date tonight.

The sound of a piano followed by a long, poignant trumpet note floated over the park. The bubble man was still blowing giant, quivering creations to the sounds of Miles Davis. The sky was turning purple, the breeze picking up. Yael watched a pigeon land on a tree branch and start to coo. A second bird landed next to it, before both flew off together. She had even packed a toothbrush in her bag, just in case.

But part of her—a large part, if she was honest with herself—asked why she was pursuing this potential romance. The risk-to-reward ratio was tilted heavily toward the former. There were at least two large obstacles. The first was that she was a UN official and Sami was the UN correspondent for the *New York Times.* His job was to dig out and expose the UN's scandals and secrets. Of those, Yael knew more than most. The suspicion nagged that Sami was only interested in her for the insider information she had. She could never let her guard down about her work or colleagues—the Al-Jazeera episode had taught her that.

But there was also the personal one, which was much more difficult to avoid. Sami was a Palestinian and she was an Israeli. And not just any Israeli. One with a past linked to his—a past that would, if discovered by Sami, blow any potential romance to pieces. For good.

So why was she drawn to him? Partly because she enjoyed his company and partly because she liked a challenge. But also, perhaps, because she knew it would never work, which meant she would never become too involved and therefore never deeply hurt. But that kind of dead-end masochism was too depressing to contemplate. She would just enjoy the evening. Perhaps it would lead somewhere, perhaps not. But either way, it was better than another night sitting in her apartment on her own. And if it didn't work, well . . . she was still only thirty-six. She was determined not to become another UN widow, one of the attractive, intelligent women working at the Secretariat headquarters with nobody to go home to and nothing to spend their substantial salaries on except ever-larger wardrobes of designer clothes. How long since she had been invited to a guy's apartment for dinner in New York? She could not remember. Although someone had bought her lunch not so long ago.

"Shalom, Ms. Azoulay. Welcome to Istanbul."

She smiled. She had finally met someone who really was tall, dark, and handsome, whose black hair fell over brown eyes shining with intelligence and good humor. And who, if she knew anything about men, liked her. But Yusuf Celmiz was five thousand miles away, so she had to work with what she had.

Yael took out her phone and reread the messages. First, hers, at 6:34 p.m.:

On my way. Forgot the wine. This time let's drink it ☺

Sami's reply had come a couple of minutes later:

Great. Ice bucket or decanter? ☺

In all the excitement of evading the tail, Yael had not got around to replying. And what should she answer? She could not turn up empty-handed, especially after telling Sami that she had returned home for the bottle. Yael looked at her watch: 7:35 p.m. Sami had told her to come over at 7:30 p.m., which meant 7:45 p.m. Where could she find some wine?

Zone, a hipster bar, was just a block away, on the corner of East Seventh Street and Avenue A. Maybe she could pick up something there. Or they could lend her a bottle. Another grin flickered across her face. Just four weeks ago, she had been there dancing with Najwa al-Sameera, the UN correspondent for Al-Jazeera. Hair flying, bodies swaying in time to the music, the two women had turned every head in the room. Sami had stared at her, entranced.

Then Yael remembered who else had been sitting at the bar, watching, and her smile vanished.

Michael Ortega walked through Riverside Park with Mr. Smith, waiting for him to speak. Mr. Smith was his second contact. The first, who had called himself Cyrus Jones, had been found in a car on the Lower East Side just over three weeks ago, shot through the head. Ortega read about his death in the *New York Times.* Ortega had asked Smith about the newspaper report. Jones had committed suicide, he had been told.

Ortega's unease grew. Taking surreptitious photographs was one thing, dead men in cars quite another, and he wanted no part of that. He was no psychiatrist, but Jones had seemed one of the least likely people he knew to commit suicide. The man was totally motivated by his mission, even obsessed with Yael Azoulay. He could see why. He thought he might be becoming a little obsessed himself. She was beautiful and intelligent, but more than that, she was thoughtful and generous. One morning, when he had still been living under the memorial, he had woken to see her placing several boxes of food by his sleeping bag, together with a bottle of water. There had even been a Post-it wishing him *Bon appetit.* A job had opened up in the building after one of the doormen had died suddenly of a heart attack. Smith had told him to apply; there had been a lot of discussion at the tenants' meeting about whether they should give a job to a homeless person, but he knew Yael's argument, that he was a military veteran and deserved a second chance, had swung it.

After Jones died, Ortega had done some research in the darker reaches of the Internet. Several conspiracy websites claimed that Jones had worked for the most secret black-ops department of the US government, called the "Department of Deniable," which officially did not exist. Ortega had heard rumors about the organization while in Iraq and Afghanistan, had seen the Special Forces and their contractor friends loading blindfolded prisoners into the C-130s at Bagram airport.

But whatever the truth about the DoD, Jones had existed. And a video of him being held by Islamists in Syria still did, easily available on the Internet. Ortega had thought about transferring all his funds from Geneva to his New York bank account, taking out the cash and running as far away as possible. But he knew he would not get very far. He was in something much bigger than he was, and for now at least, there seemed no way out.

He glanced at Smith. "I won't keep this job if you keep turning up like this. I need to be on duty. Doormen work the doors."

"You won't keep anything unless you do what you are told."

"Which is?"

"First of all, to listen to me. There is going to be a power outage. The building's CCTV will go down."

"Why?"

"Because you have a job to do."

"Which is what?"

Smith stopped walking and reached inside his pocket. He took out a small black metal box and opened it.

Ortega looked down. Inside was a tiny metal globule, barely bigger than a pinhead. Six short prongs, each as thin as a hair, pointed from it. Ortega shook his head. "Her apartment is swept once a week. They'll find it."

"Not this. It's undetectable. Guaranteed."

"How do I get inside? The apartment has a new security system. It's cable-linked to the NYPD and the UN control center."

"That's why there will be a power outage."

"There's a backup power system."

Smith shrugged. "Systems fail. We will do our job. Make sure you do yours."

"And if I say no?"

Smith closed the box and turned to look at him, his tiny blue eyes glittering amid folds of red flesh. "I don't think that word is in your vocabulary anymore."

Ortega watched a young girl, nine or ten years old, whizz by on a pink Hello Kitty scooter, blond hair streaming, her laughter spilling across the park as her mother ran after her. He felt a familiar longing for the childhood he never had. "And if I go to the NYPD, say I am being blackmailed?"

Smith laughed, a rich baritone sound, revealing two rows of crooked yellow teeth. "Then the Internal Revenue Service will take an interest in transfer B789016 from Bank Bernard et Fils to account 897655 at Bay Area Bank, Oakland. And the IRS will then alert the Department of Treasury's Office of Terrorism and Financial Intelligence that they have found a possible channel for money-laundering. And you, my friend, will no longer be living on the Upper West Side."

"It takes two parties to make a money transfer. I could go public."

"With what, exactly?" asked Smith.

It was a good question. The money came from an account registered in the name of Universal Trading Ltd. Ortega had Googled the name. Universal Trading was the name of the fake company from whose offices James Bond operated. Someone had a sense of humor. "Why do you need me for this?"

"You're part of the team now. Like D'Artagnan. Welcome aboard."

"Who?"

Smith prodded Ortega in the chest. "You've seen the Four Musketeers. 'All for one, and one for all.'" He pushed harder. "Meaning: if we go down, you come with us. Are you in?"

Ortega resisted the urge to smash Smith's hand away and take him down. He had no choice. Not yet. He nodded.

"When?" asked the fat man.

Ortega looked at his watch. It was just after seven o'clock. His shift ended in two hours. That was more than enough time. "Now. As soon as I get back."

Smith nodded. "Good."

Ortega felt Smith's hand quickly slide in and out of his jacket pocket, leaving the metal box inside. Smith's pudgy fingers were surprisingly nimble. Then, as if from nowhere, he produced a silver tube barely larger than an AAA battery, and handed it to Ortega. "You'll also need this to check the door," he said, as he turned around and waddled off, rolls of fat spilling over the top of his trousers.

Ortega looked at the cylinder in his hand. It was a mini Maglite flashlight. He twisted the top. The tiny black light bulb glowed a soft purple.

Yael shivered as she pulled her jacket around her. The sky was dark gray now, shot through with crimson streaks, and the wind had turned colder, gusting through the wide open space of the park. She watched the bubble man trying to coax forward another creation. It swelled, shimmered in the wind, then popped. He tried again, with the same result. He shook his head, kneeled down, and pressed a button on his boom box. Miles Davis stopped midnote.

She wanted to look ahead to this evening, and push that night at Zone aside. But the memories were insistent, forcing their way into her consciousness.

He is sitting by the bar, calm, confident, swirling the ice cubes in his club soda. A man used to getting what he wants. And if not, to taking it by force.

"Yael, we go back such a long way. We don't have to have this discussion now. How about dinner sometime? Tomorrow? Or we could leave now. There's great Italian two blocks away."

She steps back before she speaks. "How about if you write a letter to the family of the boy at the Gaza checkpoint, explaining what happened? He would be, what, in his late twenties now?"

Three days after her dance at Zone, Yael was in Istanbul. So was Eli, with his team, this time using different methods of persuasion.

Yael looked around the park again. The sound of childish laughter carried over from the playground. A squirrel scampered up a tree to sit on a wide branch. It chirped and seemed to look straight at her, its tiny eyes like beads of polished obsidian. Eli was safely back in Tel Aviv, on sick leave. Or so she had been told. So why was her sixth sense starting to howl? Yael watched a woman in her late thirties walk across the open space. She had thin lips, shoulder-length hair dyed the color of straw, and wore a pink jacket. She was chatting on her mobile phone, her shoulders hunched forward, her brown eyes staring resolutely ahead.

Thinking about that day in Istanbul made the voice in Yael's head even more insistent. She knew she would eventually surrender and call Joe-Don. He lived on the Lower East Side, a few minutes' drive away. Maybe he could head up here in his car and park outside Sami's apartment, keep an eye on her. She took her phone from her purse. Joe-Don's number was on speed dial. Yael's finger was poised over the screen when someone sat down next to her.

5

Thirty blocks uptown at UN headquarters, Najwa al-Sameera sipped her sparkling water, thinking fast. Had the Saudi diplomat standing next to her really said that? Yes, she decided. He had.

They were standing, drinks in hand, on the giant terrace that looked out over the East River and the rose garden. Behind them was a wall of steel and glass, two stories high. A door in the middle opened into the Delegates Lounge. The sun was setting and a breeze blew in from the water, carrying the salty tang of the distant sea.

The UN headquarters in New York covered eighteen acres of prime real estate between First Avenue and the East River, from East Forty-Second Street to East Forty-Seventh Street. The centerpiece was the Secretariat Building, a thirty-eight-story modernist skyscraper with commanding views over the city and the East River. The complex also included the General Assembly building, where all 193 member states met once a year; a conference building; the Dag Hammarskjöld Library, named for the second UN secretary-general; and numerous cafés, restaurants, and bars, the most popular of which was the Delegates Lounge.

The lounge was the see-and-be-seen place in the General Assembly Building, and Najwa had suggested that they meet there. Its front windows looked out over First Avenue, but for most of the patrons the hotbed of gossip and intrigue inside the building was far more interesting than the street outside. Bakri had agreed, but once there quickly suggested that they move out onto the terrace and she had readily assented. Although the terrace was not secluded, it would be impossible to eavesdrop there without being noticed. The view was captivating. A mile upriver, the lights along the Queensboro Bridge had just been switched on, a long string of white lamps glowing against the darkening sky. Najwa watched a UN security officer in his forties step out of the lounge and amble across the terrace. He had a heavy paunch and a thick mustache. He glanced at Najwa and her companion, then returned inside.

Najwa and Bakri had been discussing the exorbitant price of rented flats within walking distance of the Secretariat Building, the relative merits of Gramercy versus Kips Bay or even the Lower East Side. Then, as they moved to the edge of the terrace, Bakri began pointedly comparing the recent death of Henrik Schneidermann, the UN secretary-general's spokesman, to that of Abbas Velavi, a high-profile Iranian dissident who had died suddenly in Manhattan a year ago. Najwa knew about the death of Velavi, and had started asking questions soon afterward for one of many half-formed stories she intended to complete if and when the daily news deluge calmed.

Najwa raised her carefully sculpted eyebrows and leaned

forward, a puzzled expression on her face. "Riyad, are you implying that . . ."

Bakri smiled and stepped back slightly as he spoke, almost as if distancing himself from his words. "The only thing I am implying, no—stating clearly—is that $5,000 a month for a small two-bedroom apartment is absurd. But more than that, surely it's time you came to Saudi Arabia," he said, his voice suddenly lively. "There is so much to report on. So many changes. A new generation is rising."

Najwa smiled demurely, her mind completely focused as she made a mental note of what Bakri had just said. However smoothly he moved the conversation on, they both knew that he had brought it up for a reason.

Henrik Schneidermann, Fareed Hussein's spokesman, had collapsed on the corner of East Fifty-Second Street, ten blocks from the UN, two weeks earlier shortly before eight o'clock in the morning. He had been on his way to meet Sami Boustani, the *New York Times* UN correspondent, for breakfast—although that was not public knowledge. Schneidermann's death had been blamed on a massive heart attack, but he was only thirty-eight and Najwa knew he had no history of heart trouble. The tragedy had faded from the news amid the revelations of privately outsourced UN security operations and the collapse of the Istanbul Summit. Yet Schneidermann's death nagged at Najwa, although she had not made the connection with that of Velavi. Now she had a "steer," as her British colleagues would say. But what would Bakri want in return? He could see that his mention of Schneidermann had registered with Najwa, as he surely intended it to. But Najwa also understood his unspoken message: That was all he would say on the topic, at least for now.

"I would love to come to Saudi, Riyad. But first your government needs to let me in to the country." Najwa was surprised at Riyad Bakri's invitation. She had been banned from the kingdom for five years after her investigation into women's rights—or the lack of them—in the country.

Bakri leaned closer, his eyes glancing at Najwa's bust showcased in her tight black cashmere turtleneck sweater, then back at her face. "Najwa, you should know that you have many friends in Saudi, friends who applaud your work."

Najwa fixed her doe-brown eyes on Bakri. He was intelligent and sophisticated and not without a certain charm. He had a master's degree from Harvard in international relations and wore a Brioni suit rather than a white dishdasha. Clean-shaven, with dark brown eyes, his black hair tinged with gray, he also had a passing resemblance to George Clooney.

"Is that so, Riyad? Then why don't I ever hear from them?"

Najwa's follow-up program, exposing the horrendous conditions endured by domestic servants in the kingdom, had seen her ban extended to life. It had also triggered a deluge of death threats from Sunni extremists on Twitter and Facebook. Some had been reposted by accounts she knew were propaganda fronts for the Saudi foreign ministry.

Bakri sipped his drink. "We are here now, are we not, meeting, talking? Things are moving. A new generation is rising. A generation who understands our country's place in the modern world. But slowly, and behind the scenes. This is Saudi Arabia." Bakri's intimation, that he was part of this new wave, was clear. "But as you know, Najwa, I am not here to represent my country's government. I am attached to the Arab League's mission, not that of Saudi Arabia."

The Arab League had been founded in Cairo in 1945, the same year as the United Nations. But Arab unity remained as elusive as ever. The "Arab Spring" had turned into a dark winter of collapsing states, wars, militias, and even more brutal regimes. A series of UN Development Programme reports explained in detail how a culture that had once led the world in science and philosophy was now mired in illiteracy, corruption, and human rights abuses, ruled by sclerotic monarchies and dictatorships that held their citizens in contempt. The Islamists' barbarity, freely available on the Internet, seemed to attract rather than repulse youthful idealists. The ever-more powerless liberal intelligentsia and secular Arabs had been abandoned by the West in favor of "strongmen" who could supposedly staunch the rising tide of Islamism—even though it was these regimes' very corruption and repression that were the greatest recruiters for the Islamists.

And who else are you working for, Mr. Bakri? she thought, but did not ask. While the Arab League was widely derided as impotent, its UN mission was a useful listening post into the rest of the Arab world, and Najwa had heard from other contacts that he was connected to the Saudi *Mukhabarat*, its feared secret police.

As if he had read her mind, Bakri frowned and smiled, almost apologetically. "Forgive me, but there is one more thing I wanted to ask you about. Something, or rather someone, I am intrigued by."

Najwa sipped her mineral water. "Who?"

His voice was still casual, but had an eager edge he could not quite disguise. "Yael Azoulay."

Yael did not need to turn her head to know who had sat next to her. As soon as he spoke—"Hello, *Motek*"—her stomach flipped over.

Only three men in her life had ever had such a powerful effect on her. Her brother, David, was dead. The second was her father. The third was now sitting too close, his thigh resting lightly against hers.

"Try again, Eli," Yael said brightly, as though they had only last seen each other that morning. She shifted away, staring ahead as she spoke. "I already told you. I'm not your sweetie anymore."

Eli Harrari leaned back and stretched his legs out before replying. "My apologies. Yael, what a pleasure to see you again. How are you?"

Fine until you arrived, she wanted to say. She turned to look at him. The bruising on Eli's face had faded in the nine days since their encounter in Istanbul, but his skin was still discolored.

The door of the van opens. There are two more men inside, both in their twenties, dark and tough looking. "Shalom, Yael," says one. "Time to come home."

Eli steps back, easing the pressure of the gun barrel a fraction. It is all she needs.

She moves forward, drops her head, slams the back of her skull into Eli's face, and throws the weight in her hand into the van.

The stun grenade explodes with a deafening roar. The two men inside pitch forward, facedown and unconscious.

The first of Isis Franklin's betrayals had been to lure Yael to Eli's parked van in Istanbul on the pretense of sharing some new information about David's death. The second had been to poison the president.

Yael replied, "*Tov me-od*. Very good. How's your nose?"

"Sore. But luckily, you didn't break it."

"Next time."

"You did burst those boys' eardrums."

Yael shrugged. "Too bad. They should learn to take no for an answer. So should you." She glanced at Eli's wrist and right hand, encased in a support bandage.

He flexed the tops of his fingers. "Getting better every day."

"It must have hurt."

"Not much. The bullet hit the pistol. A sprained wrist and bruised fingers, but no lasting damage."

Yael had escaped toward Istanbul's bazaar, but Eli had then chased her along its roof. He was just a few yards away from her when a sniper had shot the pistol out of his hand, sending him toppling down the side of the building. Such a shot at a moving target on an irregular surface demanded an extraordinary level of skill, and the identity of the gunman was still a mystery to her.

Now, as in Istanbul, Eli was sure to have company. Yael rapidly scanned the park as she spoke. At least three possible operatives had appeared: one sat ten yards away on the other side of the long curved bench, and two more idled nearby on each side of the open space. She recognized the type instantly. She had graduated from the same school. All three were male, tanned, and fit. At first glance, they appeared relaxed but Yael knew they were on high alert as they watched the open space and the paths that led to the bench.

Yael turned to face him. "What do you want, Eli?"

He spread his arms. His blue zip-up jacket opened, revealing a shoulder holster and the butt of a pistol under his left armpit. "It's a lovely evening. Manhattan in the spring. I thought we could have a chat. Go for a walk, maybe a drink at Zone. I know you like that place. Maybe a quiet dinner somewhere."

"Thanks, but I'm busy tonight."

He looked at her appraisingly. "So I see. Who's the lucky guy?"

"Nobody you know."

Eli crossed one leg over the other. "I know all sorts of people." His tone changed as he spoke. "And if I don't know them, I know all about them. Especially Palestinians with terrorist connections and prominent jobs in the media."

Yael felt the anger ripple through her as she moved away from him. "Get out of my life, Eli. And stay the fuck out. And find some guys who blend in a little better."

"Meaning?"

She pointed at Eli's backup trio one by one, her finger resting for a couple of seconds on each. "One, two, three. This is the East Village. Not the Knesset." As if on cue, two spiky-haired young women walked past arm in arm, both wearing cargo pants and tight halter tops that framed the intricate tattoos across their shoulders. Yael continued talking. "Let's stop wasting each other's time."

Eli turned and stared at her again. "Time spent with you is never wasted."

She felt his eyes roam up and down her body, taking in the swell of her breasts under her black minidress, her flat waist, and toned legs. She closed her eyes for a second, suddenly aware of her nakedness under her clothes, feeling her skin against her dress, her stockings, her black lingerie. Even as she willed it not to, something slid away inside her. Her anger started to morph into something far more dangerous. Yael swallowed and looked away. Score one point to Eli, and he knew it.

They had been recruited together, trained together, lived together for five years in a crummy flat in south Tel Aviv. They were the agency's golden couple, and she had thought she would probably marry him. Until that day on the Gaza crossing point. And still then, after what she saw, she had wanted him as much in their last hour together as in their first.

Yael asked, "Why are you following me?"

"I already told you. It's time to come home."

"I am home. I live here now. And next time, ditch the black SUV with tinted windows. This isn't an episode of *Homeland*."

Eli looked puzzled. "What are you talking about? We had your taxi on satellite. We were a good half mile behind you. In two family sedans."

She looked sideways at him. Yael always knew when Eli was lying to her. He was telling the truth.

Despite everything that had happened between them—or because of it—Eli's sensuality was still a dark magnet, drawing her in. Even now he was salvation. Self-immolation. Both.

She cased the park again. The blond woman in jeans and a pink jacket was now sitting on a bench nearby. She looked vaguely familiar, but Yael could not immediately place her. The woman was apparently absorbed in texting on her smartphone but Yael saw her eyes flick across the path to the tattooed young women who were now standing twenty yards away, still holding hands. There were plenty of tattooed lesbians in Tel Aviv. And thirty-something blonds with mobile phones.

She glanced at Eli. He was looking at the woman in the pink jacket. His finger rose to his right ear, quickly scratched it, then dropped. The woman nodded, an almost imperceptible gesture. Yael's senses, already on alert, went up a gear.

Yael asked, "How did Isis Franklin get involved with you? Why did she bring me to you, Eli?"

Eli laughed. "You turned down my dinner invitation in New York. I thought I would try again in Istanbul. But that didn't work. So here I am again. With a new proposition." His voice turned hard. "I suggest you accept it."

6

Najwa focused before answering Bakri, glad now she had stuck to mineral water and not had the glass of wine she'd wanted.

On one level, it was hardly surprising that a Saudi diplomat, whether or not he worked for the Mukhabarat, would want to know more about a high-profile Israeli UN official like Yael Azoulay. And his interest might be personal as well as professional. In Najwa's experience, once they relaxed Israelis and Arabs were usually fascinated by each other, especially when they met on safe, neutral territory. The question was, how much would Najwa share? Especially about her own suspicions, fueled by a rumor she had recently picked up from a diplomat at the Palestinian mission to the UN.

She glanced at Bakri. His body language had changed. The relaxed charm was replaced by a palpable intensity, his eyes almost eager, his posture alert. Anything she said would be instantly absorbed, processed, used to guide the next question, and filed away.

"I know what everyone else knows. She does the secret deals behind the scenes for Fareed Hussein, and presumably, the P5. I'd love to interview her, of course, but she does not talk to the press."

Bakri nodded. She sensed his dissatisfaction.

"How does an Israeli get such a sensitive position?" he asked.

"She is also an American citizen. And Israel's a UN member state. It was founded on a UN resolution to partition Palestine."

"You sound like you are defending the Zionists."

"I'm not defending anything. Just pointing out historical reality. I've reported from Israel several times. They let me into the country," she continued, her voice pointed. "Government officials talk to us. It's the only country in the Middle East where my crew and I weren't arrested."

The mating dance between UN journalists and their sources, whether officials or accredited diplomats, was complex. Both sides had an agenda. One wanted stories, the other to put certain information in the public domain, often to their personal or political benefit. Sometimes a contact clearly detailed the material they wanted to share, even providing supporting documents. Others dropped a tantalizing hint into a conversation about something else entirely, seamlessly moving on like the words had never been uttered—as Riyad Bakri had just done.

Najwa was meeting Bakri on "deep background." Nobody ever wanted to be quoted on the record, not even UN departmental spokesmen and women. Information was the UN's currency, to be spent and traded with care, sparingly and always with regard for the possible consequences. Alliances shifted, departmental empires evaporated, powerful potentates deposed, and all so quickly that it was thought best to avoid committing to anything, at least by name. There were no outright lies, for these would be swiftly discovered and the word soon spread throughout the two hundred or so journalists accredited at the U.N. that the originator was not to be believed or trusted. Journalists used three levels of attribution. Deep background, which meant the information could be used but not attributed to anybody; a UN or diplomatic "source," which usually provided sufficient cover as tens of thousands of people worked for the UN and hundreds of diplomats were accredited there; and Najwa's favorite, "a person with knowledge of the issue," which implied someone on the inside track but could also mean anyone who had read that day's edition of the *New York Times*. But both reporters and sources knew there was one rule: if a UN official or diplomat asked to meet a reporter in private, it was for a reason. The rules said that she should give him something in return for the Velavi tip.

Najwa thought for a moment.

"She's a good dancer."

Bakri raised his eyebrows. "Especially when she has such an eye-catching partner."

Najwa held his gaze. "What do you want to know, Riyad?"

Bakri moved nearer and spoke quietly. "Who is she really working for?"

A question that Najwa often asked herself. She had long wondered about Yael's history, who she was and what drove her. Yet to Najwa's surprise, she suddenly felt almost protective of Yael. Perhaps it was their dance at Zone, or the

Amnesty International reports she had read about what happened in the basements of Saudi Mukhabarat headquarters. Either way, she would not share the tip-off she had recently received from a Palestinian diplomat.

Her mobile phone trilled three times inside her purse. That sound meant an urgent text message had arrived from her editor at the main New York bureau a few blocks away on West Forty-Fifth, which oversaw her UN operation. She looked down, then up at Bakri. "Don't think me rude, but I do need to check that."

"Please, go ahead," said Bakri, as he reached for his BlackBerry and began to check his screen.

Najwa took out her iPhone and quickly read the text message on the top half of the screen. Sensing movement to her right, she quickly scanned the entrance to the Delegates Lounge. The overweight UN security officer was back, walking out onto the terrace.

Legally, the UN was a curious anomaly. The complex was physically in the United States, but the area behind the gates was international territory and so enjoyed the same diplomatic privileges as embassies. The NYPD, FBI, and other agencies handled security around the site, but once past the gates, they had no jurisdiction. Instead, the UN relied on its own security service. However, the UN Department of Safety and Security had no authority to detain anyone suspected of breaking the law on UN territory. Crime was rare, but if one was committed, the UNDSS could only lock up the perpetrator until the NYPD took over and they entered the American judicial system.

Najwa watched the security officer stroll back and forth

for a minute or so. Was he watching her and Bakri in particular, or just checking in general? Najwa was friendly with many of the security staff, who often shared gossip or had useful inside information, but she had never seen this man before. She stared hard at him, memorizing his features: middle-aged, dark-complexioned, mustache, stomach flowing over his belt. The security officer saw her, looked away, and returned back inside the lounge.

Bakri sensed her distraction, but had not noticed the security officer. "What is it?"

Najwa thought quickly. Was she being paranoid? The whole UN building had been on a heightened security alert for at least a month after the capture of several UN aid workers by Islamists in Syria. The extra checks, bag searches, and body scans were an irritant but, she assumed, a necessary one. She was about to ask Bakri what he thought, but then decided that would sound ridiculous. Still, there was something about this security officer that made her uneasy. She frowned slightly, then slipped the phone back inside her bag.

"Bad news?" asked Bakri. "Do you have to rush off?"

Najwa shook her head. "No, not quite yet." She paused for a moment, watching a police launch bounce along the water, then made her decision. The information would be public in a few minutes and this was too good an opportunity to miss. "There's been a claim of responsibility for the DC car bomb."

"Who?" asked Bakri.

Najwa handed him her iPhone, watching him intently as he peered at the screen.

"*Jaesh al-Arbaeen.* The Army of Forty. Who are they? I

have never heard of them." Bakri's puzzlement seemed genuine, as he handed Najwa her phone back.

Najwa smiled. "Thanks for the drink. Neither have I. Which is why I have to go back to work."

Yael sat back on the park bench, watched a magpie jump across the open space. The park was deserted now, the temperature dropping rapidly. She checked her watch. It was seven fifty. She was late and getting later. Even if she stood up now and walked off she would not be at Sami's apartment for another ten minutes. She had no interest in Eli's latest proposition, whatever it was. But she was very interested in the connection between Isis Franklin and the Israelis. Sami would have to wait, which was anyway a kind of poetic justice. And if she walked fast enough, maybe she could be there in five minutes.

Yael thought quickly. She assumed that Isis had done some kind of trade with Eli, helping him to capture her in exchange for something. But what could Eli offer Isis? What was their shared interest? And then she understood. The attack ads, the op-eds accusing President Freshwater of abandoning Israel, the Twitter storms, the whispering campaigns, the Capitol Hill filibusters, the high-profile resignations of senior staffers—none of it had worked. The president's message to Jerusalem remained unaltered: Stop building settlements, withdraw from the West Bank, and reach a peace agreement with the Palestinians and the wider Arab world, or US aid would be cut in half. Jerusalem wanted Freshwater out of office and, it seemed, at any price. Isis wanted Freshwater dead in revenge for authorizing indiscriminate drone strikes, one of which had killed the little boy she was about to adopt—a death that had undone her. Tormented with grief, Isis would betray Yael and do Jerusalem's dirty work.

Yael said, "Why Isis Franklin?"

Eli shrugged. "You know the rules. Plausible deniability. She wasn't an Israeli. She wasn't Jewish. She had never even been to Israel."

"What was in it for her?"

"A new life, a new name, and a baby to adopt. More, if she wanted. All she had to do was walk away. We could have got her out of Istanbul. But she went crazy, demanding that the White House release the black files on all the drone strikes."

"Why didn't you finish the job? When Freshwater was in the hospital? Send someone in disguised as a doctor? What happened to your friends in *Kidon*?"

Hebrew for spear, Kidon was the agency's secretive elite division, tasked with eliminating the most dangerous enemies of the State of Israel. Kidon operated as an autonomous unit with Mossad, and the very mention invoked fear across the Middle East. Kidon's members ventured deep into enemy territory to place bombs in terrorists' mobile phones or the headrests of their car seats; shot Syrian generals lazing on their beachside terraces from tiny boats a mile out to sea; stuck miniature mines on the side of cars carrying Iranian nuclear scientists before vanishing into the Tehran traffic on motorbikes.

Eli turned to Yael and placed his finger on her lips. "*Mo* . . . Yael, sshhhh. We don't say that word. Especially in public places."

She opened her mouth wider. The tip of her tongue flicked against the tip of his finger. He slid his finger farther inside her mouth and closed his eyes for a second. Yael bit down, feeling bone under the soft skin.

Eli gasped in pain and yanked his hand away. In a single, swift move, he reached inside his jacket, took out a Beretta .22, and jammed the muzzle into Yael's right side, his hand still covered by the blue fabric.

She looked around the park. Eli's team had all moved nearer. A male operative stood on both ends of the long, curved bench, the third positioned in front, ten yards or so away. The two tattooed women sat on the opposite side of the open space. The middle-aged woman in the pink jacket was still walking around with her phone clamped to her ear.

Yael laughed. "Put it away, Eli. You aren't going to shoot me."

"How do you know?"

Yael dropped her hand onto his thigh. "Because you can't. And because I'm no use to you dead." She leaned closer. She had an instinctive sixth sense that told her what other people were thinking, feeling, hoping, fearing. She knew every microsign indicating whether someone was lying or telling the truth: the subtle alterations in their breathing, the pitch of their voice, their pulse. When they were lying or dissimulating, everyone had a tell. Eli had been trained to cover his, of course. But she knew him better than anyone else, and under pressure he still looked his interlocutor in the eye for a fraction of a second too long, as if to prove he had nothing to hide. It was time to take control of this conversation. To use what she had now understood.

The three male operatives started walking quickly toward the bench. Eli held his left hand up. They stopped, but watched intently.

She continued talking, her hand still resting on Eli's thigh, feeling the charge of his desire run through him. "So now that Freshwater is still alive, how are you going to start this war?"

Eli closed his eyes for a second before he spoke. Yael felt the pressure of the gun ease by a fraction. "What war?" he asked.

"Plan A, poisoning Freshwater, did not work. Plan B is war between America and Iran, which will wreck the peace process for good. The war that will keep the hard-liners in Israel and their Iranian opposites in power for a generation. They may hate each, but they share a common interest."

He slid the gun barrel down Yael's side, tracing the line of her rib cage. "Where do you get these fantasies from?"

"These are not fantasies. They are facts." A memory flashed into her mind, of the news ticker on the taxi television. "My God. That was you, and your Iranian friends, wasn't it?"

"What are you talking about?"

"The car bomb in DC. That's the start of plan B." She turned to look at him.

He stared at her, unblinking, for a fraction of a second too long. "Let's go. We can discuss this back in Tel Aviv."

"Eli," she said, her voice soft now, the undercurrent of sadness tangible. "Leave it. It's over. You, me. Israel. Everything. It's over."

Eli sat back and exhaled slowly. "Yael, let me put aside

my personal feelings here. We spent thousands of man-hours training you. You were one of the best ever. Top of your class. You remember your nickname? The Magician. Then you left, making everyone very pissed, at least until we placed you."

She sat up. "Placed me? What does that mean? I got my job on my own."

Eli laughed and put his left hand on Yael's arm, still holding the Beretta against her with his right. "Of course you did. With just a tiny bit of help. You have had your adventures. But now it's payback time."

Yael shook his arm off hers. "Listen to me, Eli, and listen hard. I am not coming back to Tel Aviv."

"Not even for a couple of days?"

"I am done with that life."

"But that life is not done with you."

"Meaning?"

"I'll give you a couple of days to think about things. Meanwhile, I have some photographs and a little film that might help you make up your mind." Eli gestured to the operative sitting at the end of the long curved bench. He stood up, walked over, and handed Eli an iPhone.

Eli passed the phone to Yael with his left hand. A video clip played, featuring a woman wearing the long sleeved blouse and ankle-length skirt of the religiously observant. She was darker and younger than Yael, but they shared the same physique and fine-boned beauty. Standing in the courtyard of a red-roofed villa, under harsh, bright sunlight, she was surrounded by children laughing and shouting.

Yael's stomach turned to ice.

Eli said, "Brave woman, living on an isolated settlement. Especially when her husband is away so often."

She looked at the side of Eli's head. Her heart was racing, her muscles tensed and ready for action. His scalp was covered with a faint black stubble. She clenched her right hand, feeling the nails push into her palm as her thumb locked the fingers into place. One swift jab, just above his ear, and Eli would topple sideways. Her left hand following instantly, a sideways hammer smashing into his nose. Or his throat. His thorax would crack and swell. Without an emergency tracheotomy he would die. A single second, that was all she needed. And a single second was about all she would have until the bodyguards, the fake lesbians, and the woman with the phone rushed her.

She controlled her breathing and let her hand slacken. "You just crossed a line, Eli."

"Good. Because if anything happens to her, it will be your fault."

"No, Eli. It will be your fault. And the whole world will know it."

Eli frowned. "Meaning?"

Yael was outnumbered and outgunned. But she had other weapons. The one thing that Eli feared was publicity. In the age of social media, a single photograph linking him to the deaths of his enemies would be all that was needed to end his career in the shadows, which was the only place where he knew how to operate. "I want to show you something. It's in my purse. Don't worry, I'm not armed. Can I get it?"

Eli nodded. "Slowly."

She reached inside her bag, took out her phone, and

pressed several icons, one after another. “Before you try and grab this you should know that it will be a waste of your time. I have uploaded this file to a secure website. I need to log on to the website every day by midnight, with a coded password that changes every day, or this file gets sent out on Twitter.” Showing Eli the phone screen, his face peering out, she swiped and a list of names, dates, and places appeared.

He tried to grab the phone, but Yael pulled it away. The website and the password were a bluff, but the information in the file was real and, she knew, enough to unnerve him.

““Your world is shrinking, Eli. I don’t think you will be returning to London, Paris, Manila, São Paulo, or Berlin for some time. But nowadays everyone leaves a data trail. Even you. People are getting interested in you, Eli. Clever people who can put two and two together.”

Eli’s eyes glittered with fury. “I already told you in Zone, Yael. Your fantasies are dangerous. Very dangerous.”

She turned to face him again. “They are not fantasies, Eli. They are facts. These people died. You were there. And then you left, went somewhere else. Where more people died. When did you turn into a killer, Eli? Did it start that day in Gaza?”

She stands next to the boy, holding his hand, stroking his hair, calming him, as the bomb-disposal expert disconnects the vest. He places it to one side and orders the boy to undress. The boy looks at Yael; she nods, squeezes his hand.

The bomb-disposal expert swiftly checks the boy all over.

Sweat runs down her back and into her eyes. The previous

month two soldiers had been killed here. The explosives had been inserted into the bomber's rectum. By the time they had stripped him and seen the wire, it was too late.

The bomb-disposal expert stands back. He signals to the second man in the Jeep: The boy is clear.

Eli's voice was cold. "That boy was wired. He would have blown us all to pieces. Or taken out a bus. Or a playground full of schoolchildren. Or a café. You remember Café Mizrahi on Shenken? We used to go there with Ilona. They reopened it. We can go back together. I'll bring flowers and spread them around where they picked up what was left of her."

Yael felt the anger and guilt rise up inside her. She dropped the phone back in her purse. "Do you think this is what she wanted, Eli? The boy didn't kill anyone. He was a *child*. A mentally handicapped child who had no idea what he was doing. And his bomb did not go off. Because I did my job," she said, her hands white as she gripped the slats of the park bench. "And then you did yours. Whatever that is."

Eli slipped the gun back into his shoulder holster. "Today is Thursday. We are reasonable people. We understand that you need to clear your desk at work. Pack up your things. Say your good-byes." He reached inside his jacket pocket and handed a piece of paper to Yael. She unfolded the printed sheet. "You are lucky. Business class. Monday afternoon. Direct to Tel Aviv from JFK. I have to travel economy."

Yael slowly tore the ticket into shreds, and let the breeze carry the scraps of paper away. Eli said nothing, only looked across the park and scratched the right side of his nose. She followed his gaze, watched the blond woman nod then press down on her phone screen.

"I'm sorry about your date." He did not sound very sorry at all. "Especially after you made *so* much effort." Eli stood up and retrieved another folded piece of paper and handed it to her. "This just arrived in Sami Boustani's e-mail in-box."

7

"Yael? Is that really you, Sis?" Noa's voice was thick with sleep. "It's four o'clock in the morning here. Are you OK?"

Yael glanced at her watch: it was just after nine. Israel was seven hours ahead. She pulled a face. "I'm so sorry. I completely forgot. I just wanted to hear your voice." The voice of someone who simply loves me and isn't trying to use, manipulate, or threaten me, she almost added.

Noa asked, "Has something happened?"

"No, nothing unusual," said Yael. Nowadays, that was true enough.

"I miss you, Sis. We all do. Amichai is twelve now. Next year will be his bar mitzvah. You will be here for that?"

Yael stared at the photograph on the sideboard of Noa, surrounded by her eight children. Amichai, the oldest, stood in the middle. Noa had her hands on his shoulders, as if showcasing him.

"Of course. What a question."

Noa lived on Har HaZion, an isolated settlement deep in the occupied West Bank, with her husband, Avi, and their family. Noa had discovered religion on a visit to Jerusalem, just after she graduated from Cornell, when she met an emissary from the Lubavitch sect of Judaism who had invited her to come for Shabbat dinner. She became captivated by the warmth and stability of the Lubavitch lifestyle—and its contrast to the turbulent childhood she and Yael had shared. Now married to a full-time student of the Torah, with no apparent income, she was blissfully fulfilled.

The two sisters chatted for a couple more minutes, before Noa said goodbye. Yael put her phone on the coffee table and sat back on the sofa, hugging her knees, trying to make sense of the evening. She had phoned Sami to cancel their date as soon as Eli and his team had left Tompkins Square Park. Sami had been polite and understanding, if somewhat cool, which was understandable. He was a journalist, he knew about the sudden demands of work, he said. Neither of them had nine-to-five jobs. They would get together soon, another time. An accomplished liar, by both training and instinct, she thought Sami had believed her. Unless, of course, he had already checked his e-mail.

After that conversation, she had taken a taxi straight home. Once back, she changed out of her dress, scrubbed off her makeup and put on an old Columbia University T-shirt and faded gray sweatpants. Then she had called her sister, experiencing an urgent need to hear her voice.

Was Noa in danger? Not yet. At least, no more than usual. The settlement was heavily guarded and Noa rarely left its confines. Eli knew very well that if anything happened to her, Yael would wreak a terrible revenge. She would release the file on him, spreading his name and photograph all over the Internet, but that would only be the beginning. She knew enough about Mossad's inner workings, and the operations in which she had been involved, to cause serious damage if she went public.

Meanwhile, a lot could happen by Monday afternoon. Yael switched on the television. CNN was showing a studio discussion about the UN's Reykjavik Sustainability Conference. One pundit, a youthful liberal blogger with a goatee, argued President Freshwater was showing strength, that she was determined to follow her own agenda, by attending. Shireen Kermanzade, Iran's new reformist president, would also be there. They might even meet, he speculated. The other guest, a middle-aged female conservative in a tight pink sweater, guffawed and said that Reykjavik was a complete irrelevance to American voters, and proved how out of touch Freshwater was with people's everyday concerns. Yael was inclined to agree. The UN organized conferences almost every day of the week. It was a mystery to her why Freshwater was bothering to spend presidential time on new methods of recycling.

Yael heard a gurgling noise. She looked around then realized it was her stomach. She picked up a small packet of crackers, marked with the Air France logo, from her coffee table and ripped it open. The contents flew out, spilling over the coffee table and onto the floor of her apartment. She sighed and picked them up piece by piece and placed them on the table. This really was not her night.

She upended the packet of crackers into her hand, tipped what remained into her mouth, and slowly chewed as she stared at the printout of the photograph that Eli had given her. Had he really e-mailed it to Sami? There was no way she could have spent the evening at Sami's apartment on a date, all the while wondering what was in his e-mail and what his reaction might be. There was a limit to even her powers of performance.

Imagine if the date had gone well. She might have stayed over, only to find Sami checking his e-mail in the morning, staring at the image, then at her. He would have felt betrayed. She would have been mortified. Yael imagined Sami printing the e-mail out before deciding what to do. He would not rush to action, she thought. This was more than just another story. This was personal, family business that had ended very badly indeed. Sami would probably approach her sometime in the next couple of days. He would be brisk and businesslike, or maybe he would try and charm more information out of her. Or he might wait for a while, as he dug deeper into her past. There was nothing she could do about it for now. Either way, tonight was a win-win for Eli.

The bottle of Puligny-Montrachet stood on the coffee table, three-quarters full, still glistening with condensation. Michael the doorman had handed it back to Yael on her return. She picked up her glass of wine, and tasted it. It was very good, as it should be for the price: lemony-crisp with an aftertaste of almonds. It was a waste to drink it on her own. She thought about calling Joe-Don. He was a bourbon man and she had a bottle tucked away somewhere. He would certainly be there very quickly indeed once he heard about her encounter with Eli in the park. At which point he would admonish her for not summoning him as soon as Eli appeared, to escort her home and stand guard at her door. But she was safe in her apartment now, and anyway, they were due to have breakfast tomorrow morning.

Who else could she call to keep her company? There were not many candidates. She took another sip of wine. In fact, there weren't any.

Sami Boustani stared at the feast cooling on the kitchen table. Lamb kebabs, both *shish* and *kofte*; three types of salads; a rice pilaf; tiny herbed falafel balls; homemade yogurt and mint sauce; and his favorite dish, his sister Leila's specialty, *kubbeh*, deep-fried crispy buckwheat, stuffed with minced lamb and pine nuts.

He checked the clock: it was just after eight thirty. By now most of the food should have been eaten, and they should be moving on to dessert, a retreat to the sofa, sliding closer, some gentle kissing, and then, perhaps . . . he glanced at his bedroom. But the food was still here, untouched. As was he. The kebabs were starting to congeal, the salads were wilting, and the rice was tepid. A bottle of unopened Lebanese rosé wine stood in the ice-bucket. He put his hand inside the container. The ice had melted and the bottle stood in a pool of water.

Sami reached into the fridge and pulled out a bottle of Brooklyn Lager. He wasn't much of a wine guy anyway. At least he hadn't opened the bottle. He could keep it in the unlikely event that he ever persuaded another woman to come round for dinner. He took a long swallow of the beer, picked up a kubbeh, and bit off the top half. It tasted dry in his mouth; the buckwheat like sawdust, the meat too rich. He forced himself to swallow it then sat down on the lumpy sofa.

Sami was thirty-five. Almost all of his friends and relatives of his age, both in the United States and in Gaza or Israel, were married with children. He still lived alone in a dark one-bedroom apartment in the basement of a brownstone on East Ninth Street that belonged to his uncle. The orange acrylic carpet was dotted with stains, and the walls, once cream, were now various shades of brown. The pipes banged and rattled, and the hot water in the bathroom spurted brown for at least a minute. There was a damp patch in the center of the lounge wall in the shape of Italy. The ramshackle furniture, including a twin bed, dated from the Reagan era but with no hint of eighties retro-chic. It was just old. Sami had lived there for more than two years but still had not got around to properly unpacking. Whenever he made time to sort out his possessions he ended up changing his mind, telling himself that this was only temporary accommodation. But each time he looked at rental websites he realized that, despite the gloom, at $1,500 a month the apartment was a bargain.

The Boustanis were Christian Palestinians who had emigrated to the United States twenty years ago from Gaza. Sami's father, Ahmad, had relatives in Manhattan, so the family settled there. Seven years later, Ahmad died of lung cancer after a lifetime of heavy smoking. Maryam, Sami's mother, had moved to Brooklyn to live with his sister Leila, her husband, and their five children. The pressure was on, if not to match Leila, then to at least enter the race.

Sami could handle pressure. He was a skilled and experienced reporter: nuanced and intuitive, yet dogged and aggressive when necessary. The UN beat demanded a subtle grasp of geopolitics and US policy: he had previously covered Congress, and had been posted to London to cover Parliament. He was now widely acknowledged to be one of the best journalists in the UN building. Navigating the complex world of competing interests with confidence and flair, he produced a stream of scoops for his newspaper and became a confidant of ambassadors and senior State Department officials. His only real rival was Jonathan Beaufort, the veteran correspondent for his newspaper's almost namesake, the *Times* of London.

But there was one thing Sami had never mastered: the rules of Manhattan's ruthless dating scene. The choreography of when to show interest, when to retreat, when to advance, and when to wait for the call—it was beyond him. He had not had a relationship of note since his return from London, although he'd enjoyed a few flings. He was regularly invited for drinks, even dinner, by female UN officials. At first he had accepted readily, then he realized that usually they were not interested in him as a person, only as a means of access to the pages of the world's most influential newspaper.

Yael was not like that. She didn't want to talk about the UN at all. Sami could not quite believe that she might be attracted to him. His mother and sister could barely contain their excitement about him having a dinner date at home, and had spent the previous day cooking for him. There was, of course, the considerable issue: he was Palestinian and she was Israeli. Or half Israeli. He had not shared this with his relatives. But he would, he thought, cross that bridge when he came to it.

Sami drank some more beer, put the bottle down on the coffee table, and sat back with his hands behind his head. Now, of course, there was no bridge to cross. He replayed his brief conversation with Yael in his head, her excuse that the secretary-general had called her in to the Secretariat Building for an emergency meeting on the Syria crisis, her apologies, the embarrassed future promises to "get together soon." It was possible, he supposed, that there was such a meeting. Yet he didn't believe her. There was something in her voice that made him think she was lying. He sat up straight. And there was an easy way to find out.

His iPhone beeped. An e-mail had arrived. He checked the header: "Story for you" from afriend99@gmail.com. Sami's e-mail address was not public, but like that of most reporters it was easy to guess, being a combination of his surname and his news organization. He frequently received e-mails from unknown people promising great revelations that rarely proved newsworthy. He would check it later. But first he would have a quick look at the news channels and see what was happening in the world outside Apartment 1G, 45 East Ninth Street.

8

Yael put her wine glass down and walked back to the sideboard. Its surface was crowded with a clutter of framed images. A black and silver art deco mirror was mounted on the wall above the display of family holidays, birthday celebrations, weddings. She stared at a photograph of a young girl with auburn hair holding hands with her father by the lake in Central Park. The child was seven or eight, her father in his late thirties. It was a picture from the pre-digital age, slightly out of focus with faded colors. She blinked, looked away, then back to pick up the largest photograph, standing in a silver frame in the center of the display. A man, clearly in his early twenties, tall, well built and good-looking, with green eyes, stood in front of a white UN Jeep near a peacekeepers' checkpoint.

She is sixteen years old, sitting in her room at the Belgrade Hyatt, when the phone rings. "Your brother has arrived," the concierge tells her.

She sprints down the corridor and takes the elevator downstairs to the glass-fronted lobby crowded with journalists, aid workers, and large, watchful men who sit there all day, chain-smoking and drinking coffee.

A UN Jeep is parked by the entrance. The vehicle is covered in mud, apart from a double curve on the windshield cleared by the wipers.

He emerges, holding a toddler in his arms.

She slides her finger into a small hole in the door. There are two more over the wheel arch and another under the window, each with the metal puckered inward. Three more women emerge from the Jeep, followed by six children and two teenage boys.

One catches Yael staring at him. He is tall, older than she first thought, perhaps eighteen or nineteen. He has high Slavic cheekbones and striking ice-blue eyes. He smiles, shyly.

She smiles back, then turns to watch her brother as he organizes the refugees and their meager bags.

She wiped her eyes and put the photograph back down. Twenty years on, the yearning was as powerful as ever. Especially on days like these.

Twelve years ago, after she graduated from Columbia University with a master's degree in international relations, Yael had started at the UN as an administrative assistant in the Department of Peacekeeping Operations. The position was more important than it sounded: she was responsible for ensuring that officials' briefings and reports were written in clear and grammatically correct English—not always the case in a polyglot organization like the UN—and distributed on time to the relevant committees and to the Security Council. The Department of Political Affairs was the most powerful in the building, but the DPKO was responsible for putting boots on the ground in the world's conflict zones. Peacekeepers fought, sometimes died, and feelings ran high in both the UN headquarters and the missions of those countries who contributed the soldiers. DPKO officials had to manage not just the complexities of multinational peace operations in war zones where fighters had no respect for the Geneva Conventions, but also balance the relentless demands of the Security Council members. Especially the P5, the permanent five: the United States, Britain, Russia, China, and France.

A steady stream of position papers and analyses, some written by UN officials, others by diplomats and intelligence officers, flowed across Yael's desk. She watched, fascinated, as some of the world's most sensitive negotiations unfolded literally in front of her via back channels to Tehran, Beijing, Pyongyang. The UN was a slow, cumbersome bureaucracy, riddled with factions and infighting, but overall, she believed, it was a force for good. She worked hard and helped out her colleagues whenever she could. Young, smart, and attractive, she was soon caught up in the building's social whirl: Friday night drinks in the Delegates Lounge, receptions at UN Missions, leaving parties, joining parties, and endless national days to be celebrated.

Yael had enjoyed her new life, until her old one began to catch up with her. After a couple of years, the UN rumor mill suddenly went into overdrive about her past, so much so that she wondered if there had been a leak from Tel Aviv, perhaps even intentional. Her bosses in Israel had been furious when she resigned. But she stuck doggedly to the cover story they had agreed upon before she left. She had done her national service, yes, as a personal assistant to a general, but it had been two years of mostly boring administrative work. The most dangerous part had been fending off the advances of male officers. The legend was well back-stopped with the necessary documents and paperwork, even a report of a complaint she had made about sexual harassment. She soon realized that many of the invitations she received were either from middle-aged male UN officials or diplomats hoping to have an affair with her, or from operatives of the numerous intelligence services, stationed under diplomatic cover, who seemed to know something about her background and wanted to use her as an asset or even recruit her.

But Yael had two powerful patrons: Quentin Braithwaite, a British army officer who was seconded to the DPKO, and the SG himself, Fareed Hussein. Braithwaite noticed that Yael's uncanny ability to sense others' moods allowed her to defuse departmental crises without offending prickly—usually male—egos. He soon moved Yael out of administration and into the operations room. One night, French peacekeepers in the Central African Republic became trapped in their base because a rebel militia was blocking the road, preventing the arrival of a UN convoy carrying supplies and troops to replace those at the end of their tour. The militia leader was demanding 500,000 euros in "customs duties." Yael called the French ambassador to the UN, whom she had met at a Bastille Day reception, and made a suggestion; five minutes later, she was able to explain to the militia leader that, if he let the convoy pass, his family would be flown to Paris where they would be issued with residence permits. Or he could await the arrival of several attack helicopters carrying French special forces from their base in neighboring Chad. She then sent him a satellite photograph of his vehicle's precise location. The convoy was allowed through.

After that, Braithwaite started to send Yael out into the field. She was so successful that Fareed Hussein poached her and made her his "special adviser," giving her an inside seat at some of the world's most sensitive diplomatic negotiations and the opportunity to broker deals herself. In Kabul, she arranged for US troops to guard the Taliban's poppy fields in exchange for the Afghan militants' promise to not blow up a new gas pipeline. In Ramallah, she persuaded the Palestinians to refrain from declaring an independent state in exchange for observer status at the UN and relaxed controls at dozens of Israeli checkpoints in the occupied West Bank. In Baghdad she had even managed to free Hussein's nephew, a twenty-one-year-old college graduate with no experience who landed a senior job with the UN and had been promptly kidnapped by Shiite insurgents.

All of her colleagues were intrigued and wanted to know more. A few were supportive, many jealous, but she couldn't tell them what she was doing, or where she was sent, and she didn't want to lie to them. So she stopped socializing. The invitations slowed, then eventually dried up. She missed the company, of course, but her job meant she was on the road much of the time anyway. The pace of life in New York was so frenetic, with people booking nights out weeks in advance, that it was almost impossible for her to arrange a social event. She rarely knew where she would be in two days' time, let alone in two weeks.

Yael glanced at the television. A photograph of the UN building covered most of the screen, with a smaller studio feed of Roger Richardson, CNN's UN correspondent, in the top right-hand corner. A caption ran along the bottom: *Senior UN official convicted of sexual assault "likely to be released soon" say law-enforcement sources.* She sat up straight, her maudlin mood gone. Richardson, a tall New Yorker with a dry sense of humor, was a veteran of the UN press corps. Yael always enjoyed his company when they met at receptions. But he was as sharp as he was amiable. Who was he referring to? As soon as Yael asked herself the question she knew the answer. There was only one candidate.

She returned to the sofa, sat down, and turned up the volume as the camera switched back to the studio.

The anchor, a striking African woman in her early thirties, looked puzzled as she spoke. "But the evidence seemed rock solid, Roger. There is a sound recording, on the Internet. Charles Bonnet's voice is clear, threatening Thanh Ly and her family unless she does as he asks. That clinched the case and got him a sentence of fifteen years for aggravated sexual assault."

Lately the network had been eclipsed by Al-Jazeera, which was pouring resources into both its Arabic and English-language services, but Yael still had an affection for the pioneer of continuous news coverage. After almost twenty years on the UN beat, Richardson also had excellent sources, Yael knew. She had occasionally leaked snippets of information to him herself.

Richardson nodded, but looked puzzled. "Yes, Aisha. It's definitely an unexpected turn of events. But my sources in law enforcement are saying Bonnet's lawyers have been pushing hard to make a case that the sound file was faked and that Thanh Ly was lying. Of course there are also diplomatic implications here."

Now displayed on the screen was a photograph of a handsome man in his early fifties, with an erect bearing, hazel eyes, and a tanned face.

The sound file was not faked. Yael had given Thanh the digital microrecorder herself. But Bonnet had powerful friends, and she'd always known it was unlikely he would serve his full sentence.

Richardson continued. "We know there have been several high-level meetings between French officials and the Department of Justice lately, supposedly about cooperation against money-laundering and terrorism. We know the US is especially concerned about Islamists in Mali and Algeria, two former French colonies. Perhaps another item was quietly slipped onto the agenda."

"It's starting to look that way. What does Ms. Ly have to say?"

"So far, nothing. She resigned from the UN and returned home to Paris."

"The plot thickens." The anchor looked at the camera as she spoke. "Ms. Ly, if by any chance you are watching this and want to tell your side of the story, do be in touch. We would love to hear from you. Meanwhile, tell us more about Charles Bonnet and his background, Roger."

"The Bonnet Group, the family firm, is one of the largest and most influential companies in France. It has substantial holdings in Africa and excellent links to the political establishment. Charles Bonnet spent time in the French Foreign Legion, and worked at the Bonnet Group headquarters in Geneva before joining the UN just over twenty years ago. He had a successful career and was most recently a very senior UN official, the Special Representative for Africa. But that particular appointment caused uproar among human rights groups."

Richardson paused for a moment.

"Why?" asked the anchor.

"They claimed that the Bonnet Group had used child labor in its coltan mines in Congo. Coltan is the world's most important mineral, vital for computers and mobile phones. The company strongly denied the allegations. Shortly afterwards, the Bonnet Group, together with the KZX Corporation, a German conglomerate, donated $5 million to UNICEF, the UN's children's charity. The controversy faded away. Bonnet kept his UN job."

"Tell us more about the man himself, Roger."

Richardson nodded. "Bonnet was also a desk officer at the Department of Peacekeeping during the genocide in Rwanda and as you know, Aisha, Rwanda was the greatest catastrophe in the UN's history. Eight hundred thousand people were killed in the genocide, including nine UN aid workers in the capital Kigali, after headquarters in New York failed to respond to their calls for help. There have been many . . ."—he paused—"*theories* about why that particular massacre, of the UN staff, happened."

Yael looked at the photograph in the silver frame. David, her brother, had been one of those nine UN aid workers. She leaned forward, listening intently to every word.

"Such as?" asked the anchor.

Richardson frowned. "Some say it was to send a message to the UN not to intervene. Others that it was simple bloodlust. There was enough of that in Rwanda then. But Bonnet's release has triggered a fresh rumor."

"Tell us more, Roger."

"That he was connected to some kind of deal behind the scenes, something to do with the nine UN workers who were taken hostage."

"Do we have any details?"

Richardson had a look of fierce concentration. He paused for a couple of seconds before he spoke. "Nothing verifiable. Fareed Hussein, the current secretary-general, was head of the Department of Peacekeeping at the time. It's highly likely that he would have known what was going on. But if there was a deal, it went horribly wrong."

Yael sat staring at her television, transfixed.

Armin Kapitanovic sat back on the wooden bench and flicked through the navy blue passport, stopping when he came to the photograph page that carried his picture. "Jovan Kovac. Translates as: John Smith. Very original."

"You don't want original," said Menachem Stein. "You want commonplace, unremarkable."

Kapitanovic stared at the embossed gold emblem on the cover. His fingers traced the words, the top line in English, the bottom in French. "Is it real?"

"Real enough," said Stein, his palm open.

Kapitanovic handed him the passport. "I used to dream of Canada, in the war. At night, in Srebrenica, I would say the names of the cities to myself: Toronto, Montreal, Vancouver, Ottowa. *Oh-tow-wa*. Like a mantra. If I kept saying the names, one day I would get there."

"Once we are done, its yours. You can go wherever you want."

The two men were sitting on a bench at the end of a short cul-de-sac on the corner of Sutton Place South and East Fifty-Seventh, looking out over the East River. A garbage scow slowly headed upriver on the black, glistening water, a yellow light blinking on the stern. Queens beckoned on the opposite shore, the apartment buildings glowing brightly. Nighttime traffic flowed along the Queensboro Bridge, headlights shining.

Kapitanovic's gaze moved to the left, to an elegant, detached townhouse that took up a good part of a block. Four stories high, it stretched from the corner of East Fifty-Seventh to the wide pavement that marked the end of the cul-de-sac. The house was built in a late Georgian style, with flat fronts and large white sash windows. A short staircase, flanked by black iron railings, led to the side door. A gray metal NYPD box with tinted windows stood on the corner, but the front entrance opened directly onto the street and was completely exposed.

"Seen enough?" asked Stein.

Kapitanovic nodded. "More than."

9

Sami scribbled "Bonnet/Than Ly—chk with Richardson—Deal?" and put down his notebook. That was good work for CNN by Roger. Sami had also heard rumors that the case against Bonnet was looking shaky, but had not dug further. Perhaps he should have, especially because of the coltan connection. And as for the rumor about the dead UN aid workers in Kigali, Sami too had heard whispers, but nothing spelled out in that level of detail. It was definitely time for a lunch in the Delegates Dining Room with the CNN correspondent—assuming that Jonathan Beaufort did not get there first.

For now, Bonnet could wait. What he really wanted to know was why a Middle Eastern feast was going cold on his kitchen table. He picked up his iPhone and pulled up the number of Roxana Voiculescu, the SG's spokeswoman. Roxana had been Schneidermann's deputy. Romanian born, attractive, and extremely ambitious even by UN standards, she had somehow bypassed the usual recruitment procedures and immediately been appointed spokeswoman after Schneidermann's death. Roxana knew all of Fareed Hussein's movements, meetings, and appointments—firsthand, 24/7, snickered some. She would certainly know if Yael was meeting the SG now, but he couldn't ask Roxana outright. Sami had heard from multiple sources that Roxana couldn't stand Yael, was jealous of her access to the SG and trying to work out how to marginalize her. Roxana would brush him off, saying such details were confidential, and then she would probe him, trying to find out why he wanted to know. He needed a plan.

He thought for a moment, and an idea began to form in his mind.

Roxana picked up on the second ring. They chatted for a minute, exchanging pleasantries, promised to meet for drinks soon. Sami still blushed at the memory of his last social encounter with Roxana. She had been nagging him for weeks to take her out. Eventually he had succumbed and spent part of the evening buying expensive cocktails at a hipster bar while Roxana flirted heavily, until she promptly abandoned him when her boyfriend appeared. Meanwhile, Sami had stolen confidential UN documents from her purse while she was in the restroom.

"Hey, Roxana, it's lovely to catch up, but I just wanted to check something," said Sami.

"How can I help?" asked Roxana, her voice bright but wary. "Is this about Roger's report? Because we don't comment on unsubstantiated rumors."

Sami stared straight ahead for a moment. The damp patch on the wall was definitely growing. *Thank you, Roxana,* he wanted to say, *for answering a question I was not going to ask and thereby confirming that Roger was onto something.*

Instead he replied, "No, nothing to do with that. I'm

writing a soft piece about Yael and the SG, how she does so much important work behind the scenes and how well they work together. It's planned for the Week In Review and the editors have asked me to fact-check something. You'll love it. I need to speak to her, just quickly on the phone. Could you give me her number?"

Roxana paused. Would the gambit work? Sami had Yael's number, but Roxana didn't know that. He could sense Roxana calibrate whether his inquiry would benefit her interest. Control of information was all, especially when dealing with unknowns.

Her reply was just as he had anticipated. "Why don't you tell me what you need, Sami, and I will ask her for you?"

"Thanks so much, but I'm right up against my deadline. I hate to interrupt her and the SG, especially when she is having an emergency meeting with him about Syria, but it's really important."

Sami heard her sharp intake of breath. "What emergency meeting? The SG's at the residence having dinner with Frank Akerman. They are probably talking about Syria as well, but not with Yael. Not as far as I know. Hold on a moment please. I'll check."

Thirty seconds later Roxana was back on the line. "Yael is not there," she said with the happy certainty of someone who knows her rival is firmly out of the loop. "It's just the SG and Frank Akerman. What did you want to check?"

Bingo, thought Sami. "Just the month when she started work at the UN. She's not on the website—I guess because of the kind of work she does."

"We are working on that, Sami, because as you know we

are fully committed to transparency for all our employees. I don't know where she is, and I cannot give you her mobile number, as I am sure you understand. I'll get back to you later tonight," said Roxana, before hanging up.

Now he had the answer he sought. He felt no guilt about deceiving Roxana, who like her predecessors daily tried to feed him any amount of disinformation. But the information brought him no joy, although there was a kind of poetic justice here. In fact, he probably deserved to get stood up.

Each time he'd had to choose between a potential romance with Yael and the demands of his job, the job had won. Last year he had published a story about a memorandum Yael had written to Fareed Hussein, protesting the deal she had been ordered to make with a Hutu warlord wanted for the Rwandan genocide. Jean-Pierre Hakizimani was the ideologue and propaganda mastermind behind the mass slaughter, urging his fellow Hutus to exterminate the Tutsis like "cockroaches." The UN, wrote Yael, was "allowing him to escape justice for tawdry reasons of realpolitik and commercial interests."

For several weeks after that Yael would not even talk to Sami. Even so, he could justify that to himself. Yes, he was interested her personally, romantically, but Yael's memo was an important story and he had to report it. Eventually he had rebuilt their fledging relationship. Then he had stood her up, appearing instead on Al-Jazeera with Najwa. Incredibly, even after that he thought he had managed to fix things. Except, clearly, he had not.

Sami finished the rest of the kubbeh, washing it down with a long swig of beer. He picked up the remote control, switched on the television, and flicked through the channels before settling on a rerun of *Sex and the City.* Perhaps he could pick up some dating tips. Or maybe it was best to focus on work. That, at least, was going very well. He picked up a DVD from a small pile on the coffee table in front of him. The cover showed African children working underground, under the title *Dying for Coltan: How the United Nations Was Almost Hijacked.* Sami had produced the documentary with Najwa.

Dying for Coltan revealed how the previous year KZX and the Bonnet Group, had conspired with rogue UN officials and Efrat Global Solutions, the world's largest private military contractor, to take over the majority supply of the mineral. KZX and the Bonnet Group had agreed to sponsor the UN's first corporate development zone in eastern Congo. Fareed Hussein and many others, none more than Caroline Masters, at that time the deputy secretary-general and infamous for encouraging privatization of UN operations, had hailed the pilot project as a new model of cooperation between the UN and the private sector. But the actual plan was for Efrat Global Solutions, with the help of Hutu militiamen, to trigger a new ethnic war in Goma that would be a rerun of the 1994 genocide in neighboring Rwanda. UN peacekeepers would have to be deployed to stop the fighting, and once they were in place KZX and the Bonnet Group could expand the Goma Development Zone across Congo while using the UN peacekeepers to stabilize the situation. Profits for the corporations. A boost to the UN's budget. A win-win all around. Except, of course, for the people who lived in Congo and mined the coltan.

The film had won several awards and was now a finalist in the Best Documentary category at the Tribeca Film Festival. Several UN and EGS officials had been imprisoned, and the planned merger between KZX and the Bonnet Group was on hold. Menachem Stein, the founder and boss of Efrat Global Solutions, had somehow escaped sanction. Fareed Hussein and Caroline Masters denied all knowledge of the planned war, although Sami and Najwa had heard, from several sources, that there was a sound recording proving Fareed Hussein had been forewarned of the planned slaughter. Such a recording, if it existed, would be the biggest story of their careers. It would certainly be the end of Fareed Hussein's career.

Sami turned the DVD over within his fingers. The film had severely angered the upper reaches of the UN bureaucracy and several foreign ministries, but that was his job. According to his journalistic idol, H. L. Mencken, a veteran reporter from the golden age of journalism before the Second World War, the relationship between the reporter and the government official should be that of the dog and the lamppost. Mencken's epithet was not exactly true, especially in a place like the UN where sources were everything. But it was still a useful motto to remember when the lure of being an insider could tempt a reporter into questionable trade-offs.

For now, the thunder had faded away. The far-reaching inquiry promised by the SG had been kicked into the very long grass that sprouted across the UN bureaucracy. The German authorities had closed down a criminal investigation into KZX's senior executives, and the company was expected to soon float on the New York Stock Exchange. KZX's relationship with the UN had survived and thrived. The firm had sponsored the UN press corps' luxurious flight from New York to Turkey, and the official press center at the Istanbul Summit.

Sami put down the DVD and picked up a piece of thick white card, embossed with gold letters.

Mr. Sami Boustani and partner are kindly requested to attend the opening reception of the new KZX School of International Development at Columbia University.

Guest of honor: Fareed Hussein, Secretary General of the United Nations

Cocktails at 7pm. Dinner to follow.

Business attire.

Partner. Who could he take? It would be a glamorous event, even by Manhattan's exacting standards. He had been musing about asking Yael, although it was perhaps a little early in their fledgling relationship for such a public outing. But that was a theoretical question now, not a practical one.

He put the invitation down and opened the new e-mail.

Subject: Of potential story interest

From: afriend99@gmail.com

To: boustani@nytimes.com

The e-mail had no text, but included an attached JPEG file. He ran them both through his security program and they came up clean. He saved the JPEG to his desktop and clicked on the file. It opened up into a photograph.

He could not stop staring at the picture, all thoughts of dinner and wrecked dates forgotten.

Yael watched for a couple of minutes as CNN moved on from Charles Bonnet to Syria, then pressed the red button on the television remote control. The screen clicked off. She did not move, turning Roger Richardson's report over and over in her mind.

A deal.

She had heard the rumors as well, of back-channel diplomacy in Kigali in 1994 that had resulted in disaster, but had never been able to get any details. Every few weeks she brought up the topic in her conversations with Fareed Hussein. He adopted his now familiar look of pious regret, slowly shook his head—and stonewalled. Now, the CNN report raised more questions than it answered. What exactly was the deal? Whose idea was it? Who had brokered it? And who was the go-between? Yael had operated in the gray area herself for long enough to know there were always cutouts. Usually her, but not in this case. Find the cutout between the UN—no, the DPKO—and Hakizimani—and she could, *would*, find out why David had died.

Could it be Bonnet? His family certainly had the connections across Africa. She reached into the drawer under the coffee table and pulled out a thick plastic file. Yael had long been suspicious of Bonnet and his family's business interests in Africa. She had compiled the bundle of printouts on the Bonnet Group from the Internet and several classified databases over several weeks last fall, before the coltan scandal broke. Founded in 1880 by Jean-Claude Bonnet, a miner from Brittany who had found a large gold deposit in what was now the Democratic Republic of Congo, the group had diversified over the decades into logging, silver and copper mining, as well as rare earths. Revenue in the Bonnet Group's mining division, headquartered in Kinshasa, had more than doubled in the last two years, the *Economist* reported.

Yael picked up her iPad, opened a new window in her browser, and typed in "un.org." The pale blue welcome page of the main UN website appeared, with the UN logo—the world encased in two olive branches—in a darker tint. A dark blue band stretched across the screen proclaiming "WELCOME" in each of the organization's six official languages. Yael clicked on the English word and a new page opened with dozens more links, photographs, and video clips leading to new pages and sections on numerous crises, wars, and general themes such as development and sustainability.

A new banner down one side featured updates about the upcoming UN Sustainability Conference in Reykjavik, Iceland, which was to be chaired by Fareed Hussein. The conference was scheduled to start in a week, but so far few A-list attendees had been confirmed apart from President Freshwater. Yael knew most countries were just sending an environment minister, many of them quite junior. She moved the cursor into the search bar and typed "Charles Bonnet." Bonnet's UN career had ended in disgrace, but he had worked at the organization for twenty years; the last time she had checked there had been a substantial and detailed biography. She clicked on the Go button. The screen flashed. Then a box appeared:

> Your search "Charles Bonnet" did not match any documents.
> No pages were found containing "Charles Bonnet"

There was no point in adjusting the search parameters. Bonnet had been airbrushed out, at least for now, as his UN history was doubtless being readjusted. But in cyberspace, some things could not be erased.

Yael opened archive.org in a new window. The wayback machine, as it was known, was an archive of the Internet, dating back to some of the first web pages and websites in the early 1990s. But it was much more than a trip down cyber-memory lane for techies and geeks. Wayback kept snapshots of every website, around a dozen days for each month, with a comprehensive search facility. Websites could delete pages, files, even the biographies of former officials who were now an embarrassment or a liability, but they lived on forever, inerasable and untouchable, if you knew where to look.

Yael decided to search un.org when Bonnet was at the height of his UN career, in August 2012, a good couple of years before the coltan scandal broke and before he had been appointed Special Representative for Africa. She settled on May 3 and typed "Charles Bonnet" into the search box. His biography immediately filled the screen. Yael read it through slowly, seeking the snippets of information that might reveal something of significance.

There was nothing, at least as far as she could see. A steady climb up the ladder before being appointed an assistant secretary-general in the Department of Peacekeeping, a position senior enough to merit a coveted corner office. She checked back through 2011, 2010, right back to 2008, when he had first been appointed as an ASG. Then she saw it. A single line that had disappeared from the subsequent biographies.

10

Najwa sat down at her desk, trying to clear a space in the chaos. UN reports, press releases, media advisories, briefing notes from think tanks and analysts, newspapers, and glossy magazines were piled up on every inch of surface space. What there was not was a notebook. Or even a clean sheet of paper. It was ten minutes to nine, and she wanted to write down a few notes on her meeting with Riyad Bakri—and by hand, not electronically—while she still remembered their conversation, before she started digging into the DC bomb and the apparent emergence of a new Middle Eastern terrorist group.

Najwa had worked at the UN for two years, appointed as Al-Jazeera's first female bureau chief after stints in Kabul, Jerusalem, and Paris. Born in Rabat, a niece of the King of Morocco, she had gone to school in Geneva and Paris, and then studied at Oxford and at Yale, where she had caused a minor scandal by modeling swimwear for a French designer. Najwa had no trouble cultivating sources. UN officials and most diplomats were often flattered to be courted, especially by attractive female journalists, and were usually ready to talk—especially over lunch or dinner in one of several excellent restaurants located in the building. Those seeking privacy could retire to one of the many eateries nearby, or one of the more obscure cafés dotted around the complex.

She picked up that week's edition of *Security Council Insider* and glanced underneath to find a half-empty packet of chewing gum. She took out a stick, unwrapped it, and began to chew as she flicked through the newsletter, temporarily distracted by its promise of "Exclusive UN insider access and information." *Security Council Insider* was a subscription-only publication that cost $500 a year. Its stories were written in a gossipy style and were usually anonymously sourced to "UN insiders," "a confidential contact," or via the passive construction "*SCI* understands." But they were almost always accurate. *SCI* was published by a company that Najwa knew was owned by the cousin of an assistant secretary general, who dealt with the Security Council, in the Department for Political Affairs. High level confidential information, for which the ASG was the obvious source, routinely appeared in the newsletter, but nobody had bothered to make the link. Or, if they had, to do anything about it. Najwa had toyed with doing a story on UN officials privately profiting from their public roles, but some of them were also her best sources. So that idea was on the back burner, at least for now.

This issue included an article that she had been meaning to read on the Reykjavik Sustainability Conference. Najwa had never been to Iceland, nor did she plan to visit. The very word *ice* was enough to put her off. She wasn't that interested in sustainability, either, but she read through the story to the end.

And watch that Icelandic time-table. SCI *understands that there are several hours between the closure of the conference and the SG's flight home. We were unable to obtain President Freshwater's schedule, but we do know that both she and Fareed Hussein enjoy a walk on the beach. And Reykjavik has plenty of those, even if they are kind of windblown.*

We suggest a stroll along the seafront to Hofoi, the lovely white house where Presidents Reagan and Gorbachev held a summit back in 1986. That meeting was the start of the end of the Cold War between the United States and the Soviet Union. Or maybe along the peninsula to Bessastadir, the beautiful but isolated presidential residence. Nowadays, of course, it's the conflict between the United States and Iran that has us all worried. Which is why we were pleased to hear that President Kermanzade might be enjoying some Atlantic air as well.

Najwa drew a red ring around the final couple of paragraphs. She had not known Kermanzade was going to Reykjavik. There was no way to check for sure, but *SCI* valued its $500-a-year subscribers and had never been wrong yet. The *SCI* story was probably enough to sway Najwa. Just a snatched appearance of the three leaders together would be enough to justify the trip.

A former academic at Tehran University who specialized in modern Iranian film before becoming the first female minister of education, Kermanzade had won a surprise victory in the recent presidential election. Iran was changing, and with 40 percent of the population under thirty-five, its citizens were chafing at the mullahs' restrictions. Not only was Kermanzade a woman, she was also a reformer elected on a platform of easing some of the restrictions of Sharia law, and reducing what she called Iran's "foreign commitments"—shorthand for cutting back support for Shia militias in Iraq and Hezbollah in Lebanon—and thawing relations with both the "Great Satan," the United States, and the "Little Satan," Great Britain. There was even talk of opening relations with Israel. Her win had sent the conservatives and hard-liners into a frenzy. Most analysts predicted Kermanzade would resign—or worse—by the end of the year.

But could the logistics work? It was short notice to plan a trip across the Atlantic. Najwa glanced at her watch. Tomorrow night was the Friday reception for the launch of the KZX Development School at Columbia University. The Sustainability Conference was due to start on Sunday morning. President Freshwater and her Iranian counterpart were due to speak on Monday, so she needed to get to Reykjavik by early Monday morning with her crew. That meant an overnight flight. There was bound to be a UN travel facility for the press, but she needed to check before she booked seats. By the time she and Sami had realized that the airplane to the Istanbul Summit was a KZX company freebie they were on board and about to take off. KZX would almost certainly sponsor the press airplane to Reykjavik, to dovetail nicely with its new partnership with Columbia University, and neither she nor Sami could accept such a free ride again. So they needed to fly commercial.

Najwa glanced around her office, in her mind already

planning her trip. Precious real estate in the Secretariat Building was allocated along strict principles: media from Western countries, especially those that dug deep into UN corruption, such as the *New York Times*, the *Times* of London, and the *Financial Times*, were granted miserly cubicles, often with no windows. Media from the developing world were given spacious offices, none more coveted than that of the Al-Jazeera bureau. Najwa and her team had three large, bright rooms. The main space was used by Najwa, the second by Maria, and the third housed an editing suite.

The white walls were decorated with framed photographs of stills from Najwa's coverage of the Arab Spring uprisings. Each staffer had a teak and steel height-adjustable workstation, with a mesh-backed office chair sprouting levers and buttons that demanded a degree in engineering to adjust. A brushed steel coffee machine stood in one corner, while the facing wall was covered with four flat LED television screens. A shelf was filled with a clutter of prizes that Najwa and her team had won for their reporting.

Najwa turned over the *SCI* newsletter and began to write on the back.

Thursday evening. Off-record, deep background conversation with Riyad Bakri. Bakri says death of Schneidermann reminded him of case of Abbas Velavi.

Why?

Bakri v. interested in Yael Azoulay—has he heard the rumors from the Palestinian delegation? What is Jaesh al-Arbaeen?

Najwa opened up the anonymizing software that allowed her to connect to the Internet through an encrypted virtual private network. The VPN masked her computer's IP address, the unique identifying number assigned to each device that connects to the Internet, then routed the connection through a series of encrypted servers around the world. In theory, she was now untraceable. She then opened her browser, which was set to Start Page, a free private search engine. Unlike other search engines, Start Page did not record any details of searches. Nor did it use cookies, those tiny bundles of data that identified users and marked when they logged into particular websites. The VPN and Start Page should, she hoped, be enough to secure her connection. All of Al-Jazeera's staff took special precautions to keep their communications as private as possible. Whether or not Bakri worked for the Saudi Mukhabarat, the UN building was home to hundreds of spies—including, she suspected, a number of her colleagues.

Najwa typed in "Abbas Velavi" into Start Page's search box. The screen instantly filled with links to news stories and articles.

She pulled up a story from the *New York Times* a year ago:

IRANIAN OPPOSITION FIGURE FOUND DEAD

By SAMI BOUSTANI

A leading figure in the Iranian opposition was found dead at home in his apartment in midtown Manhattan, police said Monday.

Abbas Velavi, 47, likely died of a massive heart attack, law enforcement sources said. The New York City Medical Examiner's Office will determine the cause of death as the investigation continues.

Mr. Velavi, who had lived in the United States since the mid-1980s, was known as an outspoken opponent of the Iranian regime. Opposition-supporting websites claimed that he had been murdered.

The United States and Iran have no diplomatic relations, although Iran maintains a mission to the United Nations in New York. Calls and emails to Iran's mission to the United Nations went unanswered.

The remainder of the article detailed Velavi's life as an opposition activist and previous threats against him. She flicked through the other links. There was little more factual material. Sami had written a short follow-up story reporting that the medical examiner had carried out an autopsy and determined that Velavi had died of natural causes. There was some shaky video footage on YouTube of a small demonstration by Iranian dissidents opposite the UN staff entrance on the corner of First Avenue and East Forty-Second Street. The protestors were holding up signs claiming that Velavi had been murdered. After that, the story had faded away from the mainstream media.

What interested Najwa was a video interview with Velavi's widow on an Iranian opposition website. She played the clip again.

The camera showed a woman in her fifties, with short gray hair. Her face was deeply lined, but her voice was determined. The footage of was reasonable quality, but the frame wobbled slightly as though it had been filmed on a mobile phone.

"What do you think happened to your husband?" asked a disembodied voice.

"He was murdered."

"The autopsy said he died of a heart attack."

The woman snorted derisively. *"He was perfectly healthy. He had just had his annual check-up. Why would he have a heart attack and die, out of nowhere? It was the visitor."*

"Tell me about the visitor."

"He was here, sitting where you are. He said his name was Parvez. He had joined the opposition in Tehran and wanted to make contact here. But Abbas was suspicious of him. He was too smooth. Too confident. Abbas asked him some questions about people in Tehran. The visitor said he knew them."

"And?"

"They didn't exist. Abbas invented them."

"What else do you remember?"

"The visitor was bald. He had a neat beard and wore fine black leather gloves. He did not take them off all the time he was here. He said he had a skin condition."

The woman's voice cracked and she began to cry. *"He killed my husband. I know it. A woman knows who killed her husband."*

Najwa added *"who is the visitor?"* on the back of the *SCI* newsletter. Had Velavi been murdered? It was certainly possible. Tehran had long arms, great expertise, and no compunction about disposing of inconvenient enemies. But like every foreign intelligence service, the Iranian Ministry of

Intelligence would be very wary of conducting an assassination on American soil. They would make certain not to leave any tracks, for fear of blowback, which meant that if Velavi had been murdered, a lot of time and planning had gone into his killing. Why?

Najwa circled his name several times with her pen on the sheet of paper. Abbas Velavi, a healthy man in his forties with no history of heart trouble, suddenly dies from a massive heart attack. Henrik Schneidermann, a healthy man in his thirties with no history of heart trouble, suddenly dies from a massive heart attack. Both men lived and died in New York. It could be a coincidence. More than eight million people lived in the city. Two loosely connected people, out of eight million, suddenly dying of the same cause a year apart was certainly possible. But Najwa's instincts told her this was not a coincidence.

She would have to talk to Sami about Velavi. Journalists always knew more about their stories than they used in, or got into, print. Sometimes the additional information could not be sufficiently verified, or it was bounced back by the lawyers. But that did not mean it wasn't true. Bakri had dropped his hint for a reason. Najwa was confident she would find out why.

And then she realized.

She was scribbling *Velavi killing—test run?* when her pen ran out of ink. There was another in her purse so she slipped her hand inside, rummaging amid the jumble of lipsticks, makeup palette, tampons, chewing gum, and packets of tissues. Her fingers finally touched a plastic cylinder that was too thin to be a lipstick. She pulled out a ballpoint pen, her hand brushing against a sheet of paper. She looked down and saw a white envelope.

Fifteen blocks north and just over half a mile west, on the corner of Third Avenue and East Fifty-Seventh, in the kitchen of a cramped two-room apartment, Menachem Stein handed Armin Kapitanovic a long, narrow wooden case covered in black leather.

The two men stood in the kitchen. Two half-drunk mugs of instant coffee slowly cooled on the small wooden table, its surface scarred by cigarette burns. A curling 2009 calendar hung from a nail in the wall. Ten floors up, the nighttime traffic roar seeped through the open window and the East River was just visible through the murky glass.

Kapitanovic put the case on the table, opened the lid, took out a wooden stock with a trigger, a long, thin barrel, and a scope. His hands moved swiftly. Less than a minute later, he held a Dragunov sniper rifle.

Kapitanovic sat down at the table, holding the rifle between his legs, pointing upward. "How long till he is out?"

Stein looked at his watch. "Probably about twenty minutes. Once the meeting is over and he gets ready to leave the residence I will get a call on this," he said, holding up an old Nokia candy-bar mobile phone.

"A call from who?"

Stein smiled. "Does it matter? Three rings and the caller will hang up. Then you go up to the roof. It's an easy shot."

"Not at night."

"The front of the house is well lit. There are street lamps."

Kapitanovic ran his finger down the barrel of the Dragunov. "It won't bring them back."

"No. It won't. But it will be a kind of justice. And a warning to others."

Kapitanovic stared ahead, suddenly far away. "Justice? Or murder?"

Stein sat down. "Tell me what happened."

The Bosnian spoke quietly. "I was working as an interpreter for the Dutch UN troops in Srebrenica. After the town fell, it was total chaos, panic everywhere. The Bosnian Serbs separated the women and girls from the men and boys. They took the men and boys away. The women were hysterical, covering their sons with girls' clothes, pulling them into the crowd. Everyone knew what was going to happen. The Dutch troops were supposed to protect us, to help us. Instead they helped the Bosnian Serbs. I hid them, my father, my brother, and my mother, in an office on the UN base."

Kapitanovic's voice trembled slightly. "Then the Dutchman came in, with a handful of his peacekeepers. I called New York, tried to speak to Fareed Hussein. He was in a meeting. Everyone was in a meeting. The Dutchman and the peacekeepers started going through every room, throwing everyone out. Eventually they found my family. We begged, offered money, everything we had. I could stay, he said. I had UN papers. My family did not. The Dutchman pushed them out of the base. I tried to follow them. My father pushed me back, as hard as he could." Kapitanovic glanced down at his chest. "He bruised my ribs."

"What could you have done?"

Kapitanovic gripped the Dragunov, his knuckles pink and white. "I had a pistol. I should have used it. My father and my brother were never seen again. They still haven't found their bodies. My mother went with the women to Tuzla. She hanged herself. From a tree. The worst thing is . . ." Kapitanovic's voice broke for a moment.

"Is what?" asked Stein, quietly.

"There was another family. Hiding in the quartermaster's stock room. The Dutch troops never found them. They all survived. If I had hidden my family . . ."

Stein laid his hand on Kapitanovic's arm. "If is a big word. The biggest."

Kapitanovic closed his eyes for a moment and breathed deeply. "I have been waiting a long time for this day."

He picked up the rifle and peered down the sight. "How did you get me out?" he asked, his voice steady now.

Stein took a sip of his coffee. "I made a trade. Information. First with the Turks, then with the Islamists."

"The Turks I understand. A Turkish army truck from Suleyman Shah's tomb back across the border, a flight from Istanbul to Montreal. But how does an Israeli do business with Islamists?"

"The same way that you exchanged stolen UN aid supplies with the Serbs in exchange for guns and ammunition."

Kapitanovic made a minute adjustment to the rifle's sight. "That's the Balkans. We knew them. They were our neighbors. We fed them. They armed us. As long as we didn't attack their position, they left us alone."

Stein put his mug down. "Balkans, Middle East, we were all once part of the same empire. We know the Islamists. They are our neighbors. We don't attack them and they don't attack us. Our border with Syria is quiet, considering. We both share a common enemy: Hezbollah. The Islamists already are at war with Hezbollah. Israel soon will be. Again. People I know keep a very close eye on Hezbollah. That information is valuable to the Islamists. So we trade information with the Islamists, and"—he glanced at Kapitanovic—"occasionally, more than that."

The Bosnian thought for several seconds. "Why did you bring me here? You could arrange a mugging, a street robbery that went wrong. A hit and run. You don't need me."

"No, I don't. But you deserve justice."

"Maybe. What else do you want?"

Stein passed the Bosnian a photograph. It showed the tanned face of a man in his early fifties, with hazel eyes and an erect bearing.

11

Yael grabbed her iPad from the coffee table, sat back on the sofa, and flicked through her archive of stories about the UN until she found the one she wanted, dated ten days earlier.

TURMOIL CONTINUES AT UNITED NATIONS

Fareed Hussein Returns, Deputy Resigns, Detained US Diplomat "Used UN Connections" to Adopt Afghan Child

By SAMI BOUSTANI

UNITED NATIONS—Fareed Hussein, the secretary-general of the United Nations, returned to his post Monday after being absent for almost two weeks on medical leave. Mr. Hussein, who had been suffering from fainting attacks, declared himself "fully recovered."

Yael speed-read the report until she reached the key paragraph.

> Confidential UN emails newly obtained by the *New York Times* reveal that, as early as a year ago, Ms. Masters was negotiating a pilot scheme with Clarence Clairborne, chairman and owner of the Prometheus Group, to supply security services for the Istanbul Summit. The emails detail how Prometheus was working behind the scenes with the world's largest private military contractor Efrat Global Solutions, which is owned by Menachem Stein.
>
> If successful, the contract, referred to in the emails as the "Washington Stratagem," would set the precedent for a wholesale privatization of UN security, and potentially international peacekeeping, a market worth billions of dollars annually.

The story had been published on the day of Henrik Schneidermann's memorial service, nine days ago. Caroline Masters had been Yael's former classmate at Columbia University, enrolling in graduate school after working as a journalist in Bosnia, Kosovo, and Central America. After graduating she joined the State Department, where she was known as a liberal interventionist, but also a realist—until she was posted to Berlin as a commercial attaché. A growing friendship with Reinhardt Daintner, head of communications at the KZX Corporation, had led to a three-month placement at KZX's new Office of Social Responsibility. During that time she became a passionate advocate of privatization, a cause that she continued to champion at the UN. The previous month, she had essentially mounted a coup, sidelining secretary-general Fareed Hussein by spreading untrue rumors of his declining health. One of her first agenda items in her brief reign as acting secretary-general had been demoting Yael to run the Trusteeship

Council, a dead-end position overseeing UN business in former colonies.

But now Masters was gone. Hussein was back in his office on the thirty-eighth floor. So was Yael, in hers. Yael knew all about the "confidential emails obtained by the *New York Times*" because she had sent them anonymously to Sami, although he had no idea of her role.

Yael picked up her wine glass, raised it to her lips, then put it back down without drinking. She needed a clear head for this. Sami was a great reporter. He understood the importance of details, but could see the big picture and its ramifications. But he only had part of the story. The Prometheus file, now locked in a safe in the SG's office, detailed how Clairborne and the Prometheus Group were doing business with Nuristan Holdings, an Iranian company that operated as a front for the Revolutionary Guard. Clairborne and his company had survived the fallout from the Istanbul Summit, but they could not survive the publication of the Prometheus file.

Sami had not yet made the connection between Prometheus, Efrat Global Solutions, and the DoD, the Department of Deniable, the most secret arm of the US government, whose operatives carried out wet-work missions of which no records were kept. Sami did not know the extent of what Clairborne, the Iranians, and the DoD had planned. But Yael did.

She is standing on the Eminönü waterfront, watching the police launch bounce across the waves. It is a perfect spring morning. The sun is warm on her face, the breeze scented with the smell of the sea. The V-shaped hull cuts through the water like a scythe at harvest time, pale spray fountaining in its wake.

The Turkish policemen grimace as they drag the dead man into the boat. His back is crisscrossed by deep welts, their ruffled edges bleached white by the water. His arms and shoulders are dotted with semicircular rows of tiny puncture marks, each two or three inches long. The commander shakes his head in disgust. He covers the body with a gray blanket, gently smoothing the fabric as though tucking a child into bed.

"We offered him a deal," says the man standing at Yael's side. He is wiry, muscled, in his mid-thirties. A long purple birthmark reaches from his left ear down the side of his neck.

"Which was?"

"Better than that," he replies, gesturing at the police launch.

"An orange jumpsuit?"

Cyrus Jones laughs. "Any color he wanted."

Yael grimaced at the memory. She closed the window with Sami's story, opened her anonymizing software program, and connected to her neighbor's Wi-Fi network. His password was based on his birthday, which she had long ago remotely extracted from a file on his computer. Despite her caution she knew nothing was totally secure, especially in the age of Edward Snowden, but the NSA software on her iPad was as good as it got.

She relaunched her web browser and typed a series of numbers and letters, interspersed with dots, into the address bar. The secure website had been set up for her by Joe-Don. A plain gray window appeared, asking for the password. The numeric code, which changed every day, was based on the first letters of the words in the headline of the lead story in that day's *New York Times*. Each letter's numeric value was based on its position in the alphabet—A being one, M thirteen, for example—and was then multiplied by that day's date. The results were added together and the total was then divided by the number of pages in the newspaper's national section. That final number was the password. Yael glanced at the news section of the newspaper on her coffee table. "Republicans Continue Push to Impeach President" was above the fold.

She picked up her phone, opened the calculator application, and started work, jotting down each set of numbers on a notepad. After a minute or two she checked the last page of the newspaper's national section, did the final calculation, and entered the result into the password field. A new window appeared. A series of folders appeared, including one holding the details of Eli's missions. But now she wanted to check a folder marked with a video player logo. There were two files inside. She clicked on the first. It showed a bare, windowless concrete room. A wiry, well-muscled man stood naked from the waist up. His head was covered with a black hood, a dark smear was visible on the lower right side of his neck, and his legs were manacled. A dog ran around the room, barking and snarling. Yael watched the clip for the twenty seconds that it lasted, then closed the window. That file was freely available in the Internet. The second one was not.

Yael watched herself appear onscreen, with her hair wild, her face scratched and sweaty as she breathed heavily. *"My name is Yael Azoulay. I work for the United Nations,"* she said to the camera, which spun around to show a man in his thirties sitting on the floor of a washroom. He was bruised and bleeding, his clothes were torn, and he was panting. His ankles were bound together with a white plastic tie, his hands cuffed over a water pipe.

Yael's voice returned. *"This is Cyrus Jones. He works for a black-ops department of the US government known as the DoD, the Department of Deniable. He is somehow connected to the Prometheus Group, which is trading illegally with Iran's Revolutionary Guard. Cyrus Jones tried to kill me today on the Staten Island Ferry."*

The camera shakily zoomed in on Jones's face so that it filled the screen. His eyes blazed with hatred and fury. The birthmark on his neck pulsed so strongly it seemed to be alive.

"This film will be uploaded to a secure server. If anything happens to me it will be posted on YouTube. Remember: Cyrus Jones. Clarence Clairborne. The Prometheus Group. The Department of Deniable."

Yael watched the clip until the end, closed the window, and logged out. She picked up a notebook from the coffee table and drew a triangle on a sheet of paper. She wrote *Prometheus* on one side and *DoD* on the other. At the top of the triangle she wrote *Efrat Global Solutions*, adding *KZX?* next to Prometheus. She understood that Prometheus, EGS, and the DoD all wanted a new war in the Middle East; Prometheus and EGS because it would be the most spectacular bonanza yet for the military-industrial complex, bringing in billions of dollars' worth of contracts. The Department of Deniable needed a new war, because without one there was no reason for it to exist. The renditioners, the waterboarders, the interrogators, the prisoner freezers, and rectal feeders, the legion of half-crazed ex–Special Forces soldiers who could never function in civilian society, had nowhere else to go.

But what was the KZX connection? KZX was the world's largest media conglomerate. The German firm had bought up newspapers and television and radio stations across eastern Europe on the cheap after the collapse of Communism, before expanding into Russia, India, and Brazil. But the firm had several other interests. KZX's pharmaceutical division was less well known but was extremely powerful on the global drugs market. That part of the company dated back to the 1930s and had recently been embroiled in a scandal in eastern Europe. There were reports that KZX scientists had attempted to produce a genetically engineered drug to reduce the fertility of Romany women, even that the science used dated back to Nazi experiments during the Second World War.* The furor had faded away after KZX announced a deluge of scholarships and endowments for Romany students and organizations.

But KZX was still aggressively seeking new pharmaceutical markets and opportunities. Yael had recently heard that company officials had secretly met with a Taliban leader in Doha, Qatar, to discuss plans for large-scale cultivation of hashish across Afghanistan, as more and more countries legalized its possession. For KZX, as well as Prometheus and EGS, instability also meant opportunity. Freshwater had made no

---

* See: *The Budapest Protocol*

secret of her dislike of international corporations and her plan to limit their global reach. It would certainly suit KZX for Freshwater to be out of the way, and have another, more pliant and amenable president in the White House.

And now there was a new addition to the mix: Eli and his friends. Masters's resignation and the ever-louder questions about the privatization of UN security and peacekeeping were all just temporary setbacks, to be expected when the stakes were this high. Prometheus, EGS, KZX, and the DoD would never give up. Nor would Eli. And she knew sooner or later, Eli and his gang would try and take her. But forewarned was forearmed, especially when she knew precisely how they operated.

Yael picked up her iPad, connected it to her speaker system, and opened a sound file. Then she sat down on the floor in a half-lotus position, breathing slowly and deeply through her nose as she began to zone out.

Clarence Clairborne glanced briefly at his wounded hand. The bandage was clean but his palm was throbbing. He could feel his pulse under the Band-Aid, his blood pressure rising before the phone call.

He looked at the two framed photographs on the corner of his desk. A family of four, half of it now reduced to two sheets of printed paper. A tall boy—with sandy hair, freckles, and a winning smile—held a soccer ball and stared out from one frame. Clarence Clairborne IV. The memories were hardwired into his brain, and no amount of bourbon could erase them. Waving good-bye to his son as the limousine rolled out of the driveway to Ronald Reagan National

Airport and the Prometheus Group's waiting executive jet; the phone call apologizing for missing his son's birthday party, with fulsome promises of the time they would soon spend together; sitting on the airplane telling himself that yes, he had locked the liquor cabinet. Most of all, he remembered the phone call he received when the airplane had landed. The cabinet had not been locked. His son had gotten drunk and drowned in the swimming pool. His wife had never recovered, and he had given up trying to reach for her through the fog of gin and tranquilizers.

A plump, pretty teenager looked out from the second frame, smiling shyly at the camera. But Emmeline Clairborne was no longer Daddy's girl. She was someone else's girl, living on Sanchez Street in San Francisco. With Abby. Her *partner.* He could barely vocalize the word, even in his head. But he was still Emmy's father. He glanced at his watch. It was six o'clock in the evening in California. They should be home by now, back from the school for children with special needs where they worked. Clairborne took a deep breath, picked up the phone on his desk, felt his cut hand throb even harder, and punched in a number. He heard the ringing, imagined the sound echoing across the kitchen. Emmy and Abby had bought the apartment for $200,000 under market value. The realtor had told them it was an emergency sale and they had to move quickly to complete the purchase. They did. Neither she nor Abby had any idea that Clairborne had flown to San Francisco, chosen the place, and paid the realtor the extra $200,000, plus another $5,000 in cash to keep his mouth shut and make sure Clairborne's daughter got to buy the apartment.

"Hello, this is Abby," said a female voice.

"This is Clarence Clairborne," he said, the receiver slippery in his palm.

"Mr. Clairborne, hello," said Abby politely. She paused. Clairborne could visualize her looking at Emmeline, the stern shake of his daughter's head. "She's not here, Mr. Clairborne."

Clairborne forced a smile to keep the desperation from his voice. "That's fine, Abby. Actually, I wanted to talk to you. Congratulations on your promotion. You are now director of the school?"

"Thank you. Yes. I am." Abby was wary.

"You may know that the Prometheus Group has a charitable foundation. We would like to make a substantial donation to the school, to be used as you see fit."

Abby did not hesitate. "No thank you, Mr. Clairborne."

The line went dead. A few seconds later the phone rang again. Clairborne pressed the speakerphone button. "Your visitor is here, Mr. Clairborne," said Samantha.

12

She is sitting on the beach where Jaffa meets Tel Aviv. The rhythm of the waves as they break is soporific. Her eyes are closed. The sun is pleasantly warm on her face, the sea breeze cooling. The water swirls around her toes, the undertow pulling gently at the sand beneath her feet.

Yael felt calm—transported, as she intended, to a conscious state somewhere between sleeping and waking.

Eli's voice boomed around the apartment. Traffic roared. Sirens wailed. Handheld radios hissed and crackled.

She focused on her breathing, feeling the flow of air in and out, in and out. After two minutes, the cacophony stopped as suddenly as it started. Five minutes later it erupted again, for another ninety seconds, then stopped. Yael opened her eyes and checked her pulse. Fifty-five. She was ready.

Ten minutes later, Yael devoured her sandwich in three bites. Ordering in was always an option in Manhattan—the restaurant flyers scattered across the coffee table offered

Thai, Italian, Korean, Mexican, sushi, and any number of regional Chinese cuisines—but that would have taken at least another thirty minutes, so a search at the very back of her kitchen cupboard had produced a packet of crispbread, a tin of sardines, and a jar of chili-flavored olives: enough for an instant, if makeshift, supper. There were two more sandwiches on her plate. They were surprisingly tasty for a slung-together meal. Or perhaps the wine had sharpened her hunger. In any event, her appetite had returned and her mind was clear as she sat at her dining table.

She picked up a postcard with a Turkish stamp, featuring a catamaran racing across the Bosporus, one of its two rudders out of the water. There was no message written on the back, but there didn't need to be. Next to the postcard lay a rectangle of thick white card, embossed with gold lettering. The invitation had arrived with a covering letter, personally signed by Daintner in his capacity as corporate communications director.

She read the first few lines:

Ms. Yael Azoulay and partner are kindly requested to attend the opening reception of the new KZX School of International Development at Columbia University.

Partner. She smiled, wryly. Actually having a date would be an event of note. She picked up the postcard of the catamaran again.

A lock of hair, so black it almost shines, falls over his head. "Shalom, Ms. Azoulay. Welcome to Istanbul."

For a second she imagined herself walking into the KZX reception accompanied by Yusuf Celmiz. It was a pleasant vision. Yael had spent three days in his company in Istanbul, and it had been a roller-coaster ride. They'd met when he kidnapped her at gunpoint and knocked her out with a stun dart, admittedly to save her from becoming a victim of some very nasty people; hidden her in a cemetery—where his relatives were buried—that belonged to the Dönme, a hybrid Jewish-Muslim sect whose members were known as "ships with two rudders"; billeted her in a safe house belonging to his employer, the Turkish intelligence service, also known as Milli İstihbarat Teşkilatı; had a furious row with his boss over her, then somehow persuaded said boss to provide Yael with an MIT identity card and a three-dimensional, computer-generated model of the Istanbul bazaar.

But Yusuf was in Istanbul, and she was here.

So, would she go? Yes, she would. She had no desire whatsoever to enjoy KZX's hospitality or drink their champagne. But she did want to gather intelligence about the firm and its relationship with the UN and other players in the nonprofit world, within which KZX was seeking to remodel itself as a generous, responsible corporate citizen. With patience, sufficient funds, and enough opinion-formers on the payroll, even the dirtiest reputation can eventually be cleansed. The framework was well established: endow a university chair, or establish a memorial library or a research institute, or all three. Best of all was to start a whole new charity requiring a legion of well-paid staff, ideally drawn from the children and friends of the key philanthropic players. Personal connections were crucial, oiled with exclusive dinners, receptions, weekend retreats to luxury hotels. This was Daintner's world, where he operated with skill and expertise. She had half-expected to see the Prometheus Group's name on the invitation as well. The firm's charitable foundation was making slow but steady inroads but was still running into resistance. For now at least, the world of New York philanthropy, no matter how money-hungry, would draw the line at Clairborne's donations. But that too, could quickly change.

Yael knew that a second, exclusive dinner was planned later on Saturday evening, around 9:30 p.m. Fareed Hussein would be the keynote speaker, but this was a private affair for just a couple of dozen people. Yael had not been invited, but she did not need to be physically present to know what was going on.

She looked down at the coffee table. A single olive had rolled onto the edge of her plate. She ate it, picked up the plate, and walked back into the kitchen. There she spooned finely ground coffee into a small brass pot with a long, thin handle, added water, and then placed it on the stove. She lit the burner, stirring the water until it bubbled and began to rise. The smell of burned grounds filled the room. Yael switched off the gas and watched the thick liquid fall back into the pot. She put it and a cup the size of a large thimble on a tray and returned to the living room.

Yael's mobile phone beeped, the sign that a text message had arrived. The number was unfamiliar but it started with +90, the code for Turkey, followed by 697, which she knew was a restricted mobile network. Only one person she knew had access to that network. She smiled, glanced again at the postcard of the catamaran.

She read the text message and her smile vanished.

Najwa slowly took out the envelope from her purse. It was long and thin, a standard letter envelope available in any Staples or Office Depot. She held it with her thumb and forefinger. Nothing was written on the front, so she held it up to the desk lamp. The backlight showed a folded piece of paper inside. She gently shook the envelope and examined the seal. No powder, white or any other color, had spilled out.

She was being paranoid, she knew. Printed anonymous tips, to avoid a cybertrail, were increasingly common. Two months ago somebody had slid a printout of an e-mail, from the private account of a senior Department of Peacekeeping official to a diamond dealer in Antwerp, under the office door. The DPKO official had been using UN flights to smuggle out diamonds from African war zones, thus allowing them to be reclassified as "non-conflict diamonds," and Najwa had broken the story. The DPKO official, a cousin of the minister of interior of Ghana, had been shifted sideways to the Department of Information. And promoted.

She gingerly opened the envelope and removed a single sheet of paper, folded twice. She unfolded it to reveal a photograph of a slender middle-aged man, bald, with a carefully trimmed beard. He wore a white collarless shirt and, over it, a gray suit jacket. Two words were written across the top of the image:

Salim Massoud

Salim Massoud. But who was he? She looked again at the photograph, taking in details of his appearance. Then Najwa opened up her saved browser window. Abbas Velavi's widow appeared, her features frozen in grief. Najwa moved the cursor back until the frame showed five seconds remaining and clicked play.

"The visitor was bald. He had a neat beard and wore fine black leather gloves. He did not take them off all the time he was here. He said he had a skin condition."

Najwa took a photograph of the printout with her iPhone, encrypted the image file, and e-mailed it to a secure server she used to back up sensitive material. What was the message here? It seemed to be that someone called Salim Massoud had killed Abbas Velavi. And there was something more, another connection that was niggling at her.

Under the pile of papers on her desk was a red plastic folder. The *Dying for Coltan* file was thick with clippings and printouts about KZX and the Bonnet Group. Many had been added since the film was broadcast last winter. She flicked through the articles until she found the printout she was looking for, from the website of Corporationsentry. The German anticapitalist campaign organization noted that KZX's pharmaceutical division still held the patents on a number of deadly toxins that had been developed under the Nazis. One of the poisons, according to the article, triggered cardiac arrest and then dissolved into body tissue, leaving no trace.

Najwa opened the browser on her computer, set the

search result filter to "ALL LANGUAGES," and typed in "KZX chemical weapons." The screen filled with links, many of them in Farsi, the Iranian language, including a number of gruesome pictures of dead, blistered bodies from the Iran-Iraq War that lasted from 1980 to 1988. Saddam Hussein's regime had used chemical weapons with abandon, not just against enemy soldiers but also against civilians, killing thousands in a gas attack on the Kurdish town of Halabja in 1988. The twentieth anniversary of the Halabja attack had triggered a new burst of media interest. Several reports, from both the German and international media, detailed how KZX had supplied Baghdad with ingredients and technology that could be used to make chemical weapons during the 1980s. The company strongly denied claims that it had facilitated the mass slaughter of the Hussein regime; Reinhardt Daintner, KZX's head of communications, was quoted in every story, stonewalling and denying. The chemicals and equipment had been supplied solely for use in industrial and manufacturing processes for pesticides.

Najwa thought for a moment, opened a new window, and typed in "KZX poison." The screen instantly displayed URLs for articles and television reports about environmental damage in Africa, South America, and Cambodia, where KZX had substantial investments. She clicked through the reports, lingering on a teenage boy's account of his fourteen-hour workday mining coltan in Congo. Buried in the long list of links was a brief 2013 article from Levant Monitor, a subscription-only website that specialized in intelligence about the Middle East. The website, based in Washington, DC, was run by several former US intelligence operatives, and was well respected. Its material was unsourced, but always accurate.

Najwa nodded as she started to read. This was what she had been looking for. Hafiz Bakshari, an Iranian defector granted asylum in the United States, claimed that he had been working on a secret Iranian government program to develop a substance that would trigger a massive cardiac arrest in the victim, then break up inside the body within a few hours so it could not be detected. The poison could be administered by drops to food and drink, by spray, injection, or even by touch. Brief contact with the victim's skin was sufficient to transfer the toxin. Bakshari said that the poison had been used on prisoners in Iranian jails who were already under death sentences, and he also admitted that he had met a German scientist who was working with the Iranians on the program to monitor the results. Bakshari could not remember the scientist's name, but one night over dinner the scientist let slip that he had formerly worked for KZX's research department.

Najwa entered "Hafiz Bakshari KZX" into the Start Page search engine. A handful of other specialist newsletters dealing with the Middle East had picked up on Bakshari's claims, as did a couple of Iranian and Iraqi opposition websites. The mainstream US media had also briefly covered the affair. In response KZX stonewalled and threatened libel writs. As Bakshari could not name the German scientist or produce another witness, the story faded away. Najwa continued scrolling until she came to a story in the *Washington Post* that gave her a chill as she read it. A month after giving his interview, Hafiz Bakshari had been killed in a hit-and-run accident in North Dakota, where he had relocated.

Clarence Clairborne sat in the leather armchair in the corner of his office, a heavy leather-bound volume in his hands. The climate in the room was carefully controlled at 68 degrees Fahrenheit, and the air was automatically replaced every four hours. But his shirt was damp and creased, sticking to the back of the armchair. He forced his right leg against the floor, trying to control the twitch in his thigh.

The ceiling lights were turned down low. A cone of light from the reading lamp next to the armchair fell on the dense text, and the heavy yellow paper glowed as though it was illuminated. Clairborne glanced at the man sitting in the armchair next to his. The visitor looked like he had stepped out of a magazine advertisement promising health and wealth to financially prudent seniors. His carefully barbered white hair shone under the light of the reading lamp, and his pink skin radiated vitality. He wore blue formal trousers and a crisp, starched button-down shirt that matched his clear blue eyes.

"Clarence, what happened to your hand?" asked Eugene Packard in his rich and sonorous baritone.

Clairborne shrugged. "It's nothing. An accident." Samantha had come in earlier to clear up the mess but Clairborne could still smell the spilled bourbon. So could Packard, judging by the way he breathed in through his nose and the knowing expression on his face. He nodded, indicated that Clairborne should read.

Clairborne picked up the book. "And there were lightnings, and voices, and thunders . . ." His voice, usually a deep boom, was a weak murmur. Clairborne coughed and drank deeply from the glass of water on the side table. His leg twitched again.

Eugene Packard smiled and laid a manicured hand on Clairborne's arm, as though he was reading his mind. "Clarence, take a breath. Slow down. We all have our own ways to get through the trials and tribulations the good Lord sends us." He laid his fingers on the edge of the book. "This has been with us for two thousand years. It's not going anywhere. Start again."

Clairborne nodded. He closed his eyes for a moment, opened them, and then focused on the text in front of him. "And there were lightnings, and voices, and thunders. And there was a great earthquake, such a one as had never been since men were put on the earth, such an earthquake, so great." He sounded more confident now, drawing strength from the presence of the man sitting next to him. "And the great city was divided into three parts and the cities of the Gentiles fell. And great Babylon came in remembrance before God, to give her the cup of the wine of the indignation of his wrath. And every island fled away, and the mountains were not found."

Packard smiled. "The islands fled away, and the mountains were not found. Such language. Very good, Clarence. Carry on."

Clairborne continued. "And great hail like a talent, came down from heaven upon men, and men blasphemed God for the hail, because it was exceedingly great."

Packard held up his hand.

Clairborne stopped reading. He looked at Packard.

Packard's smile had vanished. His eyes were now glacial, his voice flat. "But the hail did not come down from heaven, did it Clarence? It did not come down from anywhere. And certainly not from a car that had been parked in a garage on New York Avenue in Washington, DC."

Clairborne swallowed, his tongue dry against his palate. "Yes. No. I'm sorry. I don't know what happened." He reached for his glass of water.

Packard's hand snapped around his wrist, holding it suspended above the side table. "What went wrong, Clarence? Do we have a leak?" The preacher's eyes drilled into his. "A traitor, perhaps?"

"No, no, of course not. It was just bad luck. An attendant in the garage was suspicious. He called the cops. Everything is on high alert here."

"Are you still a believer, Clarence?" asked Packard.

Clairborne glanced at the photographs on the wall of him with three previous presidents. These men, each in his time the leader of the free world, had all sought his company and counsel. Soon after their conversations, inconvenient regimes had collapsed, revolutions had imploded, social justice movements had withered away, activists had been arrested or killed in mysterious auto accidents. Clairborne had helped remake the world in his own image. He had built his company from nothing. He had more money than he could ever spend, but could continue to name his price for any one of the multiple services his company provided, to be paid by bank transfer to a range of accounts or even in cash. Yet this elderly preacher made him feel like a nervous teenager. He nodded decisively. "Yes, sir, I am. In Jesus Christ our Lord, absolutely."

"And in the prophecies of John of Patmos?"

"Those too. More than ever, as the day approaches."

"Why?"

"Because they are true."

"And what do they tell us?" Packard's grip tightened on Clairborne's arm.

"Rapture is coming."

"Rapture." Packard smiled, an almost dreamy look in eyes. "Do you remember the last verse of Revelations, Clarence?"

Clairborne nodded again. "I do."

"Recite."

Clairborne sat up, his back straight, his voice louder now. "And he said to me: Seal not the words of the prophecy of his book: for the time is at hand."

Packard released Clairborne's wrist. "The time is at hand, to vanquish the Antichrist. But sometimes even the Lord needs a helping hand. A hand to clear away obstacles." He reached into his briefcase and handed Clairborne a brown paper file, a small photograph stapled to its front. "You know what to do with this?"

Clairborne glanced at the photograph. Yael, frozen in midstep, as she walked toward her apartment building. "Yes, sir," he said, "yes, I do."

13

Najwa scribbled on her pad, trying to put her thoughts in order: *Abbas Velavi, Hafiz Bakshari dead. Salim Massoud?—KZX?* Like spies, journalists sought patterns, similar incidents involving the same, or connected, actors. The pattern was forming now. Was the envelope from Bakri? He was certainly the most likely suspect, especially as the writing was in Arabic. If so, he was telling her that Salim Massoud, whoever he was, was killing Iranian dissidents and had also killed Henrik Schneidermann. But why? And what was Bakri's agenda? Despite his admiring glances, he certainly wasn't passing this material to Najwa to boost her career.

The Arab League might be derided as a hopeless talking shop, but it was also a place where neighboring countries met and agreed on a common agenda. None more common than that shared in the Gulf, where Saudi Arabia and its neighbors were united in their fear and hatred of Iran. The rivalry between the Arabs and Persians for control of the Gulf, indeed for the whole of the Middle East, reached back centuries. The Persians, whose culture had produced masterpieces of art, architecture, and poetry, looked down on the ascetic Bedouin of the Arabian Peninsula. Religion introduced an extra dimension to a classic regional power struggle. The Saudis were Sunnis and the Iranians were Shiites. Because of a schism rooted in the death of the Prophet Muhammad, who was predeceased by his sons and did not designate a successor, each regarded the other as apostates.

Most of Muhammad's followers supported Abu Bakr, his father-in-law, and became known as Sunni Muslims after the *sunna*, the teachings of Muhammad. But a smaller group, the *shiaat Ali*, or partisans of Ali, claimed Muhammad had anointed Ali, his son-in-law, as his successor. The two branches went to war. Ali's son Hussein, Muhammad's grandson, and his companions were massacred at the battle of Karbala, now in Iraq, in 680. Millions of Shia Muslims traveled there every year for Ashura, which commemorated the battle.

So it was in Bakri's interest to direct Najwa toward an Iranian connection to Schneidermann's death. The Saudis were enraged by the nuclear deal between the United States and Iran. In exchange for strict controls of Iran's nuclear program, sanctions were being lifted. Anything that was bad for the Iranians was de facto good for the Saudis. But there had to be something in his steer. And Najwa's instincts told her that there was indeed an Iranian link. The Middle East was in turmoil as the Islamists advanced. Old certainties were evaporating, new alliances sprouting. Tehran was winning its struggle for influence and the Shia crescent now ran through Iraq, Syria, and Lebanon. Just this week she had watched a report on how America and Iran were cooperating against the Islamists in Syria and Iraq. The Pentagon denied it, but there were increasing reports about intelligence-sharing, even special forces working together.

The Saudis and their allies were left standing on the sidelines, furious and fearful that Iran's strategic victories might foment an uprising among their own restless Shia minorities. After all, Shia Islam had been the engine of the revolution in Iran that overthrew the Shah and brought the ayatollahs to power. Centuries of oppression and persecution at the hands of Sunni rulers hardened the Shia, who celebrated martyrdom and were known for being skilled at subterfuge, conspiracy, and secrecy. And amid this state of flux and confusion, the White House was flailing, assailed by enemies within and allies without. The Saudis and their neighbors were deeply worried by the uncertainty in Washington, and were developing ever-stronger secret ties with Israel's defense and intelligence establishments. The news of the car bomb in DC would only increase their anxiety.

Along with about 80 percent of the Muslim world, Najwa had been brought up as an observant Sunni. Sunni Islam was an egalitarian faith without a formal clergy, whereas Shia Islam had a clergy and a carefully delineated hierarchy, at the top of which sat the ayatollahs. As an adult, she did not pray or go to the mosque, but neither did she deny her faith and her roots. If asked, she answered that she was a Sunni Muslim. Her Western education and time living in Europe and the United States triggered complex emotions about her heritage. She felt a powerful loyalty to the Arab world, but burned with frustration, even anger, at the chaos and bloodshed across the region and the failure of so many Arab governments to provide even basic services for their citizens, let alone human rights and freedoms.

Najwa picked up the remote control on her desk, pointed it at the LED screens on the wall, and pressed a button. Each television was tuned to a different station: Al-Jazeera English, Al-Jazeera Arabic, BBC, and CNN, but all four showed the same footage. Renee Freshwater, dressed in a white blouse and black jacket, with her black hair tied back and her strong features tight with determination, sitting at her desk in the Oval Office. Najwa turned up the volume:

> "We utterly condemn the barbarous attempt at a terrorist outrage tonight in our nation's capital. A catastrophe has been averted, a catastrophe that would have taken dozens of lives and maimed many more."

A former United States ambassador to the United Nations, Freshwater had begun her career in the State Department, where her reputation as a liberal was solidified after she called for the United States to intervene in the Rwandan genocide. Her election had enraged Republicans, and more than a few southern and conservative Democrats, but in the beginning she rode a powerful wave of public support. Her first couple of years had seen a tsunami of legislation as she forced through an amnesty for illegal immigrants and reforms for labor law and banking regulation, infuriating both Wall Street and K Street, the avenue in Washington, D.C., where powerful lobbyists congregated. Now, after three years in office, the luster of being America's first female president—one with Native American ancestry—had long faded. The Republicans had declared open war on her administration, aided by their covert allies in the Democratic Party. Her proposed bill to bring back all outsourced military and security functions from the private sector to government had been quickly vaporized by a bipartisan filibuster. In Syria, Freshwater had pushed hard to back the moderate Syrian opposition and called for airstrikes after the Assad regime gassed its own people. But the moderates were abandoned and the airstrikes never happened, and Najwa had heard from several sources that sections of the American intelligence agencies saw President Assad as a bulwark against the Islamists and were secretly cooperating with him.

Either way, power was leaking away from the White House and down the corridors of Capitol Hill to those of K Street. Freshwater's husband Eric had been killed in a strange skiing accident ten months ago. Despite her efforts, and the involvement of multiple government agencies, there had still been no concrete answer as to why his bindings had failed and he had hit a tree. The president herself was still recovering from Isis Franklin's attempt to poison her. Losing Eric had garnered sympathy and brought a truce from her political enemies for a couple of months. The assassination attempt in Istanbul had brought temporary respite—but this time for just a few days. After that, her enemies used it to pillory her, asking how she could protect America if she could not protect herself. The president was once again dubbed "Dead-in-the-Water," hobbled by Congress, dismissed by the ever-louder right-wing media as a one-term wonder before America recovered its senses.

Freshwater continued talking, her praise of the police and

emergency services presumably read from a teleprompter in front of her desk. Then she paused and looked directly into the camera, her dark eyes blazing with anger. "Whoever planted this cowardly bomb: I know you are watching. So listen up, because I have a message for you. I don't care whether you have an army of forty or forty thousand. Know this: We are coming for you. We will never give up. The United States of America will hunt you down, will find you, and make you play." She blinked once, then paused for a fraction of a second. "Make you *pay*." Each channel switched back to the studio.

Najwa grimaced. She switched off three monitors and changed the channel on the fourth to Fox News. The blowback about the president's stumble would be instant. A ticker across the bottom of the screen already announced: *Freshwater blunders over DC car bomb, promises to play with terrorists.* The host currently live was Beau Clarkson, a former communications director for the Prometheus Group. A portly man nudging sixty, he turned to his guest, Heather Bowles, a Tea Party–backed congressional candidate.

"Heather, how is our commander in chief going to track down the DC bomber when she cannot even finish a sentence?" he asked.

Bowles, a rangy brunette in her forties, laughed out loud, throwing her head back before she spoke. "Beau, this is what I have been saying all along. It's barely ten days since the president survived an attempted assassination. Lord knows, I have plenty of issues with the president, but this was a heinous attack not just on her, but on America and its values. She can't speak properly, let alone command an intensive counterterrorism operation. She needs a rest. A long one."

Clarkson nodded, and looked serious. "But the White House doctors say she is fit to return to work."

"The White House doctors." Bowles snorted derisively. "You and I both know she was never fit to start work. We still don't even know what kind of toxin was administered. Ten days ago the president nearly died, and we are supposed to believe that she can run the country when we are under attack? The DC bomb could have been the worst terrorist outrage since 9/11, in the heart of our capital. We need leadership from the White House. We don't need an invalid in the Oval Office."

Fox News was leading the charge, but Najwa knew an army would quickly go on the attack. She watched Clarkson and Bowles's back-and-forth for a couple more minutes, then checked her Twitter feed on her computer. A hashtag was already trending: *#playdeadinthewater*

She shook her head and switched off the television. Najwa was an experienced reporter, but the public capacity to generate vitriol and hatred still had the power to unsettle her. The speed and timing of the tweets indicated a high level of planning and organization. Whoever was directing the Twitter storm had been waiting to pounce. Even if Freshwater had not stumbled, the attack would have been launched anyway on some other pretext. It would not be difficult, she knew, to whip the same people up into a frenzy against Al-Jazeera, or even her personally.

She glanced at the door to the office. Not for the first time, she worried about security. This building was full of spies, many of whom were intensely interested in the work of the Arab world's most influential television station. She had thought about asking for a CCTV link to the Safety and Security Service operations room, but that would mean staff there could watch her and her colleagues while they were at work so it wasn't an option. And in any case, who knew who was watching the UN? Back in 2004, a British politician in then prime minister Tony Blair's government had caused a scandal by revealing that the SG's office was bugged by MI6, the British foreign intelligence service. The ensuing furor resulted in wry smiles throughout the complex, for this was hardly news to UN insiders. A door code and an alarm were adequate protection against thieves. But a hostile organization, like the Saudi Mukhabarat or Iran's secret service, known as VAJA, would easily be able to get past them.

Her phone beeped, so she picked it up and looked at the screen. A new tweet from a prioritized account: @darkstone

> *D.C. bomb was loaded with shrapnel. Pieces now being tested for possible chemical/bio-contaminants. Who or what is Al-Jaysh al-Arbaeen?*

Najwa processed what she had just read. Contaminated shrapnel. Ugh. New York Avenue led directly onto Pennsylvania Avenue near the site of the White House. The streets around the president's residence were always packed, with tourists and locals, and the carnage would have been terrible. The claim of responsibility by the Army of Forty had appeared from nowhere, sent to the news agencies. @darkstone was asking the right question. All Najwa knew was that *Jaysh* was Arabic for army while *Arbaeen* meant forty.

She spent the next twenty minutes trying to find out more. Modern-day terror groups, especially Islamic ones, were usually deft users of the Internet and social media. But the Army of Forty had no website, Twitter handle, Facebook page, or Instagram account. Her Arabic-language Internet searches did not yield anything. Nor were there any leads in the jihadi deepweb, the clandestine corner of the Internet where the extremists gathered on restricted-entry forums using code names. Then it came to her.

The *Shia* holy day of Ashura.

After which came the Shia holy day of Arbaeen.

She opened a new window in her browser and typed in "www.farsi.com." A virtual Farsi-character keyboard appeared, and she began typing rapidly.

14

Yael stared again at the screen of her phone, half-hoping she had imagined the message. She had not. Isis Franklin was dead, found hanged in her prison cell in Istanbul. Yael placed her phone on the table in front of her, trying to disentangle the flurry of emotions and memories.

Isis sitting next to her on the bench on Dag Hammarskjöld Plaza, just by the UN building, trying to persuade her to come out to party at Zone. The gold flecks in her dark eyes shining, her black hair pulled back tight from her forehead.

"Don't be coy, babe. You are a star. The whole building's talking about you. Everyone wants to meet you. Don't think. Just do."

Isis talking about the new information she'd said she had on why no peacekeepers were sent to save David and the other UN aid workers.

"I don't want to get your hopes up. It's all secondhand at this stage. I can't confirm anything, yet. I will tell you more when I have something."

Isis and Yael having lunch in the UN canteen, sharing the latest gossip about who was up and who was down, who was in and who was out. The two of them in the lounge at the UN base in Kandahar, watching DVDs of *Friends* and fending off advances from the "Oakleys," as Yael had dubbed the legion of soldiers, spies, mercenaries, and military contractors who all seemed to wear that brand of wraparound sunglasses. Two women with similar jobs, backgrounds, and interests, enjoying each other's company. Two women who were starting to trust each other, sharing confidences. Or were they? Perhaps Isis had sensed Yael's craving for companionship. Perhaps she exploited it for her own ends, to draw out the information that Yael had, and that so many others wanted.

Had she and Isis ever really been friends?

Yael thought so. She hoped so. Surely her sixth sense would have alerted her if Isis had an agenda. *All* relationships were based on a degree of mutual exploitation; the only question was, how much? Lord knew Yael had used her looks, charm, and considerable skills of emotional manipulation often enough to get what she wanted. Yael didn't remember Isis probing, or trying to extract secrets from her. So, yes. They had been friends.

But then there was the other Isis, the Isis in Istanbul calling her on the phone, taking advantage of Yael's determination to find out why her brother died to lure her into Eli's trap.

"Walk towards me. I'll meet you on the corner, where Tigcilar turns onto Mercan Caddesi. We can talk in the van."

The curse of Azoulay was as strong as ever, it seemed. It already reached from Kandahar to New York and was now looping back to Istanbul. Isis was its third victim. The second was Olivia de Souza. Olivia had been Fareed Hussein's personal assistant. She and Yael had become friends, a relationship that was steadily deepening until last fall, when Mahesh Kapoor, Hussein's chief of staff, had hurled Olivia off a balcony on the thirty-eighth floor of the UN's New York headquarters. Kapoor was now in prison for murder. As for the first victim, his death, and its consequences, was the most painful of all.

Yael walked over to the large picture window. She lived in a good-sized one-bedroom apartment with thick walls, high ceilings, the noisiest water pipes on the Upper West Side, and a breathtaking view of the Hudson River, and had done so for more than a decade, moving in after her grandmother had passed away. Her grandmother had bequeathed it to her with two instructions: take care of the art deco furniture that she had brought from Budapest after the end of the Second World War, and start a family. Yael ran her finger over the surface of the sleek, curved dining table by the window. The furniture, at least, was in fine condition.

She rested her forehead on the window, the glass cool against her skin. The river shone black and silver. A speedboat swept past, bouncing on the water, its searchlight skittering across the water. The lights of the apartment blocks across the water in New Jersey were glowing in the distance, their reflections shimmering on the water's surface. Would she also die alone, like Isis? Perhaps in a prison cell, or, more likely, here on West Eighty-First Street, a childless spinster who spent her weekends reading the *New York Review of Books*, going for epic walks in Central Park, having lunch at the long shared table in the cramped café at Zabar's in the vain hope she sat next to or opposite someone decent-looking and interesting?

And if she did die childless, it would be partly her own fault. Her mind drifted back, to a night seven years ago, on assignment for the UN, stranded overnight in a remote village controlled by the Taliban, high in the Afghan mountains. A night of fear, freezing cold, and a colossal blunder. Sharif's tent had been pitched next to hers. A snap decision, a walk of two steps and she was inside the tent, then soon inside his sleeping bag. Yael was the first woman he had slept with. Her interpreter had instantly fallen in love with her, announced that they would soon be married.

Yael walked back to the mirror above the sideboard. She pulled off her T-shirt, unclipped her bra, let it fall to the floor, cupped her breasts and released them. A little more give, perhaps, but they still sat high on her chest. She pulled at the skin over her cheeks, kneading it this way and that, then let go. It bounced back into place, but lately she noticed that the web of fine lines radiating from the corners of her eyes seemed more pronounced. She needed an eye cream, that was all. She piled her hair up, turned right and left, let it down again, as the memories poured through her head.

Yael had explained, as gently as she could to Sharif, that she could not marry him. He had been devastated, had begged her to just go through with the ceremony for the sake of his family's honor. "Please, Miss Yael, just pretend, for one day," he had pleaded, "then you can go back to New York and we never have to see each other again. One day, that's all I ask. To spare us humiliation." She had been twenty-nine, self-righteous and full of politically correct ideas about the need to modernize Afghanistan. She had refused. Sharif disappeared. Her contacts in the Taliban told Yael that he had completed the martyrdom ceremony. She made some calls, discovered his planned route, shared the information with one of her contacts. A sniper had shot Sharif dead on the road to the Kandahar bazaar. She had not pushed to find out any more details. Back in New York, she had discovered she was pregnant. Ten days later, after two appointments at a clinic, she was not.

Perhaps Eli was right. Maybe she should have married him. She would be living in Tel Aviv now, in a big villa near the coast. She would have children. Their father would be an assassin. An assassin who never gave up.

Eli's operation in Istanbul, and more recently her encounter with him in the park, were the latest and most extreme of a series of attempts by Mossad to bring Yael back to Israel. They had first approached her twelve years ago, while she was studying for her master's in international relations at Columbia University. Then they had tried to play on her patriotism, assuring her that what happened at the Gaza crossing point was a terrible mistake, that lessons had been learned and those responsible disciplined. They did not ask for information—although Yael knew they were interested in two high-profile Palestinian academics who taught at the university—just for her to keep in touch.

Now they wanted Yael back not just because she had been the star of her training class, but also because of the gold-standard information she had access to at the UN. At first they love-bombed her with a stream of invitations to lunches, dinners, receptions, and cultural events. Alone in New York trying to build a new life for herself, sometimes homesick and lonely, she was tempted. But the memory of that day in Gaza, and what she later discovered, steeled her resolve. Eventually the invitations faded away, and for a while Yael thought she was free. Until she realized she was being followed and that her apartment was being watched. Each morning when she left for work, she saw a white van parked across the street. Yael did not alter her routine, or carry out anti-surveillance maneuvers, unless she was headed to a sensitive or confidential meeting. But she did alert a former Columbia classmate who had joined FBI Counterintelligence.

The FBI's New York field office kept a very close watch on the Israeli mission to the UN, in part to ensure that it was not under surveillance or threat from hostile powers or agents. But also because Israel maintained one of the largest and most active espionage operations conducted by a foreign power in the United States. Israel and the United States were close allies, and the United States was also a free and open society—a paradise for Israeli spies who mined it for vast amounts of industrial, technological, and military intelligence, much of it from open sources such as specialist publications and websites.

One morning Yael walked out of her apartment building to see two NYPD vehicles parked by the white van.

When she came home that evening, the white van was still there and so were the NYPD patrol cars. The same thing happened the next day. By the third, the NYPD cars were gone and so was the white van. After that, there had been no more invitations and no more strange vehicles parked nearby. That is, until Yael's involvement a few months ago in the coltan scandal, which had almost brought down the secretary-general and nearly triggered a new genocide in Africa. Then the invitations, the "chance" encounters with Israeli diplomats in the UN buildings and its surrounds, started again.

Yael put her T-shirt back on, tucked it into her sweatpants and walked back to the living room. She leaned back on the sofa, her eyes closed. Images tumbled through her mind like a kaleidoscope, fragments of voices, sounds, places. Congo. New York. Geneva. Istanbul.

Jean-Pierre Hakizimani, the Rwandan warlord wanted for genocide, tearing up the file detailing his crimes against humanity in a Goma hotel room. Hakizimani trussed on the floor of the Hotel Millennium in New York, pleading as Yael held a lighter to his only picture of his three dead daughters.

Her legs locked tight around the American thrashing underneath her in Lake Geneva, pushing his face down into the water as his body convulsed, then stilled.

Sprinting along the roof of the bazaar in Istanbul with Eli behind her. The crack of the rifle. Looking around to see that Eli had vanished.

The memory faded, replaced by understanding. She knew who had shot the gun from Eli's hand.

Najwa was trying to decipher an Iranian opposition website when a window appeared on her computer screen.

<good work. You are on the right track>

She closed her eyes, rubbed them, and drank some more of the coffee she had just made. She looked again. The window was still there, two inches by three, the cursor blinking. Najwa considered her options. She could close the window. Or switch off her computer. Or call UN security. Or Al-Jazeera's computer experts. This was creepy. But it was also intriguing. Who could do this? A government, or an intelligence agency perhaps. Or a very adept hacker.

Najwa typed: **<who are you?>**

The answer came back a second later: **< a friend>**

<what kind of friend hacks into someone else's computer? And won't tell their name?>

<the helpful kind. Who has a tip-off for you. An exclusive>

Najwa smiled despite her rising annoyance. Her new friend knew how to bait the hook. **<why me?>**

<because you do good work>

<I'm listening>

<I need your word that you won't record this dialogue or keep any records of our conversation. It's in your best interest as well as mine.>

<I'll think about it>

Najwa finished typing. A screen grab would doubtless alert her interlocutor, so she grabbed her iPhone, started the camera, and positioned the lens in front of her monitor.

Her monitor screen turned black.

She sat bolt upright, dropping her phone onto the desk. The small blue light in the lower right corner of the monitor frame glowed softly. It was still switched on. She picked up her iPhone and checked the Wi-Fi connection: five solid bars. She checked the hard drive: it was switched on. So there was nothing wrong with the computer. She glanced at the top of the monitor. A tiny pinprick of red light glowed next to the lens of the webcam. Najwa reached around the back of the hard drive and pulled out the webcam cable.

A minute passed, then two and three. Finally, her computer beeped, alerting her that an e-mail had arrived. The screen returned to life, showing her desktop wallpaper of grinning Syrian children in a refugee camp.

The e-mail had no header or sender. But there was an attachment: a JPEG image.

She clicked.

A photograph of a young woman appeared. She was strikingly pretty, with olive skin, dark brown eyes, and long black hair.

Najwa gasped. Letters began to appear in the message window.

<we can play hardball. Or we can be nice. Which would you prefer?>

Najwa glanced at the image again, and swallowed. **<nice.>**

<Good. You will keep your webcam plugged in at all times when we communicate. OK?>

<OK>

<Plug the webcam back in.>

Najwa took the webcam cable and reached around the

back of her drive. She found the USB port but her hand was shaking and she kept missing the slot. She took a deep breath to calm herself. Eventually, the cable jack slid into the USB port.

<Mabrouk, congratulations. Nice outfit, BTW.>

<thanks. What's the tip?>

<two, actually>

<I'm all ears>

<One, Bakri is reliable>

Najwa ignored the flurry of questions that message triggered. Instead she typed: **<two?>**

<Take your crew to the SG's residence immediately.>

Yael switched on her television and flicked through the news channels. President Freshwater's stumble played again and again. There was more coverage about the DC car bomb as numerous pundits speculated as to who, or what, the Army of Forty was. There was no mention anywhere of Isis Franklin's death, but that was not surprising. Nine o'clock at night in New York was four o'clock in the morning in Istanbul, and Isis had been held in a high-security prison. The news would eventually leak out overnight, either from someone inside the prison or the American diplomats who were dealing with Isis's case. She could leak the news herself, of course, and tip off Najwa, or Sami, or both. A little credit in the favor bank with two influential journalists was always useful. She certainly owed Sami a favor. She glanced at her phone. But she owed Yusuf a much large one. She would keep quiet.

She continued channel-hopping until she pulled up Al-Jazeera America. The television screen showed a photograph of a man in late middle age. He was tall and broad-shouldered, with a square jaw and thinning gray hair. Underneath was written: *Breaking: Dutch UN official killed by unknown gunman near Secretary-General's residence.* The photograph vanished, replaced by a live feed of Najwa standing outside the SG's home on Sutton Place in midtown Manhattan. The whole area had been taped off, and police checkpoints had clearly been erected on the corner of East Fifty-Fourth Street and First Avenue. Crowds of onlookers watched, held back by officers wearing Kevlar helmets and full body armor.

"What do we know about this apparent killing, Najwa?" asked a male voice, presumably that of the studio anchor.

"Frank Akerman was leaving a meeting with Fareed Hussein, the UN secretary-general here, about half an hour ago—" Najwa spoke as a police helicopter swooped overhead, the roar of its rotor blades suddenly drowning out her voice, sending her long dark hair flying in every direction. She waited for a few seconds until the helicopter flew on: "—when he was shot dead."

The screen cut to the anchor, a middle-aged Pakistani man, in the New York studio. "Do we have any information about the type of weapon used? Or who might have been responsible?"

Najwa nodded. "Yes, and no, Faisal. My understanding is that he was killed with one shot to the chest, which may have been a high-caliber sniper bullet. But no claims yet of responsibility and no arrests. The police have yet to release a statement."

"So we may be looking at a targeted assassination. Who was Frank Akerman? And why might somebody set a hit man on him?"

"Akerman was assistant secretary-general of the UN's Department of Political Affairs. The DPA deals with the most sensitive international issues. Akerman was a Middle East specialist who just this morning returned from a trip to Istanbul."

Yael stared, her eyes wide in disbelief. Akerman was dead. And he had been in Istanbul? Istanbul was a common neutral meeting point for confidential discussions on Iran. But why hadn't she been informed? She and Akerman had met several times to talk about his role as a back channel between the White House and Tehran. She hadn't seen him around since she'd returned, but had no idea he had recently been dispatched to Istanbul, especially as he had not been at the summit. At well over six feet Akerman was tall, even for a Dutchman, with a laconic style that was almost monosyllabic. They'd never really connected even though, or more likely because, their briefs overlapped. Yael tried not to get involved in turf wars because her mandate from the SG allowed her to act fairly autonomously, and she did get to see Akerman's reports to the SG. At least, the SG *said* they were Akerman's reports. Apart from brief summaries of his meetings with US officials in Washington and Iranians in Tehran, they never seemed to contain much of interest that could not be gleaned from media coverage and specialist newsletters.

The anchor asked, "What was Mr. Akerman doing there, Najwa?"

"That is a very good question, Faisal. We don't know for sure, but my sources tell me that he may have been acting as an intermediary between the United States and Iran. Both sides deny that they have been in contact, but there has been increasing talk of high-level discussions, especially now that they both want to see the defeat of the Sunni extremists and the jihadists in Iraq. We've already seen reports of American and Iranian intelligence agencies and special forces working together against the Islamists, which both parties refute. But the UN would be the obvious channel for these kind of negotiations."

Yael watched, riveted and annoyed. Najwa was better informed than she was, at least about Akerman's movements. Where was she getting this?

"So we could be looking at an alliance between America and Iran? The enemy of my enemy is my friend," said the anchor.

Najwa nodded. "That's how it works, especially in the Middle East."

The anchor continued. "And what is the UN itself saying about this apparent assassination of one its senior officials?"

"Nothing yet, but—wait a second." Najwa paused. "Roxana Voiculescu, the secretary-general's spokeswoman, has just come out of the residence."

The entrance of an imposing five-story mansion appeared on the screen. Roxana Voiculescu stood outside and began speaking. "We utterly condemn the . . ."

A loud crack sounded and a shower of wood splinters erupted around her. Roxana's startled face filled the screen, then was replaced by the sky, a blur of images, the pavement.

There were screams, shouts, a male voice yelling, "Get down, get *down*!" Bystanders and journalists were lying on the pavement, scrabbling for cover behind cars.

Yael leaned forward and placed her wine glass on the coffee table, trying to process what she had just seen. The glass would not stand flat and tilted to one side, spilling a little wine on the wood. She picked it up and immediately saw why the glass was crooked.

A tiny scrunched up fragment of brown paper rested on the table.

15

Rain lashed the windows of La Caridad. The sky was dusk-dark, thick clouds muffling the feeble morning sunshine. Water fell from the sky in a biblical torrent, sweeping along Broadway in great gusts of wet wind. Morning commuters huddled under shop awnings, fingers and thumbs gliding over their phones as though their messages and e-mails would somehow stop the deluge.

The weather suited Yael's mood. She checked her watch. Where was Joe-Don? She had a lot to discuss with him. They had planned to meet for breakfast at eight and it was now almost a quarter past. He was never late. In fact he was usually ten minutes early, checking out the place where they were meeting, even if it was just the same diner they'd been going to for years. And today of all days. She reflexively checked the inside pocket of her denim jacket, where a small plastic envelope held the scrap of paper she had found on the coffee table last night. The confrontation with Eli, the CNN report about the deal in Rwanda that had gone wrong, Akerman's shooting, finding her tell, all had unnerved her. She had hardly slept. Her phone beeped. She glanced down at the text message.

Sorry for delay. On my way. Fighting with OHRM-called me in later.

Yael frowned. What did the UN's Office of Human Resources Management want? An unexpected summons to the personnel department was never a good sign in any organization, especially one announced before nine o'clock in the morning. The waiter, a stooped, elderly Chinese man, arrived with black tea in a small aluminum pot. Yael smiled and thanked him. She declined his offer of a menu. Her breakfast order had not changed in a decade.

La Caridad was one of the last Chinese-Cuban diners on the Upper West Side. Situated on the ground floor of a brownstone apartment building, it looked out over Broadway and West Seventy-Eighth. The diner was renowned for its enormous portions, low prices, and rapid, brusque service. Yael had been coming here for breakfast since she was a child growing up in New York, always sitting at the same corner table. Sometimes, if she closed her eyes and concentrated hard enough through the clamor of the diners' conversations and the staccato Chinese and rapid-fire Mexican Spanish of the waiters, she could think herself back in time to when her parents, David, and Noa piled with her through the door for a weekend brunch treat, she and her siblings loudly declaring what they would order.

She felt the longing inside her. There was no point fighting it and so she let it course through her. It seemed such a long time ago. Another lifetime. Hers, yes, but one lived so differently. David was gone. Noa had moved to Israel. Her father was no longer part of her life. Her mother . . . *Her mother.*

Caught up in last night's news of the bomb in DC and Akerman's murder, Yael had forgotten that her mother was arriving tonight from San Francisco. One part of Yael was pleased and excited. Another was nervous. Nervous and resentful at the way they had grown apart over the years—or rather, the way her mother had *let* them grow apart. Or that she had allowed her mother to let them grow apart. Everything that had happened between them was too dense, too complicated, and too fraught to untangle. But maybe, this weekend, they could start to fix things. And then Yael remembered her conversation with her mother in Gurdeep's taxi last night, before she had noticed the black SUV. Her mother had explained that they needed to talk—about Yael's least favorite topic.

Yael had not spoken to her father for eight years. Just the mention of him triggered a slew of competing emotions. Especially because lately, she had sensed his presence. Once, in her apartment, almost physically, as though he had left his energy there to disturb the air. At other times, that he was somehow involved in the events in which she was caught up. Even watching her, looking out for her. Perhaps she needed that now, when she felt under threat. Yael's father had never liked Eli. Intoxicated by love, sex, and their glittering future, she had brushed off her father's warnings that Eli was not what he seemed. Maybe she should have listened. Now

Eli was back and she was in danger again. Was that why her mother was coming now?

She watched a policeman standing by the broken traffic light on the corner of West Eightieth Street, stoic as he directed traffic, clear rivulets streaming from his cap and cape.

Had Mossad really placed her in the UN, manipulated her up to the thirty-eighth floor, into the SG's office and his deepest confidence? Over the course of a decade? Could they do that? Maybe. Especially if they had something on Fareed Hussein, and Lord knew there was enough out there to compromise him. One sound file in particular, which Yael had in her possession, and which she had nicknamed "Doomsday," would destroy the SG and his reputation for good.

Joe-Don, with his network of contacts through the UN and numerous US government agencies, could find out if Eli was telling the truth. But whatever the truth of his claim, she was not going back to work for her old employer. Ever. For a moment she was back at the crossing point between Gaza and Israel, a stifling hot day fourteen years ago when she made up her mind to leave Eli, and Israel, for good.

The man in the Jeep turns to the passenger in the back, an Arab woman.

She jumps out of the vehicle and runs forward, her head scarf flapping in the breeze. Yael lets go of the boy's hand. The boy sprints toward her. They embrace, crying and sobbing.

The second man climbs out of the vehicle.

Yael smiles at him, happy the mission is over. He smiles back and raises his hand in greeting, but walks toward the boy and his mother.

He says something to the boy and takes his arm. The boy starts sobbing again, shaking, saying no, over and again, holding on to his mother. The mother keens.

Yael closed her eyes for a few seconds. She could still hear the sound of the woman's cries as her son was taken away.

She looked out of the window. A harried-looking young mother pushed a double stroller in front of her, trying to negotiate a path through the rain. A hipster on a commuter bicycle with tiny wheels weaved in and out of the traffic on Broadway, barely missing a blue Toyota trying to squeeze into a parking space. The cyclist banged the roof of the car hard enough to leave a dent and the driver leaned out of the window, yelling abuse as the cyclist sped off. Manhattan was not happy in the rain.

The door opened and Joe-Don Pabst strode over to her table, rain dripping off his hooded green US Army–issue parka. He hung his coat on a nearby stand and sat down in front of her. Yael smiled at the sight of her bodyguard. She hated eating alone in public places. Joe-Don's presence was as welcome as it was reassuring, especially after finding the paper tells on her coffee table. "Hey. I'm so glad you are here. What did personnel want?" she said, her hand moving inside her jacket toward the plastic envelope.

"I don't know. I put them off until midday. I'm not worried about that right now."

She looked at his face. She knew every one of his expressions. He was unsettled, even angry. She took her hand out of her jacket. The paper tells could wait. "So what are you worried about?"

Joe-Don opened his bag and looked around the room to check that no waiters were approaching. "This," he said as he placed half a dozen photographs on the table.

McLaughlin's was a ramshackle Irish bar on the corner of Second Avenue and Forty-Seventh. At eight thirty in the morning it was underlit and underheated, the damp air heavy with the smell of yeast. Smoking had been banned in Manhattan bars since 2003, but the top part of the walls and the ceiling were stained dark yellow with tobacco and nicotine. Last night's glasses were piled up in the bar sink and on several tables. Van Morrison crooned softly in the background, a small concession to the morning after the night before. There were no waitstaff to be seen until a tall man in his early thirties walked out from a door behind the bar. He had scruffy black hair and wore a T-shirt that proclaimed *No Fucking Way, Jose!*

"Breakfast?" he asked.

Najwa nodded.

He ran his fingers through his hair. "There's no menu. We have—"

"Eggs, oatmeal, corn-beef hash, I know," said Najwa. "Oatmeal, please." She looked at Sami.

"Same. With fruit, if you have any."

The waiter looked doubtful. "I'll try."

"Coffee for both of us," Najwa added.

They waited until the waiter had gone.

Sami stared at Najwa. "Are you OK? You look pale. Did you sleep last night?"

She smiled. "Not much. Big story."

Najwa had returned home around two o'clock in the morning, and spent the hours until dawn trying to find out more about the Army of Forty. Her Farsi-language Internet search had proved fruitful once she started looking in the right places, among Iranian opposition websites and forums. She had found a mix of rumors and speculation but much of it pointed in one direction: Tehran. Getting anything on Frank Akerman had proved much more difficult. It was six hours ahead in Europe, so the London, Berlin, and Sarajevo Al-Jazeera bureaus all had reporters on the task as well, but so far they had garnered little, except a rehash of old rumors that Akerman worked, or had worked, for the Dutch military intelligence service, which was hardly surprising. The best potential lead seemed to reach to the Balkans. The Sarajevo correspondent was chasing down a tip that Akerman served in Bosnia during the war in the early 1990s, as a "military adviser" to the UN peacekeeping mission. They had agreed that Najwa would dig deeper at the New York end. There would be some kind of record of Akerman's assignment in the archives.

Any potential Dutch military connection to Bosnia set Najwa's journalistic antenna twitching. The army's reputation, indeed that of the whole country, had never recovered from the July 1995 disaster in Srebrenica. After the city fell to the Bosnian Serbs, the Dutch UN peacekeepers stationed there had handed over eight thousand Bosnian Muslim men and boys before retreating to Zagreb, the Croatian capital, where they drank beer and danced in a line to celebrate their freedom. The Bosnian men and boys were also lined up, but not to celebrate. Fareed Hussein had been the head of the DPKO at the time. Srebrenica was the second genocide on his watch, but the consequence for his career was the same: he was later exonerated by a UN commission of inquiry.

"A very big story," said Sami. "That must have been scary last night."

Najwa shrugged. "One bullet passing by twenty yards away isn't scary. Try being the only woman on Tahrir Square, surrounded by Egyptian men drunk on revolution and their idea of free love—that's scary. I'm just pissed that one of our cameras got damaged."

Sami nodded, but Najwa sensed he was not entirely convinced.

"So who shot at—" he started to say.

"Wait a second," she broke in. Sami was right. She did feel unsettled. Very unsettled, but not because someone hit the SG's front door with a sniper bullet while she was standing nearby. She could still see the JPEG file opening when she clicked on it, the photograph image on her desktop. Reaching inside her purse, she took out two identical black pouches. Made of a heavy fabric, each was slightly larger than a mobile phone, with a long fold-over flap at the top. Two Velcro straps, one horizontal and the other vertical, looped around the outside. She passed one of the pouches to Sami.

He opened the top flap and peered inside. "What's this?"

Najwa pointed at Sami's iPhone on the table.

His eyes widened. "Are you serious?"

She picked up the second pouch, heavy and distended by her phone, and weighed it in her hand. "Once they start shooting people, totally."

Sami picked up his phone, slid it inside the pouch, then dropped it into his messenger bag. "Now we are done with Jason Bourne stuff, can we talk?"

"Sure. Work or love life? How was last night?"

Sami sat back and crossed his arms, his black eyes boring into her. "Work."

To her surprise and embarrassment, Najwa blushed. She understood immediately why he was angry.

Just then the waiter arrived. She thought quickly as he placed two large white mugs of black, scalding hot liquid on the table along with a small jug of milk. There was no point playing the innocent. Najwa received eight calls from Sami after her news story about the shooting. She had eventually called him back after midnight. Her excuse was that she had been tied up in the studio, but the real reason was that she had been so unnerved by the photograph file she could barely concentrate on getting her story reported, edited, and broadcast. But she couldn't tell Sami that. He was right to be angry. Her behavior was a grievous breach of their agreement; not long ago they had sat at this same table as she upbraided him for not telling her about the breakfast he had arranged in secret with Henrik Schneidermann.

Najwa and Sami were technically competitors, but had found a way to pool their resources to mutual advantage. If Najwa had a story, for example, about corruption among UN peacekeepers, she gave Sami a heads-up about the broad outline of her report and when she would be filing it. This allowed him to prepare a follow-up in advance and have it ready to go soon after Najwa's story was broadcast, went online, or both. And when Sami had a story he did the same for Najwa. They shared some of their contacts—although usually kept the best for themselves—and generally did not cooperate with any other reporters. Especially not with their greatest rival, Jonathan Beaufort. Sami and Najwa's editors would have baulked at *any* kind of cooperation with a rival news organization, but as Najwa had explained to Sami, they didn't need to know.

She tipped some milk into her coffee and sipped it. Nor would her vamp act be enough to fix things. Najwa knew Sami was attracted to her, and today she was dressed in one of her favorite outfits: an olive cashmere V-neck sweater that highlighted her generous curves and dark coloring, a matching pencil skirt, and her trademark knee-high black patent leather boots. She had noticed Sami's quick, appreciative glances when she walked through the door. But the two reporters were more like a long-married couple bickering and reconciling than potential lovers.

Najwa put her coffee down. "I'm sorry," she said, in her most apologetic tone, reaching for Sami's hand across the table. "I owe you an apology."

Sami glanced at her hand for several seconds, then shook it off. "Too late. You owed me a *prompt* call back last night. You tweeted twelve times about the shooting but couldn't find the time to pick up your phone?"

Najwa tilted her head to one side, appraising him. Sami had always been sharp, digging up a stream of stories about UN corruption, incompetence, or both, interspersed with occasional feel-good pieces about brave peacekeepers and the good work done by the organization's humanitarian wing. But when they worked together, Najwa had always set the pace. Until recently. What a difference a month and a stream of stories on the front page above the fold made. The disheveled reporter who, in Gap shirts and baggy jeans, looked like a graduate student trying to find the library was gone. Sami's hair, once a wild mass of unruly curls, had been neatly trimmed. This morning he wore a dark blue light wool suit jacket and a crisp light blue shirt. He sat up straight with an easy confidence.

Najwa leaned forward, fixing on him her most demure expression. "Sami. I'm sorry. What more can I say? I didn't have a spare second. The editors were crazy for the story. I am in your debt," she said, resting her hand on his again. "You said you had to talk to me about something important. How was dinner?"

"It wasn't. She canceled."

"*No.* I am so sorry. Why?"

"She said she had an urgent meeting with the SG."

Najwa frowned, thinking for a moment. "But she wasn't there last night. There was just the SG, Akerman, and Roxana." She brightened. "Roxana's pretty. Why don't you ask her round for dinner instead?"

"Ha-ha."

Najwa squeezed Sami's hand. "I still want to introduce you to my cousin. She is very beautiful. Or maybe we should wait until you are recovered. *Habibi*, are you heartbroken?"

Sami laughed despite himself. "No. I'm not. And we

haven't finished talking about your evening. Let's loop back to the beginning. To before the beginning." He slid his hand out, but gently this time. "Here's what I'm wondering. How did you happen to be at the SG's residence, with a film crew, just after Frank Akerman was shot?"

She had anticipated this question. There was only one possible answer: the truth. "A tip-off."

"From who?"

"I don't know."

Sami looked skeptical. "Some random person just happened to contact you and say 'Hi Najwa, why don't you drop whatever you are doing and rush up to the SG's residence because someone's about to get shot when they walk out of the front door?'"

Najwa flushed. "Not exactly."

"So what did they say?"

Najwa paused for a couple of seconds before she spoke. "Enough to make me take my cameraman there."

"But why did you believe them? Any stranger can ring up a news office and say rush here or there. Most journalists don't do that. Why did you?"

"Instinct. Haven't you ever taken a chance on a tip?"

"Yes, of course. But you have no idea who it was?"

Najwa shook her head.

"Did someone call you? Or was it an e-mail, or a text message?"

Take your crew to the SG's residence immediately.

"I told you. I got a tip. I acted on it." Najwa was not about to share the provenance of the information, and what came with it. Not yet, anyway. Better to turn the conversation around. "That was an interesting quote from the 'western diplomatic source' you had in your story. Care to share?"

"Maybe. Tell me about the Army of Forty. I couldn't find any trace of them on the net."

"Then you weren't looking in the right places. Maybe you should brush up on your Farsi."

"I don't speak Farsi. Do you?"

Najwa picked up her coffee and took a sip. "Not fluently. But enough to get by. In fact you don't need Farsi to make the basic connections."

Sami looked puzzled. "Try me."

"You have heard of Ashura?"

He nodded. "Of course."

"And forty days after Ashura is?"

Understanding spread across Sami's face. "The Shia holy day of Arbaeen, commemorating the martyrdom of Hussein ibn Ali, grandson of the Prophet Muhammad."

16

Yael leafed through the photographs. The detail was pin-sharp. She could see the outline of Eli's .22 Beretta behind his jacket as he jammed it against her ribs, read the emotions frozen on his face: anger, resentment, hunger.

Joe-Don stared at Yael, his small blue eyes bright with exasperation. "First Akerman. Now this."

Yael turned red. "Where did you get these?"

"I found them in my post-box this morning. In this envelope." He handed Yael a white envelope embossed with the UN emblem. "Put them away now. The waiter is coming."

She swiftly folded the photos and placed them back inside the envelope. The elderly Chinese man arrived with a cup of coffee for Joe-Don.

"Ready now, miss?" he asked Yael. She nodded, although her appetite was fading fast. "Something to eat?" the waiter asked Joe-Don.

"No thanks. Just coffee."

The waiter looked annoyed. "Peak time now. You gotta order something."

Joe-Don looked around the restaurant, which was half empty. "But . . ."

"I'll have the usual. He'll have pancakes. With jam. Blueberry," said Yael, before Joe-Don could finish his sentence.

Joe-Don silently nodded his assent.

Yael waited until the waiter had gone before she spoke. She sounded as contrite as she could. "I'm sorry."

"Why? I like blueberry jam."

She looked down at the table. "You know what I mean."

Joe-Don glared at her. "You should be sorry. How can I protect you if I don't know you are in danger? Or where you are. I thought you were going on a date last night. A cab door to door, you promised me. And a call or text if you were . . . weren't . . ." He looked away, embarrassed.

Yael was about to tell him about the paper tell when she suddenly felt an overwhelming rush of affection for the craggy-faced, socially awkward, intensely loyal man sitting in front of her. She placed her hand on his. "Do you know how much you mean to me?"

Now Joe-Don turned pink. "Yeah. Sure. Anyway, what the hell were you doing with Eli and his team of hoods in Tompkins Square Park?"

She took a deep breath. She told him about the SUV that had been following her, how she had gone to the park to take a few minutes out before going over to Sami's place when Eli and his team had appeared, how he had threatened Noa and demanded Yael return to Israel. She pulled out her iPhone from her purse and called up the photographs she had taken last night from the taxi. Her phone looked like any commercially available iPhone, but it was not. As well as the ultrasensitive voice-recording app, it had also been fitted with NSA-standard encryption software and a broadcast-quality, high-definition still and video camera.

She handed the phone to Joe-Don.

He flicked through the shots, then handed it back to Yael. "Not very subtle. Looks like the kind of car that musician guy you work out to would drive. What's his name? M&M's?"

She laughed. "Eminem."

"Was the SUV Eli's people?"

Yael shook her head. "I don't think so. It's not how we were taught, or how they operate. He said they were way behind me in two ordinary sedans. I always know when he is lying. He was telling the truth."

"So who was it?"

"Whoever took the photos, I guess."

"And who's that?"

"Someone I pissed off along the way." Yael shrugged.

Joe-Don smiled. "Well, that narrows the field. How long did Eli give you?"

"Ninety-six hours. Four days. A ticket is booked for me on the El-Al flight to Tel Aviv on Monday evening."

Joe-Don sipped his coffee as he processed the latest news from his wayward charge. Born in Minnesota, the taciturn US Special Forces veteran had worked for the UN's Department of Safety and Security for more than a decade, the last six as Yael's bodyguard. Barely five feet nine, he had sloping shoulders and the physique of a boxer who had mellowed somewhat with age but was still hard-packed muscle at the core. Now in his late fifties, his face was scored with deep lines from his nose to his mouth. His thick, callused fingers and almost simian appearance led some to dismiss him as a muscle-bound goon, which was a mistake. His instinct for danger and sharp, subtle intelligence had saved his life, and Yael's, on numerous occasions. He beat back kidnap attempts by insurgents in Kandahar and Kabul, and he still walked with a slight limp after taking a bullet in his leg when he threw himself on top of Yael during a Gaza firefight between Hamas and Fatah gunmen. Despite his bravery and his complete lack of self-interest—or perhaps because of them—Joe-Don had many enemies at the UN, none more than Fareed Hussein. When he was serving in Baghdad, Joe-Don sent a long memo to Hussein, who was then at the Department of Political Affairs, warning him that the city's UN headquarters needed properly manned checkpoints at staggered perimeters, zig-zag approach roads, blast walls, and shatterproof windows.

Hussein had not replied, but the following year, 2004, a suicide bomber smashed a truck through the wall of the building, killing twenty-three people and injuring many more. Joe-Don was immediately fired for "dereliction of duty." He protested, producing copies of his 2003 memo to Fareed Hussein, and was instead relegated to an advisory position with reduced security clearance. After a reminder from the US ambassador to the UN that the United States paid 25 percent of the UN budget, Joe-Don was properly reinstated, with top-level clearance that gave him access to any UN mission or building anywhere in the world. Nor was Hussein in any position to object when Joe-Don, impressed with Yael, decided to work with her.

The waiter reappeared with a tray of food. He placed a tortilla, tomato salad, and a portion of red beans in front of Yael, and the pancakes in front of Joe-Don.

Joe-Don upended a small container of blueberry jam over the thick pancake. "So let's count the candidates. You derailed KZX's coltan plan. You saved Freshwater. But these are tactical victories. Everything is still in play. Clairborne. Prometheus. KZX. Eli and his friends. They are all still out there. We know they want their war. They won't stop and they won't give up."

"Did they kill Akerman?" asked Yael.

"I'm not sure. Akerman had a lot of enemies with long memories. Very long memories. I saw the NYPD firearms trajectory analysis early this morning."

"And?"

"A single shot, probably from the roof of an apartment building a block or two away. They think the corner of East Fifty-Fourth and Second Avenue. The New York JTTF has opened a case file. It was a tricky shot, on a moving target."

Each of the FBI's fifty-six field offices hosted a Joint Terrorism Task Force, bringing together dozens of US local and national law enforcement and intelligence agencies. The New York JTTF office, the first to be established in 1980, was one of the most high-profile.

"Did you know Akerman had been in Istanbul?" Yael asked.

Joe-Don shook his head. "No. Only after he was shot. It was an overnighter. In and out. Did you?"

"No. And I didn't know Akerman was meeting Fareed last night. What is Fareed up to?"

Joe-Don speared some more pancake and raised his fork. "Want some?"

"No. Fareed?"

"What's Fareed up to? Let's see. Number one. Guarding his back. Number two. Guarding his back. Number three. Sharpening a knife and keeping it nearby in case it is needed in anyone else's back. But to answer your question, it looks like Fareed is opening a private back channel to someone in Tehran."

"Without telling me."

"Exactly. You might ask him about that."

"I will." Yael cut off a slice of tortilla. It was delicious, rich and eggy, with thick slices of potato. "Eli told me something else."

"What?"

"That Mossad placed me at the UN. Is that possible?"

"Sure. Anything is possible. Especially at the UN."

False flag operations, when an asset was recruited by an agent purporting to be from one country or secret service while really working for another, were well known in the world of shadows. Mossad was renowned for them.

"How?" asked Yael.

Joe-Don shrugged. "It's not hard to get someone a job at the UN. A fat envelope or the right connections is enough. The real question is, why did Fareed Hussein pluck you from the masses and fast-track your career?"

Yael smiled. "Because of my natural talents, charm, and puritan work ethic?"

"Sure. All of those. Or maybe because Mossad has something on the SG. They could have played a long game. And now it's coming to the end." Joe-Don paused. "There is more bad news. From Istanbul."

Yael nodded. "I know. I got a text from Yusuf. Is it true?"

"It's true she is dead. Isis hanged herself in her cell. Whether she was helped along the way is an open question."

"Clairborne?"

"Clairborne and/or his Iranian friends. She was no more use to them, and she knew too much."

Yael looked thoughtful. "Is my father wrapped up in this mess?"

"It's starting to look that way. You should talk to your mom. She is still due in tonight?"

"Yes, she is. And I will. Meanwhile, KZX are hosting a reception tomorrow night. At Columbia University."

"I know. Are you going?"

"Yes. I think I'll take her. She'll enjoy the glamour and the glitz. There is also a dinner later. Fareed Hussein and KZX and their friends. I'm not invited."

"Are you surprised?"

Yael laughed. "Not very. But I want to know what they talk about. Can you fix it?"

"Sure. Anything else?"

"Yes. There is. But that's harder to fix." Yael put her fork down into the tortilla, watched it slowly topple over. She looked outside. The sky was even darker. The rain smashed onto the cars and sidewalks as though it was being fired from the heavens.

Joe-Don sensed her mood. "Tell me."

"I don't know, J.D. I think I'm reaching my limit. I've had enough of being followed, threatened, kidnapped, shot at. I'm thirty-six. I want to go shopping. I want to go to the movies. I want a hot guy to take me out for dinner. Someone who has never heard of the UN. Someone who doesn't even read the newspapers. Plus . . ."

"Plus what?"

"Body clock. Tick-tock."

"So go to the movies. Take a day off. You deserve it."

"Not on my own. Not again."

"Then stand down. Or just take a long break." Joe-Don's eyes probed Yael's. "You've done enough. Much more than most. Find a guy. They should be queuing up for a girl like you."

"Yes. They should." Yael looked around, smiling. "Do you see them? Because I don't. Meanwhile, I just have to prevent the outbreak of World War Three. Then I promise I will take a long holiday." She glanced down at her breakfast. "There's more."

"Go on."

Yael reached inside her jacket, extracted the plastic envelope and upended the contents onto her palm. She handed a scrunched up scrap of paper to Joe-Don.

Thunder cracked the sky, the boom so loud it made Yael jump.

The waiter presented two steaming bowls of oatmeal to Najwa and Sami. In the center of each was a single triangle of canned pineapple. Najwa looked at him, and started laughing.

"What's so funny?" he asked indignantly. "Oatmeal. With fruit. That's what you ordered, isn't it?"

She gave him her best smile. "We did. Absolutely. Thank you."

He left, still bristling.

Najwa sprinkled brown sugar on her oatmeal and slowly stirred it, watching the sugar trails dissolve in the mush. "Schneidermann," she said.

Sami shook his head. "It's really sad. And now it's like he was never there. Roxana's in his office. Even Francine's gone."

In theory, the UN spokesman was available to journalists whenever they needed to speak to him or her. In practice, access had been strictly controlled by Francine de le Court, his secretary. An immaculately dressed Haitian of a certain age, she was known as "Madam Non" among the UN press corps.

"I know," said Najwa. "Actually, I kind of miss our duels."

"Where is she now?"

"At home, I guess. She left last week."

"Jumped or pushed?"

"Pushed, I heard. A hefty shove from Roxana and a payoff from HR. No leftovers from the ancien régime allowed." She took a spoonful of oatmeal. "Remind me—what did the Schneidermann autopsy say?"

"Natural causes. A massive heart attack."

She nodded. "Do you believe that? Really believe it?"

Sami was thoughtful. "I'm not sure. We know he had no history of heart trouble. He was a bit overweight, but that's all."

"I'm not sure I believe it either. Remember your article about Abbas Velavi?"

"The Iranian dissident?"

Najwa took out a small tablet computer from her purse and handed it to Sami. "That's the one. Press play."

Sami watched Abbas Velavi's wife recount the arrival of the mysterious visitor and her belief that her husband was murdered.

"The visitor was bald. He had a neat beard and wore fine black leather gloves. He did not take them off all the time he was here. He said he had a skin condition."

Najwa put the tablet back inside her purse and took out the photograph of Salim Massoud. She slid it across the table to Sami.

He looked down at the picture, then up at Najwa. "There are lots of bald men with beards and black gloves. How do we know it's . . ." he glanced at the Arabic script. "Salim Massoud, whoever he is? Where did you get this?"

She ignored his questions and closed her eyes for a few seconds, concentrating hard, before she spoke. "Let's talk this through. We know that the Prometheus Group and Efrat Global Solutions were working with Caroline Masters on a pilot plan to privatize UN security as a stepping-stone to outsourcing all peacekeeping to private military contractors. That was the Washington Stratagem, worth billions of dollars. You wrote about that. Controversial, but not illegal. But what if there was something else? We know that Schneidermann had been at the SG's residence before he came to meet you for breakfast. Why?"

Sami drank his coffee. "Schneidermann told me the day before that he—meaning the SG—wanted to give me proof of an Iranian connection to the Prometheus Group, and somehow, to the UN."

Najwa stared at him. "Iran, again. You didn't tell me this before. And why did the SG want you to have this proof?"

"Hussein was ambivalent about the Washington Stratagem; he would probably have gone along with it if it suited his interests, and if it hadn't been Masters's idea. He hates her. The feeling is mutual. But because it came from Masters, it would be her triumph. If he could show an Iranian connection to the Prometheus Group it would bring her down. But you still haven't told me how you got this photograph."

"From a source. A reliable source. It's good enough for me, so should be for you. Don't worry about that. We need proof of the Iran-Prometheus connection. The SG must have other copies of the documents."

"Of course. And all we have to do is persuade him to hand over another set."

Najwa spooned up some more oatmeal. "That's all. But he doesn't need to now that Masters is out of the picture. It's not in his interest any more. Of course you could ask Roxana. I'm sure she'll help. Maybe you could take her out for some more cocktails."

"Or maybe you could," said Sami, drily.

Najwa's spoon was suspended in midair. "Good idea. But wait a moment. You were meeting Schneidermann here. The SG's residence is on Sutton Place and First Avenue. That's what, seven blocks up and one across. So he probably walked down First Avenue."

"And?"

"CCTV. There must be CCTV footage. It was only two weeks ago." She put her spoon down. "This is how it's going to work. I'm going to chase down the CCTV footage. You can find Francine and Velavi's widow."

"Well, thank you, Ms. Al-Jazeera bureau chief. But the last time I checked, I was employed by the *New York Times*."

Najwa fixed her doe eyes on him. "Please? Anyway, I believe you owe me an iPad Air, an iPhone 6, a Montblanc pen, and a leather portfolio. All inscribed with my name. This will cancel our debt."

Sami, Najwa, and the rest of the UN press corps had flown from New York to Istanbul on an airplane sponsored by KZX, who provided a lavish goodie bag for each journalist. Sami handed his back. So had Najwa, in solidarity and with only the slightest of pouts.

Sami laughed. "Deal. But I have a question."

Najwa nodded.

"When was Akerman shot?"

"At five minutes past nine. I got that from the cops."

"And when did you get the tip-off?"

Najwa thought for a moment. "I don't know exactly. The communication method was . . . unorthodox. Let me think for a moment." She stirred her coffee as she ran through the events of the previous evening in her mind. The complicated communication method, and especially the photograph, had thrown her off track.

She couldn't say for sure, at least with the precision Sami and she were looking for. The communications had disappeared from her computer. *But*: she would have phoned Maria and Philippe, her French cameraman, immediately after the message appeared on her screen. Najwa removed her phone from the pouch and flicked through to her call log. "Oh," she said, looking down at the screen. She sat back, her face creased in worry. "What time did I say Akerman was shot?"

"Ten minutes past nine."

Najwa gave her phone to Sami. "That's when I called Maria."

"Ten to nine. That's creepy." He handed it back.

"I know. And problematic."

"Very. If the cops start asking questions about why you called your producer twenty minutes before Akerman was shot, then rushed to the residence . . . Is there a record of an incoming call? Was it a phone tip-off?"

"No. Nobody called me, which helps. If they ask, I'll just say we had a tip-off that Akerman was. . . ."

"About to be shot dead?" said Sami, brightly.

"*No.* That Akerman was having a secret meeting with the SG. That's a legitimate story." Najwa studied him, a quizzical expression on her face. "Why didn't you come up to the residence once the story broke? You could have been there by ten. I would have told you everything. You were free. Yael canceled."

He looked away, his voice suddenly tight. "I got an e-mail last night. That's why I didn't go up to the residence."

"And?"

"Take a look," said Sami, as he handed Najwa a sheet of paper.

17

Yael walked to the front of the line in the security tent and showed her UN identity card to the uniformed security officer. "The SG is expecting me. We have a meeting at ten thirty," she explained politely.

The security officer, a middle-aged man with olive skin, a thick mustache, and a heavy paunch, handed Yael's card back without looking at it. His Velcro name tag said "Nero."

"Sorry, ma'am. We are on the highest state of alert." Nero's voice was gruff, almost hoarse. He did not sound very sorry. "There is no way to speed up the security procedure. Please take your place in the line. Thank you for your help today."

Yael did not feel especially helpful. She looked at her watch. It was 9:45 a.m. She had passed through the main entrance on East Forty-Second and First Avenue more than a quarter of an hour ago. The walk from there, through the open courtyard, to the door of the General Assembly Building usually took a minute or so. There was sometimes a short wait for the elevators, especially to the thirty-eighth floor, but she should have been in her office by now, with plenty of time to get to the SG's suite a few doors away.

Instead she had been standing in a queue for a metal detector in a freezing, shaky tent in the middle of the courtyard for fifteen minutes, waiting to go through the same procedure she had just completed at the UN's main entrance. She was cold, wet, pissed, and unsettled. Who had taken the photographs of her and Eli? The same person, or group, who had been inside her apartment? Generally she did not like to jump queues and use her connections with the SG just for convenience's sake. But at this rate she would miss her meeting with him, and that would likely be it for the rest of the day, at least. Last night's CNN report was still echoing through her head. If anyone would know the details of the deal that may have resulted in her brother's death, it would be Fareed.

Thunder rumbled, echoing over the East River. Yael shivered. The weather had not improved, drops of water the size of hard candies gushing through the pavement and gutters, drumming on the canvas walls of the security tent as the wind pulled the walls in and out like a pair of giant bellows.

Helicopters clattered overhead; NYPD checkpoints sealed off FDR Drive, the highway running up Manhattan's east side, five blocks above and below the UN complex, causing a mile-long backup as they checked the papers and the vehicles of anyone wanting to enter the area. Police launches cruised up and down the East River. The Queensboro Bridge at East Fifty-Ninth Street was closed, causing massive traffic jams deep into Queens. Even the cable car to Roosevelt Island had been shut down.

To slow approaching traffic the NYPD had set up concrete blocks in a zigzag pattern along First Avenue, while officers on foot frisked everyone walking by the Secretariat Building or waiting to enter it. Local radio stations broadcast a continuous alert, strongly advising locals to avoid the whole midtown area, especially on the East Side, unless they had "urgent and necessary business" there. Queues at the visitor's entrance security tent on First Avenue and East Forty-Third reached down almost two blocks.

Yael had traveled on the subway, taking the 1 to Times Square, and then a bus to the corner of East Forty-Second Street and First Avenue. She wore a poncho and rubber boots, and carried an umbrella, but even that was insufficient protection for the short walk from the bus stop and the wait to pass through security. Her damp jeans were cold against her legs. Her blouse stuck to her lower back, where the rain had somehow found a path inside. She stood aside, took out her phone, and called Fareed Hussein on his private number, one shared with just a handful of people. No answer. She stared at the screen as if to force him to pick up. Nothing happened. He hadn't taken her call last night, either. In the chaotic aftermath of the shooting, that was understandable, but why not now? Where was he? Yael tried Grace Olewanda, his secretary. Grace, a lively Congolese woman, was usually an ally, always willing to find a few minutes for Yael in the SG's schedule. Her number was busy. Again. Yael waited a minute and hit redial. This time Grace picked up, and Yael quickly explained her situation. A few seconds after they hung up, the phone on the desk rang. The desk security officer, a stocky African-American woman in her early forties, looked around the tent until she saw Yael, then she nodded and put the handset down, beckoning her forward.

Yael emptied her pockets into a plastic tray, dropped her purse onto the conveyor belt, and stepped through the metal detector. The light flashed green. She handed her identity card to Nero. Clearly unhappy that she had pulled rank on him, he checked her name against a list, her face against a computerized database on his tablet computer, drawing out the process as long as he could. Yael knew most of the security staff, but she had never seen him before. She gathered her possessions from the plastic tray and he handed her identity card back, then she walked through into the entrance foyer of the Secretariat Building, down the long, glass-walled corridor that overlooked First Avenue, and over to the elevators. A sign announced that, due to the security situation, there were no direct elevators to the thirty-eighth floor. All staff and visitors had to go to the thirty-seventh floor, pass through a further security check, and then be escorted to the SG's office. The new procedure added a further delay.

She was walking to the elevator bank when she saw Roger Richardson striding across the foyer in a drenched fawn double-breasted mackintosh. She waved to him. He smiled, walked over to her. They both instinctively stepped aside, away from the crowd, chatting about the appalling weather as they walked toward the glass wall that looked out over First Avenue.

They stopped there. Yael waited as the CNN correspondent took off his round, tortoiseshell spectacles and wiped the rain off. "I don't have any more, Yael," Richardson said.

"There was supposedly a deal. But who, what, when, where, why, I'm still working on it. You heard everything I know."

Yael nodded, slowly. "Of course. Look, I know you cannot reveal your source. But is there . . . someone I could I ask for more information?"

Richardson smiled, put his now clean spectacles back on. "Not much happens here without Fareed knowing about it."

Najwa stared at Sami's printout. Yael Azoulay was clearly recognizable, her hair was pulled back in a ponytail. In a white T-shirt and loose blue cotton trousers, she knelt down next to an Arab boy in a large open area. Warning signs nearby were written in Hebrew and Arabic. The boy looked to be in his early teens. He wore badly fitting jeans, a T-shirt, and over that a khaki vest with six front pockets. Each was filled with light brown blocks, from which a series of linked wires extended.

She said, "Talk me through it, again. When did you get this?"

"At eight thirty last night. It was from 'afriend99@gmail.com.' I have a friend who works at Google, so I checked and it's fake. They have no record of any such account or e-mail address."

"So we are probably dealing with a government intelligence service."

Sami nodded. "Considering where the photo was taken, I don't think we need to look very far."

"I agree." Najwa looked down at the printout again. "She looks much younger. Very determined. But kind of satisfied as well."

"She should do. She did a good job. The bomb was defused."

"How do you know about this?"

"I remember the incident. It was fourteen years ago. We were already here, but all our relatives in Gaza were talking about it. There was some media coverage in the US as well, although nothing mentioned Yael."

"How old was he?"

"Fourteen. He was mentally handicapped. Islamic Jihad got hold of him. They kidnapped him, set him up."

"OK, so we have some nice background for a feature. 'The secret past of the SG's negotiator.' How she talked down a suicide bomber and saved dozens of lives." She paused, her brow furrowed. "But why is someone sending you this?"

"I'll get to that. Actually, it's not such a heartwarming story. The problem is what happened next. The boy disappeared. The Israelis took him. They had a couple of minutes together and then he was taken away. His mother was hysterical. She never saw him again."

"How do you know all this?" asked Najwa.

Sami looked away and shook his head, his voice cracking slightly as he spoke. "Because he was my cousin."

Twenty minutes later, once again composed and professional, Sami escorted Najwa into the *New York Times*' new United Nations bureau. The old office had been a musty, cramped cell, barely ten feet by ten, with cables sagging from the roof, leaking ceiling tiles, and a cracked window that overlooked an airshaft. Sami's rickety desk was always piled high with papers next to a heavy, old-fashioned computer monitor that took up most of the space. There was only one chair, and usually Najwa needed to clear away various half-eaten donuts, cookies, and sandwich crusts before she could find a place to sit on Sami's desk.

The new United Nations bureau of the *New York Times* appeared to have been transplanted directly from an office furniture showroom. It was pristine, clean, and light. A pair of light gray wooden desks stood in the center of a room at least four times the size of the old office, its large windows overlooking First Avenue. Two LED flat-screen monitors stood back-to-back on top of the desks, cables all but invisible, Apple brushed-aluminum keyboards in front of them. One wall was lined with graphite-colored metal filing cabinets that matched the two $1,000 Mirra office chairs in front of each desk. Najwa knew they cost $1,000 as she had just ordered six for her bureau. Two flat-screen televisions were attached to the wall, one showing BBC World News and the other, she was glad to see, tuned to Al-Jazeera America. A top-of-the-line Nespresso machine stood on top of one of the cabinets. There was even a bowl of fresh fruit.

But the most noticeable addition was the young woman sitting in front of her computer screen. She carried on typing as Sami and Najwa walked in. "Hi. I have some more on Frank Akerman," she said, without looking up, "he was . . . hold on a second . . . something at the Dutch ministry of . . . I've got it . . ." She closed her document and turned around in her chair to see Sami accompanied by Najwa. "Oh," she said, startled for a moment. She glanced at Sami, as if waiting for instructions.

"Hold that for a moment. Collette, this is Najwa al-Sameera."

Collette Moreau stood up and extended a graceful, well-manicured hand. "What a pleasure to meet you in person," she said, her smile revealing two rows of even white teeth and a dimple on the right side of her mouth.

"Thanks. And welcome aboard. When did you start?" asked Najwa. Collette's grip was warm, dry, and just firm enough to be assertive without being aggressive.

Collette let go of Najwa's hand and looked at her watch. "Fifty eight minutes ago. At nine o'clock. Are you OK? That must have been terrifying last night."

"I'm fine. The gunman wasn't aiming at me."

"What a story. Do you think they were trying to kill the SG? Or Roxana?"

Najwa shook her head as the two women stepped apart. "No. He wanted to kill Frank Akerman, and he did. It was a single shot at the SG's door. He wanted to scare him and Roxana."

"Then it worked. The SG arrived here in a convoy of armored vehicles this morning. I'm one of your biggest fans, by the way."

"Thanks," said Najwa, as she rapidly reappraised Sami's new deputy. She had expected a wide-eyed newbie, one step up from an intern, overawed to be working for the *New York Times* and mixing with the titans of the UN press corps. She did not anticipate this sleek, efficient vision of Parisian chic wearing Chanel pumps and a Rado watch. Collette Moreau was young, petite, and fizzing with energy. She had wide brown eyes, a bob of thick, mahogany-colored hair, carefully groomed eyebrows, a subtle dusting of makeup, and a French accent that Najwa knew every man in the building would find cute. Her fitted white blouse and tight blue tapered slacks highlighted her almost boyish figure. Najwa was bursting to ask Collette what she had discovered about Akerman. But this was Sami's colleague, and Sami's territory. He had first rights. And it was never a good idea to look too eager.

Sami looked at both women, both of whom were waiting for him to tell Collette to share what she had found out. "Come," he said to Najwa, a mischievous smile on his face. "Tour time."

She flashed him an angry glance, but had no choice other than to go along with the game. "*Mabrouk*, Sami. It's beautiful. Like moving from a prison cell to a five-star suite. But I thought you were going to move into the office next to our bureau. It's been empty for ages."

"This is what they came up with. I took it while the offer was still open."

Najwa paused before she spoke. "How, exactly, did you do that? The *Financial Times* and the *Times* of London are still stuck in their poky holes. Who was here before?"

"Healthwire. The agency in Paris that Henrik Schneidermann worked for before he became the SG's spokesman. They closed their operation, so this space freed up. Complete with their furniture and computers."

She thought for a moment before she replied. "Sure, but there was a long queue ahead of you. And you already had an office, even if it was a dump."

Sami shrugged. "Add it to the list of UN mysteries. I'm not complaining."

Collette was sitting back down and tapping away again at her keyboard as she stared at her screen. But Najwa could see from her posture, straight and alert, that she was listening hard to every word.

Najwa's phone beeped. She scrolled through the messages until she found the latest arrival, which she read quickly. "Just in time for the presser with Roxana. From our Sarajevo bureau." She glanced up to see Sami staring hungrily at her phone. She inclined her head toward Collette, as if to say, *You know what to do.*

Sami turned to Collette. "What did you get on Akerman?"

Collette spun around, with a printout in her hand. "Captain Frank Akerman. Dutch Military intelligence, 1992 to 1994. Liaison officer with UNPROFOR, the peacekeeping mission in Bosnia. He was also an UNMO."

UNMO stood for United Nations military observer. UNMOs were, in essence, licensed spies who could cross back and forth across front lines in conflict zones where the UN had a presence. They used their privileged UN status to gather information for the Department of Peacekeeping, and UNMO reports were a treasure trove of military intelligence, recording highly coveted data like troop numbers and deployments, weapons capability, and command structures. Everyone understood that the UNMOs' reports would soon find their way to the defense and intelligence services of those countries who had an interest, or troops deployed, in the conflict zone.

"And then?" asked Sami.

Collette said, "Trail goes cold. I'm working on it."

"It just heated up," said Najwa as she handed her phone to Sami.

Clarence Clairborne watched his visitor lift the antique volume off the bookshelf and slowly open it. Despite the prodigious amount of bourbon he had drunk yesterday, he felt relaxed and refreshed. Clairborne always slept well after a visit from Eugene Packard. The doubts, the nagging voices in his head, all were quelled by the pastor's certainty. He was doing the right thing, for himself, for Prometheus, and, most of all, for America. For this was God's work, even if it demanded some curious allies, like the man currently in his office.

Menachem Stein nodded. "I am impressed. I didn't know you were a fan of Rumi." The leather binding creaked as he gently opened the book.

"Careful, now," said Clairborne, "that's five hundred years old."

The work by Persia's most famous poet had pride of place in Clairborne's office library. It was displayed full on, flanked by other works on the Middle East in Arabic, Farsi, German, and English that had been tracked down by Clairborne's international network of antiquarian booksellers.

Stein slowly closed the book and returned it to its shelf. He looked around, his surprise showing on his face. Clairborne was used to Stein's reaction, as the rare visitors allowed into his office were often taken aback by the understated furnishings. He was never sure quite what they expected—a Confederate flag, perhaps, a poster advertising a lynching, or a piped recording of a rendition of "Dixie"—

but not this. The dark floor of Vermont oak was covered with an enormous Persian rug, woven for the royal court. A pattern of roses and jasmine flowers swirled around the center medallion. The walls were covered with wooden paneling from the same forest as the flooring. Clairborne's heavy, old-fashioned desk once belonged to Richard Nixon, before he became president. Apart from the framed photographs of Clairborne with three presidents and Eugene Packard, the only sign of ego was the P and G monogram on the wooden humidor.

Clairborne gestured to Stein to sit next to him in one of the two leather armchairs in the corner. "What can I get you, Menachem? Coffee, water, both, something stronger? I have an excellent bourbon, from a boutique distillery in Kentucky. Something to smoke?" Clairborne asked.

"Thank you. Nothing. I'm fine."

No, you are not, Clairborne wanted to say. The last time he had seen the chairman of Efrat Global Solutions, barely a month ago, they had been hunting on his estate in West Virginia. Five hundred acres of prime farmland and forest, with a twelve-room lodge. Stein had shot several ducks out of the sky, but Clairborne none. Most incredibly of all, Stein had actually lowered the barrel of Clairborne's gun when he was about to take a shot, just to emphasize his point.

Clairborne did not like Stein. He was no fan of Israel or Israelis, and thought the Palestinians had a rough deal. But there was no money to be made in Palestine. However, although he felt no warmth toward Stein, Clairborne did admire him. Stein, like Clairborne, was a survivor. EGS had been deeply implicated in the coltan scandal when, less than a year ago, two of its most senior officials had been arrested in Congo while handing out arms to a Hutu militia so its members could trigger a new genocide. Stein himself barely escaped an Interpol warrant.

That scandal, like several others, had not affected EGS's share price or its contracts. In fact, it only seemed to boost their value. EGS was the largest private military contractor in the world, its headquarters five minutes' walk from Capitol Hill. For Stein, like Clairborne, the instability in the Middle East had been very good for business. Despite the Israeli connection, EGS had just signed a multi-billion-dollar contract to train the Emirates' new military and paramilitary forces.

Stein sat down next to Clairborne. Stein was in his early sixties, dressed casually in jeans, Timberland boots, and a white shirt under a blue V-neck sweater. He had close-cropped silver hair, which highlighted the most remarkable thing about him: his eyes. One blue and one gray, they had the intensity of lasers.

Normally they unsettled Clairborne. But today he had ammunition.

"Let's get down to business, Menachem. The car bomb in DC. That was your responsibility. It would have been a damn useful backdrop to the Reykjavik meeting. Blood and shrapnel, a few yards from the White House. A trail of terror from Tehran to Pennsylvania Avenue. What happened?"

Stein frowned, tapped his fingers on the armchair. "I am not sure. Everything was in place. You saw what the cops found. There was no reason for anyone to be suspicious of the vehicle. A gray Ford. But someone made a call, alerted the cops."

"Does EGS have a leak?"

Stein shook his head. "Impossible. Maybe the leak is at your end, Clarence."

"Out of the question. I am the only one who knew about it."

"Really? What about your friend? Packard the preacher? He was here yesterday, I believe." Stein patted the arm of the chair. "Sitting here, I am sure, calling down fire and brimstone."

Clairborne was about to ask how Stein knew about Packard, but immediately realized there was no point. EGS obviously had the Prometheus Group under surveillance. If he had done the same to EGS, he might know more about why the car bomb failed to detonate. "Packard does not know operational details," said Clairborne. "And even though the bomb did not go off, at least we have laid a trail back to Tehran. What about the girl?"

Stein looked at his watch. "Meeting with the SG by now. He will give her the Reykjavik assignment."

"I'll miss her once she's gone. She's a firecracker."

Stein smiled. "Yes. She is."

18

The SG was waiting for Yael by the elevator, a rare honor. They briefly hugged, his soft belly pushing against her for a couple of seconds. She could smell his coconut hair lotion. There was the hint of new aftershave or cologne as well. It was light and floral for a male fragrance, but somehow familiar.

They stepped apart. Hussein stood in front of Yael, his hands resting lightly around hers. "Thank you so much for your calls last night. That meant a lot to me."

"Of course. I was so worried about you." Her next question, as to why he had not picked up and actually spoken to her, was left hanging in the air.

Every successful politician and diplomat had the ability to make the person they were with feel like they were the center of the universe, even if only for a few seconds, but Hussein's skill in drawing in his companion was unrivaled. Yael had experienced every weapon in his charm armory, and while that knowledge blunted their efficiency, it did not neutralize them. Their relationship was complex and intense, but was laced through with genuine mutual affection. Each found in the other something missing from their personal lives. Hussein kept one hand on Yael's upper arm as he escorted her through to his office. The warmth of his palm was still curiously comforting.

Grace Olewanda looked up as Yael and the SG stepped into the anteroom where she worked. Yael mouthed the word "Thanks." Grace nodded and mouthed "Anytime" in reply as Yael and the SG walked through into his suite.

Even in a city that prized real estate like no other, and rewarded its power brokers accordingly, the office of the secretary-general of the United Nations stood out for its size and views. It took up most of the length of the thirty-eighth floor of the Secretariat Building, and all of its width. The front windows looked out over First Avenue and the East Forties, steel-and-glass canyons of office blocks and apartment buildings. The rear view took in the East River and the shoreline of Queens with its giant billboard advertising Pepsi Cola. The side windows showcased First Avenue and Roosevelt Island—a narrow strip of land just off the Manhattan side of the East River—and the Queensboro Bridge with the cable-car service that connected the two.

The SG normally took pride in his office, showing off the view even to his regular visitors. But not today. Yael glanced at Hussein. There were dark shadows under his eyes and his skin had a grayish pall. He was walking with a slight stoop. "Fareed, are you sure you're OK?"

"Physically, yes. I'm fine. But I'm very shaken. It's such a tragic waste. And at such an incredibly sensitive time. Frank was a very talented diplomat. He will be much missed."

As they spoke, Yael suddenly realized what the second fragrance was. A few days earlier she had stopped by Bloomingdales on her way home. A sales assistant at the perfume counter had sprayed Zest, "for the busy urban woman," on Yael's wrist. Why was the SG wearing, or carrying a trace of, a woman's fragrance on his skin? His wife, Zeinab, had not been seen in New York, let alone the building, for months. After Sami reported that she held shares in Geneva Holdings, a company in Kinshasa that was connected to the coltan scandal, Zeinab had returned to Pakistan to "take care of pressing family matters."

But Yael had more important questions on her mind than lingering perfumes. Firstly, what did Fareed know about the Rwanda deal that Roger Richardson had discussed on CNN last night? And secondly, why had she not been informed of Akerman's mission to Istanbul—or his meeting last night with the SG, especially as Roxana had been there?

And this was more important than a usual turf war. The SG had already sent her to persuade Clarence Clairborne to stop trading with the Revolutionary Guard. How could she deal with Clairborne if other UN officials were parleying with interested parties behind her back?

There was no point protesting or demanding an answer. Providing an opening for Hussein would likely prove more productive than a direct attack. Once they had discussed Iran, and he hopefully felt more at ease, then she could ask about the CNN report.

"Perhaps I can help fill the gap. I'm up to speed on Iran," said Yael.

"Come, let's sit down," said Hussein as he guided her across the room, thus buying himself a few seconds. She sensed him instantly calculating permutations and their probable cost-benefit ratios, and watched him carefully as she waited for his reply.

Apart perhaps from the White House, few organizations were defined by a hierarchy as finely delineated as that of the UN. After twelve years at the UN, Yael was completely attuned to the coded messages of inclusion and exclusion. Nowhere was this more apparent than in the SG's inner sanctum. Hussein had evolved his own system for processing guests and visitors, the precisely calibrated nuances of which were discussed across the building with the kind of fervor usually reserved for fans dissecting a recent football game.

Those not in favor would be left to stand in front of the SG's giant black desk, made from environmentally certified Brazilian hardwood. Most visitors were seated in front of the SG, on a very comfortable chair with a seat exactly three inches lower than his. For those with something to offer, the real question was: sofa or armchair?

The sofa stood against one sidewall of the office. The SG liked to sit there and pose for photographs with visiting statesmen because it created a faux atmosphere of intimacy. Only the SG's most prized confidants were invited to the corner where three leather armchairs clustered around a low table, and Hussein made the drinks himself. Yael usually met with the SG there, as the coffee machine sighed and oozed occasional puffs of steam, gently flavored with the SG's own special blend of fair-trade Ethiopian beans. There was also a white china teapot for those who did not drink coffee, and even a jar of tea for Yael, a powerful blend of Kenyan and Assam nicknamed "builders' brew" after the

British tea she had come to love while living in London. It was a unique and much-envied privilege.

Hussein was apologetic as he sat down on one of the leather armchairs and beckoned her to sit next to him. "Forgive me if I am somewhat out of sorts this morning. Frank Akerman was a dear friend as well as a fine colleague. We had known each other for many years." He sat back and closed his eyes for a moment, before he looked at Yael. "There is something I need to discuss with you, a matter of the utmost sensitivity. But before that, my dear Yael, we should speak about last night."

Yael kept her face expressionless. Hussein could talk his way out of a speeding ticket if he was caught driving at one hundred miles an hour. Still, part of her always enjoyed his performances. Sometimes she even learned something from the veteran arch-manipulator. The contrition gambit, she guessed. Admit responsibility. Explain the problems. Finally, throw yourself on his or her mercy.

A second later she felt the SG's fingers on the back of her hand, as he began to speak. "It all happened so quickly that there was simply no time to keep you informed. It's my fault entirely. I saw Akerman's work as complementing your substantial achievements. I had intended to bring you and Frank together as soon as possible. Ideally, this evening. But now that won't be possible. And I am sorry for that."

She smiled. Just as she had predicted, but still a bravura performance—especially as it was not clear whether the SG was sorry that Akerman was dead or that Yael had not met with the Dutchman. Yael was used to Hussein talking his way out of difficult spots. She would allow him this mea culpa but was still determined to get the information she needed. But she would let him run a bit first. "Apology accepted. So where do we go from here? Any news from the FBI? Or the OGAs?"

OGAs stood for other government agencies. In the singular, OGA was usually shorthand for the CIA. But there were likely to be many OGAs marking out their territory around Akerman's death. As he was a high-ranking UN official with diplomatic immunity, the US Secret Service would also be involved, along with the UNDSS and, because the victim was a foreign national, the State Department's Bureau of Diplomatic Security. Those were just the official players. Behind the scenes, Yael knew Akerman's Iranian connection would attract the interest of the NSA, the Department of Homeland Security, the Pentagon, and doubtless Cyrus Jones's former employer, the Department of Deniable. It was all a recipe for ferocious bureaucratic infighting. Which was good news because the backbiting between the agencies would give her some useful room to maneuver.

"Yes, we'll get to that," Hussein said. "Meanwhile, would you like some tea?"

She nodded.

As Hussein filled the kettle and prepared her drink, Yael looked around the familiar office, the familiar questions running through her head. What drove the seventh secretary-general of the United Nations? The more time Yael spent with him, the more she realized how little she really knew of him. Trying to pin down the SG was like trying to catch smoke. Hussein proclaimed himself a fighter for peace, yet he had done little to try and prevent the genocides in Rwanda and Srebrenica. He championed the poor and the underprivileged, but he also loved luxury and the company of celebrities. All of his visitors were given a signed copy of his memoir, *My Journey for Peace*. Recounting his life from his childhood in Delhi to the present day, it was littered with dropped names of former and present presidents and prime ministers, actors and actresses who had been schmoozed into sprinkling stardust onto a UN campaign. However, even Yael had to admit that the parts about his early years, where Hussein dropped his mask, were moving.

He had been born in India, in 1940, to a Hindu mother and Muslim father. Both sets of parents had frowned on the marriage but the young couple had threatened to elope, and eventually, their families surrendered. In the cosmopolitan world of pre-Partition Delhi, his father, Ahmad, was a prosperous financier. The clients of his small private bank were drawn from the city's financial elite. In part because of his own experience, Ahmad insisted that the family home was always open to visitors, with no regard to race or religion. Fareed and his brother, Omar, were privately educated at a small British-run school modeled on Eton College, where Britain's elite were educated. Hussein still affected an upper-class British accent and dropped slang expressions of the 1940s Raj into conversation, both traits he secretly nurtured by reading P.G. Wodehouse novels.

Partition destroyed the family's cozy world. In that summer of 1947, hundreds of thousands of citizens were expelled, forced to flee from the homes where their families had lived for centuries. The streets ran with blood as fanatics on both sides descended into a frenzy, slaughtering in their quest for racial and ethnic purity. Families of mixed heritages were especially targeted, so Ahmad Hussein took his family to Switzerland. Fearful of what might be coming, he had already moved most of the family's money out of the country, but they still lost the bank, the family home, the summer house in the mountains, and all their belongings other than those they could carry.

But the Hussein family's greatest loss was not material. Amid the chaos of a Delhi railway station, Omar's hand had been wrenched from his brother's by a surging mob, and he was never seen or heard from again. There was a photograph of him on Fareed Hussein's desk: a skinny six-year-old with a gap-toothed grin. Next to the picture of Omar was another frame, which held half of a post card of the Taj Mahal. A few months before Partition, already sensing that bad times were coming, Fareed bought the post card, summoned his younger brother to the terrace of their house, and tore the picture in two. Then he and Omar made a solemn promise to keep their halves for the rest of their lives, just in case they were ever separated. One late evening, a year or so ago, Yael had walked into Hussein's office to find him staring at Omar's photograph, tears coursing down his face.

After a decade in Zurich, Ahmad moved his family to London. Fareed studied at the London School of Economics, then worked as an investment banker in New York and Frankfurt. To all outward appearances, he was a successful financier. But he was still psychologically scarred by the events of Partition and wanted to make a difference. In 1991, his fortune made, he joined the UN High Commissioner for Refugees as finance director. His appointment raised eyebrows across the UN empire; no one doubted his business skills, but he had no experience in any kind of humanitarian or public policy organization. His opponents mocked him behind his back for his mannerisms. But, one by one, they were sidelined, sacked, or encouraged to resign. Hussein shook up the torpid world of the UN bureaucracy. He soon gained a reputation as a mover and a shaker, one whose charming exterior hid a determined, sometimes ruthless operator.

After two years at the UNHCR, Hussein shifted to the Department of Political Affairs. DPA officials worked closely with the superpowers to prepare the agenda of the Security Council, whose decisions had the force of international law. Hussein carved out a niche for himself as the go-between between the United States, Britain, and France on one side and Russia and China on the other. By 1992, there were so many peacekeeping operations that a dedicated department, separate from the DPA, was set up to oversee the Blue Helmets. Worried that this new Department of Peacekeeping Operations might take a more muscular approach, the P5 made sure that Hussein was appointed as its head. As Yugoslavia burned and the Hutu *genocidaires* stockpiled their machetes, Hussein's foremost priority was to ensure that what he called the UN's "sacred neutrality" was not damaged.

Yael knew the world lived, operated, in shades of gray. Hussein might be obsessed with the UN's neutrality, which had helped cause catastrophes in Rwanda and Srebrenica. But without that neutrality the organization would not be allowed into war zones to do its humanitarian work. And that same neutrality had given her a life of great excitement and fulfillment. Hussein had plucked Yael from the thousands of people working in the Secretariat Building and made her his personal envoy, giving her a career that she could never have even dreamed of.

She had seen, firsthand and up close, the reality of realpolitik; how the superpowers, even Western ones, quickly sacrificed their principles for political advantage, human rights for corporate profits. And she too had facilitated, even sped up that process. She had helped killers walk free, baptized warlords as statesmen, transformed insurgent groups into governments. She had sacrificed justice for peace, but she slept easily. Wars had been stopped, ceasefires held, countless lives had been saved. Like all human constructs, the UN was imperfect, but she had spent a decade of her life working for a good and right cause: saving lives. There were no perfect answers, only compromises. Each carried a price. The means may be imperfect, but the important point was the end that was achieved. And for all Hussein's public insistence on the UN's impartiality, he had many times let her bend the rules to achieve a greater moral good. Just as long as there was no e-mail or paper trail back to his office.

Hussein's office walls were covered with signed photographs of him with presidents, prime ministers, actors, and film stars. Yael saw there was a new photograph, of Hussein standing with an attractive woman in her early fifties, on the shores of Lake Geneva. The elegantly dressed woman wore a brightly patterned green and black headscarf: Shireen Kermanzade, the new reformist president of Iran. The matter of "the utmost confidentiality" that Hussein had mentioned was surely related to Akerman's mission to Istanbul and Iran.

Hussein's phone rang. He glanced at the number, then at Yael, who gestured at him to take the call. The comfortable chair, the warm office, the smell of coffee were all pleasant and welcome rewards after that morning's weather and the hassle of getting into the building. Perhaps she should back off Hussein a little. It would be shocking to have a sniper kill someone at your front door, and it was natural for the SG to be preoccupied, even nervous. The next bullet could very well be aimed at him. But still, CNN. *David.*

Yael sat back and closed her eyes for a moment, replaying her memory of Roger Richardson's report last night. It was entirely possible that there had been some kind of deal, one that had gone terribly wrong. Deep inside her, Yael believed—*knew*—that Hussein's obsession with the UN's neutrality had played a role in her brother's death. The question was, how much of one? Yael worked at the UN because she believed in its ideals. But more than that, she wanted know why her brother had died at the hands of Jean-Pierre Hakizimani's militiamen and who was personally responsible for allowing the UN workers to be slaughtered. And once she had those answers she wanted those guilty to face justice. Even if they included her boss.

Her phone beeped. A text message had arrived. It was only six words long, but she read it and reread it until the words became a blur.

19

As Roxana Voiculescu walked into the press room, Najwa watched her with a mix of amusement and admiration. The SG's spokeswoman took her place behind the pale wooden lectern and surveyed the assembled reporters. Her expression was pensive and determined, befitting someone who witnessed a murder the previous night and who had herself been shot at. She wore a black Prada jacket and matching below-the-knee skirt that emphasized her shapely figure, a gray blouse, and gray Louboutins with red soles and modest heels. Her long black hair was pulled back in a ponytail, and she wore just a touch of mascara to emphasize her blue-gray eyes.

Yet despite Roxana's somber appearance, Najwa sensed an undercurrent of something—satisfaction, perhaps even triumph—in her posture and her eyes. The bullet that smashed into the SG's door had anointed her. There could be no more whispers about her skills, suitability, or experience: she had risked her life for the UN.

Soon after Roxana had succeeded Schneidermann, she had invited Najwa, Sami, Jonathan Beaufort, and several other correspondents from major media and news agencies to what she called a "getting to know you dinner" in the SG's private dining room. It had been a strange evening, as Roxana had rebuffed the journalists' questions apart from the most anodyne, but with charm and skill had extracted all sorts of personal information from many of the reporters present, all of whom, except for Najwa, were male. Only Sami and Jonathan Beaufort had resisted Roxana's alcohol-fueled charm offensive.

Three things about Roxana in particular interested Najwa. Roxana was obsessed with Yael Azoulay. She spent much of the dinner trying to dig out any scraps of gossip or information about the SG's special envoy, and had repeatedly circled the conversation back to an altercation in Geneva, when Yael had drowned her would-be killer, and the incident at the Millennium Hotel, when Yael had posed as an escort to gain entry to the suite occupied by Jean-Pierre Hakizimani, who was later found dead. Roxana's steer was not very subtle, especially because these events were already known and so regarded as old news. The second was the rumor that, despite an age difference of more than forty years, she had quickly forged a very close connection indeed with Fareed Hussein. And third, how could Roxana afford $2,000 shoes and a Patek Philippe watch? UN salaries were generous, but not that abundant.

Najwa looked up and down the press room. She had never seen it so crowded. Most of those present were genuine reporters, but there were a good number whose byline never appeared because they either reported to their national intelligence services or were relatives of UN diplomats and used accreditation to obtain an American visa. Usually a few dozen journalists turned up for Roxana's daily briefings, lately sometimes even less now the novelty of having an attractive new spokesperson had worn off. But today there was barely space to step inside the room, let alone gain a seat. The electric undercurrent of excitement and anticipation underneath the whispered gossip was palpable.

Reporters stood in huddles, some hunched over their cell phones, tapping away, others expounding complicated theories as to who shot Frank Akerman and why. One strand of thinking had it as an attempted hit on the SG that went wrong; another, that Akerman had somehow uncovered Iranian nuclear secrets and paid the ultimate price. The correspondents from Reuters, Associated Press, and Bloomberg Business News were standing together and they waved at Najwa, but she did not stop to chat. Jonathan Beaufort, she saw, was deep in conversation with the new bureau chief for *Russia Today*, a long-legged blond who was rumored to be a niece of the head of Gazprom, the Russian state energy company. Beaufort beckoned Najwa over, but she declined. She needed to stay focused for what was coming.

Television crews lined the sides and the back of the room, their halogen lights making the space even warmer than usual. More cameramen and news photographers were standing at the front, the harsh light glinting off their lenses. Maria, Najwa's producer, had already staked out a prime position in the center of the front row. The table in front of Roxana's lectern was thick with black cables and microphones adorned with network logos. Najwa counted ABC, CNN, BBC, Reuters, Russia Today, Associated Press, and Nigerian,

Turkish, and Japanese crews, along with Xinhua, the Chinese state news agency. Even Vice, a hipster network not usually known for its interest in the United Nations, had sent a crew.

Roxana nodded at the sound technician at the side of the room. The reporters quickly fell silent, glancing at each other expectantly before staring at the SG's spokeswoman.

"I have a short statement about the tragic events of last night, but as this is an ongoing police investigation I will not be taking questions, so as not to prejudice the legal proceedings."

Najwa watched, amused, as the room filled with outraged muttering. She checked her phone. The screen showed the profile of @najwaun. The tweet had already been written; the link to the video clip, just uploaded onto Al-Jazeera's website, added. She looked up as Jonathan Beaufort raised his arm and started to shout a question, his stentorian voice cutting through the complaining journalists. "This is absurd. A UN official was shot dead by the SG's residence last night. A sniper was taking potshots at the door, and you won't take questions?"

A half smile played on Roxana's mouth. "One shot at the door, actually, Jonathan. I'm very pressed for time today. So if you don't stop shouting and waving your arms around and sit down, I won't be able to read the statement. Which for technical reasons won't be on the website for several hours. You might like to consider the interests of your colleagues and their deadlines."

Beaufort sat down, his face crimson with anger.

Roxana began to speak. "At ten minutes past nine last night, Frank Akerman was brutally murdered as he stepped onto the pavement outside the door of the SG's residence. We strongly condemn this cowardly killing of a dedicated UN official and public servant. UN officials must be free to carry out their duties without suffering threats or violence, or, in this case, murder. The Joint Terrorism Task Force, based at the New York Field Office of the Federal Bureau of Investigation, is investigating the killing of Mr. Akerman. Please direct all your inquiries to their press office."

"That's it?" asked Beaufort.

Roxana smiled beatifically as she gathered her papers. "That's it for today, Jonathan."

The reporters looked at each other in amazement, their indignation tangible. Then came the eruption. A barrage of questions in a babel of languages resounded across the room. Roxana ignored it all and walked toward the door, her portfolio under her arm.

Najwa quickly reread her tweet, double-checked that the link was complete, and pressed the button. @najwaun had more than forty-eight thousand followers. She watched with satisfaction as just a few seconds later many of the journalists pulled out their phones, stared at them, then pressed down on their screens to watch the attached video. Najwa waited until the hubbub had died down and Roxana was almost out of the room. She walked up to the lectern, switched the microphone back on, and tapped it twice. The noise echoed around the room and the journalists looked at her, wondering what was happening now. Roxana spun on her heel and turned back to face Najwa, her face indignant.

Najwa said, "Thanks for the briefing. You might like to check your Twitter feed."

An hour later Quentin Braithwaite greeted Najwa with a wry grin as he walked into McLaughlin's. "Good morning. Or should I say mabrouk, congratulations? You've ruined Roxana's day. Not to mention a number of people's placid retirement," he said, his blue eyes aglow with amusement. He pulled up a chair and sat down opposite her. "I was wondering how long it would take you, or one of your colleagues, to find that video of Akerman."

Najwa smiled. "Our Sarajevo bureau received an anonymous e-mail. After that it was easy."

"It always is when you know where to look."

"A little guidance goes a long way," she said, watching Braithwaite's face as she spoke.

"It does indeed," he deadpanned.

Colonel Quentin Braithwaite was tall and sturdy with red hair, freckles, weathered cheeks, and a brisk manner. He wore his usual green tweed jacket with leather elbow patches over a white shirt whose collar was fraying slightly, and a striped university scarf. Braithwaite was the leader of the interventionist faction in the Department of Peacekeeping Operations. His world view had been shaped twenty years ago by his time as a peacekeeper in Bosnia, when his Warrior fighting vehicle had smashed its way through a Bosnian Serb checkpoint. A furious Fareed Hussein had denounced what he called a "reckless and foolhardy violation of the UN's neutrality" and tried to get Braithwaite removed. But Britain and the United States had rebuffed Hussein's lobbying and Braithwaite had later moved to a senior position at the DPKO.

Braithwaite sat back and looked around, taking in the

smoke-stained walls, sniffing then exhaling. "Ah . . . nothing like the smell of yesterday's beer in the morning. I've often walked past this place, but never been inside." He paused for a moment to give Najwa a searching glance. "I wouldn't have thought this was your natural habitat."

She raised her eyebrows, a glimmer of a smile on her lips. "Precisely."

The waiter ambled over, still wearing yesterday's T-shirt. "Breakfast's finished. Lunch service starts in an hour."

"Thanks," said Najwa. "We'll just have coffee."

Braithwaite waited until the waiter walked away. "How can I help? I seem to have plenty of time on my hands at the moment."

Fareed Hussein had recently appointed Braithwaite to lead the UN's Commission of Enquiry into the coltan scandal. The SG had been praised for appointing someone of principles and integrity to get to the bottom of the affair. But Braithwaite soon realized, as he was stalled and diverted at every move by the UN bureaucracy, that his appointment was a neat way of both marginalizing and neutralizing him.

"So I hear," said Najwa, with a grin. "Which is why I brought you this."

She reached inside her purse to retrieve the photograph she had found in the white envelope, and slid it across the table.

Salim Massoud walked through the scuffed front door and glanced around the one-room studio: gray walls, a single bed that visibly sagged in the middle, a Formica coffee table, a threadbare sofa with a front almost shredded by a pet cat, the stink of garlic and ginger from the nearby restaurants in Chinatown, a whiff of drains and stale water from the tiny shower cubicle. Perfect for his needs. He sat down at the small kitchen table by the window and rifled through his canvas bag until he found a large brown envelope. He tipped the contents onto the table: a bundle of birthday cards, held together by a red elastic band. He carefully slid off the elastic band and opened the top card. Nothing was written inside, but there was a photograph of a thin, dark-haired young man, with hollow eyes and sallow skin, holding up that day's issue of the *New York Times*.

Massoud put the photograph back inside the card and picked up another one. It was identical—"Happy Birthday to a Great Dad" emblazoned in garish writing on the cover and nothing written inside, but it contained a similar photograph of the same young man holding the *New York Times*, marked with the same date a year earlier. Massoud swallowed, slid the cards back into the envelope, and replaced it inside the bag.

He closed his eyes for several seconds then looked out the kitchen window. A sliver of the East River could be glimpsed between the gray walls of the Lower East Side apartment blocks. The landlord had shown no interest in his new tenant, only in the $800 Massoud had paid up front for a week and another $800 as a security deposit, which was how Massoud liked it. He took out a Canadian passport from his jacket pocket and flicked through the pages. There had been no questions at the border, a little-used land crossing, when Toronto-based businessman Parvez Marwan came back into the United States. Still, the passport was probably coming to the end of its useful life. In seventy-two hours the question would anyway be academic. His home country and the United States would be at war.

He opened his laptop and flicked through the Iranian news websites. The smiling, attractive face of Shireen Kermanzade looked out from almost every home page. In each she wore her trademark green and gold headscarf, pulled so far back from her forehead that several years ago she would have been arrested. In a lifetime spent within the darkest, innermost circles of the Iranian regime, Massoud had never known such a sense of betrayal. From the voters, certainly, but most of all from Kermanzade herself. The nuclear deal with the United States was a catastrophe. Not because of its terms, although these had been broken as soon as the ink was dry. The Israelis were right: Iran would get a bomb, sooner or later, and an accord with Washington would slow that process but not stop it. Luckily, the more Tel Aviv shouted, the less anyone listened.

No, the real catastrophe of the nuclear deal was the opening to the West that it brought. In exchange for the lifting of sanctions, Kermanzade had allowed outside inspectors into Iran's most secret military and nuclear installations and had launched an unprecedented program of liberalization. Everything that his generation had fought, and died, for was crumbling. Western firms were opening "liaison" offices with local partners to help them penetrate a market of seventy-six million people, a majority of whom were under thirty-five and connected to the Internet. An Internet stripped of its controls, where students and activists now poured out their demands on Facebook, Twitter, and Instagram. Demands for full democracy, human rights, civil freedoms. Demands that just a few months ago would have earned a session in the basement of Evin Prison, or even a noose on the end of a crane. The Basij, a motorcycle militia that had crushed the 2009 protests, was disbanded and its leaders arrested. Even members of the Revolutionary Guard were being investigated. It would not be long, Massoud knew, before his time came. He had no regrets, except his son.

Farzad had been missing for five years. Completely uninterested in politics, he had wanted only to do good. His value as a prisoner was solely as Salim Massoud's son. Massoud had managed to trace his journey to Kabul, Bagram air base, a black-site prison in Romania, and then silence. Apart from the cards. Presumably he was being held somewhere in America. But the messengers, intermediaries, the Swiss diplomats and German businessmen who had contacted the Americans had all failed. No part of the government had any knowledge of Farzad Massoud or his whereabouts, or so they said. Clairborne too had failed to obtain any information. There was no demand, no request for a meeting. But someone, somewhere in the Great Satan knew. The message was clear enough: *We are holding your son because we can.* He could do nothing for his son. Until now.

20

Yael glanced at the SG, who was still deep in conversation. Eli's words echoed through her head.

"We placed you."

Was it really conceivable that, all this time, she had also been working to someone else's agenda? That she had risked her life, faced down killers and become one herself, reached the wrong side of thirty-five still single and childless, all so her old employers could lure or force her back home and find out everything she knew? The Mossad was especially skilled in false-flag operations. Few foreigners wanted to spy for Israel, especially those based in Arab or Islamic countries, but Israel was a nation of immigrants, and the children of immigrants. Its spy services had recruits from a myriad of backgrounds, who could pretend to be agents of other countries. But a decade-long false flag, in which the target did not even know that they were an asset, took things to a whole new level.

As if this was not enough to process, there was the text message that had arrived that morning.

Fareed Hussein let your brother die.

The message had come out of the blue. Yael had no idea who sent it because the outgoing number was blocked. On one level the words were shocking. On another, they did not surprise her. Was it true? She knew that David and the other UN workers trapped in Kigali had sent a stream of increasingly desperate telegrams and messages, and made numerous phone calls, to the UN headquarters in Geneva and New York and the peacekeepers in Kigali. Fareed Hussein was then the head of the DPKO, and as such he could have ordered the peacekeepers, stationed just a few miles away, to rescue David and his colleagues. But he didn't. The UN's own inquiry into the disaster had vindicated Hussein personally, but found that he sat at the top of a chain of command with poor communication, blurred lines of responsibility, and unwillingness to take responsibility or decisive leadership. The inquiry made some recommendations about how the UN should respond to emergency situations. In short, a classic UN snarl-up, followed by a classic UN fudge.

The great unanswered question was: What, precisely, was the SG's role in the catastrophe? Was it his personal decision not to intervene, or was he merely following orders? If so, whose orders? Could he have refused? Or screamed, shouted, held a press conference to demand action? Or had he worked behind the scenes, as Yael did so often, to save David and his colleagues, but been stymied by the usual mix of bureaucratic infighting?

That was twenty years ago. Little had changed at the UN. But Rwanda had altered Yael's life, forever. She was left completely bereft by her brother's death. Her mother, Barbara, suffered a nervous breakdown. She ended her relationship with Yael's father and relocated to Berkeley, where she eventually moved in with her female therapist, a Hungarian called Nora. Her father had taken his own dark path, one that had eventually caused Yael to break off all ties with him.

Yael knew she was not the only one haunted by the UN's complicity in genocide. Both Rwanda and Srebrenica hung over the Secretariat Building like giant, ghostly bloodstains. No amount of redecorating or renovation could scrub away the shame, and still the reverberations continued. Kicked out of Rwanda, the genocidaires had simply regrouped in Congo, using the UN refugee camps as bases to launch raids into Rwanda. Eventually the Hutu militias brought the whole region to the brink of another war, which was why the SG sent Yael to make a deal with Jean-Pierre Hakizimani, a mission she had protested. If he stopped the raids and dismantled his militias, he would receive a lighter sentence and a comfortable prison in Paris when he was tried by the International Criminal Tribunal for Rwanda.

But Hakizimani had known something. Something that could bring down the SG, or worse. A memory of something Hakizimani had said in that hotel room flashed into Yael's mind.

Hakizimani speaks slowly and carefully: "You tell your SG this. If he starts altering the terms now, I will personally ensure that our communications during 1944 and subsequent years are leaked to the press."

What were those communications? What did Hakizimani have on the SG? She had not asked Hussein. There was no point. He would just brush off her questions, deny everything. Hakizimani could not tell her about his communications with Hussein because he was dead. That much Yael knew, because she had killed him. She still did not know if his death had been her intentional revenge for David's death, or an accident. But the end result was the same. The answer, Yael sensed, was somehow connected to the "Doomsday" sound file, implicating Fareed in a planned mass murder, that she had transferred to her phone that morning.

Yael looked again at the SG. He was still talking on the phone, ending his first conversation then starting a new one as he greeted a second person. Meanwhile, she could at least utilize the waiting time. Yael called up the Doomsday file. She inserted her earbuds, jumped back to the start, and pressed play.

FRENCH MAN: We need at least five hundred. That will have maximum impact.

HUSSEIN: No, no, that is unnecessary. It's far too much. A couple of hundred at most would be sufficient for our purposes. Less would suffice. Even a few dozen.

AMERICAN WOMAN: We disagree, Mr. Secretary-General. Five hundred is really the absolute minimum, if this is going to work. More, ideally.

HUSSEIN: I am more and more inclined to stop the whole thing. I think—

FRENCH MAN: We understand, Mr. Secretary-General, that you have some doubts. We all do. That is only natural. Otherwise we would not be human. But you—all of us—need to think of the bigger picture. That will be our legacy—peace in Congo. Millions, not even born yet, will have the chance for a happy, productive life.

GERMAN/AUSTRIAN MAN: Yes, Mr. Secretary-General. That is what matters, surely. The bigger picture. How many people have died in the wars in Congo? Four million? Five? Nobody even knows, and, sadly, even fewer care. Now you have a chance to go down in history as the UN secretary-general who stopped the longest and bloodiest conflict since 1945. This is a small price to pay.

Thanks to Yael, the "small price," of a massacre of five hundred people by Hakizimani's militia, had not been paid. The American woman was Erin Rembaugh, former head of the Department of Political Affairs, who had been killed in a hit-and-run accident outside her home in Connecticut. The Frenchman was Charles Bonnet. The German or Austrian man, she thought, might be KZX communications chief Reinhardt Daintner. The recording had been sent anonymously to her last year, before the coltan scandal broke, and it had not yet been made public. Nor had Yael mentioned the sound file to anyone, though lately she had been hearing increasing rumors about its existence, which meant that other people knew about it.

Yael slipped her phone into her purse. Her glance fell

on the SG's desk. There were two framed pictures there, she knew. One of Omar, and another that showed a pretty young Indian woman in her graduation gown: Rina, the SG's estranged daughter and one of Yael's rare failures. She was a human rights activist who spent much of her time denouncing her father as "an accomplice to genocide." Hussein had asked Yael to befriend his daughter and then gently raise the topic of a reconciliation, so she had met with Rina several times. This was one assignment Yael felt no ambiguity about: reconciling a daughter with her father was a straightforward good thing. It also made Yael wonder about her own decision to break off relations with her own father. What she had read about him still shocked her, but some of Fareed Hussein's history was also shocking, if presented as black and white. Perhaps her father also had a case to make—if she let him.

But more than that, Yael felt she had finally made a friend, one she could trust. They had enjoyed each other's company; Rina was witty and intelligent, with a wry, sharp view of the world, especially as seen by a smart, thirtyish single woman in Manhattan. Still, a shadow fell over the evenings they spent together—Yael knew that eventually she would have to mention the SG. She put it off as long as she could, but the SG was pressing her. Just as Yael had feared, Rina did not take the news well. One night, over dinner in a trendy Harlem restaurant, Yael had tentatively raised the topic of Rina's father and his hopes. Rina had picked up her purse, walked out, and not spoken to Yael since. She did not respond to Yael's e-mails, text messages, or calls. Eventually, Yael gave up. She had once seen Rina on a protest outside the UN headquarters. She considered going up to her to say hello, but when she caught Rina's eye the SG's daughter had looked straight through her. Yael still missed their nights out.

Yael took out her mobile phone. She scrolled through the numbers. Rina's was still there. She called up the text message about David. Sometimes it was better to act than think too much. She added a line, and forwarded it to Rina.

Just as she pressed "SEND," Hussein sat back down. He looked sternly at Yael before he started speaking. "Those were two interesting conversations."

Yael brought herself back back the present, focused on the SG. "Who with?"

"First, with the FBI liaison for the Host Country Unit at the US mission."

"What did they want to talk about?"

"You."

Clairborne stared at his computer monitor and waited for his contact to come online. The two men had first met in Tehran in 1978, where Clairborne had been ostensibly sent as a cultural attaché. In reality he was a CIA officer, liaising with SAVAK, the Shah's brutal secret police. Clairborne was training SAVAK officers in "enhanced interrogation techniques"—including electric shocks, severe beatings, and tapping lengths of wooden dowel through the ear canal into the brain—he had learned while serving in Vietnam on the Phoenix program. All the SAVAK officers were enthusiastic students, but Clairborne was especially interested in a quiet, diligent operative who had managed to penetrate the Islamic revolutionaries. Clairborne and his contact were soon trading: Clairborne supplied satellite imagery of the Iraqi army, which was preparing for war with Iran, and made regular payments into a Swiss bank account in the SAVAK agent's name, while the SAVAK agent passed Clairborne detailed intelligence about the coming Islamic revolution.

Clairborne's long, detailed memos to Langley, predicting the demise of the Shah and the coming Islamic revolution, were ignored. So were his recommendations that the United States cooperate with the Ayatollah Khomeini behind the scenes to build goodwill. The SAVAK officer's predictions came true soon after Khomeini's triumphant return. Iran declared itself an Islamic republic. That November, revolutionaries attacked the American embassy, holding fifty-two hostages for 444 days. Despite this, and all the denunciations of the Great Satan, back-channel connections between Tehran and Washington, DC, continued. Clairborne's contact, like many of his colleagues, smoothly transitioned from SAVAK to VEVAK, its successor organization.

The two men kept in touch over the years, meeting in Beirut, Geneva, or Paris. Still working for the CIA, Clairborne continued to supply intelligence about the Iraqi military and receive detailed information on the inner workings and power struggles of the Islamic regime in return. On September 12, 2001, he had received a message that could have changed the course of modern history: in exchange for the resumption of diplomatic relations, Tehran would help the United States depose the Taliban in Afghanistan. Clairborne recommended that the offer be seriously considered, but he was brushed aside. The next day he resigned and set up the Prometheus Group.

Despite their differences, the Christian American and the Shia Muslim from Iran shared a similar belief. Clairborne and Eugene Packard called it the Rapture or the End of Days, the Second Coming of Jesus Christ: a righteous fire that would cleanse the world and deliver salvation to the true believers. For Salim Massoud, it was the appearance of the Mahdi, the redeemer of Islam. Sunni Muslims believed the Mahdi was yet to come, but for Shia Muslims the Mahdi was already on Earth, hiding until the time came to join Jesus in saving humanity. But whatever the theological nuances, both Clairborne and Massoud agreed that it was their solemn duty to accelerate Armageddon. Now everything had been set in motion. There were only three more days to wait.

Clairborne pressed a series of buttons on his keyboard. A window opened, showing a thin young man with sallow skin lying on his back in a windowless gray concrete cell and staring at the ceiling. Clairborne damped down his guilt. He had arranged for the boy to be kidnapped to give him leverage over Massoud, to keep him vulnerable and off-balance. The Iranian had never suspected that Clairborne, the very man he asked for help to find his son, was holding him prisoner. Clairborne stared more closely at the computer monitor. The boy's eyes were empty, almost dead. Once the war had started, he would release him. He certainly would.

Yael looked at the SG. It was never good news to be the subject of a conversation with the FBI, especially a section of the bureau so close to home. The Host Country Affairs Section at the US mission dealt with protocol, accreditation, and immunity for foreign diplomats posted to the UN. Like embassies, foreign missions to the UN enjoyed full diplomatic immunity under US law. Diplomats accredited to the UN, and their families, also had full diplomatic immunity. While most were law-abiding citizens, a small minority took advantage of their status to break the law with impunity; there had recently been several cases of diplomats from the developing world keeping domestic staff in conditions of near slavery. Governments could waive their diplomats' immunity and allow them to be prosecuted, but that almost never happened. Usually, the offenders were given a couple of weeks to pack their bags and return home.

Until the previous month, Yael had rarely thought about her legal protection. Within the UN, the SG and four top officials, including her, had full diplomatic immunity, which meant they could not be arrested even if they committed a crime outside UN territory. But in her brief interlude as acting secretary-general, Caroline Masters had threatened to strip Yael of her immunity and extradite her to Switzerland, where authorities wanted to question her about the man she had had drowned in Lake Geneva. Yael's defense, that she had taken the man's life in self-defense after he'd kidnapped her and tried to murder her, would likely prove adequate, but she had no desire to test it in a Swiss court.

Fareed Hussein had never made such threats. For the moment she was back in favor, especially after saving President Freshwater's life, but Yael knew all that could change in an instant, depending on the vagaries of international diplomacy—and the SG's interests. Life in the upper reaches of the UN reminded her of the accounts she had read of the courts of Roman emperors or Ottoman sultans: danger increased with proximity to power. Olivia de Souza, the SG's personal assistant, had been hurled off a balcony on the thirty-eighth floor. Yael did not fear for her life, but she had little doubt that despite their intense, shared history, the SG would, if necessary, throw her overboard to save himself. If the Doomsday sound file was genuine he was prepared to sacrifice the lives of five hundred people. If the text message was true Hussein was also implicated in the death of her brother. Even if it was not, if she was sacked from the UN she would never be able to find out how and why David had died.

Yael felt distinctly uneasy, but she made sure not to let it show. "Anything in particular about me, or just a general chat?"

"They have received an inquiry from the NYPD about your legal status."

Yael's discomfort grew. Masters had also threatened to hand Yael over to the NYPD so they could investigate her part in the death of Jean-Pierre Hakizimani in the Hotel Millennium, which was a much more alarming prospect because she wouldn't have to be extradited anywhere. She lived in New York. And also because Yael had killed him by repeatedly shocking him with a stun gun. While he was tied up, so there was no defense of self-defense.

Yael remained impassive. "OK. What did you tell them?"

"That I would talk to the NYPD to get the facts of the matter firsthand."

"Which are?"

"The NYPD wants to issue tickets to a taxi driver called Gurdeep Patel, and two of his cousins, for dangerous driving. You were Patel's passenger. He says that you declared that his car, and those of his cousins, were part of your security detail and UN territory and were thus immune from traffic laws."

Yael's tension drained away. "So what if I did? I have full immunity. I was being followed. I needed to get away. To do that I needed to give them a guarantee. It seemed the simplest thing to do. Otherwise why would Gurdeep and his cousins risk it for me?"

Hussein frowned. "It is legal nonsense for you to declare three random New York taxis to be UN territory for the duration of your ride, as you well know."

"They were not random taxis. They were helping me avoid a car that was following me. I had good reason to believe I was under threat because of my work for the UN. I had a right to ensure my security. Give me a moment, please."

She picked up her cell phone and scrolled through the menus until she found the video clip. She pressed play and handed it to the SG. "The black SUV. It was near my apartment, then tracked me down Broadway until we got away."

Hussein stared at the screen as the video clip played, then handed the phone back to her.

Yael watched him as she spoke. "Fareed, you can make this go away with a phone call. Please?"

The SG blinked as he answered. "This time, yes. But don't make a habit of this. You have a bodyguard. Try using him. Anyway, we have something much more important to discuss."

Yael leaned forward. "I'm listening."

The SG spoke for several minutes, explaining what he wanted Yael to do. Her eyes widened in surprise. Even with Akerman's death, she had not seen this coming.

Hussein sat back. "So you see now, why Akerman was in Istanbul, and why I could not tell you until now."

She was about to reply when the door opened and Roxana walked in, holding her mobile phone, wafting perfume through the air. The fragrance smelled familiar. She smiled and nodded briefly at Yael in greeting, then looked at the SG. "I need to talk to you."

"Please, Roxana, sit down," Hussein said.

Roxana remained standing, looked at Yael again, then back at the SG. "Fareed, we have a situation here."

Yael looked at Roxana, then at the SG. Roxana's dominating body language, her demanding tone of voice, were both extraordinary and telling. And Yael definitely knew that smell: it was Zest.

Hussein sat still for several seconds. He looked at Yael. "Would you excuse us, please."

21

Yael and Joe-Don sat at a table by the window in Patsy's Pizzeria, three empty cans of Diet Coke and the remains of a large Margherita pizza—a few crusts and a lone slice—in front of them. The rush hour traffic was pouring down Second Avenue, but they had a clear view of number 800, and the gray police booth that stood by the entrance, across the street.

Joe-Don handed Yael a printout of a photograph. "You've seen this before. But here's a reminder."

"Salim Massoud," she said. "Number two in the Revolutionary Guard. The money man, with the occasional assassination on the side. Is he back?"

He took a sip of his Diet-Coke. "We don't think so. But he hasn't given up. He is still in communication with Clairborne. They want their war."

Yael stared closely at the photograph. She pointed at the side of Massoud's right eyebrow where an inch or so of skin was ridged and puckered. "What's that?"

"A scar, from the Iran-Iraq war. He was a commando.

Three of his brothers were killed. He is the last one of his family. Apart from his son."

"Tell me about him."

"Farzad Massoud. A teacher, went to Afghanistan to help. The Americans lifted him at a checkpoint in Kandahar five years ago. He was clean; his only value is his connection to his father."

"Is he still alive?"

"Sure. Thinner, but alive. Every year his father gets a birthday card from him. Same as yours—August twenty-first."

Yael handed the photograph back to Joe-Don. "How old is he?"

"Twenty-six. So he was born when?"

"Er, 1985?" Yael's inability to do simple mathematics was a running joke between them.

"Try again."

"Eighty-eight?"

Joe-Don smiled. "Eighty-seven."

"Whatever. Where is he?"

"Somewhere in the US. In a DoD black prison. So black it's off the books. Run by a private corporation. Guess which one?"

Yael said, "Begins with P?" She looked outside again, across the road. 800 Second Avenue spanned the length of the block between East Forty-First and East Forty-Second. Apart from the police booth, the building appeared to be just another of the standard office and apartment blocks that filled this unremarkable quarter of Manhattan. The UN

Plaza Pharmacy occupied one corner of the ground floor, Calico Jack's Cantina the other. But heavy concrete blocks had been staggered in front of the building and along the sidewalk that ran down its right-hand side. They had been painted gray, and some had plants growing out of the center, but there was no mistaking their purpose: to prevent car bombers from smashing through the doors. The only direct clue that this was the Israeli mission to the United Nations was a small blue street sign, on the corner of East Forty-Second Street, for Yitzhak Rabin Way, named after the Israeli prime minister assassinated by a right-wing Jewish fanatic.

Yael glanced at her watch. It was ten minutes to four. The mission's end-of-week review and security update took place every Friday at four o'clock. He should be here at any moment. She gestured at the last slice of pizza, keeping one eye on the building entrance.

Joe-Don shook his head. "Please, be my guest. How can you eat that much?"

"I get hungry when I'm stressed."

"Are you sure this is a good idea? I can't help you in there, if it goes wrong."

She took a large bite out of the slice. "Sure. I need to speak to him—and on his home territory. I can pick up all sorts of stuff about what's going on once I'm there. I'll tell him you are waiting for me. I'll be fine."

Joe-Don looked doubtful, but said nothing.

Yael continued talking. "What have you got on the SUV's license plate?"

"Black Ford Expedition, three years old. Registered to a

firm in Montana. The firm ceased trading a year ago. The trail goes cold."

"What's the name of the company?"

"Davidson Outdoor Devices."

She frowned, thinking hard for a few seconds. "Oh. Of course."

"Of course what?

"D.O.D."

Joe-Don nodded, sipped his Diet Coke. "Figures."

"Was it them inside my apartment?"

"Maybe. But it's clean. I swept it this morning. No bugs, no cameras."

"So why did my visitor leave the paper tell on the table?"

"Because he could? To send a message?"

"What kind of message?"

"That your apartment is not as secure as you think."

"Clearly. But why would someone do that? And how did he get in without triggering the alarms? The UN security people said the system was foolproof."

"Nothing is foolproof. You know that. There was a brief power outage last night on the Upper West Side. A few seconds, but long enough to disable the system."

She dunked a piece of pizza crust into a puddle of tomato sauce and bit the end off. Then she put it down and took out her cell phone. The screen showed a frozen frame in a video clip. "Have you seen this?"

"Not yet."

"You need to. Najwa got it." She slid it across the table and pressed play.

Surrounded by rolling hills and pine trees, a much

younger version of Frank Akerman was standing by a shallow stream. He was dressed in the UN Peacekeeper's uniform of khaki military fatigues, a UN armband, and a blue beret. The camera panned to the bank of the stream, where a thin man in his thirties, wearing dirty jeans and a track top, lay facedown in the mud. There was a large, dark stain in the center of his back. A few feet away a younger man lay on his back, staring sightlessly at the sky.

Akerman was talking to an older man. Shorter and stockier, the man had a puffy red face and wore a Bosnian Serb army uniform. Both he and Akerman were holding small glasses filled with clear liquid. The two men clinked glasses and downed their contents in one. They then hugged and slapped each on the back.

Joe-Don exhaled loudly. "Wow."

Yael pointed at the date stamp on the film. "Tuesday July eighth, 16:04 1995. Srebrenica had fallen by then. The Bosnian Serbs were taking away the men and boys. The killing had already started."

"How did she get this?"

"I don't know. They have a bureau in Sarajevo. She's good." Yael shook her head admiringly. "RIP Frank Akerman. And his reputation." She kept one eye on Second Avenue as she spoke. A well-built man, dark and tough-looking, was approaching the entrance of number 800. He looked familiar.

"What is it?" asked Joe-Don.

"Hold on. Yes. That's one of Eli's goons. I saw him in the park last night. Eli should be here soon. But I forgot to ask—what did HR want when they called you?"

"Me to retire."

"We both knew that was coming. You'll be sixty next year. I might join you. We could go into business together. Set up a consultancy."

"Or a think tank. The Institute for How the World Really Works."

"A great idea. We can ask Fareed to get the UN to sponsor it."

Joe-Don stirred his coffee. "I was thinking about Clarence Clairborne. Or maybe Reinhardt Daintner," he said, his voice droll.

Yael laughed. "Sure. Daintner would go for that. KZX would love it."

Joe-Don smiled wryly. "You can ask him on Saturday. Meanwhile, you still haven't told me what the SG wants you to do."

"I'll get to that. I also promised Eli that at three p.m. on Monday afternoon I would be standing in the foyer of my apartment building, with my bags packed. He kindly offered to arrange a lift to the airport. He's booked me a ticket to Tel Aviv. Business class. El-Al, but still business class."

Joe-Don started in surprise. "You're going back?"

"Of course not. We will either be at the airport by then or en route. Pack warm clothes and waterproofs. And the other stuff."

"Sure. Where are we going?"

"Reykjavik."

Joe-Don frowned. "Is that part of your brief now, sustainability?"

Yael drained her can of Diet Coke. "It's part of everyone's brief, J.D. Our world has limited resources. There are too many of us. Consumer culture is killing the planet."

"Sure. Is that why you have twenty-four pairs of shoes?"

"Twenty-five, actually. Although that does include boots and sports shoes."

"Right. Now tell me. Why are we going to Reykjavik?"

Yael's voice turned serious. "President Freshwater knows she is being undermined from inside her own party. She is pissed that the Istanbul Summit collapsed. She wants to define her legacy, make a symbolic statement for history. Iceland's good for that, it's where Reagan and Gorbachev met in 1986. The Cold War ended soon after."

Joe-Don snorted. "Sure. And look where that got us. A lot of hot wars instead. And what's all this got to do with sustainability?"

"The conference is just the public premise for the trip. The real reason she is going to Reykjavik is to meet with Shireen Kermanzade. Fareed has been working on this for ages. That's why Akerman was in Istanbul. It's all double-ultra-secret."

"And what will the two presidents be doing in Reykjavik?"

Yael picked up the last piece of crust. She looked at the crispy dough for a few seconds and offered it to Joe-Don. "Are you sure you don't want some?"

"No. And you didn't answer my question."

She glanced at the building entrance, then at Joe-Don. "Sorry. He's here. I'll tell you more when I get back."

Standing up, she emptied her pockets of her keys, wallet,

and cell phone and slid them over the table. "If I'm not out in an hour, come and get me."

Joe-Don put her possessions into her purse and sat with the bag on his lap, shaking his head. Yael squeezed his shoulder and hurried out, with adrenalin, excitement, and, yes, anticipation coursing through her.

Three minutes' walk away, Najwa and her crew were standing on First Avenue outside the UN headquarters. The sky was still overcast, the line of flags hanging limp and wet, but the rain had stopped. Shining from the downpour, the sidewalk was jammed with television journalists, all reporting or following up on Najwa's footage of Frank Akerman. Part of the street was blocked off by a line of television trucks, parked face-on toward the curb, each with a giant white satellite dish on its roof. Held back behind metal barriers, a couple of dozen demonstrators had gathered on the other side of the road, waving banners demanding "Justice for Srebrenica" and "Where was the UN?" A woman in her early thirties, wearing a red beret, held a megaphone and led a chant, "Fareed Hussein, Resign in Shame."

Security was still intense. The NYPD had now set up a temporary station in two Portacabins on the UN plaza. A second layer of concrete barricades had been placed in front of the main entrance. White NYPD pods on metal stilts, bristling with CCTV cameras, stood thirty feet in the air on every corner. The black slabs of glass on each of the pod's four sides stared down like the eyes of giant insects. A half-dozen police officers watched the demonstration, one filming the protesters.

Najwa looked into the camera as she signed off her report. "The UN Department of Peacekeeping said it was unable to provide a spokesperson to respond to the film we obtained of Frank Akerman. Roxana Voiculescu, the spokeswoman for the secretary-general, has issued a one-line statement saying that the UN is investigating the authenticity of the footage. But as you can see and hear from the protestors behind me, it has blown open a two-decades-old controversy over one of the UN's great failures. Many in the building hoped that, twenty years after the Bosnian war, the Srebrenica massacre was filed away. For now, at least, that seems unlikely. This is Najwa al-Sameera, reporting for Al-Jazeera from the United Nations."

"Mabrouk, congratulations. You got two scoops in a week," said Maria, as Najwa unhooked her microphone. Originally from Madrid, Maria was petite, black-haired, and the sharpest producer with whom Najwa had ever worked.

Najwa glanced back at the protesters. The women in the red beret was walking away. Something about her looked familiar, but then she was gone, absorbed in the crowd. "We got them," she said, smiling at Philippe, the cameraman. "All three of us. Al-Jazeera. Not me."

Philippe was a stocky Frenchman in his fifties, a veteran of numerous Middle Eastern war zones who had been relocated to New York from Beirut, against his wishes, after narrowly escaping a kidnap attempt while on assignment in Iraq. "Maybe, but it was your instincts. We have the highest-ever levels of traffic to the website. The clip has gone viral. Every major news agency has picked it up."

Maria glanced at her cell phone. "Here's Reuters: 'Slain

UN official toasted fall of Srebrenica with Mastermind of Massacre.'"

Najwa smiled. "That's about it."

All three wished each other a great weekend as they packed up. Najwa stood for a few seconds, watching her colleagues walk up First Avenue, before she turned and walked through the main entrance. She braced herself for long waits at the security checks here and at the tent. The first she passed through reasonably quickly, because at four o'clock on a Friday afternoon the flow of people was overwhelmingly out of the building. There was a short line at the security tent in the open courtyard, but by now the system had been honed. There were three lines: for UN officials, visitors, and accredited press. There was nobody in the press queue and so she walked to the front. A UN security guard checked her ID, and she glanced at him as he ran her details through the computer: heavy paunch, luxuriant mustache, a name tag reading Nero. He looked familiar, and then she realized that she had seen him on the terrace of the Delegates Lounge while she was meeting with Bakri. Nero waved her through the metal detector, noting down the time of her arrival.

She looked at him questioningly. "Keeping tabs on me?"

"Nothing personal. Extra security measures, ma'am. All entries to the building have to be logged."

Najwa shrugged and slid her purse onto the conveyer belt of the X-ray machine. It passed through without incident, and Nero waved her through.

She strode ahead into the building. Impatient to get to her office, she walked quickly to the escalators and did not notice a female security guard pick up the phone and speak in an urgent whisper as she passed.

Al-Jazeera and other major news organizations had their offices on the first floor. Najwa stepped off the escalator, her heels clicking on the polished black granite. She should have been feeling triumphant, but instead she felt uneasy, even claustrophobic. There were no outside windows in this part of the building, except in the journalists' individual offices, and the white ceiling of the hallway and its square neon lights now seemed to bear down on her, the pale cream walls shrinking inward.

The door to the office next to the Al-Jazeera bureau was open, Najwa noticed with surprise. The room had been empty for several months and she knew that numerous news organizations had applied to use it, although none had been successful. She pushed it gently and it swung inward, so she poked her head around the door. It was a much smaller space than her office. A young woman was standing at the large window that looked out over the East River and the Queens shoreline, with her back to the door. Her bob of brown hair looked familiar.

Najwa asked, "Hello, anyone at home?"

The woman turned around. "Hi," said Collette Moreau, smiling brightly.

Najwa started in surprise. "Hi . . . what brings you here?"

Collette smiled as she stepped forward. "We are thinking of further expanding the bureau. The building manager said this room had been free for ages. He gave me the key."

Najwa shrugged. "OK. Good luck. Hey, don't think me rude, but I'm in a rush. Keep me posted if we are going to be neighbors."

"Sure. I hope we soon will be," said Collette, as she closed the door gently but firmly.

Once inside her office, Najwa pulled down the blinds on all the windows. She locked the door, then pulled the handle to check that it was properly closed. Her encounter with Collette did not really make sense. The *Times* had just moved to a new office with plenty of space. Why would they need another room? No newspaper editorial budget nowadays could justify three reporters to cover the UN.

However, she had more urgent matters to take care of. Braithwaite had shared some information about Salim Massoud. Najwa knew he knew much more than he was telling, but it was a start. Massoud, he explained, was the number two figure in the Revolutionary Guard, an extremely dangerous man who had evaded surveillance on several occasions. He also had powerful allies in the United States, and was somehow connected to a secret government agency known as the DoD, the Department of Deniable. Massoud's current location was not known, but he was believed to be out of the United States.

Najwa opened her purse and took out two phones, an obsolete Nokia candy-bar model and her iPhone. She removed the SIM card from her iPhone and put it on her desk. The phone's screen showed eleven Wi-Fi networks. The strongest, Fatima79, had five solid bars. Najwa reached around her desk, unplugged the Wi-Fi router and the modem, then checked her phone again. Fatima79 showed an empty triangle. By now, most savvy mobile phone users knew that their conversations were not secure. Not only could a mobile phone be tapped, it could also be used remotely as a microphone, to bug a room or record a conversation, even when switched off.

But Najwa also knew from a recent reporting trip to Israel that a cell phone could now also be used to hack a nearby computer. Invented by Israeli researchers, "air-gap network hacking" allowed a cell phone, fitted with the requisite software, to connect to a computer from a range of up to six yards, get inside it, and transmit the computer's data. The software could be remotely installed on a cell phone without the owner's knowledge, and there was no need for a USB, or even a Bluetooth, connection between the phone and the computer. Air-gapped computers, ones not connected to the Internet via Wi-Fi or a modem, or to any other devices, were thought to be secure. But even when a computer was air-gapped, the keyboard, monitor, hard drive, and memory chips still poured out a stream of microsignals and electronic vibrations. Every stroke on a keyboard, for example, transmitted an electronic signal on a particular frequency. The hacked cell phones covertly scanned for electromagnetic waves, and if a hacker had access to those emanations, he could gain access to usernames and passwords. Many of those working on the hacking software had previously served with Unit 5200, the highly secretive cyber unit of the Israeli military.

Najwa switched off the Wi-Fi on her iPhone and placed it inside the secure bag that she had showed to Sami at McLaughlin's. She then removed the SIM card from the Nokia, cut it in half and dropped the pieces in the trash can. She opened up the Nokia's message folder. There was one message:

All Akerman's UNMO files missing.

She took the battery out of the Nokia as well, and then put the phone in her purse. The news did not surprise her. All sorts of files, it seemed, had a habit of disappearing from the UN archives. Access to many records of the DPKO's involvement in both Rwanda and Srebrenica was highly restricted, and each archive kept records of anyone even requesting sight of the reports. But there were rumors that several files, detailing Fareed Hussein's involvement in both catastrophes, had not been seen since the mid-1990s.

Najwa unlocked a drawer in her desk and took out a Toshiba laptop. It was thick, heavy, and at least fifteen years out of date. With no built-in Wi-Fi, it could only connect to the Internet through a dial-up modem, but it did have a USB port. She powered it up and plugged a memory stick into the port. A window opened on the screen, playing a file of fifteen minutes of CCTV footage from the corner of East Fifty-Second Street and First Avenue. The clip was date- and time-stamped Thursday April 17, 8:00 a.m.—two weeks earlier.

She sat staring at the footage for thirteen minutes. It showed the bustle of early morning commuters on a busy Manhattan thoroughfare. Every other person mouthed silently into the cell phone clamped to their ear. Most were carrying large cups of coffee as they weaved a path through the crowd. An elderly lady walked a tiny dog on a leash. A tall black man in a green vest handed out copies of *Metro*, a free daily newspaper. Nothing seemed out of the ordinary.

When the footage reached its last ninety seconds, Najwa

straightened, suddenly alert. Henrik Schneidermann appeared, his briefcase in his hand. He looked curiously cheerful and purposeful, quite different from the morose Belgian she was used to dealing with at the UN press office. She felt a sudden pang at the thought of never seeing him again except in this video clip, forever striding forward, full of energy. She watched, transfixed, as a man bumped into Schneidermann's left side and fell onto the sidewalk. He was bald with a neatly trimmed salt-and-pepper beard. Schneidermann reached down to help the man get up. Najwa could see their mouths move as they spoke.

The man held his hand out as he scrabbled to right himself.

Najwa pressed pause.

The screen froze, revealing the man's fingers, in black leather gloves, grasping Schneidermann's hand as he rose from the pavement.

22

Yael stepped out of the lift on the seventeenth floor of 800 Second Avenue and walked into the entrance foyer of the Israeli UN mission. Two CCTV cameras were mounted on the top corners of the heavy steel door. Two more CCTV cameras pointed down from the ceiling. The room was a small, windowless space, around twenty feet by twenty, with light blue walls and a gray floor. On one wall, a poster of smiling, attractive young people in a nightclub advertised Tel Aviv, "the 24 hour city." Part of another wall was made of tinted glass, an inch thick. A single door opened onto a corridor of more offices.

Yael walked up to the glass wall. Behind it sat a plump young woman with short black hair and thick, black-framed glasses. She stared at Yael. "Can I help you?" Her voice was tinny, coming out of a hidden speaker.

"I hope so. I'm here to see Eli Harrari."

"Who?"

"Eli Harrari. The chief of staff to the ambassador."

The young woman stared at Yael. "Mr. Harrari has left New York. He has returned to Tel Aviv."

"Really? Then how did I see him walk into the building five minutes ago?"

"You didn't."

"Actually, I did. At 3:57 p.m. Check the log."

Even with the wall of glass between them, Yael sensed the young woman's mind spinning. "I don't know what you are talking about. Please leave or I will call security," she said, as she picked up the phone.

"Sure. Do it. Have me thrown out. See what Eli says then. And see how long you will still be working in New York."

The young woman looked at Yael again, less sure of herself. "Who are you?"

"Motek."

"Your name, I mean."

"That's what he calls me."

Her eyes opened wider as she placed the phone handset back in its cradle. "Pass your ID, wallet, and cell phone under the glass."

"I don't have any of those with me."

"How did you get into the building without ID?"

Yael had shown her driver's license to the police outside and to the security guard at the reception, but she was not going to hand it over. She would never see it again.

Yael leaned forward, switched to rapid Hebrew. "Are you really as dumb as you look? How many times do I have to tell you? Eli is waiting for me."

The young woman flinched, switched off the microphone, picked up the phone receiver again, and spoke rapidly. She stopped talking, listened for several seconds, then looked at Yael. She turned the speaker back on. "Wait here."

Joe-Don looked at his watch, the knot in his stomach twisting tighter by the moment. The battered Rolex Oyster showed five minutes past five. He returned to staring at the entrance of number 800. The door opened. Two young women walked out. Neither was Yael.

"If I'm not out in an hour, come and get me."

She had been joking. But this was not funny. No matter how smart or how brave she was, she was on Eli's territory now. The instant she stepped inside the mission, US law no longer applied. Not that laws were really the issue here if something went wrong. He would have to get past the cops at the building entrance, force his way into one of the most secure diplomatic buildings in the United States, find her, take down whoever was holding her, and then get both of them out. While he was unarmed. The odds were, to put it mildly, against him.

He scanned the contact numbers in his phone. There was someone he could call, an old friend from his Special Forces Group days in Central America who could be here in twenty minutes with a weapon, maybe sooner. But it might be easier for him to get one of the cops' guns. It would certainly be faster. He looked over the road to the UN Plaza Pharmacy. A can of hair spray, a polite request for directions, a sudden face-full of L'Oreal, a haymaker. He could grab the officer's gun and use it to take down his partner. And probably spend the rest of his life in prison.

Joe-Don shook his head. It would never work. Especially not on his own. There would be backup systems for a building like this. And the Israeli mission would certainly have a CCTV feed onto the street. They would see what was happening, go into lockdown mode, sound the alarm. The NYPD, FBI, Secret Service, and who knew what else would be here instantly.

He had to damp down his rising anxiety and think this through. Logic, not emotion, was needed now. He watched a laundry truck stop on the corner of Fortieth and Second Avenue. The deliverymen worked with mechanical efficiency, hurling large sacks of clothes into the back before slamming the door and jumping back into the truck as it headed into the traffic.

That was it. If she really was a prisoner, eventually they would have to get her out of the building and into a vehicle. It was just a question of waiting. Entering and exiting buildings and vehicles always made for the most vulnerable moments. Former Serbian prime minister Zoran Djindjic had one of the heaviest security details in the world, but it had not prevented a sniper from killing him as he stepped out of his car one afternoon in Belgrade.

Joe-Don had checked the building plan earlier and number 800 had no back entrance. If they had Yael, they would need to come out of the front, or more likely the side entrance on East Forty-Second Street. Maybe he *would* make that call to his old friend, but give him a longer shopping list. He would need a vehicle, weapons, and some backup. He began to calculate the permutations: the number of men, the weapons, the positions they would need to hold. He picked up his phone and called up the number of his contact. He was about to press the dial button when the door of the pizzeria swung open.

Reinhardt Daintner checked over the guest list for the twelfth time that day, nodding to himself in quiet satisfaction. Almost every one of the city's great and good were attending. Both the Democratic mayor and the Republican governor had promised to be there, even though it was well known that they cordially loathed being in the same room as one another. The chairman of the board for both the Museum of Modern Art and the Metropolitan Museum, the chairman of the Board of Education, almost every city councilor and state senator, as well as numerous journalists from the major newspapers, television networks, and websites, had all gladly accepted KZX's invitation. Even Page Six was sending two reporters.

Twelve hours ago, it had looked like he would have to cancel. The NYPD and the FBI demanded that the event be postponed, claiming the threat level was too high after Akerman's shooting. But after a series of phone calls to some of the most prominent guests, and promises of substantial donations to the NYPD's and the FBI's Benevolent Funds, they had agreed to go ahead. Daintner put the list down on the faux-antique desk in his executive suite at the Waldorf Astoria and looked around. Composed of two rooms, a bedroom and a sitting room, it was furnished with the bland corporate elegance that now seemed to be his permanent habitat: a dark blue carpet, lighter walls, two plush cream-colored sofas, the walls decorated with unthreatening works of abstract modern art.

He leaned back, yawned, and stretched his long limbs. Daintner had arrived in New York three days ago. He'd factored in a couple of days to get over the jet lag, but the journey had certainly been eased by the fact that he was the only passenger on KZX's corporate jet, a Bombardier Global Express. The onboard chef had prepared him a light dinner of grilled sea bass, washed down with a superb Chablis. A good night's sleep in the airplane's bedroom was followed by a swift VIP processing at Teterboro Airport, just outside New York, and a limousine to his hotel.

He reached across the desk for the fine white china teapot, poured himself another cup of Japanese Sencha green tea, and walked over to the large corner window. The sky was still gray but the rain had stopped and pedestrians were striding along without umbrellas. He watched a pizza deliveryman effortlessly zip through the crowds on Rollerblades, all the while holding two cardboard boxes in front of him. How easy it looked. How easy Daintner's own work had been, directing the tide of money that quickly washed away the stains on KZX's reputation.

A series of dinners at Michelin-starred restaurants over the last year, hosted by the PR department of KZX's New York office, and several substantial corporate donations to the favorite charities of the cabal of elderly ladies who reigned over New York City's philanthropy circuit had opened all the necessary doors. The coltan scandal; the recent unpleasantness in eastern Europe with the Romany people; the messy connection with the Prometheus Group over privatizing UN security and peacekeeping—all this was now old news. The new news was tomorrow evening's opening reception of the KZX School of International Development at Columbia University, with Fareed Hussein as the guest of honor. Daintner looked at his watch, a sleek black Rado. It was now five o'clock. Twenty-six hours to go.

He sipped his tea, relishing the sharp, almost bitter taste. Tomorrow night would be the crowning glory of his career. Sometimes he admitted to himself that the reach of his company, the sheer power of money, scared him a little. What if, one day, his bosses tired of him? For now, at least, that seemed unlikely, but if they did there were the files, backed up somewhere deep in cyberspace, the hard copies in the safe sunk into the floor of his penthouse apartment overlooking Lake Geneva.

Daintner put the cup down on the desk and walked into the bedroom.

The floor on his side of the king-sized bed was empty. Three identical gray silk suits hung from the railing in the wardrobe, together with six white shirts. Each had been hand-stitched by Daintner's tailor on London's Savile Row. Two identical pairs of black brogues stood on the floor, both handmade by Lobbs. He walked around the bed. That month's issue of *Vogue* lay open on the floor, on top of that day's *New York Times*. He picked up a black bra that lay crumpled in a corner and placed it on the bed.

He slowly shook his head in irritation, walked into the marble-lined bathroom, splashed his face with cold water and stared at himself in the mirror. Reinhardt Daintner's unusual appearance almost always turned heads. Just over six feet tall, he was stick-thin, with slightly stooped shoulders and light gray eyes, and so pale he was almost an albino. His white-blond hair stopped on his forehead in a widow's peak, above eyebrows of the same color. On the rare occasions that he was worried, and he let it show, his tongue flicked out through his lips like a hungry lizard's. Yet he could, when he chose, be charm itself.

Daintner had joined KZX as a trainee in the communications department after graduating from Heidelberg University. He lived to work and his dedication was appreciated; after twenty years he was now director of corporate communications, with a network of media and political contacts across the world that many of the prime ministers, presidents, and CEOs on the list would envy. An invitation to lunch or dinner came almost every week from an elite head-hunting agency representing countries and corporations keen to hire him. He never accepted any of them, partly because, despite the promises of confidentiality, word of his disloyalty would soon get out. But mostly because KZX was one of the most powerful corporations in the world. It had its own intelligence department, which was far better informed that those of many countries. KZX's media holdings were always in the headlines, but its pharmaceutical division garnered less attention—which was how Daintner liked it.

Daintner had recently returned from a secret meeting with Taliban leaders in Qatar. Once marijuana and hashish were fully legalized, other drugs would soon follow, and the potential market was worth billions. Which was why the KZX School of International Development had already commissioned a series of pilot studies, from several leading academics and economists, under the guise of helping the pharmaceutical industry act in a socially responsible way once legalization took place. The reports had titles like "The likely socio-economic impact on the micro-economy of an Afghan village of the potential impact of the legalization of heroin," but buried within the touchy-feely stuff about the poor peasants were numerous nuggets of hard intelligence and financial information that would be the building blocks of the company's future strategy. Once KZX's links were formalized with the Prometheus Group, the two firms would be unstoppable. Prometheus would supply what was known as "force projection" to secure a market in opiates, minerals, or whatever other resources were in demand, and KZX would then take care of the business side of the global drugs market.

Daintner found Clarence Clairborne's millenarian fantasies about the coming "Rapture" laughable. But you worked with who was available and could get the job done. Of that, he had no doubt. The coming war would shake up the old order, destabilize the Middle East, and leave the requisite power vacuum that would immediately be filled by Prometheus and KZX. The plan itself was buried so deep in cyberspace, and encrypted to such a level that even the NSA would struggle to find and decode it. However, others had sensed the coming storm: Henrik Schneidermann, for example. His instincts had been completely correct. If only Schneidermann had kept them to himself. Had he not put them into an analysis for Fareed Hussein, he might still be alive. His death had been regrettable, but even with him taken care of there were still several pieces of grit in the machine.

Daintner returned to his desk. Three files lay on the surface, each with a small passport-sized photograph stapled to the front and ULTRACONFIDENTIAL printed at angle across the cover. The top file had a photograph of Yael, the second one of Sami, and the third one of Najwa. He picked up the top file and flicked through the pages, lingering with a smile over the account of how, several years ago, Yael had arranged for US Special Forces to guard the Taliban's opium fields so they would not blow up a gas pipeline. That was not the first time she had been unwittingly helpful. Daintner glanced at the second file. Sami Boustani was an irritant, and persistent, but essentially manageable. He would be receiving several visits from "immigration officials" in the next couple of days, officials especially interested in his family connection to an attempted suicide bombing on the Gaza border. That was more than a decade ago, but there was no statute of limitations on terrorism.

It was Najwa al-Sameera who proved more troublesome than expected. He grabbed her file and scanned the heading of the latest addition:

Report of Meeting between NAJWA AL-SAMEERA and RIYAD BAKRI

The only useful thing about the account of the meeting between Najwa and the Saudi diplomat was the fact that it had taken place. His operative had not managed to overhear any of their conversation. The giant terrace outside the Delegates Lounge was an inspired choice because it was impossible to stand close enough to anyone there to eavesdrop. All KZX's informant could provide was the place, time, and duration of the meeting, but even that was useful. Bakri was a person of growing interest. The Saudi Mukhabarat had superb networks inside Iran.

Daintner switched on his laptop, a thin machine in a titanium case that had been custom manufactured for him by one of KZX's subsidiaries. He entered his password and checked his secure e-mail inbox. There was a new message. No sender was shown, but the e-mail had two links. He clicked on the first. It opened a window with Najwa's name and a list of her recent Internet searches. Daintner was alarmed to see that Najwa's data trail led to the video interview with the widow of Abbas Velavi.

He sat staring at the screen for more than a minute, then opened the second link. The footage had been shot from above, perhaps twenty-five or thirty feet above ground, Daintner guessed. It showed Najwa doing her stand-up on First Avenue outside the UN headquarters, first from a distance, then zooming in closer. Daintner froze the frame as it focused on Najwa's face. She was certainly attractive, if a little Rubenesque for his taste. He thumbed through her file: "Despite all the talk of a boyfriend/fiancée, al-Sameera has never been seen in public with a partner."

His ringing phone interrupted his reverie. He looked at the number and immediately took the call.

A female voice with a French accent said, "We have a situation, sir."

Yael dipped the tea bag in the cup. The water turned a pale brown. She dipped the tip of her index finger into the drink and kept it there. "Why can't Americans make tea? It's really easy. You just put boiling water on a tea bag and leave it for a couple of minutes. I've had baths hotter than this."

Joe-Don's face was tight with anxiety. He stared at Yael, who looked surprisingly calm. Her skin was soft and relaxed, gently flushed. Her eyes were shining. "Are you going to tell me what happened in there?" he demanded.

She pressed a teaspoon against the tea bag, tasted the drink, and scowled. "They made me wait. Pretended they had never heard of Eli. Eventually they let me in. He was there. We talked in his office for a while." She paused, looked down at her drink, suddenly shy. "Quite a while."

Joe-Don stared harder. A thin film of perspiration covered her upper lip. He exhaled long and hard. "Tell me you didn't . . ."

Yael caught his eye, blushed. She put her hand on his. "I did what was needed."

He quickly withdrew his hand from under hers. "I don't believe it."

She smiled. "Hey. It worked. We made a deal."

Joe-Don shook his head in mock despair. "Which was?"

Yael turned to face him, her voice businesslike now. "I promised to wipe the file I have of Eli's movements and the dead people that keep turning up wherever he does. I also agreed to be ready in the foyer of my apartment at three o'clock with my bags packed, awaiting my transport to the airport, on Monday for my brief holiday in Tel Aviv. In exchange he guaranteed Noa's safety."

"Do you believe him?"

"I am not sure. But I told him that I had informed my father about his threat. And that if anything happened to

Noa or any of her children, Eli knew what to expect. He is one of the few people in the world that scares Eli."

"And where will Eli be next week?"

"That is the tricky part," said Yael.

"Where?" demanded Joe-Don.

"Reykjavik."

23

"You promised to tell me about your date," said Barbara.

Yael smiled ruefully. "Sure. Have you got five seconds?"

It was eleven o'clock on Saturday morning. Yael and her mother were standing on Bow Bridge in the middle of Central Park, looking out over the water. Barbara's flight had been late coming into LaGuardia and she had not arrived until after midnight. They had woken late, grabbed lox bagels and coffee from Zabar's, and walked to the park.

Bow Bridge spanned a narrow stretch of the lake, surrounded by trees and greenery. It was a minor landmark, a graceful arch of pale gray stone popular with tourists and New Yorkers alike. The sky was bright blue, studded with puffy white clouds. A gentle breeze blew over the water, ruffling the gray-green surface of the lake. The air smelled clean and fresh. Beyond the edge of the park, granite apartment blocks pointed skyward, the bright morning sun glinting on their windows.

"I'm sorry," said Barbara. "I know you were looking forward to it. What happened?"

Yael turned to look at her mother. She was just the right side of seventy, but looked several years younger. Barbara Weiss—she had reverted to her maiden name after her divorce—was tall and still slender. She had blue-green eyes and gray hair cut short in a stacked bob that subtly emphasized her graceful neck. She was dressed in a blue turtleneck sweater and jeans and a gray American Apparel zip-up jacket. This was the first time Yael had seen her mother for three years. One part of her wanted to hug her, be hugged, and never let go. The other wanted to up-end her and tip her over the bridge and into the water.

"It's a long story," said Yael. She watched a white electric park maintenance vehicle silently glide by, the minitrailer stacked high with branches and leaves. She instinctively checked the inside compartment. The driver, the only one inside, wore wrap-around sunglasses and a baseball cap. Was it a deliberate attempt to obscure his face? Or was she being paranoid? She had not sensed any surveillance that morning, but that was no guarantee that there was no threat.

Barbara took Yael's arm, breaking her chain of thought. She beckoned her daughter to a nearby bench. "Tell me. We have time. All day, if you need."

Yael sat down. The park vehicle was now several hundred yards away. She relaxed. The wooden slats felt familiar against her back. Perhaps they had both sat on this very bench at some point in the past. Yael had spent much time in Central Park, with her parents when she was still a child, and later with David. Her parents had met in 1969, at a New York reception for former Israeli prime minister Golda Meir. Barbara was then a reporter on the Metro desk of the *New York Times*, and assigned to cover the event. They fell quickly, deeply, in love, and when Barbara got pregnant they had married. David was born in 1970. Barbara ran the business and administration side of Aleph Research, Yael's father's company that supplied business intelligence to governments, firms, and select individuals, but that was a poor substitute for the buzz of the *New York Times* newsroom.

Aleph was not listed in the phone directory or on corporate contact lists, but it never lacked for clients. It was known for accuracy, both of its research reports and its forecasts. Yael's father brought in much of the information, together with a team of researchers, most of whom seemed to be Israeli or to have lived in Israel. There was a stream of visitors from all over the world. Yael got used to hearing French, German, Spanish, Russian, even Arabic. When she asked her parents who the visitors were, they told her they were "clients." As a child of eight or nine, Yael had delighted in helping with the filing. She even had her own desk with a small brass nameplate inscribed: "Yael Azoulay: Office Manager." By her teenage years, she believed that Aleph was either a front company for the Israeli intelligence establishment, or was so close to it that it didn't matter.

But by the 1980s, Barbara was increasingly unhappy: about having to raise three children on her own, about the kind of work Aleph was doing, often for the darker reaches of the US government. During the 1980s governments toppled across the developing world in coups, and in almost every instance Aleph had submitted a detailed report on the country before the violence had erupted.

Yael watched a heron swoop low over the water before instantly changing direction and soaring skyward. Her mother's smell, a mix of White Linen perfume and lemon-scented soap, was familiar, even comforting. She had once been very close to her mother. Her father traveled all around the world for Aleph, so much that she hardly saw him.

Barbara put her hand on Yael's arm. "Your date?"

Yael started to talk, and then she couldn't stop. She felt overwhelmed at the emotions welling up inside her. So many feelings, stopped up for so long. It all poured out, from Goma to Geneva, from Istanbul to Tompkins Square Park. The coltan scandal. The Sami disaster. Her friendships with Isis Franklin and Olivia de Souza and their terrible ends. Rina Hussein. The dark force that still drew her to Eli. But she did not mention Eli's threat against Noa, or her agreement with him.

When she was finished, she wiped her eyes, stared at the lake. A young couple sat in a boat, going round and round in circles as the man ineptly tried to row. His girlfriend was laughing, the wind in her hair, filming his efforts on her camera. Yael felt suddenly, intensely jealous. She blew her nose, and turned to her mother. "Where *were* you?"

"I'm sorry. I thought you didn't want to see me or talk to me anymore."

As Yael got older, she slowly grew apart from her mother. Barbara focused on David, the eldest son, and Noa, the youngest daughter, leaving her middle child to her own devices. Yael felt that her mother resented her, even started to view her as a rival for her father's attention and affection. In reaction, she reached out to her father, further alienating her mother and launching a self-perpetuating circle of mutual resentment. After David died, when Yael was sixteen, her parents separated. Her father returned to Israel, and she went with him; two years later she followed him to London. Yael stayed with her father in London until she moved back to Israel and did her military service.

"I did. I didn't. It doesn't matter what I wanted. You're my *mom*." Yael was almost shouting now. "You are supposed to come and find me. To make it better. That's what moms do. Why didn't you?"

Barbara swallowed, blinked, looked out over the park as she spoke. "You never picked up the phone when I called. You didn't reply to my letters. You never called."

Yael started coughing, laughing through her tears. "Now you really sound like a Jewish mother."

Barbara's face was tight. "It's very . . . *difficult* for me, for all of us at this time of year. He would have been forty-four by now. And when I think how he . . . what happened there . . ."

She grasped her mother's hand, the skin was warm to her touch. "Don't. *Don't.* Don't think about that. Remember him as he was." Their fingers intertwined, locked solid. "I still miss him so much. I lost my brother. I'm permanently single. Nobody calls me. Every time I make a friend they end up dead. I'm the kiss of death." She blew her nose again. "I'm so sick of being on my own. Eating alone. Sleeping alone. At least you have Nora."

"Not anymore. We broke up."

"I'm sorry to hear that. Why?"

"Everyone likes to experiment. My phase came a little late in life. But look at you. You are beautiful. There must be someone out there."

Yael released her mother's hand. She reached inside her purse, took out the postcard of the catamaran and handed it to Barbara.

"A boat with an Istanbul postmark," she said, intrigued. She turned it over. "And it's wordless. How mysterious. Who's it from?"

"A friend."

"Obviously. What kind of friend? A male friend?"

Yael looked out over the lake. The oarsman had control now, gliding along the surface of the water. His girlfriend leaned back, the sun on her face, looking contented.

She watches Yusuf finish his pide. His fingers are long and slender, his dark eyes, somewhere between brown and black, warm and intelligent. A lock of hair, so black it almost shines, falls over his forehead.

Her voice was almost wistful. "Male, yes, definitely. But he's there and I am here."

"Why don't you go? Istanbul's not that far. You must be owed weeks of vacation."

Yael smiled. "Yes, I am. And I find myself thinking about him. More and more often. Maybe I will go. But not this weekend."

She turned to look at her mother. "Mom, I'm really happy you're here."

"Me too."

"But why now, all of a sudden?"

"Because . . ." Barbara paused. "Because there's something I need to talk to you about."

"Go on."

Barbara took both of Yael's hands in hers. "Your father."

Najwa stepped back and checked the blue awning that reached from the front of the apartment block on East Sixty-Sixth Street to the curb. Number *One Hundred and Twenty* was written along the side in cursive. She was in the right place. It was a classic Manhattan building: gray granite on the outside, cream and brown marble foyer on the inside. A uniformed doorman stood at the entrance in matching livery, watching her.

Najwa looked around as she walked down the entrance corridor. The building was not quite as grand as it seemed from the outside. The cream walls were covered with numerous scuff marks and needed repainting. The black granite floor was chipped and worn, spotted with gray and white patches. There was a faint but noticeable smell of disinfectant. CCTV cameras covered the entrance, the corridor, and the lobby.

A second, older doorman stood behind a tall wooden desk that reached up to his chest. He had small, suspicious eyes set in a broad, fleshy face. The sports section of the *New York Post* was open on the lectern.

"Can I help you, ma'am?" he asked, looking Najwa up and down, clearly assessing her curves.

She smiled. "I hope so. I'm here to see Francine de la Court."

The doorman scowled and returned to his newspaper. "You're outta luck. She's out," he said in a strong Queens accent.

Najwa glanced at the row of television monitors by the side of the desk. They were all blank apart from the words "Source fault." On the contrary, she was very much in luck. "That's a shame. I'd like to go up anyway. She has a book of mine. She said if she had to go out she would leave it with a neighbor. He's waiting for me to pick it up."

The doorman looked up. "Who?"

"Joel Greenberg. Could you call him?"

"Mr. Greenberg don't like to be disturbed by unexpected visitors. Try later."

"Please? I am here now, I cannot come back later," she said, dropping a fifty-dollar bill onto the newspaper. The doorman did not lift his eyes, merely gestured backward with his head to indicate she could go ahead.

Francine lived on the sixth floor, in apartment 6F. Najwa stepped out of the elevator and walked down the hallway. The floor was lined with a brown runner, held in place by brass rails, but the brass was dull and mottled and the edges of the long, stained carpet were fraying. Apartment 6F was just two doors down from the elevator. It was an old and noisy contraption, and she could feel the floor vibrate as it descended back to the lobby.

The door of 6F was painted light green. She knocked. There was no answer. She knocked again. Still no answer. This was not unexpected. Najwa had called several times over the past couple of days, and nobody had picked up the phone. The bad-tempered doorman was correct. She moved on to knock on the door of apartment 6E, which she had already established was occupied by Joel Greenberg.

A voice shouted, "Hold on, I'm coming," echoing down

the corridor. A few seconds later the door opened to reveal an elderly man. He wore a pressed light-blue denim shirt that matched his lively blue eyes, and was trim and well groomed. He looked at Najwa, clearly pleased to have such a visitor. "Hello. How can I help you, my dear?"

She gave him her most dazzling smile. "I'm Najwa, a friend of Francine's from the UN."

"Joel Greenberg, pleased to meet you."

They shook hands. Greenberg's palm was cool, his grip firm.

"I'm worried about her," Najwa said. "She doesn't answer any of her phones. I've left several messages. She hasn't called back."

Greenberg frowned. "I thought it was terrible what they did to her. First her boss dies, then they sack her, just like that after all those years of service. I told her to get a lawyer but she didn't want to know. I used to be a lawyer, did a lot of labor work, for the unions as well, and I told her, she would have a very good case for—"

She sensed he was about to launch into a monologue and cut in quickly. "I completely agree, Joel." She paused. "May I call you Joel?" she asked, already knowing the answer.

Greenberg nodded. "Of course."

Najwa continued talking. "We all said she should fight it. Even the UN staff union wanted to take it up. But she didn't want to . . . do you know where she is now?"

"She said she was going away for a while, to stay with friends. Didn't say where. We were good friends, you know. Then she just disappears like that . . ."

"The thing is, Joel," Najwa leaned forward conspiratorially. She could hear the NPR midday news playing in the background. "I lent her a book and I really need it back." She stepped back, paused. "No, no, it's too much to ask."

"What? Ask already."

"I couldn't . . ."

"Ask."

"A key. Did she leave you a key? It would be for a couple of minutes, just till I find the book."

Greenberg gave Najwa a piercing look as if to say, *I may be old, but I know when I am being played.* "A friend of hers from the UN, you say?"

"That's me. We spent a lot of time together." *Mostly trying to get past her to get to Henrik Schneidermann,* Najwa thought, but there was no need to go into that.

He paused for a moment. "Then you must know her daughter. A beautiful girl."

"Francine doesn't have a daughter. Not as far as I know. She does have a son, Luc. He goes to Brooklyn Community College."

Greenberg stared at Najwa, taking his time. She held his gaze, feeling the familiar, confident excitement that things were going her way.

"Hold on," the old man said. He stepped inside his apartment. Najwa watched him walk into a well-equipped kitchen, heard him rummage in a drawer for several seconds before he returned. He held a key in his thumb and forefinger. "OK. I'm trusting you with this. Five minutes."

24

Najwa stepped inside the front door of 6F, a small two-bedroom that smelled faintly of perfume and flowers. The scuffed parquet slats creaked underfoot. The air was still, undisturbed. She looked around with interest, quickly reassessing her opinion of the apartment's owner. To the right was an outdated kitchen with a stove and orange Formica cupboards that dated back to the 1960s. A fridge buzzed and gurgled in the corner. To the left, a small dark corridor led to the living room on one side, and two bedrooms on the other. Najwa told herself the intrusion was for a good cause, to find out the truth about Schneidermann's death. She had not broken in. The neighbor had given her a key. But she felt like an invader as she stepped into the kitchen.

Madam Non's *froideur* was doubtless the best defense against a horde of pushy, demanding, wiseass reporters. But away from the UN building, she was very human indeed. A piece of homemade fruit cake was drying out on a serving plate. Daffodils wilted in a vase. Several pictures of Francine and a teenage boy were pinned on a corkboard. There did not seem to be an adult man in their lives. A brass bowl held a pile of receipts, and Najwa flicked through the scraps of paper. There were several from the Café Port-au-Prince. She grabbed one and put in her pocket.

She stepped out of the kitchen and walked down the corridor into the living area. The room was neat and tidy but lacking natural light, with gloomy, old-fashioned furniture. A framed photograph of Francine shaking hands with Fareed Hussein stood on top of a dark, heavy sideboard. Most of one wall was taken up with bookshelves. Najwa scanned the contents: a mix of romantic novels, Central and South American poetry volumes, and several books on international relations and the role of the UN. She needed a book to show to Joel Greenberg, and her glance fell on a work she knew, an interminably dull academic history of peacekeeping operations. She grabbed it and had just placed it on the sideboard when she heard the door open, and two voices. Neither belonged to Joel Greenberg.

A dozen blocks south, Fareed Hussein stood by his desk in his bedroom, staring through the window down onto the patio and garden. His arms, back, legs—everywhere, it seemed—ached. There was no fool like an old fool, he well knew. And he was both. He raised his fingers to his nose: perfume, sweat, a sharp female tang, salty and metallic. The girl's demands were incessant in bed—and, increasingly, out of it.

His wife, Zeinab, seemed to have lost interest in sex more than a decade ago, and anyway he had not seen her for months, since she returned last fall to Pakistan. He had long thought that his sex drive had been sublimated into his privileged place on the global A-list. Security Council intrigues; cosy tête-à-têtes at the White House, Ten Downing Street, the Kremlin, and the Élysée Palace; the VIP list at Hollywood receptions; a place-card at the most sought after dinners in Davos. But he was wrong about his libido, and he had been pleasantly surprised at his performance, even if it had been aided by the small blue miracle pills. Still, it was with distinct relief that he had said good-bye to her an hour ago. This affair, fling, seduction, call it what you will, had been a mistake. He would end it as soon as the KZX reception tonight was out of the way. He could not afford any kind of scene there. Or here, for that matter.

Like the Secretariat Building, the grand townhouse at Number 2 Sutton Place was a snake pit of gossip, intrigue, and backbiting. Word had doubtless already leaked about her overnight stays, and nobody was fooled by the rumpled sheets in the guest bedroom. Built in 1921 for a daughter of J. P. Morgan, the fourteen-thousand-square-foot building was five stories tall, built around an imposing wooden staircase that seemed to have been transplanted from an English stately home. The residence had recently been redecorated by an expensive Park Avenue interior design firm, the $3 million bill setting off a firestorm among the right-wing media until a Silicon Valley software billionaire picked it up, in exchange for a lifetime guarantee of invitations to the SG's most exclusive dinners and receptions.

Hussein rested his hand on the corner of his desk, wincing when something small and hard pressed into his palm.

He looked down to see a tiny red and black USB stick. He picked it up and examined it. It did not look familiar. Where had it come from? Perhaps Roxana left it behind, he thought momentarily. He would call her and ask, but later. This morning, especially, he needed to be alone for a while. He put the memory stick back on his desk and looked down at the garden again.

The patio appeared cool and tranquil, its spotless gray flagstones almost shining in the midmorning sun. A small circular table, covered with a thick white tablecloth, was set for a late breakfast. In the center was a white vase holding a single red rose. The sides of the terrace were lined with bushes and trees, and a lush lawn reached from the end of the patio to the end of the garden. Hussein watched one of the three gardeners prune the rose bushes, suddenly back on the terrace of his father's house in Delhi—before the deluge and the bloodletting, when the family was whole.

Roxana's early morning demands usually made him hungry. But today he had no appetite. The pain, the memories, did not dim with time. On the contrary, as the years passed they seemed to be stronger, more vivid, more real.

Omar would have been seventy-four today. Perhaps he was. It was the not knowing that was the worst. He could have been killed in the crush, the blood frenzy. Or he may have lived, hiding until the madness wore itself out and then been taken in by another family, adopting another name, forgetting his history. He might even have a family of his own, children, grandchildren. Hussein would never know. Hussein clenched his fingers, digging them so hard into his palm that he winced. Could he have held on harder to his brother's hand?

Hussein rarely spoke of Omar. His memoir was the only time he had discussed his brother and his disappearance. But people were speaking—he sensed, he *knew*—about his other secrets. Justifiable at the time, every decision taken left a dark residue that over the years turned into a brittle carapace of guilt and shame. One that could—would, he thought—eventually crack and shatter, taking his reputation along with it. He stared at the indents in the skin of his hand, the same hand that had briefly grasped Yael's brother's arm when he departed for Kigali.

Hussein sat down by his desk, glanced at the photograph in the silver frame, a copy of the one in his office. It was almost too painful to look at. He had one arm around Zeinab's shoulder and the other around Rina's, on the day of her graduation. All three were smiling happily. Now his wife was gone. His daughter would not communicate with him, other than to denounce him on social media. All he had left was his name and his future legacy. And the means of their destruction. That, at least, was secure, securely stored in the steel filing cabinet built into the left-hand side of his desk, protected by a biometric lock.

He picked up the red and black USB stick. He was about to call Roxana to ask if it was hers when older, more cautious habits kicked in.

Who else had access to his bedroom? The room was kept locked when he was not there. Only the housekeeper, Evangelina, a Filipina in her fifties, had a key. She had worked in the residence for more than twenty years, was the very soul of discretion, and was approaching retirement. And as far as he knew Evangelina's computer skills did not extend much beyond e-mail.

He turned the USB stick over in his hand. It was tiny, barely larger than his thumbnail. He still found it difficult to believe how much data could be stored on such a miniscule object. But how had it got here? Unknown objects should not be appearing on his private desk at his home. He trusted Evangelina completely, but somebody could have forced her to leave the memory stick on his desk. Or maybe someone had broken into the house. In theory, that was impossible. But complete security was never possible. Random strangers still managed to wander into the private areas of the White House, supposedly one of the world's most secure buildings.

There was one way to find out what this was about. And even if the memory stick was Roxana's, it would do no harm to find out what she was up to. He slid it into the port on his laptop. A folder containing two icons appeared on the desktop, one labeled "Rwanda" and the other "Srebrenica."

His finger trembled as it hovered over the track pad. He waited a second, slid the cursor onto the first icon, exhaled hard, and clicked.

A PDF of a scanned UN internal report opened up:

ULTRA CONFIDENTIAL: REPORT INTO THE DEATHS OF NINE UN WORKERS IN KIGALI ON APRIL 10 1994.

He already knew what was in the second file without having to open it. He clicked on the icon anyway. A second PDF opened up:

ULTRA CONFIDENTIAL: AN ACCOUNT OF A MEETING WITH THE BOSNIAN SERB LEADERSHIP ON MARCH 25 1995.

For several seconds he could not breathe. He forced himself to inhale, exhale, take control. He placed his elbows on his desk and sat with his head in his hands for several minutes, waiting until the thoughts whirling through his brain began to calm. In a way, he felt a kind of relief. He had feared—*known*—for a long time that this day was coming. All trace of the two documents had supposedly been removed from the UN archives in New York, Geneva, and Nairobi. The company that Hussein hired, at great personal expense, assured him it had recovered the originals and all extant copies. Efrat Global Solution's corporate security division had a rock-solid reputation for accomplishing sensitive, illegal operations. But Hussein knew that while the past could be rewritten, spun, reconfigured, it could never be completely wiped. Every cover-up left traces, hints that led to a trail.

He would have to contact EGS. The situation was manageable, he told himself. He had been through worse. Perhaps Yael would help. Then he glanced again at the Rwanda document, remembered what it contained. Yael would not help this time.

Najwa looked around Francine's living room, seeking a hiding place, but saw none. The voices were louder now, one male and one female. Both sounded familiar, the female voice especially so. Their speech was clipped as they moved around the kitchen—the woman was giving orders—and Najwa sensed their tense aggression. They were looking for something; opening drawers and cupboards, swiftly rifling through the contents then closing them, careful not to leave a sign that they had been there. She had no doubt that she was in danger.

Under the bed? That would be the best option. The only one, in fact. Until they looked there. But she would deal with that if and when it happened. Najwa quickly pulled her sports shoes off and cat-stepped into the bedroom, praying that the parquet would not give her away. It was a small room, and painted a faint shade of pink. A faded kilim took up most of the floor. A large window, diagonally bisected by a rusty fire escape, looked out onto the back of the neighboring apartment blocks. She could see a middle-aged man chopping vegetables in his kitchen. He turned and saw her, his knife raised in midair. Then she glanced at the bed. It was a twin. With two drawers underneath.

A large stand-alone antique closet stood in the corner of the room. The two voices sounded nearer so Najwa stepped inside it, pressing herself against the soft rows of dresses and jackets. She slowly pulled the door closed, her hand on its edge, hoping it would slide into place and stay shut. It swung open. Najwa closed it again. It opened again. There was no handle on the inside, and the voices were getting closer. There was a large crack across the door panel, so she hooked a fingernail inside the gap and managed to draw the door shut. Part of the room was visible through the crack.

Then they were in the room.

Najwa's eyes opened wide.

"It could be anywhere," said Nero.

"I know. Keep looking. How long will the CCTV be down?"

"Another three minutes. Then we have to . . ."

A loud knock at the door interrupted him. "Hey, that's way over five minutes," exclaimed Joel Greenberg. "What's going on in there? Who's there with you? It sounds like a herd of elephants. I have another spare key. I'm coming in."

Najwa watched Nero yank open the window and climb out on to the fire escape, Roxana following immediately behind him.

Ten minutes later, Najwa was standing on the corner of Fifty-Ninth and Second Avenue, the hair on the back of her neck slowly rising up. Her skin prickled, as though she was about to start a fever. At first she thought it was leftover adrenaline from her adventure in Francine's apartment, but this felt different. She was used to attracting gazes, mostly of men, sometimes of women, and this was not the same; she sensed a strange field of dark energy around her.

She looked around, taking in what seemed to be a typical Saturday morning. The sidewalks were crowded with pedestrians, the road hummed with traffic. Two women, who looked like students, headed toward the subway station at Lexington and Fifty-Ninth, loudly discussing the previous night's party. A stooped elderly man, in sports shoes and a blue hooded top, walked a small dog on an extendable leash. A middle-aged black woman trudged along Second Avenue, weighed down with brown paper grocery bags. To Najwa at least, none of them looked remotely suspicious. There was no sign of Roxana, or Nero.

She stepped away from the road and started walking through a small square toward the Roosevelt Island Tramway. Tramway was a misnomer; Najwa was educated in Europe, where trams ran along rails embedded into the ground, and this was a cable car, with glass walls in a steel frame painted a bright, jolly red. From a terminal on the shore of the East River, it soared above Manhattan to Roosevelt Island, a long spit of land forty blocks long and 260 yards wide. The Tramway ran parallel with the Queensboro Bridge, which connected Manhattan with the island and then, on the far side of the river, Queens.

A row of benches lined either side of the open space. Najwa sat down in the middle of a bench on the right-hand side and looked around, she hoped not too obviously. A small circular rose garden stood in the middle, surrounded by gray stone tiles. On the facing row of benches sat a young woman. She had short blond hair, pale skin, and wore a black Geox jacket and blue Nike running shoes, with transparent bubble soles. Najwa had just bought the same shoes as part of her latest fitness plan. Three benches away, on Najwa's right side, was a well-groomed woman in her fifties, with short brown hair. She wore a blue woolen coat and was reading the *New York Times*. There was a large Gucci bag at her feet, a few inches of denim showing among the shopping.

Both women had been here when Najwa sat down. So

why was the hair on the back of her neck still standing up? Najwa trusted her instincts, which so far had never failed her. She took out her phone, switched to the front camera, held it up, and smiled, as though she was about to take a selfie. The screen showed a thickset man wearing badly fitting jeans and a black leather jacket, walking into the square. He sat down one bench behind Najwa, glanced at her, and nodded. Her eyes widened in surprise. The legendary Joe-Don Pabst. What was he doing here? Najwa was about to turn around and ask when he subtly shook his head. She quickly returned her phone to her purse.

As soon as Nero and Roxana climbed out of Francine's bedroom, Najwa had walked to the front door. There she found an indignant and by now very suspicious Joel Greenberg. He was about to call the police, but Najwa managed to talk him out of that idea. The NYPD descending was the last thing she needed. She placated Greenberg by *promising*, her hand on his arm, her eyes on his, to call as soon as she had any news of Francine. It was a promise she intended to keep.

Now she reached into her pocket and took out the crumpled receipt she had taken from Francine's kitchen. The top read: Café Port-au-Prince. It was a bill for $42.95: two entrees, desserts, and coffees. Najwa had already located the place on Google Maps and found the name of the owner, Carlotta. The café was on Roosevelt Island, ten minutes' walk from the terminal on the other side. She glanced sideways at Joe-Don. He was absorbed in his cigarette, watching the tramcar rise up over Fifty-Ninth Street, slide swiftly along the black lines of cables, and head out into space.

Najwa stood up, crossed the plaza, and started up the stairs that led to the tramway entrance. She glanced around, reassured to see Joe-Don take a last drag on his cigarette, drop the stub on the floor, crush it with his foot, and walk after her.

25

She is seventeen years old, standing at the shooting range with a Jericho 941 pistol in each hand.

The target pops up.

Her father says one word: "Right."

She fires with her right hand. A rip in the target's shoulder.

"Right," her father orders.

She fires again. A hole appears in the center of the target's heart.

"Left."

A hole in the target's left arm.

"Left," he repeats.

Six inches above the heart.

"Left. Double tap."

Two holes appear: the first through the heart, the second through the head.

"Left, right, left."

Three targets, three bull's-eyes.

She follows his orders with ease, the guns an extension of her arms, firing smoothly and accurately each time.

Eventually, he bids her to stop. "Mazel tov, congratulations," he says.

Happy and proud, she takes his arm in her hand as they walk out.

"Come," said Barbara as she stood up, taking Yael's arm in her hand. "Let's walk."

They stepped across the path and onto the sidewalk by West Drive. Full of Saturday morning joggers and cyclists, the tree-lined road ran along the side of Central Park. Yael idly watched a middle-aged man run past wearing a sweat-sodden singlet and loose nylon shorts, his face red with exertion. What did her mother have to tell her? And why now?

"Your father says you haven't spoken since your security vetting," Barbara began.

"He's right," replied Yael, her voice tight.

She had expected her father to be proud of her when she joined the UN. Instead, he had been furious. His angry demands that she quit still resounded in her ears: the UN had taken his son and now he had to sacrifice his daughter as well? Yael tried to heal the rift. Trying to reassure him, she called and e-mailed often with detailed accounts of where she had been and what she had been doing. At that early stage in her career, her responsibilities were mostly administrative, and although she went out on occasional field missions she was in no real danger. But as Yael progressed professionally, her father became less and less communicative. Each time she was promoted, he seemed to withdraw more.

It was hurtful of course. She tried to find out why he was pulling away from her but never got a proper answer.

Eventually, she gave up. She was so busy with work that there was little time to dwell on their difficult relationship.

Eight years ago, however, just before her vetting for the top-level security clearance she needed to join the SG's innermost team, her father made contact. He was in Manhattan and invited her for dinner. She gladly accepted, but it was an uncomfortable, even unpleasant meeting. He'd spent most of the evening trying to persuade Yael to leave the UN. He repeatedly talked about David and what he would have wanted. At first this irritated her, then it made her angry. David, she was sure, would have wanted her to make her own path in life. She was puzzled, as well. He seemed almost scared—but of what? Then, a few days later, her security clearance arrived. Still brooding over the encounter, she had entered her father's name into the UN database, which received information from all the main Western intelligence services and which she could now access. She could still remember what she had read. Despite his repeated efforts to make contact, she had not spoken to him since.

"He misses you," said Barbara.

Yael turned to her mother, frowning in surprise. "How do you know? I thought you hated each other."

Barbara smiled. "We never hated each other. Our lives went in different directions. But we still have a shared history. Three children, eight grandchildren. Of course we talk."

"What about?"

"You, lately."

Yael stopped walking and stood in the middle of the sidewalk. A young woman on Rollerblades shouted, "Hey," as she swooshed around her, missing her by only a few inches.

"Why?"

"Because we are your parents. We could have been better parents, for sure. But that's how it is. And we worry about you. We think it's time to end your UN adventures. You've played the odds. So far you have won every time. But you only need to lose once. We have already lost your brother. We don't want to lose you. It's time to find someone nice, settle down. Give us some more grandchildren."

Yael stared at her mother with incredulity. "It's a bit late for this, don't you think?"

Barbara softly squeezed Yael's arm as they walked. "No, darling. It's never too late."

Yael did not answer as she tried to disentangle her emotions. She was indignant, even angry. The last she had heard, her parents were only communicating through lawyers. Now they were having cozy chats about her future and trying to tell her how to live? But part of her was also pleased. Her mother's hand on her arm felt right. She did love her. And she cared about that, very much. And another part agreed about playing the odds, although she was not about to admit that. But the secret files about her father that she had read on the UN database could not be wished away.

"My father can mind his own business. He's been on the wrong side of every conflict for the last decade. Kosovo, Sri Lanka, Colombia, Darfur, Iraq, Syria, shall I go on?"

"No, there's no need. I know what he did. But it's not as simple as you think."

"Really? Tell me why not."

Barbara talked for some time as they continued walking. Yael listened. Absorbed in her conversation, she did not notice the electric maintenance vehicle glide by again, its minitrailer still stacked high with branches. The driver was hunched over the steering wheel talking on his cell phone, still wearing his baseball cap and sunglasses.

"I have visual," said Michael Ortega.

Yael's phone beeped, interrupting Barbara as they walked. She quickly scanned the text message, her eyes widening in surprise.

"Bad news?" asked Barbara.

Yael shook her head. "No. Not at all. And I'll think about what you said." She kissed her mother. "I'm sorry, Mom. I've got to go. It's nothing serious or dangerous, really. I'll see you at home in a couple of hours. And we are going to have fun tonight. Promise."

The Roosevelt Island Tramway carriage was packed with excited tourists and locals returning home after a morning trip to Manhattan. Najwa had a place at the front, peering through the large windows at a spectacular view over Manhattan and the East River. The tramway was certainly the cleanest, most modern public transport system that she had ever used in New York. The red metal frame shone like new, the glass walls were spotless.

A forty-ish black man wearing wraparound sunglasses sat on a high stool in front of a control panel. "All aboard, all aboard, ready for takeoff," he declared mock-sternly, triggering a wave of giggles among the tourists.

The sliding doors had just begun to move when the last

passenger jumped on board. Joe-Don. Najwa watched the operator press down on the green button. The doors slid shut and the carriage moved smoothly forward, climbing steadily over the riverbank. She looked around the carriage. She heard English, French, and Spanish as the carriage soared further upward, the tourists holding out their smartphones to take photographs and videos of the view. The East River was blue and gray, shimmering in the morning sunshine. Roosevelt Island beckoned, its low-rise apartment buildings spread out along the riverbank.

Najwa glanced up. An emergency exit panel of clear plastic had been cut into the roof. The carriage was now as high as the Queensboro Bridge. Girders, ladders, crossbeams, and cables flew by. The carriage stopped for a second, swaying in the breeze. In the far corner of the carriage, a young woman, perhaps in her twenties, stood with her back to the crowd, watching the Manhattan shoreline as it retreated into the distance. Something about her posture, the way she held her back very straight, looked familiar. She wore a gray beanie hat covering her hair, sunglasses, and a denim jacket. Had Najwa seen her before?

Joe-Don caught Najwa's eye and looked at the far corner, nodded his head down. Najwa followed his gaze. The woman in the beanie hat was wearing blue Nike sneakers with transparent bubble soles.

Roosevelt Island quickly came into view, a mini-Manhattan of apartment blocks, roads, warehouses, and shops. The carriage bumped slightly and began its descent. A memory flashed in Najwa's mind, of the woman with the short brown hair who had been sitting nearby, of the flash of blue in her Gucci bag.

Joe-Don eased his way through the crowd, loudly apologizing, until he stood next to the woman in the beanie hat. She turned to look at him, her face curious and mildly concerned. He spoke softly in her ear. Her body stiffened, and she seemed about to call out when his left hand moved inside the pocket of his leather jacket. He gently pressed something into her side while he continued speaking. The young woman nodded, rigid, still staring straight ahead as the tramway slid into the terminal.

Najwa stepped off the tram and walked out into the open space around the terminal. She glanced forward at the shoreline of the East River and the UN building for a couple of seconds, then back at the terminal. The young woman in the Nikes came out, walked straight back inside, passed through the ticket gates and waited for the tramway to return to Manhattan. Joe-Don was nowhere to be seen.

Like many New Yorkers, whether new arrivals or native-born, Najwa had never been to Roosevelt Island. The thin strip of land was a curious hybrid, linked to Manhattan by bridges and the tramway, yet somehow separate. There were hardly any cars on the clean, wide road. The sidewalks were spotless. The air seemed cleaner, fresher, cooled by the river. Cyclists meandered past at a moderate pace. Passers-by stopped to greet each other and chat. It was like traveling back in time. Manhattan was just a quarter of a mile away, but its frenetic energy, the sense that someone, somewhere, would always be privy to something newer, better, even more exclusive, had evaporated over the narrow channel of the East River. Even the name of the biggest thoroughfare, Main Street, conjured up a vision of an America now largely vanished.

Najwa came to a small square ringed by modern apartment blocks, with the usual branded shops and cafés on the ground floor. She went over to Starbucks and pretended to peer inside, using the glass as a mirror, to see if she was being followed. No sign of a tail, or at least nothing obvious. Nor was there any sign of Joe-Don but she was sure he was somewhere nearby. Then Najwa walked another hundred yards until she came to the Port-au-Prince Café, and stepped inside. It was small, with a dozen Formica tables and tubular metal chairs. The tables were covered with shiny red plastic cloths and there seemed to be no menu, only a series of specials chalked on a blackboard mounted on the sidewall: a medley of goat and chicken, cod and beef. A glass display case showed fresh fish and seafood.

Najwa headed straight to the wooden counter at the back of the room. A plump woman in her sixties stood behind it, next to the cash register and in front of a narrow door set in the wall. Her black hair, shot through with gray streaks, was tied behind her head. She had coffee-colored skin, blue eyes, and a welcoming smile.

"What can I get you?" she asked, a bright yellow dishcloth in her hand.

"Nothing yet, thank you. You must be the owner, Carlotta," said Najwa, extending her hand.

Carlotta put her dishcloth down and shook Najwa's hand, clearly wondering who she was.

"My name is Najwa. I've heard so much about you. It all looks great. Real Haitian home cooking. I'm looking for a friend of mine. If she's around, I hope we'll eat together. It all looks great."

"Who?" Carlotta asked.

Najwa glanced around. The restaurant was empty, apart from an elderly man sitting at a corner table, nursing a Coca-Cola as he looked out of the window. Any doubts that she—and Francine—were in danger had been erased by the events on the Tramway. "Francine," she said. "Francine de la Court."

Carlotta stiffened for a fraction of a second, shook her head, looked down, and began needlessly polishing the counter surface with the yellow cloth. "Never heard of her."

Najwa smiled. Carlotta was not a very good liar. "Are you sure? Francine who worked at the UN? She was always talking about this place."

"I told you, lady. I don't know her. And we're closing now."

Najwa looked at her watch. "But it's twelve thirty. Lunch time."

Carlotta stepped out from behind the counter, walked over to the door, and flipped the sign around so that OPEN showed on the back before returning. "No lunch service on Saturdays." She picked up the dishcloth and began polishing the already sparkling-clean surface again, rubbing hard at a nonexistent stain.

Najwa knew that fifty dollars would not work here. The truth, however, might. She leaned forward, changed the tone of her voice. "I really need to speak to Francine. She is in danger."

The woman stared at Najwa, her body tense. "I told you. I never heard of her. Now go please."

"Carlotta, if you care about Francine, let me help."

Carlotta did not reply, but pressed a button by the cash register. The door behind her opened and a black man in a skin-tight T-shirt and jeans, revealing the overdeveloped physique of a bodybuilder, came out. He looked at Najwa, then at Carlotta. "Problem?" he asked.

"Yes," said Najwa. "There is. My name is Najwa. I am a friend of Francine's, from the UN. I know Francine is a regular here. I know you both know her and you probably know where she is. She is in danger. I need to speak to her."

"The lady is leaving," said Carlotta. She turned to Najwa. "Wayne will show you the way out."

"But . . . !" Najwa protested.

"But nothing. We don't know any Francine. We never heard of her. And we are closed."

Wayne came out from behind the counter.

Najwa held her hands up. "I'm going. But I will leave my card with you. In case anyone comes in who does know where Francine is. You give it to them and tell her to call me. It's just a card. Is that OK?"

Wayne looked at Carlotta. She nodded. Najwa reached into her purse for her business card holder. She had just taken one out when the narrow door opened.

"It's OK. Let her through," said Francine.

26

Yael quickly reread the message.

I sent you this. If you want 2 talk meet me @ Eagle statue at Battery Park memorial at 3.

<Fareed Hussein let your brother die>

She leaned back against the low stone barrier and scanned the area again. The East Coast Memorial, as it was properly known, was located on the southernmost tip of Manhattan. Two rows of four massive slabs of granite, inscribed with names of hundreds of US servicemen who lost their lives in the Atlantic Ocean, stood several yards apart on either side of an open space. At one end, a small flight of steps led down onto the seafront promenade and out to the Atlantic. At the other was a giant modernist bronze sculpture of an eagle, mounted on a black granite base, which was where Yael had been ordered to wait.

The text message had arrived a little over an hour ago. From West Seventy-Second Yael had taken the 3 express train, the fastest way to get downtown. It only stopped at

Times Square, Thirty-Fourth Street, and Fourteenth Street before slowing down again for the local stops. She carried out several anti-surveillance maneuvers on the journey down from Central Park, alighting from the subway at the last moment and doubling back on herself. At Chambers Street, she had changed to the 1. During the week, the trains south were packed with Wall Street commuters, but at two o'clock on a Saturday afternoon her car, and the two on either side, were almost empty. The staircase at South Ferry was the only exit, a natural chokepoint. As far as Yael could tell, nobody had followed her up the stairs. But it was impossible to know for sure.

The memorial would not have been Yael's choice of meeting point. Although it would be impossible to eavesdrop on anyone without being spotted, there was no real cover. It was surrounded by the rest of Battery Park, and behind the greenery stood a cluster of steel and glass office blocks that marked the start of the Financial District. Any one of the offices would be a good base for an observer with high-powered binoculars. She checked her watch: it was two fifty-five. Then she looked up to see a woman walking purposefully across the plaza between the memorial slabs. She wore a red beret over her long black hair, black ankle boots, and a blue down jacket. She stopped in front of Yael and smiled nervously.

The back office of the Café Port-au-Prince was a small, gloomy room, about fifteen feet by twelve, next to the kitchen. The light green paint on the wall had darkened with age and the floor was covered with red linoleum. Metal shelves lined the back wall, each jammed with worn box folders holding annual accounts, correspondence, and ancient bills that poked out of the top. Although the kitchen's extractor fan hummed in the background, the room still smelled of cooked food and oil.

Francine was sitting on an ancient sofa in the corner, its cracked beige leatherette cover revealing the yellow foam inside. Poised, smartly dressed, perfectly coiffured Madam Non was nowhere to be seen; Francine's brown eyes were red-rimmed and her face was pale and drawn. She wore navy sweatpants and a baggy blue T-shirt. Her black hair was straggly. She stared at Najwa, trying to assess what kind of new threat the Al-Jazeera journalist represented. "How did you find me?" she demanded.

Najwa waited a moment, then told her the truth. That she had been worried, that Joel Greenberg had let her into the apartment, and she had found the café's receipts in the kitchen.

Francine's voice was tight with anger. "You broke in?"

"I had a key."

"So what? I didn't give it to you. Nosing around my apartment. Who the hell do you think you are?"

"I wasn't the only one."

"Meaning?"

"Roxana was there with a UN security officer."

"Which one?"

"Nero. I think he's new."

"I don't know him. But I do know that girl is a devil." Francine sagged, sat back. "What do you want?"

"To find out what happened to Henrik."

Francine looked away. "He died."

"I know," said Najwa softly. "But how? What do you think happened?"

"What do I think? I won't tell you what I think. I will tell you what I know. There was nothing wrong with his heart. He was murdered. Why do you think I am here, and not at home in my apartment? A couple of weeks ago, the day after Henrik's funeral, a woman came by. She asked me if Henrik had ever given me anything, a disc, or a USB stick, or a password."

"Had he?"

Francine paused for several seconds. She looked Najwa up and down, as if making up her mind about something. "We never got on, did we?"

Najwa smiled. "It was nothing personal. We both had our jobs to do. I thought you did yours very well."

Francine nodded. "Thanks. You too. I liked the way you never gave up, just kept digging till you got what you wanted. Where was I? Oh yes, I told the woman no, Henrik had not given me anything. She made me promise to tell her if I found anything."

"How?"

"She showed me some video footage of Luc at college, hanging out with his friends, on the lawn. Told me how well he was doing, how healthy he looked, what a fine young man he was. As soon as she left I packed a bag and I came here."

"Where is Luc?"

"Safe. Staying with relatives in Haiti. I sent him away till this blows over."

"What was the woman like?"

"Fifties, maybe. Short brown hair. Blue wraparound coat."

"She knows you're here. I was followed here, on the tramway. She was at the Manhattan terminal. There were two of them, her and a younger one. The younger one got on the tramway with me. So did Joe-Don."

Francine smiled for the first time since Najwa arrived. "Joe-Don? He's here?"

Najwa nodded. "Somewhere. I'm not sure exactly where, or why, but yes."

"Then don't worry about me. I'll be fine. In any case my friends will look after me. Now you should go." Francine stood up and shook Najwa's hand. Her grip was light, almost delicate, so as not to push the small object in her palm any harder into Najwa's.

Let's walk," said Yael.

Rina Hussein fell into step next to her as they headed toward the promenade. Yael sensed Rina watching her, suspicious and wary. A row of benches stretched along the seafront, wooden slats on iron frames with no backs. There the two women sat down, facing the sea. The Statue of Liberty was visible in the distance. Giant wooden breakwaters, each the size of several tree trunks, stood in front of a metal fence. A Coast Guard launch flew by, white spray in its wake. Yael opened her mouth to speak, but for once the words would not come.

What was she scared of? Finding the truth about how and why her brother died? She had sought it for years, telling herself it was the one reason why she stayed at the UN and, especially, why she continued to work for Fareed Hussein. One reason, perhaps, but not the only one. The SG had chosen Yael from the mass of ambitious UN employees, made her his protégé. She knew of numerous occasions when Hussein had watched her back, sometimes even gone out on a limb. Knew too, that there was a limit to his patronage. He had sacked her during the coltan scandal, tried to blame her in part for the mess. But when the SG had welcomed her back, made the right kind of reassuring noises, she had returned willingly. Part of her, she sometimes thought, was still the dutiful daughter helping with office duties; the teenager on the firing range, seeking her father's approval.

But what if, as she sometimes suspected, the trail that connected the SG with David's death led to tawdry sacrifice and betrayal—and betrayal by Hussein? How could she carry on working at the United Nations? She could not. She told herself that she would bring Hussein, and anyone else responsible, to justice. But if she left the UN, what would she do? Many of her contemporaries were married, settled with a family. She told herself that she too wanted love, domesticity, stability. But did she, did she really? Or did she prefer the dark thrill of touching evil? Either way, she certainly would like a friend. Olivia de Souza was dead. So was Isis Franklin. At least Rina Hussein was still alive, and making contact.

Yael went into work mode, put her emotions aside. There was a job to be done here. The first priority was to get the truth about Rina's text message and David. She knew that until she broke off contact, Rina had enjoyed their time together. That was the way in to the conversation.

Yael turned to Rina. "It was fun hanging out, you know. I don't have a lot of friends. I would have been happy to see you even if your father had not sent me."

Rina looked confused. "I know. Me too. But I wasn't sure what you wanted. Whether you were really interested in meeting me, or I was just another mission."

"It started as a mission. But one I was glad to take and enjoyed very much."

"I'm glad to hear that."

"Rina, I'm really glad to see you again. We can meet whenever you like. But . . ." Yael paused. "Your text message . . ."

Rina stiffened. She turned to Yael. "It's true. I wouldn't make up something like that. Roger Richardson was correct. There was a deal in Rwanda, and it went wrong. But it was all my father's idea."

Yael nodded, focused now. "Go on."

"But the journalists will never be able to prove it. My father has pulled out all the crucial records from the archives detailing his involvement in Rwanda and Srebrenica."

"How do you know?"

Rina pulled her beret down hard around her ears. "Because I checked the archives. According to the official record, the documents were never there, they never even *existed*. But they do. I have read them. I found them in his office at home, years ago, before he became SG, when he was still at Peacekeeping."

Yael stared out to sea.

The wind was blowing harder now, sending the waves crashing against the wooden breakwaters. Yael shivered. "Where are they now?"

"In the residence, I think. He would not leave them in the office."

Yael thought quickly. How could she get to them, and ideally for long enough to make a copy? Fareed would never release the papers to her willingly. It would have to be a trade-off, in exchange for something he valued more than his career, his name, his legacy. An idea began to form in her mind. She closed her eyes for a moment, appalled at herself. Yes, she would use her nascent friendship with Rina to get the truth about David. But when had she become this kind of monster? All that talk about how she had enjoyed Rina's company. And now she was about to manipulate this vulnerable woman in the most cynical way possible.

What other option was there?

Yael opened her eyes and looked at Rina, her face softer now. "He wants to see you. He's lonely, especially since your mother went back to Pakistan."

Rina swallowed before she spoke. "I miss him too sometimes. He wasn't much of a father. I always though he barely noticed me. I always thought he wanted a son, instead. But there was only me."

"He notices you now," said Yael. "Especially at demonstrations. And on Twitter."

Rina laughed. "Good."

"You know it would be the end of everything if the documents were released. His reputation, his legacy . . ."

Rina frowned, "I'm not so sure. He's survived this far. He's Teflon-coated."

"Maybe you are right." Yael nodded slowly. She turned to look at Rina. The strident, self-righteous activist was gone, replaced by a young, uncertain woman who missed her father. Yael knew that feeling. She ignored the rising feeling of self-disgust and tried to sound thoughtful, reasonable, as she spoke. "It would certainly clear the air once they were out. Exorcise the ghosts."

"Yes. It would. That needs to happen."

Yael moved a little closer. "And once he retires he would have much more time for you."

"Would he really?" She turned to Yael, her voice eager. "What do you think? You know him, how his mind works."

Yael steeled herself. This was the moment. It was horrible, awful, but it had to be done. At least it was for a good cause. It might even work out in the end. Fareed and Rina would be reconciled. Yael would finally have someone to hang out with. Happy ever after. Anyone would do the same to find out why their brother had died. Wouldn't they? But Rina had to get there herself—all she needed was a little guidance.

Yael put her hand on Rina's arm. Rina flinched, very slightly, her nerves drawn tight, then relaxed. She smiled at Yael.

Yael said, "Your dad is a diplomat. He makes deals. Offer him something he wants to release the documents. What does he want, more than anything?"

Rina drew her arm away and tightened the belt of her coat, her fingers twisting the fabric. "His daughter back."

Najwa sat at her desk at home, scanning her e-mail. There was nothing new in her inbox except a confirmation from Sami that he would be over later. She could use the company. As a journalist she was excited to be on the trail of a major story—and this was major, of that she had no doubt. Two deaths, an innocent woman and her son driven from their home, a surveillance team on her, *and* Joe-Don with a gun on the Roosevelt Island Tramway were proof of that. But as a woman, one living alone in a large, anonymous city, Najwa was also nervous. She was poking a snake, and so far she had no means of cutting off its head. She was also using up her favor bank: Obtaining the CCTV coverage of Schneidermann and the man with the gloves at the Fifty-Ninth Street subway station had cost her much of her capital with her NYPD contact. The download may well have triggered an alarm there.

She glanced again—unnecessarily, she knew—at her front door. It was locked, bolted, and made of steel. She checked her watch: three thirty. She had stayed talking to Francine for about twenty minutes, then taken a cab home across the Queensboro Bridge, then along FDR Drive before turning down East Twenty-First and into Irving Place, where she lived. Had she been followed? She wasn't sure, but she didn't think so. There had been a black SUV with tinted windows behind her as her taxi pulled away and headed toward the bridge. She had scribbled down the number plate: EXW 2575. But when she looked around as they crossed over the river, the car had disappeared.

Najwa reached inside her purse and took out her black leather personal organizer. She had tucked Francine's USB stick inside the back pocket. She flipped the cover open when a photograph fell out. It showed two young girls at a beach, both in their early teens, on a beach. Najwa stared at the photograph for several seconds, kissed the second girl in the picture, and put it down on her desk. She took out the USB stick and placed it next to the photograph. Whatever Francine had given her, it could wait for a little while.

Najwa turned to her computer and clicked on a JPEG file on her desktop, the JPEG sent by the unknown person communicating with her. The file opened to show a picture of a young Arab woman, a grown-up version of the second girl on the beach. As if on cue, a new window opened on her screen.

<Welcome home. Keep your crew at the KZX reception tonight until the end>

Najwa typed: **<I wasn't planning on taking one. No news usually at these events.>**

<There will be>

The window closed. Najwa sat back and closed her eyes. Her heart was pounding, her stomach twisting. Having someone in her computer, someone who seemed to know her deepest family secret, was bad enough and it creeped her out. But more than that, she was now compromised. Again.

She reached for the packet of Marlboro Lights and Zippo lighter resting by her monitor and took out a cigarette. She sat still for a moment, her hand in the air. The cigarette tip was shaking. Then she lit up and took a deep drag, feeling the nicotine instantly kick in. Not a heavy smoker, Najwa usually only indulged at parties, after a good meal, or when she was stressed. Like now.

She watched the gray cloud float over the desk. Once again she had been forewarned. Forewarned digitally, in writing. The message window had instantly vanished, but she had no doubt that a record of the exchange lived on, somewhere in cyberspace or on a distant hard drive. She should alert the authorities so they could take the necessary precautions. But what could she tell them? That an unknown person had hacked her computer? That the last time he, or she, had been in communication, Najwa was told to head to the SG's residence, arriving just as a gunman killed a senior UN official on the steps and left another bullet embedded in the front door frame? She would be questioned at length. Her life would be turned upside down and inside out. She would almost certainly be arrested. The Al-Jazeera connection and her Arab background would trigger a frenzy of terrorism accusations. She would be suspended from her job and likely lose her green card as well. Then what? She glanced again at the photograph of the two young girls on her desk. The guilt ebbed and faded, a slow tide inside her, but it never went away completely. Not that she wanted it to.

Or, she could keep quiet and hope for the best. The KZX reception was a grand-enough event that she could justify bringing Maria and Philippe along, especially as it might generate more leads on the coltan scandal and a follow-up to her and Sami's documentary. But which did she value more? The life of an unknown potential victim? Or her career and comfortable existence?

A sharp pain shot through her fingertip. She was squeezing the USB stick so hard the metal corner was digging into her skin. Later, she told herself. She would decide later.

First, she would see what was on Francine's USB drive. She opened her air-gapped Toshiba laptop. Lines of code flew across the screen as it lumbered into life. She reached around the back and slid the USB drive into the port. A video file icon appeared. She clicked on it and a blurry image of Henrik Schneidermann filled the screen.

27

Renee Freshwater stood in front of the three tall, white-framed windows at the back of the Oval Office looking out over the Rose Garden. The rainbow palette of flowers glistened against lush greenery in the bright sunlight, still shiny after that morning's spring shower. Twenty years ago, King Hussein of Jordan and Yitzhak Rabin had stood here and shaken hands, ending forty-six years of war. A full peace treaty had followed soon after. Although a comprehensive solution to the Israeli-Palestinian conflict seemed as distant as ever, the treaty had held.

The roses were in full bloom, a riot of pink with splashes of deep red, almost as dark as blood, next to the low manicured hedges. A breeze ruffled the white crabapple blossoms. Freshwater watched a flower tumble from a branch before the wind carried it off, dancing on the air currents. What would be her legacy? At first her nickname, Dead-in-the-Water, had been confined to the Beltway crowd of politicians and lobbyists, journalists and government officials that lived and worked in the capital. But it had soon spread out to the talk show hosts, the crazies that sent death threats every day by the thousand, the Twitter furies and the website creators whose pages showed her dark, almond eyes, strong cheekbones, and glossy black hair superimposed on a target.

She knew, of course, that the United States' first female president, one from the left wing of the Democratic Party who was proud of her Native American roots, would not be universally loved. But nothing could have prepared her for the depth of hatred, the tidal wave of venom. It had been easier when Eric was still alive. God, she missed him. Their girls still cried most nights for their father and so did she, silently and alone. She had never felt so isolated, so vulnerable. The wolves were closing in, she knew, the most vicious of all from her own party. They scented blood and the feeding frenzy would soon start. But she would go down fighting, and not before she finished what she set out to do.

She turned around to face her security chief. Dave Reardon was sitting on the edge of a plush, gold colored sofa, one of two matching pieces facing each other with a coffee table in between.

"Reykjavik. What do you think, Dave?"

Reardon glanced down at the sheaf of papers on his lap and pulled one to the top. "What I think, Madam President—what I know—is that the last time you asked my advice I told you not to go shopping in Istanbul. But you did, and you nearly died. Two days ago a car bomb was discovered a couple of hundred yards from the White House. Frank Akerman, the UN intermediary between you and the Iranian president, has been shot dead. The Internet is seething with death threats. You are surrounded by enemies, many of them pretending to be your friends. Some even sit in your cabinet. I think you should stay here. And move away from that window."

Freshwater laughed uneasily. "You are joking? About the window?"

"For now, yes. But that too could change. And we still don't know where Isis Franklin got the poison from, not for certain. But we have a lead."

"To where?"

"Tehran."

Reardon was one of the very few people that Freshwater trusted. He and the president had known each other for twenty years, were students together at Princeton. One night a group of drunken frat boys had encountered Freshwater walking back to her dormitory alone after a late session in the library. They had hustled her back behind some trees; she managed to punch one out, but was clearly outnumbered. Reardon happened to be walking past. What happened next had been hushed up by the authorities, despite the arrival of an ambulance and the subsequent expulsion of the fraternity members, but Freshwater was not bothered again.

A stocky, black ex-Marine, Reardon had served in Iraq and Afghanistan, reaching the rank of colonel. His time on the front lines had fine-tuned his radar for threats and provided a network of useful contacts across America's intelligence agencies. The latest he had heard regarding Renee Freshwater was not good. If he had his way, she would stay locked in a room till the end of her term. And then move to another country.

"Continue," she said.

"Abbas Velavi, an Iranian dissident, died of a heart attack after a visit from an Iranian wearing black leather gloves like Isis Franklin's. But there's more." Reardon flicked through his papers until he brought up a typewritten sheet marked Top Secret. "We think that Henrik Schneidermann, the UN secretary-general's spokesman, was also murdered using the same method. There is CCTV footage of him at the Fifty-Ninth street subway station, helping up a man who appears to have slipped. A man wearing . . ."

She frowned, walked over to the facing sofa, and sat down opposite Reardon. A coffee pot and a tray of cookies stood between them on the low table. "I can guess. Black leather gloves."

"So I think that you should stay here in DC, where I can look after you. But I don't suppose you want to do that."

Freshwater smiled. "I can't hide, Dave, and you know it."

She thought for a long moment. Presidents, she had soon discovered, were limited in what they could accomplish. Congress, lobbyists, the traditional media, social media, all had shackled her ambitions. But at least she could redecorate the Oval Office. She had made minimal changes: The heavy brown and cream drapes by the windows remained, as did the cream and white walls. But several paintings had gone, and on one wall a century-old tapestry showing the Native American tribes and their original homelands across North America, before they were forced into reservations, now hung. On the other was a portrait of Chief Red Cloud, one of the most adept Native American military commanders. Red Cloud had ambushed US army soldiers across Wyoming and Montana, but eventually made peace with them and lived to be eighty-eight. And she had kept the desk. Intricately carved, it was built from the timbers of *The Resolute*, a nineteenth-century British Arctic exploration ship. *The Resolute* had gone missing and was presumed lost until it was rescued by the captain of an American whaler. The recovery was well timed, as tensions were rising between United States and Britain. Diplomatic relations had been broken off, and ambassadors expelled, when a hawkish senator suddenly proposed that America refurbish *The Resolute* and return her to Britain as a gift. It worked. War was averted. Could Freshwater accomplish the same with Iran?

Perhaps was her best answer. But she had to try. So far, the most powerful woman in the world could not even find out why her husband had died. The investigation into Eric's death was stuck in a morass of interagency rivalry, but her personal sources and Reardon's contacts seemed evermore convinced that his bindings had been tampered with. And there was more. She picked up her BlackBerry and scrolled through the saved links until she came to a story on the *Newsweek* website. She handed the phone to Reardon. "Read this."

FLASH OF LIGHT PRECEDED DEATH OF PRESIDENT'S HUSBAND, CLAIMS WITNESS

By CORDELIA ADDIS

A blinding flash of light may have caused Eric Cortez, the late husband of President Freshwater, to crash into a tree while skiing off-piste at Aspen, a new witness has claimed. Cortez was killed in the accident last September, and a spokesman for the White House said the investigation into his death is still ongoing.

"I could see Mr. Cortez on the mountain. He was a very stylish skier. I was on the nearby black diamond run when there was a tremendous flash of light. I was almost blinded," said Eva Ferguson. "At first we thought it was lightning, but there was no thunder and the skies were clear. I heard a loud crash and the next thing I saw was him lying in the snow, next to a tree. His helmet was several feet away."

There have been repeated rumors about a flash of light preceding Cortez's death, but Eva Ferguson is the first witness willing to go on the record. "It's been nagging at me for a long time. I thought I should tell what I saw."

The following paragraphs recounted the desperate attempts to save Eric, and his flight by medevac helicopter to the University of Colorado Hospital in Aurora, where he was pronounced dead.

Freshwater had heard about the claims, referenced in the article, that a flash of light had preceded the death of Princess Diana in a car crash in a tunnel in Paris. That had never been proven but had still triggered all sorts of conspiracy theories. She had no idea, however, that Western intelligence services reportedly considered using a similar technique to kill former Serbian dictator Slobodan Milosevic while he was attending a peace conference in Geneva. Someone, it seemed, had been working on this technique. If Eric really had been killed at such close quarters, then the danger was very close to home. Perhaps Reardon was right. But she refused to cower in the White House.

Reardon quickly read the article and handed the BlackBerry back to Freshwater.

"Do you believe it?" she asked.

"I believe it's possible. I believe, I know, we have a problem. I don't who we can trust. If it hadn't been for Yael Azoulay, you might be dead. I let you down."

"No, you didn't. I insisted on the shopping trip, against your advice. I should have listened to you. And we need to do something for Yael. A medal. Or a dinner. Or both."

"Sure, once you get back from Reykjavik. You will see her there. She's replacing Akerman."

Freshwater poured them both coffee. She picked up her cup, was silent for several long seconds.

Reardon sipped his coffee, then gave her a quizzical look. "What it is? I can hear the cogs turning."

Freshwater looked at him directly and smiled. "Dave, you agree we are threatened from the enemy within, as well as without?"

Reardon nodded, warily.

"Good. So you are not, repeat *not*, to take this as any kind of slight. I put my complete trust in you . . ."

"Please, Renee, not a PMC."

Freshwater shook her head. "No, no private military contractors. Not in my White House. Of course not. But I do think we need some outside help. Which is why I wanted you to be here now."

He exhaled loudly. "Outside help from where, exactly?"

"A place with the best security in the world."

"Yes, but . . ."

"Dave, I'm just asking you to listen. It's a preliminary talk, we just hear what our visitor has to say. And then we—*we*—decide whether to take his advice. But I am going to Reykjavik. For *all* the reasons that you know about. And I plan to come home in one piece. "

"OK . . ." Reardon sounded doubtful.

The phone on the coffee table trilled. Freshwater flicked a button. "Your noon appointment is here, ma'am," said a male voice.

The door opened. A man in his late thirties walked in, a broad smile on his handsome face.

"Madam President, what a pleasure to see you again," said Eli Harrari.

Najwa pressed play. Schneidermann's voice came out of the Toshiba's lo-fi speaker. *"Is that recording now?"* he asked, before muttering, *"Yes."*

Najwa smiled as the image stabilized and Schneidermann's familiar, pale features came into focus. She suddenly felt a powerful nostalgia, wishing herself back in the press briefing room, watching him duel with her pushy, demanding colleagues—and with herself as well. By the end he had become a bravura performer. He could be difficult, obstructive, and just plain bloody-minded. But he certainly had not deserved to be murdered.

She sat with her chin in her cupped hands, staring intently at her computer monitor.

"Well, you know us Belgians, we are not known for drama.

Chocolate and bureaucrats. We are good at that. So please believe what I have to say. The best evidence of the truth is that you are watching this video file. If so, I am almost certainly dead." Schneidermann looked down, blinked, then stared back at the camera. "*That is not a very easy thing to say. But there you are. I have said it. And you know if it's true or not. So who would want to kill me, and why? I am not exactly sure. But I think it's connected to the death of Olivia de Souza. Poor Olivia, you will remember, was thrown off a balcony on the thirty-eighth floor by Mahesh Kapoor, the SG's former chief of staff. Olivia had found out too much about the coltan plot, the details of which are now well known.*"

He coughed and reached for a glass of water. The picture suddenly swerved sideways and there was a loud banging noise as the camera toppled over. The film stopped for a few seconds before Schneidermann reappeared.

"KZX's response has been very clever: a deluge of money for scholarships, academic studies, and most of all the new school for development studies at Columbia University. But behind the scenes, the company remains as determined and voracious as ever. The coltan plot was just part of the plan. I have discovered that two senior UN officials, one in the Department of Economic and Social Affairs, and another in the Office on Drugs and Crime, recently met with a representative of KZX in Qatar to discuss the company's future role in a global, legalized drug market."

Najwa clicked pause while she scribbled a note on her nearby pad: *KZX/Qatar/UN official*. She hit play again, and the video resumed.

Schneidermann ran his fingers through his sparse, light brown hair as he spoke. *"Well, drugs are only part of the case. The main plan is connected to the Prometheus Group. Caroline Masters was the engine behind bringing in Prometheus to the UN. The idea was to outsource and privatize the UN security service first, then the whole peacekeeping operation. That plan took a hit with the collapse of the Istanbul Summit. But there is much more, and it has a certain logic. Before you have peacekeepers deployed, you need a war to stop."* He looked around, as though he was afraid of being overheard. *"What I am going to say sounds crazy I know, but it makes perfect sense. I think Prometheus, KZX, and Iranian hard-liners are all planning a massive war in the Middle East. They hate each other, of course, but their interests coincide. The Iranian hard-liners want to get rid of Shireen Kermanzade. Prometheus and KZX want to get rid of President Freshwater. The last thing they want is a rapprochement between America and Iran. And wars are always good for business."* Schneidermann wiped his brow, picked up his glass of water, and took a deep drink. He stared at the camera and seemed about to speak again, then the screen went blank.

Najwa drummed her fingers on the table, staring intently at the monitor. The video file returned, juddered, stopped again. She moved the cursor to the play button and clicked several times on her mouse.

Finally, the frame filled again with Schneidermann's pale, worried face. He bit his lip, shook his head, and looked around before coming back to the camera.

"Sorry about that. Someone just rang the doorbell. What was I saying? The SG sent Yael Azoulay to try and persuade Clarence Clairborne, the boss of the Prometheus Group, to stop trading with the Revolutionary Guard. That didn't work. So now Fareed Hussein is working on something with Freshwater and Shireen Ker-

manzade. He has copies of e-mails and records of meetings between KZX, Prometheus, and the Iranians. I haven't seen them, but I am pretty sure they are somewhere in his office. I'm going to look for them. I will meet Sami Boustani for breakfast later this week. I am going to tell him everything."

He looked from side to side once more. Just as the video file ended the entry phone rang. Najwa walked over to the door and pressed the speakerphone button.

"Sami is here, Ms. al-Sameera," said the doorman.

Najwa lived in a duplex loft overlooking Gramercy Park, twenty blocks south of the UN. The lower floor had white walls, large windows, a dark wood parquet floor and a kitchen with an island. One corner of the apartment was devoted to Najwa's office, with an outsized computer monitor on a desk and a fifty-two-inch LED television mounted on the wall. The facing corner was a lounge area, with a sofa and two armchairs. Several lush, towering house plants, along with Turkish kilims on the floor, added splashes of color. The upstairs area was reached by a spiral staircase. The rare visitors to her home never failed to be impressed.

Najwa opened the door and welcomed Sami inside. He was unshaven and looked preoccupied. "Coffee?" she asked. "Beer? Whiskey?"

"I feel like a whiskey," Sami replied. "But coffee is fine."

She walked over to the kitchen and popped a capsule into the Nespresso machine. Completely undomesticated, she could not cook. Maria or Philippe took care of the steam-oozing monster in the Al-Jazeera office. Sami wandered over to her desk as she rummaged in her cupboards for something to serve with the coffee.

He picked up the photograph of the girls on the beach. "Lovely picture. This is you and . . . ?"

Najwa thought about her answer for several seconds. The truth, she decided. "Fatima. My twin sister."

Sami smiled and put the photograph down. "Gosh. There's two of you? Where is she? I'd love to meet her."

"She's in Jeddah. In a compound, with two other wives. So I don't think that's going to happen, habibi."

Najwa walked in with a tray holding coffee, cups, cookies, and dried fruit. She sat down on the sofa, beckoned Sami over and handed him his coffee.

He looked puzzled as he sat down next to her. "Can I ask a personal question?"

"Sure."

"You get to go to school in Geneva, graduate from Oxford and Yale, live in a loft in Manhattan and work as a journalist, but your sister is in purdah?"

Najwa paused before she answered. "I'll take the fifth on that. Sugar?"

"Two. So how was your day so far?"

She told him.

28

The last time Yael saw Charles Bonnet, she had kicked a cup of coffee out of his hand, punched him in the side of his neck, slammed his head against the edge of a desk to knock him unconscious, and trussed him up. That was nine months ago, when she encountered him in an obscure wing of the UN headquarters in Geneva. Arriving at eight o'clock in the morning, she'd pretended to be a cleaning lady to gain entry.

She rummages through the contents of his desk: leaflets advertising Michelin-starred restaurants and a spa hotel, a leasing agreement for a Mercedes V8 convertible, a photograph of Bonnet with his African wife and their son and daughter.

Her mission was to find the plan giving KZX and the Bonnet Group control over Congo's coltan supplies. Bonnet was not known for his work ethic, and she didn't expect to find him in the offices that early.

Now the sight of the Frenchman, recently released from prison where he had been serving time for a crime she knew he had committed, triggered in her a powerful urge to repeat her actions. Instead, she greeted him with a nod and wary half smile. Tonight she needed information.

Bonnet raised his champagne glass in response. "*Bon soir*, Yael. Let's celebrate my freedom. And the independence of the American judicial system."

Yael did not reply.

"You will let me finish my drink this time?" He tilted his glass forward as if to clink it against hers.

She stepped back, holding her drink close to her chest. "That depends."

"On what?"

"Your behavior. And level of contrition."

"Contrition." Bonnet gave a thin smile. "I am, what do you Americans say, 'processing' recent events. My lawyer advised me that I could sue, both my accuser Thanh Ly and the authorities. What do you think?"

"I think you don't want to know what I think."

He nodded. "No, I probably do not." He sipped his drink, was silent for several seconds before he continued. "May I speak frankly?"

"Please do."

"Yes, strings were pulled. And yes, my behavior was appalling. But I have paid a high price. Deserved, of course. But still . . ." He glanced upward as the overhead roar of a helicopter drowned out his voice, waited until it faded. "My wife has left me. I am a sex offender. I cannot see my children. There is a restraining order against me. I have lost my job. I am informed, through unofficial channels, that I have a fortnight to sort out my affairs, and then I must leave the United

States. My UN career is over. So is my social life. I have been here an hour. You are the first person to talk to me."

She looked around. Bonnet was right. The reception was packed but there was nobody within ten feet of the Frenchman. Yael looked him up and down. The mahogany permatan had been replaced by a prison pallor. Bonnet's mane of dark, wavy hair was now a short crop, shot through with gray. His blue pin-striped suit, handmade on Savile Row, sagged on him and his shirt collar was loose around his neck. Its edge was covered with a light dusting of the face powder he used to disguise the scars of childhood acne. But even after spending most of a year inside the American penal system, much of it in isolation, his posture remained that of a former Foreign Legionnaire.

She did not believe for a moment that the sexual assault case against Bonnet had genuinely collapsed. He might appear repentant, but he was still a sexual predator. Nevertheless, she needed to talk to him. And talking to bad men was what she was good at. Especially when one held the key—or part of it—to her brother's death.

Yael lowered her glass and stepped slightly closer. "I am sorry, Charles, that things turned out like this," she said sympathetically.

Bonnet looked back warily at her, his expression one part relief because someone was talking to him and another part a rapid calibration of why. A phone ringing cut through the buzz of the party. He reached into his pocket, and saw his screen was flashing. "Please excuse me for a second."

She nodded, and looked around her as he stepped away. The giant marquee covered most of the large open space in front of the steps ascending to the university library. Its light blue walls, the color of both the university and the UN, were subtly emblazoned with the UN symbol, Columbia's emblem of a crown, and the letters *KZX*. Outside the air had turned chilly, but every few yards a standing space heater radiated warmth. The air smelled lightly of food and perfume. Waiters circulated with silver trays of drinks and bottles of champagne. White-jacketed chefs wheeled out steel trays of appetizers and enormous bowls of salad to add to the buffet being set up against the far wall, their barked instructions cutting through the buzz of conversation and background music. Fustat, a six piece Arab-African band, played in the corner of the marquee. Yael caught the eye of the vocalist, a plump twenty-something with wild black curly hair, and they exchanged smiles. Exactly two weeks ago she had watched Fustat play at Zone and danced with Najwa. But Yael did not think she would be dancing tonight.

The invitation had specified a starting time of seven o'clock, but it was now 8 p.m. and guests were still lined up three-deep on the red-tiled pathway leading from the university's entrance on Broadway to the marquee. Security was intense. Invitees had to pass through two metal detectors, one at the entrance to the campus on Broadway and the second in front of the marquee, before they were hand-frisked. The thoroughfare had been sealed off to traffic ten blocks north, and also south, of the subway station at West 110th Street. Snipers had set up nests on the roofs of the library and every building nearby. Police checkpoints ringed the campus. Helicopters swooped and banked above. Every side street was packed with police cars and vans.

Despite the queues, body frisks, and scans—or perhaps because of them—the atmosphere crackled with anticipation. This Saturday night in Manhattan, the KZX-UN reception was *the* event. There was nothing the city loved more than money and glamour, and here there was plenty of both. Yael saw Fareed Hussein deep in conversation with Lucy Tremlett, the British actress and UN ambassador. Tremlett had brought along several A-list Hollywood friends, each of whom was trailed by several paparazzi. In one corner the editors of *Vogue* and *Newsweek* huddled together conspiratorially. In another stood several regal-looking elderly ladies, the queens of New York philanthropy, wearing either Chanel or Balenciaga.

A few yards away, Jonathan Beaufort was making what looked like a play for Collette Moreau, summoning the waiter for more champagne. Roxana was standing too close to the mayor, who was trying not to be distracted by the amount of cleavage her deep scoop-necked blue silk dress displayed as they talked. Roger Richardson was bringing a glass of champagne for Grace Olewanda, the SG's secretary, resplendent in her green and gold traditional African outfit. Philippe, the Al-Jazeera cameraman, was filming Najwa as she interviewed the governor of New York. Yael felt a flicker of jealousy at seeing Sami Boustani, looking sharp in his black linen suit, ensconced with the blond correspondent for *Russia Today*, who was nodding enthusiastically at whatever he had to say. Yael caught Sami's eye and mouthed the word *later.* He nodded, not very enthusiastically, then turned back to his companion. But what did she expect, after standing him up two nights ago—and Eli's e-mail?

Lacking what the invitation described as a "partner," she had brought her mother. Yael lent Barbara one of her several black dresses, in which she looked annoyingly glamorous. Where was she? Yael scanned the crowd. Barbara was standing on the other side of the party, deep in conversation with Reinhardt Daintner. The KZX executive loomed over her like a tall, pale praying mantis. Barbara nodded thoughtfully as he spoke, apparently fascinated by everything he had to say. Yael stared in amazement at Daintner's hand resting on her mother's upper arm. Their proximity, and relaxed body language, indicated an easy familiarity. Until Caroline Masters strode over, when Daintner instantly dropped his hand and stepped back.

Bonnet ended his call and put his phone in his pocket. He followed Yael's gaze. "Who is that talking to Reinhardt?"

"My mother," said Yael, still taken aback.

"Of course. So they are still friendly," said Bonnet, his voice amused.

"Still?"

Bonnet ignored her question. He gave Barbara a swift, Gallic appraisal. "She is very beautiful. Lucky you." He turned and looked at Yael. "You have good genes. And you share her looks." He sipped his champagne, tilting his head to the side before he spoke. "*Ma chère* Yael, I am not complaining, of course, about being in your company. There is no queue to replace you. But," his voice hardened slightly as he continued, "I am wondering why, in a room of glamorous, successful New York movers and shakers, any one of whom would be glad of your company, you are here talking to me, a disgraced, burnt-out has-been. At least this time you have let me finish my drink. Speaking of which . . ." Bonnet raised his empty glass and looked around the marquee.

A waiter appeared almost instantly. Yael glanced at his face, then his name badge, and smiled; not too obviously, she hoped. The last time she saw "Miguel" had been last fall, when he and Joe-Don helped her escape from the Millennium Hotel after killing Jean-Pierre Hakizimani. Joe-Don had wanted to come with her tonight, of course, but Yael had insisted she would be safe. There was nowhere in New York more secure than the KZX reception. Still, it was a good feeling to know that Joe-Don had her back even when he was not around. Miguel filled Bonnet's empty glass with champagne, then raised the bottle over Yael's glass, which was still almost full. She shook her head. She needed to keep a clear head for what was coming next. Miguel winked at her and walked off.

Bonnet drank half his champagne in one go. The alcohol seemed to give him courage. "I may be vain. But I am not stupid. What do you want?"

"You saw Roger's report on CNN last night?"

Bonnet nodded.

"He said there was some kind of deal, to do with the nine aid workers that were killed. You were on the Rwanda desk then. Was there?"

The Frenchman stiffened, almost imperceptibly. He looked at his champagne glass, raised it, then lowered it again without drinking. "Why are you interested in this? You were a teenager then."

"I knew one of them."

She is seven years old, sitting on her brother's shoulders and giggling with delight as he strides across Central Park, pretending to be a giant, striding between the trees.

As far as Yael knew, only Fareed Hussein knew that David Weiss was her brother. David too became estranged from his father, wanting nothing to do with Aleph Research, and took his mother's maiden name. The SG would likely have kept that information to himself. The last thing he'd want was any more discussion of Rwanda and his role during the genocide, especially in the office.

Yael watched Bonnet. There was no flash of recognition in his eyes, but he was suddenly wary. He looked around, stared at her for several seconds, made a decision. "Not here," he said, and started to walk out.

She followed him through the crowd. Bonnet turned left and walked around the side of the library, through a manicured garden with low hedges. There he sat on a stone bench. A policeman walked by, his radio crackling. He glanced at Yael and Bonnet, nodded briefly in greeting, then walked on.

Bonnet waited until the policeman had gone. "It was a tragedy. We had hoped, planned, for a very different outcome." He looked into the distance as he calmly rifled through his memories.

Yael asked, "It is true then, what Roger reported on CNN? That there was a deal?"

He sat back. "You have a cigarette, maybe?"

Yael reached inside her purse and took out a pack of Marlboro Lights. She handed him the box and her Zippo lighter. He extracted a cigarette and lit it, and closed his eyes for a few seconds, drawing deep. The tobacco crackled, the end of the cigarette glowing red as it trembled. The breeze was cooler now. Yael pulled her shawl around her. Her black minidress, the same one that she had worn for her canceled date with Sami, was designed for being inside a party. Her toes were chilled in her open sandals. She waited for Bonnet to speak.

He exhaled a long plume of smoke through his nose, then turned to her. "Fareed said it was his idea, but I don't know if that's true. You know how it works. A chance remark in a meeting, a proposal in a memo, then suddenly it's policy, actually happening. Either way, it would have been a win for me, and for France, and a large deposit in Hussein's favored bank from one of the P5."

Yael nodded, her heart racing, but trying to seem curious but dispassionate. "How was it supposed to work?"

"The UN workers were to be taken hostage, then rescued by French peacekeepers."

"But why? In exchange for what?"

"You will have to ask Fareed that. Or whoever was giving him orders."

"And you did what?"

Bonnet shrugged. "What I had to. What I was told to do. Like a good soldier. Or peacekeeper. We know when not to intervene. Which, then, was most of the time." He took another drag and watched the smoke trail into the air. Yael stayed silent.

"I . . ." he swallowed, trying to get the words out. He closed his eyes, and exhaled hard. The words came in a torrent. "I liaised with the Tutsis. With Hakizimani. The UN staff's captor." He swallowed again, paused. "Their murderer."

For a second Yael was back in the Millennium Hotel, listening to Hakizimani.

"You tell your SG this. If he starts altering the terms now, I will personally ensure that our communications in 1994 and subsequent years are leaked to the press."

So you handed them over to be killed," she said, surprising herself at how calm she remained.

"Not intentionally. They were supposed to be hostages. They were to be held for a day or two, then released."

"But why? What was the point? What were the terms?"

Bonnet shrugged. "I don't know. Really. I'm telling you the truth. Ask Fareed. Or the P5. I was just the facilitator. There was always a danger, of course, we knew that. We took a gamble. We lost. They were casualties of war. What do the Americans say? Collateral damage. Nine deaths among hundreds of thousands. It was chaos, we had no means of stopping it. It was not my fault. So I tell myself. Sometimes I even believe it. Whose fault was it? Everybody's. Nobody's." He paused, turned to face her. "But you, Yael, you know all about secret deals."

Yael bristled. "I have never handed over anybody to be killed."

Bonnet laughed, a brittle sound. "Please. We are having an adult conversation, are we not? How many killers have you let walk free on Fareed's orders? Killers who later continued their slaughter. How many warlords have escaped justice because the P5 or the global corporations decided it would be *inconvenient* to call them to account? And then got you to do the dirty work."

She did not reply. She looked at the ground. Bonnet's questions were precisely the ones she had been asking herself lately. She did not like the answers.

He paused, and looked at his cigarette. "You said you knew one of them. Which one?"

"David. David Weiss."

"How? You were what then, fifteen, sixteen years old? How does a teenage girl living in London know an American aid worker in Kigali? I remember the boy. He was good-looking. Green eyes, like yours." He stared at Yael. "Like yours . . ." A slow realization dawned across his face. "Of course. So that's why you dig so hard. David Weiss was your . . ."

There was no point in lying. "Brother."

Bonnet looked away, clearly shocked. "I had no idea. I am sorry."

"So am I. You lost a gamble. They lost their lives." Anger and regret curdled inside her. Had the man sitting next to her acted differently, shown some courage, not followed instructions, her brother might still be alive. But there was no point attacking him now. Especially when she needed more information. "I have another question."

"Go ahead," said Bonnet.

"What were you doing when you were seconded to the Prometheus Group from the DPKO?"

His weary cynicism evaporated. He suddenly looked alarmed. "How on earth did you . . ."

"An old version of the UN website. It must have been posted by mistake. It was taken down, but it's still out there in cyberspace, if you know where to look."

Bonnet dropped his cigarette on the ground. "I always admired you. Really, it's not just a Frenchman's flattery, although it would have been nice if that had worked." He crushed the butt with his shoe. "But be warned. You are poking a hornet's nest. Nobody has your back. Fareed will throw you overboard in a second."

From here, Yael could see out over the campus's gardens, the carefully trimmed hedges; the grand stairs to the library entrance with its row of columns; even right across Broadway, to the apartment blocks that overlooked the thoroughfare. For a moment she thought she saw something or someone moving on a roof, a glint of light, a reflection on glass. Night was falling but there was still plenty of illumination from the streetlights, shops, and apartment windows. She glanced back. Nothing. It must have been a shadow.

Yael had enjoyed her time at Columbia, worked hard for her master's. But her real education had started at the Department of Peacekeeping. Would Fareed "throw her overboard"? He had done so once already. But now their lives were more entangled than ever. She was about to reply when a movement in the distance caught her eye. She looked out again across Broadway, to the roof of the apartment block. Not one, but two people. Her heart sped up. She knew exactly what was going to happen next.

Time slowed, almost stopped.

Yael glanced at Bonnet.

A red dot appeared on his chest.

Collateral damage.

She glanced again at the roof of the apartment building.

A photograph of Bonnet with his African wife and their son and daughter.

She shoved him sideways as hard as she could and dived to the ground.

PART TWO

REYKJAVIK

29

Yael watched Magnus Olafsson as he came to the end of his final security briefing. There were a dozen people in the Hotel Borg's conference room and the air was thick with hostility. Olafsson sat at the head of the long, polished wooden table, his deputy Karin Bjornsdottir on his right. Four men sat on each side of the table. Those on the left all seemed in their forties or early fifties, were pale and clean-shaven. They wore navy two-piece suits, button-down shirts, and plain ties. Their counterparts opposite, mostly of a similar age, had darker complexions. They wore gray or black suits and white collarless shirts. Two had beards, including the obvious leader of the group, who was older and plumper, with silver hair. All eight had cold, wary eyes.

The two sides stared at each other, as though convinced that the other was planning to assassinate their head of state, if not start shooting there and then. A coffee pot, bottles of mineral water, and a teapot sat atop one of the tables together with white china cups and saucers, fruit, cookies, and muffins. None had been touched.

Olafsson, the commander of Iceland's elite counterterrorist unit, the Vikingasveitin, or Viking Squad, had short blond hair, dark blue eyes, a sharp, almost pointed chin, and a long day's worth of stubble. He spoke thoughtfully, weighing his words, a sea captain staying unruffled as the waves pound the deck. "Gentlemen. We have been through the plan several times. You have a detailed, minute-by-minute timetable in the folders on the table in front of you. Because there will be overlap between your presidents' visits to our president at the Bessastadir residence, we need to coordinate and work together."

A visit from the UN secretary-general, not to mention any president, always entailed extensive cooperation between the accompanying security details and the host country's police, military, and intelligence services. But Iceland, perched in the freezing waters of the North Atlantic, was different from other countries. Just 332,000 people lived on the volcanic island of 40,000 square miles, about the size of Kentucky, most in and around the capital, Reykjavik. Vast swathes of the landscape were icebound, barren tundra, or lava fields where nothing could grow. Not only did Iceland lack any kind of standing military force, despite being a NATO member, its police were unarmed and guns were rare. It also lacked an intelligence service, but it did have the Vikingasveitin to ensure the security of visiting foreign dignitaries.

Olafsson gestured at Yael and Joe-Don, sitting in two leather armchairs a few feet away. "Yael Azoulay and Joe-Don Pabst are here to coordinate the UN's involvement and to ensure the safety of Fareed Hussein. So, gentlemen, can I have your assurances that we can all work together?"

"No," said the American sitting directly to the left of Olafsson.

Every eye in the room turned to stare. Kent Maxwell, a heavyset older man with thinning gray hair and a red face lined with veins, was the US Secret Service's liaison officer with the Viking Squad.

"Pardon?" said Olafsson.

"No. I said no," replied Maxwell. "The United States of America does not 'work together' with state sponsors of terrorism."

The Iranians remained impassive. Each looked at the older man. He nodded almost imperceptibly. All four began to gather their folders and made ready to stand up.

Olafsson raised his hands in supplication. "Gentlemen, I understand the difficult history of your countries and the agencies which you represent. But, with respect, that is not my concern here today. In the last few days a senior UN official has been murdered, another shot at. My concern is to ensure a safe and secure environment for your heads of state, especially when they meet our president. And for that to happen, you need to put aside your differences."

"We will put aside 'our differences' when the Iranian government puts aside its suicide bombers and truck bombs," Maxwell said.

The man with silver hair looked disdainfully at Maxwell. "And when you put aside your drones and torture chambers and summary executions." He paused and looked at Olafsson. "However, *we* appreciate that we are guests here. If you apologize, we will overlook your insult."

"Sure," said Maxwell. "When you apologize for holding my countrymen hostage for 444 days in our own embassy."

Olafsson raised his hands, palm out, and glanced at his deputy. "OK. OK. If that's the way you want it. I hereby announce that the government of Iceland withdraws all security cooperation. We can no longer guarantee the safety of either president and we will make an announcement immediately to that effect. From this moment on, you are on your own. Good luck." He started to slide his chair back.

"Wait," said Yael, as she stood up and walked over to the table. "Everyone stay where you are." She looked at the Americans, then the Iranians. "The United Nations, on whose security council both of your countries sit, requests a couple of minutes for a time out."

The Americans glanced at Maxwell, the Iranians at the silver-haired man. Both Maxwell and the silver-haired man nodded.

Yael continued talking. "We all know that both of your teams could manage Bessastadir, on your own, without coordinating with your opposite numbers. But there is one thing you all need and that is Magnus, Karin, and the Viking Squad. How do you think your presidents will react when they learn their visit to the presidential residence has been canceled because of their security details' macho posturing? I doubt very much that any of you will have a job when you return home." Yael paused to let her words settle. "We need to fix this, and quickly. Please, reach across the table and shake the hand of the person sitting opposite you."

All eight men looked at their colleagues with varying degrees of alarm, murmuring in English and Farsi.

"An excellent idea," said Olafsson. "Both of your technicians have swept this room. Nobody is watching, listening or recording. A little trust goes a long way. Especially when you are all so far from home, on a lump of rock and lava in the middle of the Atlantic Ocean."

Yael watched the four Iranians as Olafsson spoke. The older man seemed familiar; nothing specific, but something about his appearance nagged at her. She frowned, trying to remember if and where she had seen him before.

Maxwell shrugged, glanced around the room as if to check no camera crews had sneaked in, and tentatively reached across the table. The Iranian facing him had hooded eyes. He looked to the silver-haired man sitting next to him, as if to seek his permission. A subtle nod, and the American's hand was grasped. Within a few seconds, all eight men were shaking hands.

Coffee and tea was poured, cookies and muffins passed around. Yael sat back down, stifling a yawn. It was three o'clock on Monday afternoon. She drank some more tea, hoping that the caffeine would reenergize her. After a rough six-hour flight punctuated by brief bursts of snatched, uncomfortable sleep, her body clock was still on Manhattan time, five hours behind. Unlike heads of state or prime ministers, the UN secretary-general did not have his own airplane. He and his party either traveled on commercial airlines or on transport provided by the country of his destination. They had planned to fly on Icelandair, but after Friday, Olga Gunnarsdottir, the president, immediately offered her own private jet—an offer that was gratefully accepted.

The Gulfstream arrived at Teterboro, a small private airport in New Jersey, on Sunday evening at seven. The SG's party had been airborne an hour later, landing at Keflavik at seven o'clock on Monday morning local time. There were four passengers: Yael, Joe-Don, the SG, and Roxana. The rest of the SG's party had flown commercial. Roxana had hovered around the SG for most of the flight, but eventually she fell asleep, finally giving Yael the chance to speak with him without Roxana listening.

The flight might have been uncomfortable, but their accommodation was not. Opened in 1930, the Hotel Borg was Iceland's first luxury hotel. Over the years it had evolved its own neo–art deco style. The walls were painted a light chocolate brown, the doors and the ceiling were white, the dark wood floor polished till it shone. Yael cast an envious eye on the chairs around the table. Their bold curves and mahogany-and-cream color scheme would fit very nicely in her apartment.

Olafsson tapped his pen on the side of his water glass. "Let's get back to work. To recap: the United Nations Sustainability Summit started yesterday, Sunday, at the Harpa conference center by Reykjavik port at ten o'clock in the morning, on schedule. The first day ended at seven o'clock in the evening. There are nine hundred delegates here, as well as hundreds more representing various NGOs, plus the media contingent of about two hundred people. The conference is due to finish at four o'clock this afternoon. Security is at Code Red, the highest level, especially after the shooting in New York on Friday. There was pressure from your governments to cancel or postpone the conference. But

Fareed Hussein and Presidents Freshwater and Kermanzade were both determined that it go ahead."

He looked around the table. The atmosphere had eased, suspicion and hostility fading to a wary alertness. Olafsson watched the leader of the Iranian delegation reach for a tangerine and begin to slowly peel it before he continued talking. "There have been no changes in schedule or personnel since our previous briefing at eight o'clock this morning. However, I also wanted to introduce you to my deputy, Karin Bjornsdottir, as she could not attend this morning's briefing. Karin will be your second point of contact. All her details are enclosed in your update file."

Karin Bjornsdottir was a round-faced blond in her early thirties with high cheekbones and ice-blue eyes. She looked around the table appraising what she saw. The two Americans nearest her shook her hand, the other two nodded, as did all the Iranians.

"Fareed Hussein has now given his closing address," Olafsson continued. "He and President Gunnarsdottir are now at the final press conference. To recap, the SG, President Freshwater, and President Kermanzade are each scheduled for a ten-minute meeting with President Gunnarsdottir at Bessastadir. Realistically, knowing that the one thing all politicians, no matter what their nationality, tend to do is run over time"—both sides exchanged knowing looks across the table—"we have scheduled their visits to allow for this. Each of the three will travel in a separate armored motorcade after their closing speech. The journey takes about twenty minutes. Fareed Hussein will arrive first at six o'clock, followed by President Kermanzade, and then President Freshwater.

"And then, my friends, hopefully, soon after seven o'clock, we can all head home." Olafsson gathered his papers and slid them into a plastic folder. "Any questions?"

None came. "Then I thank you, gentlemen," Olafsson finished.

"And we thank you," said the plump Iranian.

"Copy that," said Kent Maxwell.

Yael glanced at Joe-Don. He gave her a knowing smile. They both watched Olafsson and Bjornsdottir stand and walk the two groups to the door.

Yael waited until the security officials had left and then picked up a cookie, took a large bite, and walked over to the floor-to-ceiling windows. The heavy brown drapes had been drawn tightly closed, so she opened them and looked out.

The view from the Tower Suite was captivating, bathed in afternoon sunlight of crystalline purity. Reykjavik was built on a long finger of land surrounded on three sides by the Atlantic Ocean. The sea was the color of sapphires, topped with white, foaming waves. Neat rows of nineteenth-century houses, their corrugated iron walls painted orange and blue, yellow and pink, radiated out from the city center. Tiny parks were scattered across downtown, splashes of green amid the steel and glass. The harbor was crowded with ocean liners and fishing trawlers, whalers and yachts. Lake Tjörnin rippled gray and silver, its banks jammed with great flocks of seabirds and swans. Across the square stood the Althingi, the Parliament House, a two-story building of gray stone with curved white windows. Even the sidewalks were smart, their gray edges running along a center strip of red-brown stones.

"Yael, please close the curtains and step away from the window," said Olafsson. "We don't want you attracting any more bullets."

She nodded and slowly began to close the drapes, still checking the area around the hotel and giving a quick, final glance up and down Pósthússtræti, which ran in front of the hotel. Just one detail marred the idyllic scene: The dumpy, middle-aged woman sitting on a bench fifty yards from the entrance. Her pink coat, and her companions, last seen with Eli Harrari in Tompkins Square Park, had gone, Yael saw. The woman now wore a heavy black parka. But her hair, the color of straw, poked out from under a brown cap.

Olafsson poured himself a cup of coffee. "Thanks, Yael, for your help. Soon they will all head to the airport, secretary-generals, presidents, and their security guards and normal life resumes." He checked his watch. "In just over two hours."

Yael finished closing the drapes and turned around. "Actually, Magnus, it might be a little longer than that."

Najwa stepped inside the Kaldalón auditorium and quickly looked around for Sami. He was, as instructed, sitting in the front row with his messenger bag reserving an empty seat next to him. She briskly walked in front of the seats to her place. The closing press conference of the Sustainability Summit was coming to an end, and the SG sat in the center of a steel and glass table, talking about the valuable work that had been done in the last two days. He was flanked on one side by Olga Gunnarsdottir and her press attaché, a skinny brown-haired man in a tight navy suit who looked about twenty years old, and on the other by Roxana.

Until the events of last week, the Reykjavik Summit had garnered little interest among the UN press corps. Reykjavik, they predicted, would go the way of all other UN gatherings dealing with the big issues of the day: doom-laden warnings that Something Must Be Done; behind-the-scenes wrangling over quotas for reductions or increases, as required; followed by a solemn pledge from the attending nations to implement whatever had been agreed, which would be immediately ignored as soon the delegations returned home. Sensing the lack of excitement, the SG's press office had not even offered a "travel facility."

But by Friday morning, after Frank Akerman's murder, the mood had changed. If someone was shooting at the SG, then perhaps it was worth following him to Reykjavik. Any doubts were swept away by the attempted killing of Charles Bonnet. The UN was hot. Which was why the Kaldalón auditorium was standing room only. Najwa counted at least two hundred reporters sitting in the chairs and dozens more standing at the sides in between the rows of camera crews.

The Kaldalón was the smallest of the four auditoriums in the Harpa concert center. Perched on the very edge of downtown Reykjavik, by the harbor, the Harpa complex was a hypermodern asymmetrical construct with sloping walls and windows that changed color according to the position of the sun. Like the rest of the Harpa center, Kaldalón looked like the star feature in an architecture magazine. The bare stone floor was a lighter shade of gray, matching the gray and gold fabric wall coverings. The dark gray cinema-style chairs, each with its own foldaway writing table and outlet, were laid out in stepped rows so the journalists were looking down at the table where the SG and President Gunnarsdottir were holding the press conference.

Fareed Hussein finished by recapping the "vital" international agreement that had been reached and thanking President Gunnarsdottir and Iceland for hosting the summit, before handing the microphone to Roxana. She did not look quite as poised as usual, Najwa noticed. Still wearing the black Prada jacket and skirt she'd had on last Friday at the New York press conference, her blue blouse was creased and she had rings around her eyes that a liberal application of makeup could not quite disguise.

"Thank you, secretary-general and President Gunnarsdottir," said Roxana. "I am very pleased to see such a large turnout from the press for this vital international summit. I would ask you, as a courtesy to our hosts, to keep your questions related to sustainability and international development. Please state your name and the media outlet you represent."

A sea of hands shot up. Roxana ignored all the members of the New York UN press corps and instead pointed to a thirtyish woman with cropped blond hair and rimless glasses sitting on the end of one of the middle rows.

"Thank you. Sabine Altheusser, from *Environment International*. How can the United Nations ensure that the countries here today will implement the quotas for the reduction of plastic bags, for example?"

Najwa glanced at Jonathan Beaufort, who rolled his eyes. She looked at her watch. It was ten minutes past three. The press conference had started at two fifty and was scheduled to end in five minutes. Both the SG and President Gunnarsdottir had been late and spoken for too long, cutting into the time allotted to the press for questions. Najwa had little interest in sustainability, but she was very interested indeed in the death—or murder, as it now appeared—of Henrik Schneidermann and Frank Akerman and the attempt on Charles Bonnet's life. For the moment, she would keep what she had discovered about Schneidermann and the Iranian connection to herself. She had plenty of questions, but would not ask them at a press conference with dozens of other reporters present. Although, putting more pressure on now, she mused, might flush out more information.

More questions followed, all of them from environmental reporters. The UN press corps was becoming increasingly irritated by Roxana's blunt but effective stonewalling. But even the highest, thickest stone wall could be scaled—or stepped around. Najwa knew that protocol required Roxana to take at least one question from the host country's national television network. Which was why Najwa had invited the political correspondent of Iceland's RUV for breakfast at her hotel that morning. The Icelandic reporters were all friendly and helpful, keen to put their island home on the international media map and flattered by the arrival of the major television networks and newspapers. Rafnhildur Eriksdottir, a vivacious brunette, had been pleased by Najwa's interest and even more pleased when she explained her plan.

Roxana looked around the room. The clock showed

three fifteen. The press conference was over time, but she still needed to take a question from RUV. Roxana looked at Eriksdottir.

The Icelandic journalist stood up. "Rafnhildur Eriksdottir, RUV. I have a question." She paused for effect, enjoying the attention. "It's not about the Sustainability Summit."

The room quieted. Roxana and Fareed Hussein glanced at each other, a frisson of concern on their faces. Najwa caught Jonathan Beaufort's eye again and smiled. He grinned back and made the thumbs-up sign.

Rafnhildur continued talking, "With all due respect to my colleagues who are focusing on sustainability, the real news about the United Nations, as we know, is the murder of the senior UN officials Frank Akerman and the attempt to kill Charles Bonnet."

Roxana's faced creased in annoyance. "Charles Bonnet is no longer working for the UN. This is not a question. It is a statement. Your question please. We are running out of time."

Rafnhildur said, "Why have all the documents on Frank Akerman's role as a military observer in Bosnia been removed from the UN archives?"

30

"Now? You are telling me this now?"

Olafsson was more puzzled than indignant, although he had every right to be angry. Presidents did alter their schedules at the last moment to squeeze an extra few minutes together or make room for an unexpected encounter. But this was an entirely different order of magnitude.

"I'm sorry," said Yael. "But I couldn't mention it before. And especially not with the others in here."

Olafsson exhaled sharply. "But that was exactly when you should have raised this. Yael, I know you love to live on the edge, but really, this can't be done. It is impossible. These are heads of states. Two states almost at war with each other. Here. In Iceland. Where we don't even have an army. Everything to do with their visit has been planned out for weeks in advance, here and in DC and Tehran. Right down to the last minute. Last second, ideally."

Yael stirred her tea for several seconds before she spoke. A former UN civil affairs officer, Olafsson was a grandson of a former president of Iceland. He had spent much of his childhood at Bessastadir and knew the building better than anyone else alive. Olafsson and Yael had first met in Afghanistan. There he had been training the Afghan police force in human rights and anticorruption measures, a task he once described to her as like trying to melt a glacier with a candle.

The Icelander continued talking. "You are telling me that the president of the United States of America and the president of the Islamic Republic of Iran are going to hold an impromptu press conference at the residence of their Icelandic counterpart, where they will announce the resumption of diplomatic relations, the lifting of sanctions, and the release of all Iranian political prisoners?" Olafsson looked at his watch. "In just over two hours, without telling either of their security details? Or their governments?"

Yael nodded. "That's it. But what's changed? You already knew that the three of them were getting together in the same place. The Americans are handling the security for Freshwater, the Iranians for Kermanzade. Each president will tell their people they are staying at Bessastadir longer than they planned. The only difference is—"

"That the leaders of two countries who are deadly enemies will be making an announcement that will make a lot of people very angry indeed," he interrupted. "This love-in will take place inside or outside the residence?"

"First inside, then they will take a walk outside."

Olafsson groaned out loud.

Yael gave him her brightest, and, she hoped, most convincing smile. "Magnus. This is history in the making. Like Gorbachev and Reagan at their summit that ended the Cold War. This will prevent a hot war between America and Iran. It will put Iceland on the map again."

Olaffson shook his head. "Especially if one of them, or Fareed Hussein, gets shot. Which seems to be happening quite frequently nowadays." Olafsson looked at his deputy.

Karin Bjornsdottir slowly moved her head from side to side, her blond ponytail swinging as she chewed her lip. "Well . . . it is only an extra hour. And they will all be there anyway."

Olafsson poured himself some more coffee. "The longest hour of our lives." He sat still for several seconds. "It seems I cannot refuse. If that is what the three presidents want. Although a heads-up would have been nice."

Yael grinned. "I just gave you one."

"From *them*. And slightly more notice would have been appreciated."

"Next time, I promise," she said, proffering the plate of snacks. "Cookie? Once we're done you can write another book. A thriller. What's the phrase . . . 'inspired by real events'? Hollywood will love it."

Icelanders wrote, read, and published more books per capita than anywhere else in the world. Even Magnus had written one, a children's saga set in medieval times. One night in Kandahar he had showed Yael a copy of the book, which was a best seller.

Olafsson grabbed a chocolate muffin and ate it in three bites. "Talk me through Friday evening again. I need to go over the background once more."

"Why don't we start with Al-Jazeera?" said Yael. "They were the only major network there with a camera crew. The report is accurate and gives you a good sense of what happened. It's all online." She reached inside her purse, took out her iPad, and started tapping. A browser window opened, followed by the Al-Jazeera website. She placed the iPad on the table, upright in its case. The screen showed the evening news anchor, Faisal, sitting in the studio and discussing the fighting in Syria with a correspondent when a graphic flashed across the screen: *Breaking News*.

The screen switched back to the anchor, who was touching his earpiece and nodding. A ticker was running across the bottom: *Reports of shooting at UN New York event, second in 48 hours*. "We are going straight to our correspondent Najwa al-Sameera, who is on the scene. Najwa?"

The camera cut to Najwa, who was standing on the steps leading to the Columbia University library, its tall Greek columns looming behind her. "Yes, Faisal. Dramatic events here in Manhattan at the UN-KZX launch of the School for International Development. A sniper has opened fire. The party is over and the whole area, as you can see, is being evacuated."

Police were ushering a stream of guests out of the marquee. Almost all were holding mobile phones close to their heads and talking rapidly. Several looked dazed. A few were crying. Sirens wailed. A helicopter ambulance stood near the marquee.

"Has anyone been killed or injured?" Faisal asked.

"Nothing is confirmed but there are reports that Charles Bonnet, a former senior UN official, may have been shot. All the dignitaries and UN officials, including secretary general Fareed Hussein, have been evacuated."

Faisal nodded. "This is the second UN official to be targeted by sniper fire in three days. The first, Frank Akerman, was shot dead outside the secretary-general's residence. Are the shootings connected?"

"There is no evidence yet, but it is certainly possible."

"Najwa, yesterday you tweeted a link to a video that showed Frank Akerman clinking glasses with a Bosnian Serb general after the fall of Srebrenica, just a few feet from the bodies of murdered civilians. Bonnet has also been in the news because of events two decades ago. Tell us about that."

Yael glanced across the table. Olafsson, Bjornsdottir, and Joe-Don were all absorbed in the television report. She dropped her hand into her purse and took out a small pill container, opened it, took out two tablets. She swallowed the tablets with a glass of water, then slipped the container back into her purse.

Najwa was still talking. "Charles Bonnet has just been released from prison, where he had been serving a sentence for aggravated sexual assault. A judge ruled this week that the evidence was inadmissible. But more than that, it seems that Mr. Bonnet was involved in some kind of backroom deal over the UN's greatest catastrophe, the genocide in Rwanda."

A policeman appeared, his gruff voice cutting over Najwa's. "Ma'am, you need to stop filming and leave the area."

"But we are live . . ." she protested.

"Leave or I will arrest you all."

The screen cut back to the studio.

Yael pressed pause. The screen froze, showing the anchor. Yael said, "The rest is speculation. The gunman missed. He didn't fire again. Bonnet is fine. He flew to Paris the next day."

"Why was he shot at?" asked Olafsson.

She tried not to hesitate before she answered, to put aside her emotions and thoughts of David. "Because of Rwanda, I guess. We're coming up to the twentieth anniversary of the genocide. Anniversaries always make people look back, think what might have been. What they have lost."

Joe-Don looked at Yael, as if to say, *I'm taking over now.* She nodded as he reached inside a folder and handed out four sets of three printed sheets stapled together. Joe-Don began speaking: "Let's focus on what we know. This is the Joint Terrorism Task Force sitrep. It covers ballistics, initial analysis, and threat projection forecasts. The FBI is the lead agency, but there has been input from the NYPD, the State Department Diplomatic Security Service, the Secret Service, the CIA, and the NSA. Shall I talk you through it?" he asked, while the two Icelanders slowly read through each page. Yael scanned the report, which she had already read and discussed in detail with Joe-Don on the flight to Reykjavik.

"Please do," said Olafsson.

Joe-Don picked up the jug of coffee on the table and looked around the table. Yael shook her head, as did the others. He slowly poured himself another cup, took a long drink, and began to speak.

"Let's start with Frank Akerman. He was killed by a single 7N1 bullet. The 7N1 is an extremely accurate bullet, produced in small numbers especially for the Russian Dragunov sniper rifle. It has a steel core and a hollow spot in the nose with a lead knocker behind it. The knocker moves on impact into the hollow spot, causing the bullet to destabilize, spin around inside the body, and cause massive internal injury. Akerman was hit in the lower right-hand shoulder. The bullet eventually lodged in his rib cage and he died almost immediately."

He looked up to see three faces staring at him. Satisfied he had his audience's attention, he carried on reading. "The 7N1 was superseded in 1997 by the 7N14, which means that the ammunition used to kill Akerman probably dates from the early or mid-1990s. The Dragunov has an effective range of almost nine hundred yards, or more than half a mile. It was the standard sniper rifle in the Warsaw Pact countries before the dissolution of the Soviet Union, and was also used by all sides during the wars in the former Yugoslavia in the 1990s.

"The bullet fired on Friday at Charles Bonnet was recovered. It is of the same caliber and has the same rifling patterns, so we can assume that it was fired from the same weapon. In both cases the gunman fled the scene and no trace has been found."

Olafsson shook his head. "I cannot tell you how uneasy I am about this last-minute change to the Bessastadir schedule. What if this gunman is here? In Reykjavik? The airport is on the highest state of alert, but we are an island, with a long coastline."

"The only way the gunman could have got here in time is by airplane. Keflavik is locked down," Yael said.

"And if he travels on a false passport?" asked Olafsson. "And a weapon has been arranged in advance for him?"

"All we can do is our best," Yael continued, "and minimize the risk."

The four of them talked some more, going through the protocols and permutations. Just two reporters would be invited, they agreed, who would then pool their material: Najwa al-Sameera for the international press, and Rafnhildur Eriksdottir from RUV.

Olafsson looked down at his coffee cup. It was empty. He held it upside down. "The threat level does not alter. Only the time of exposure to danger."

Yael nodded. "Exactly." But she said nothing about the woman with straw-colored hair sitting on Pósthússtræti. Nor would she. She would stop Eli. And she would do it her way.

Alone.

Half a mile away in the Kaldi café on Laugavegur, Reykjavik's main shopping street, Sami was trying his best to persuade Najwa to temporarily enlist him as an Al-Jazeera staffer. "I could be your. . . ." he paused. "Assistant producer. Actually, I am already a coproducer, on the coltan film. You have to take me."

Najwa stirred her coffee, licked her spoon, then glanced at the ceiling. "Do I? I'm just trying to remember our most recent conversation about a division of labor. In McLaughlin's."

Sami knew what was coming. "Yes, but—"

"Exactly. Your words. *Yes, but. 'Yes, but the last time I checked, I was employed by the* New York Times, *not by Al-Jazeera.*'" Najwa smiled, enjoying herself. "All our vacancies are listed on our website. Habibi."

"Well, *now*, I would *love* to be employed by Al-Jazeera . . ."

Najwa put her hand on his. "I'm sorry. The terms are set in stone. Two reporters for the pool. One local, and one international. And anyway, what's the big fuss? It will just be more blah-blah about sustainability."

He shook off Najwa's hand. "Two television reporters. What about print?"

"Print. You are *so* twentieth century. You can write us up once we have broadcast our stories."

He frowned. "This is ridiculous. My editors are calling every twenty minutes demanding updates for the website. And now the American and Iranian presidents are going to be in the same building. What if they issue a joint statement, or say something?"

"About what? Plastic bags? Freshwater visits Gunnarsdottir. Kermanzade visits Gunnarsdottir. And the SG adds his buck's worth of platitudes. Blah, blah, recycle more, save the whales, then we are back to New York." She looked around. "Although actually, I am getting to like it here. It's kind of like Brooklyn without the jerks. Everyone I meet here seems to be a writer. But they actually produce books and get them published."

From the outside Kaldi looked like a house: three stories tall, with a small front door painted white to match the large windows looking onto the street. The front of the building, and that of its immediate neighbors, was covered in sheets of corrugated iron, painted brown, to protect it from the elements. Inside it was a relaxed, comfortable place, eclectically decorated with blue walls, a white ceiling with exposed wooden beams, and stripped brickwork. A wooden upright piano stood by the long copper bar. The music of Sigur Rós, one of Iceland's best-known groups, swirled gently around the room.

Najwa took another sip of her drink. "Who knew that they had such good coffee in Iceland?" She looked back at Sami. "I'm sorry, habibi. I can't. I even have to use Rafnhildur's cameraman. No producer. Maria and Philippe are already pissed. I can't leave them and take you. Anyway, you have your story."

Sami sipped his coffee. "Which one?"

"You know very well what I am talking about. The photo of Yael in Gaza. What are you going to do about it? She is here, you know. Why don't you try and talk to her. Get her side of the story? Does she know you have it?"

"I think so. I saw her on Friday, at Columbia, before the shooting. She looked embarrassed."

"Embarrassed is good. You can leverage that up into a full and frank account of what happened. Exploit her guilt."

"Does she feel guilty?"

"Of course she feels guilty. She's an Israeli liberal. You are a Palestinian."

"It will have to wait until New York." He picked up his messenger bag. "I'm going back to the hotel to write my story. Beaufort wants to meet for a coffee."

Najwa put her cup down. "Beaufort?" she asked, trying to sound casual.

"Jonathan Beaufort. The correspondent for the *Times* of London. I believe you know him," said Sami dryly.

"What does he want?"

"It's not what he wants. It's what he's got." He looked thoughtful for a moment. "He says he has a lead that he really wants to talk about, maybe share the story."

"A lead on what?"

"Akerman. Or Bonnet, I guess. Or both."

Najwa stared at him. "Beaufort and you? Sharing?"

"What's the big surprise? You and I used to share."

Najwa was alarmed. "Used to?"

"Yes," said Sami, looking at his watch. "Until I applied for a job."

"I'll talk to HR. Why would Beaufort share with you?"

She stared at Sami. He looked relaxed, in control. *Was he playing her?* She thought so. But now, after the shootings, there were so many rumors flying around the UN building and the press corps that it was best not to rule out anything, no matter how outlandish it sounded. Everyone sensed the web drawing more tightly around Fareed Hussein. His and Roxana's blustering performance in the press conference would only fuel the fire. Neither had a decent answer to Rafnhildur's question about Akerman's records. They had kept looking at each other uncertainly, and eventually took refuge in a bromide about investigating the claim.

"It's a swap," said Sami. "I give him the Yael photo. He gives me what he's got. He breaks his story first. I have my follow-up already written as soon as his goes online and vice-versa when I write the Yael story. Do you want in?"

"Of course."

Sami handed her a mobile phone. A tiny microphone was attached to the handset by a thin black cable. "You clip this to your jacket, put the phone in the inside pocket. You call me as soon as you arrive at Bessastadir, and leave the line open."

Najwa slowly stirred her coffee. "First you retweet and favorite my tweets. And you include my handle in all of your tweets. For ten minutes. Then you can use whatever you hear to send your own."

Sami paused for a moment. "OK for the retweets and the favorites and your handle. But two minutes max. Then it's open season."

"Eight."

"Four."

"Six."

Sami extended his hand across the table. "Deal."

31

She is walking down Yefet Street, deep into Jaffa, far from the tourist shops and restaurants. She treads carefully on the cracked sidewalks, past the kebab stands, the car repair workshops, the drug dealers idling in the doorways. She turns right at the bakery, heading toward the dilapidated villas overlooking the beach. It is a bright autumn afternoon, still warm enough for bathers. The sunshine sparkles on the waves, the air carries the smell of salt. A boy, twelve or thirteen, leads a foal across the sand, its hooves leaving delicate, precise imprints.

She is on the way to meet a new friend. Khamis is an Arab Israeli, a postgraduate student at Tel Aviv University, studying the 1948 war. A handsome, quiet man with long eyelashes, he is already captivated by the beautiful, wide-eyed American student newly arrived in Israel and yearning for justice for the Palestinians, whose hands keep brushing against him. He wants to take her to his favorite hummus restaurant.

She glances up and down the road. She has been to Jaffa many times, but never this far south, into the rundown side streets. A gang of teenagers sits on a low wall, smoking, whistling, and cat-calling when they see her. A car drives past, missing her by inches, Arab music blaring from the windows. The acrid smell of hashish mixes with the scent of the sea.

Eli's words echo in her head. "You won't see us. But we see you, wherever you are. Don't worry. We are watching."

Yael stood at the railing on the bank of Lake Tjörnin, watching the seabirds soar and swoop. The lake was in the heart of downtown Reykjavik, just a few minutes' walk from the Hotel Borg. The shore was lined with large, detached houses painted in bright colors, their reflections shimmering on water the color of gunmetal. The sky was a patchwork of clouds, daubs of white on a vast gray canvas. The wind gusted back and forth, sending gentle waves lapping at the shore.

Seabirds and swans hopped along the cobbles of the path, chirping and cawing. Yael had only been in the country a few hours, but she was already captivated. She had been to many remote places, ones that could only be reached by propeller planes landing on airstrips hewn from the jungle. Keflavik International Airport was like any other—slick, modern, full of shops. But the landscape, almost lunar in its rawness, was not. The road into Reykjavik wound through great fields of black lava. There were no trees or bushes; the sole vegetation seemed to be a hardy orange-brown grass. Iceland was part of the modern world, with mobile phones, American hotel chains, bearded baristas, and high-speed Internet, yet still there was something elemental about the place, almost primeval. A reminder that the daily squabbles and struggles of human existence—all the striving, intrigue, plots, and cabals—were ultimately pointless and irrelevant.

The only thing that mattered was the planet itself, a chunk of rock spinning through space.

Yael looked down at the row of framed pictures on the railing that showcased the avian varieties. Who knew bird-watching could be so engrossing? A whooper swan glided across the water, its long white neck regally straight. A short and stubby greylag goose bobbed past, its beady black eyes looking from side to side. A mallard watched her warily from the stone bank, its green head tucked into its curved body. The sun suddenly emerged and the lake shimmered. The breeze faded away. The air was cool and fresh.

She was a long way from Jaffa. But part of her was still walking down Yefet Street, knowing that Eli was watching. Khamis, she later learned, was really called Mahmoud, and he was not from Jaffa. There had been signs: Arabs from Jaffa were usually fluent in Hebrew, their Arabic inflected with slang from neighboring Tel Aviv, and he could not speak Hebrew properly. At times he seemed not to know his way around the backstreets. This was because he was from Gaza, Eli had revealed. He had infiltrated Israel and was part of a Hamas cell that planned to kidnap Yael and hold her hostage in exchange for several high-ranking political prisoners. So he told her. Then, at least, she had believed Eli.

A small part of Eli's story was true. Mahmoud really was from Gaza, she'd eventually discovered. The rest was a lie. He was gay and had fled to Israel, the only country in the region where it was possible to live freely as a homosexual. But there was a price for admittance: in Gaza they called it collaboration, and in Tel Aviv they called it cooperation.

Mahmoud was to make himself useful in training exercises. Word soon trickled back to the refugee camps, and Hamas issued a death sentence. Mahmoud refused to carry on working with Eli. He hanged himself in his prison cell the night before he was to be sent back.

Yael watched the mallard uncurl its neck, admiring the bird's smooth confidence as it slid into the water and paddled out into the lake. She was prepared: a Nokia burner was taped above her ankle inside her right boot. Two pairs of plastic cuffs were jammed down the side of the left. She knew what Eli would use and she had taken the antidote in the hotel. She did not feel nervous. Rather, she felt a calm certainty that Reykjavik would be where she finished her business with Eli. For good.

Her mind drifted back to the meeting with Magnus and Karin. Then she remembered what had been nagging at her. The portly man with the silver hair, the head of the Iranian delegation. An inch of skin by his right eyebrow, puckered and scarred. She had seen that scar before. She took out her phone and called up Joe-Don's number. Nothing happened. Joe-Don did not know she was out by the lake. She had told him she needed a nap for an hour before they headed to Bessastadir, and he had believed her, more or less. She had slipped the DO NOT DISTURB sign on her door and snuck out of the back entrance of the hotel. He would be furious, she knew, especially after the shooting at Columbia University.

She looked down. There were no bars on the network connection indicator. She tried again. Still nothing. There was no point trying to use it. Something was blocking the signal. It was starting.

An insect bit her neck. She raised her hand to swat it away.

"Hello, Motek," said a familiar voice behind her.

Yael wheeled around and her legs gave way.

Three miles away, Fareed Hussein paced back and forth across the presidential suite at the Hilton Reykjavik Nordica, his face twisted in anger as he gripped a sheaf of papers.

"How?" he demanded. "How could you allow that—that *fiasco*—to happen?"

"I resent that," said Roxana, her eyes glittering dangerously. "It was not a fiasco. Everything was fine until the last question."

Hussein sat down by the desk, pointing the papers at Roxana like a weapon. "Exactly. The last question. How did that Icelandic journalist know about Akerman's documents?"

He stared at Roxana. He had never seen her like this before. She was rattled, disheveled, her hair in disarray. She even smelled different, a heavy application of Zest barely disguising yesterday's sweat.

Roxana shrugged. "Information leaks. We cannot always stop it. Akerman is news. He's shot dead outside your front door, then it turns out he was drinking and backslapping with Bosnian Serbs while they were taking the Muslim prisoners away to be shot." She paused, ran her fingers through her hair, to no noticeable effect. "On your watch. While you were running peacekeeping. Here's a heads-up, Fareed. This story has legs. Twenty-year-old legs, reanimated. It's a zombie. And I cannot control it."

Hussein's anger seemed to suddenly evaporate, and with it, his self-confidence. His shoulders slumped, his face gray and lined under the bright lights of the hotel room. "So what should I do?"

"That depends."

"On what?"

"On how many more unexploded mines there are, waiting to go off. I cannot plan your media strategy if you don't tell what's waiting out there, in the archives. Or not in the archives."

Hussein looked around the presidential suite while he gathered his thoughts. The suite covered a thousand square feet, with a bedroom at one end and kitchen dining area at the other. It was a symphony in shades of white: walls, curtains, furniture, ceiling. Even the painting on the wall was a shade of white. The floor was dark polished wood, covered with pale rugs. The sofas and armchairs at least were a soft shade of brown.

He walked over to the glass wall that looked out across the city to Reykjavik bay and all the way to Mount Esja. He watched a six-deck cruise ship slowly pull out of the harbor, a large part of him wishing he was on board. He could tell her, he supposed. Tell her that two documents existed. One put on the record his catastrophic failure to intervene in Rwanda, to even save the UN aid workers. Another recorded that a year later, he had tried to make a second deal behind the scenes, this time with the Bosnian Serbs, again to protect the UN's neutrality. And how, just, like in Rwanda, the Bosnian deal too had gone horribly wrong.

Hussein returned to the sofa, switched on the flat-screen

television and flipped through the news channels. Akerman's death and the files that had gone missing from the UN archives were being discussed on the BBC, Euronews, CNN, MSNBC, every news channel that he tried. He put down the remote control, picked up the list of accredited journalists and flicked through it. Roxana had spent a good part of the flight over memorizing the names and faces of reporters that she would allow to ask a question. All of them were earnest environmental reporters, completely uninterested in Akerman, Bonnet, Srebrenica, and Rwanda. "This Icelandic reporter, Rafnhildur," he asked. "Who is she? Does she have an agenda?"

Roxana shook her head. "I am as surprised as you are. I met with her first thing this morning at seven thirty, before breakfast. I suggested a softball question about the summit putting Iceland on the map that I guaranteed that you would answer. I hinted strongly that if it went well, she could have an exclusive interview with you at the end of today about the summit. She agreed!"

Hussein sank back on the sofa, exhaled slowly. Another summit, another bland, luxurious hotel room. There would not be many more, he sensed. His time on the thirty-eighth floor was coming to an end.

The murder of a UN official, his personal envoy, outside his front door, was a very clear message. He personally did not fear assassination. There was no point. It was impossible to completely protect a dignitary from a determined killer. But he did fear the destruction of everything for which he had worked, his good name and future legacy. Reykjavik was supposed to be the pinnacle of his career. The Istanbul

Summit had failed. Its vast multilateral agenda—bringing peace across the Middle East—had always been overambitious. But Reykjavik, he knew, could work. A straightforward reconciliation between two enemies whose maneuvers threatened to bring the world to the brink of war, all under the aegis of the UN. A major step toward world peace. This was to be his legacy, not the catastrophes of his time as head of peacekeeping, but now events were spinning out of control. Maybe he should give Rafnhildur that interview. Just hand over the two documents, give her the scoop of a lifetime, then sit back and watch the deluge, ending this misery of uncertainty.

But the two documents were not the worst of it. They could probably be explained away; blame shifted onto his subordinates, the wavering P5, most of all, the member states' pusillanimity. If the USA, Britain, France, any of the P5, had really wanted to prevent the genocides in Rwanda and at Srebrenica, they would have. A few battalions of ground troops in Kigali; a wave of air strikes against the Bosnian Serbs—these were all that was needed. Either way, the media storm would eventually pass. Two UN reports had officially exonerated him. The SG was supposed to execute policy, not make it—although the reality was different. The worst of it was the recording. The recording where he had discussed—permitted, authorized—the death of five hundred people. That could not be explained away. The recording at least, remained secret.

Meanwhile, he had to make a choice, a choice that could not be finessed, side-stepped, or delegated. It was his, and his alone.

Yael had told him of Rina's offer—her demand—on the flight to Reykjavik. He had lost his brother. His wife had left him. His only child had disowned him. Even Yael had not been able to get Rina back—until now, when she would reconcile but only on her terms: release the two documents about Rwanda and Srebrenica. So which would he sacrifice? His good name or his daughter?

The choice, he sensed, was being made for him. The ghosts that haunted the thirty-eighth floor, the whole of the Secretariat Building, were coming to life. The Tutsi families slaughtered at the Hutu checkpoints, the Bosnian men and boys lined up in a field, they were all rolling down the corridors, calling his name, demanding a reckoning. But why here, of all places?

Hussein said, "An Icelandic political reporter is suddenly up to speed on the inner workings of the UN archive? Who prepped her?"

"James Beaufort, maybe. Or Najwa. I will find out," said Roxana.

Hussein held his head in one hand, rubbing his eyes with the other. "It doesn't matter anymore. I have done what I could. I will resign on our return to New York."

"No, Fareed! You will not. You will stay in office, until you hear otherwise."

He looked at her with amazement. "Who are you, to threaten me? And what with?"

Roxana took out a small blue digital recorder from her pocket and pressed play.

Charles Bonnet's voice said, *"We need at least five hundred. That will have maximum impact."*

Hussein heard himself reply. "*No, no, that is unnecessary. It's far too much. A couple of hundred at most would be sufficient for our purposes. Less would suffice. Even a few dozen.*"

Yael surfaced slowly, rotating through her senses, one by one, focusing on keeping her breathing deep and even, her limbs soft and relaxed. She was sitting in a car being driven carefully, no sudden acceleration or stops. Nothing to draw the attention of the police. Her hands, tied together with a plastic cuff, rested on her lap. The thin band cut into her skin. She moved her feet, subtly, and realized they were unbound. Her fingers, too, responded.

There were two voices in the car, Eli's and a woman's. Yael opened her eyes a tiny fraction for a second. The car was a gray four-door Ford family sedan, well used, with sagging blue upholstery. A good choice, unobtrusive. The woman was driving. She had straw-blond hair and wore a black parka. Eli was sitting next to her, close enough to Yael that she could smell his Issey Miyake cologne.

"Now what?" asked the woman.

As soon as she spoke, Yael remembered her. Michal. She had had short black hair when she joined a year after Yael. She completed the course, then had never been seen again on operations. Until now. Which meant one thing: *Kidon*.

Eli continued speaking. "We go ahead as planned. Everything is in place. Once the operation is completed the United States will immediately start mobilizing to attack Iran. There will be an official declaration of war. Bombing will start in a few hours. And we go home. Mission accomplished."

"And *Motek* here?"

"Home, debrief."

"And then?"

"She will have several options. None of them involve working for the UN. Or ever leaving Israel again."

"It will be a long download," said Michal, laughing.

"Twelve years' worth," said Eli.

Michal glanced at Yael in the mirror. "Are you sure she's not awake?"

Eli reached back and opened Yael's right eye. She did not flinch, kept her breathing rhythmic. She glimpsed the outskirts of Reykjavik. The streets had turned from picturesque to drab. They were passing through a housing estate: gray box dwellings, each with a patch of green in front.

Two seconds later Eli let go of her eyelid. The housing estate disappeared. Eli continued talking. "Absolutely. It's a knockout for at least eight hours. The next time she wakes up it will be somewhere over the Mediterranean."

Salim Massoud watched Clarence Clairborne come into focus on his computer screen.

"*Sobh bekheir,* old friend. You are looking older," said Clairborne.

Massoud smiled. "That's the plan."

Clairborne stared at his computer. "Silver hair suits you. But you may need to lose a little weight."

Massoud reached inside his mouth and removed two pieces of rubber. "Better?"

"Much. The girl?"

"Like a moth to a flame. Exactly as the Israeli predicted. Out of the way and on her way home, for good."

"The statement of responsibility is written?" asked Clairborne.

"Yes. Jaysh al-Arbaeen has long arms."

Clairborne frowned. "One thing I am worried about."

"Speak freely, please."

"Menachem Stein."

Yael made tiny fluttering movements with her eyelids, as though as she was dreaming. It was enough to allow her to see inside the car and get a glimpse of the outside. They had turned off onto a side road a little while ago.

Eli had her iPhone in his hand and was flicking through the menus. Michal was focused on her driving. The road was empty, flanked on both sides by grass shoulders. Yael flexed her fingers, felt the plastic cuff bite her wrist. Eli whipped around.

She dived forward and yanked the hand brake up.

32

Magnus Olafsson and Joe-Don stood by the door to the presidential residence. The American and Iranian security teams patrolled, one on either side of the building. The horizon, streaked with gray clouds, had darkened. Wind gusted as though the sky itself was breathing in and out, dumping flurries of raindrops that splashed on the glimmering black stone road. The two groups of security officials regarded each other warily as they huddled under their ponchos, muttering into their earpieces. Their gazes swooped left and right and left again while they walked up and down the property.

"Any word yet?" asked Olafsson.

Joe-Don shook his head. "None. She said she needed to sleep. The DO NOT DISTURB sign was hanging from the handle. I checked her room. She's not there and she's not answering her phone."

"GPS?"

"Nothing. She's gone dark."

Olafsson laid a large hand on Joe-Don's shoulder. "Don't worry too much. She knows what she is doing. I'm sure she'll turn up soon. We are covered here." His radio crackled with a burst of Icelandic. "I have to check in with my police colleagues. They are parked half a kilometer away. Coming?"

"Sure," said Joe-Don, not letting his anxiety show. His own sixth sense, the one that had kept him alive through decades of war zones, told him that she was in trouble. The worst kind. Eli trouble. He looked around the flatlands as they walked to the car, as though she might suddenly appear on the tundra, or out of the sea that stretched almost to the snow-capped mountains on the horizon.

Bessastadir was only twenty minutes' drive from downtown Reykjavik, but the sense of isolation was palpable. It was a tiny settlement, a handful of buildings and a church, built on a long, thin promontory of land that poked into the Atlantic like a crooked finger. Such isolation was not rare in Iceland, but more surprising was the lack of security at the residence. The flat terrain around it was wide open, the gray-green grass, liberally spattered with seabird droppings, turning into a swampy black mud where it met the water.

A low white gate controlled vehicular access to the black stone road, but it would barely slow a family sedan, let alone a determined attacker. There were no fences or gates or flip-up barriers to stop a vehicle crashing into the building. The windows seemed to be normal glass. Overhead a helicopter swooped low, banked steeply, and then headed out to sea. With the Americans and the Iranians coordinating with the Viking Squad, the residence was ringed with well-trained, armed agents from all three countries. But the basic topography could not be changed. Bessastadir was an assassin's dream.

Olga Gunnarsdottir led her visitors through a corridor from Bessastadir's formal reception room into her personal living quarters. The family sitting room was long and narrow, with pale wooden floors and lined on two sides with crowded bookshelves that reached almost to the ceiling. The other walls, hung with old maps and lithographs of historic Iceland, were painted cream, the ceiling a darker brown. More books were piled up on one side of an antique desk. A well-worn long wooden table was flanked by a sofa on one side and half a dozen padded dining chairs on the other. It was a comfortable, lived-in space, silent but for the loud ticking of a wooden grandfather clock in the corner next to her desk.

Gunnarsdottir was a tall blond in her early sixties with shoulder-length hair, green eyes, and the brisk, no-nonsense manner on which Icelanders prided themselves. A former diplomat who had once served as Iceland's ambassador to the United Nations, she knew Fareed Hussein of old. This should have been a day of triumph for him, but she had never seen him looking so unsettled. He was normally so fastidious, but today his trademark Nehru jacket was creased, his shirt collar bent.

She had seen the television coverage of the press conference of course, and the deluge of coverage that followed. But Hussein was an experienced operator. He had been here before, knew enough about the media cycle to know that interest in the fate of Akerman's UNMO reports, indeed in that of Akerman himself, would soon fade away. So why was he looking so worried?

For now, though, she had more important matters on which to concentrate. Gunnarsdottir gestured at the table. "Please, make yourselves comfortable," she instructed, as she took the seat at the head.

President Freshwater sat on one side, Shireen Kermanzade on the other. Dave Reardon stood by the wall, tense and alert, his eyes sweeping the room. Freshwater was dressed in a dark blue business suit and white blouse that accentuated her dark hair and eyes. She wore silver earrings and a simple silver necklace with a black stone. Kermanzade was older, her dark brown hair graying. She wore her trademark green and gold headscarf, pulled far back from her forehead and a white high-necked blouse buttoned to the top. The two women, Gunnarsdottir was pleased to see, seemed at ease with each other. Kermanzade had waved away her security detail, asking them to stay outside the room.

"There is no written agenda for what happens next," said Gunnarsdottir, "but let me say how pleased and honored I am that you both"—she looked at Freshwater and Kermanzade—"have chosen my country to announce a historic reconciliation that will change the face of not just the Middle East, but the world in which we all live."

President Freshwater gestured to her Iranian counterpart that she should reply.

"Thank you, Madam President," said Kermanzade, her voice light and musical.

Gunnarsdottir smiled. "Please, call me Olga. You are guests in my house."

Kermanzade seemed about to continue when a phone rang inside Gunnarsdottir's purse. She pulled out the handset, looked at the number, and took the call. "*Ja, ja*, yes, yes. *Nu*, now? OK." She hung up. "Ladies and gentlemen, I am sure there is nothing to be alarmed about," she said, her face drawn and tense.

Yael pulled harder on the hand brake with all her strength, her cuffed hands locked onto the grip as the car instantly decelerated. Suddenly deprived of its forward momentum, the vehicle skidded round and round, the G-forces throwing Eli and Michal—neither of whom were wearing seatbelts—against the wall and the windows, giving Yael a second's advantage. She knew what was coming. She used the hand brake to stabilize herself, pushed her knees against the side of the front seats, ducked low and braced herself. The front of the car careened into a tree and bounced off, sending the vehicle into a spin. Michal flew forward, her head smashing against the windshield, which shattered.

Eli went sideways, crashing into Michal. He tried to sit up but the car was still sliding across the road and he fell forward. Yael, shaken but unhurt, looked up to see Michal unconscious, blood streaming from a gash above her right eyebrow. Eli spun around so he was facing Yael and flailed at her with his right fist. She dodged the blow, let go of the hand brake, moved under Eli's arm and opened her palms as far as she could. She drove both her thumbs up into Eli's eye sockets, feeling the bone against her fingers as she pushed hard under the orbs. He yelped in pain and fell away. Yael slid back and kicked him hard in the stomach, slamming him back against the dashboard. The car's spins slowed, then stopped, and it came to rest on a grass shoulder at the side of the road.

Eli sat back, panting hard, holding his hands over his eyes. "*Kusemmak*, fuck your mother, what have you done to me?"

"You'll survive. And so will your eyesight."

She glanced at Michal, who slowly stirred and moaned. Yael swung her arms around to grab Michal's hair and banged her head, once, hard against the steering wheel. She slumped forward. Then Yael reached across to the broken windshield and rapidly sawed the plastic cuff around her hands against a sharp edge of glass. The cuffs sprung apart. She reached inside Michal's coat and took out a Jericho 941 pistol, slipping the gun into her own jacket pocket. She pulled out a plastic cuff from her left boot, wrapped it around Michal's limp wrists, pulled it tight. She reached across to the door handle, opened it, then sat back and put her foot against Michal's thigh and pushed. Michal hit the ground on her side and lay still.

The second Yael's back was turned, Eli reached inside the left shoulder of his jacket to draw his own Jericho 941. But she saw him in the driver's mirror, spun around, and grabbed the barrel of the gun with both hands, forcing it upward. Eli fired twice, the sound thunderous inside the vehicle as the two bullets pierced the roof. The last time she had seen Eli, five days ago on Thursday night in Tompkins Square Park, his hand had been bandaged. The bandage was gone now, but she could feel that he still lacked full strength.

Now she had the advantage. She twisted her hands sideways. Either he would release the gun, or his fingers would break.

He let go.

She slipped her finger into the Jericho's trigger guard and pointed it at Eli, while she closed the car door with her left hand.

He laughed. "You kept the antidote. Clever."

Yael shrugged. "Not really. You are just predictable."

"So are you." He blinked several times, rubbed his eyes. "Now I can see you properly. Another gun? You won't use it," Eli said mockingly. "You couldn't shoot me in Istanbul. You can't shoot me here. You can't shoot me anywhere, Motek. Come home, and we'll make babies."

Sensing movement outside the car, she did not answer, instead glancing at the road while still holding Eli's pistol in her right hand, keeping it trained on him. Michal had stood up. She was unsteady on her feet but was now rummaging inside her jacket for her gun.

"*Ze po*, it's here," murmured Yael, her left hand sliding inside her jacket and taking out Michal's pistol.

Eli laughed. "You look like a cowboy, Motek."

"Shut up, Eli," said Yael.

She fired once, swiveled round at Michal, fired again.

Najwa checked her watch. It was just coming up to five o'clock. She glanced at Harald Ingmarsson, the Icelandic president's press secretary. *What now?*

He smiled back. "I'm sorry. They are running late. I'm sure it will only be a few more minutes."

They were waiting in Bessasstadir's formal reception

room that looked out over the surrounding flatlands. A chandelier hung from the ceiling, its thick wooden beams painted off-white. The cream-colored walls were covered with bright, impressionistic works by Icelandic artists. The furniture was old-fashioned, but elegant: two pale blue sofas with thin, gilded arms and legs; a green marble-topped coffee table; a dark wooden kitchen dresser, its shelves filled with glasses and porcelain; an oval side table with a black granite top. Rafnhildur sat on one sofa and her camerawoman, Ingilin, sat on the other, checking the settings on her camera. Two minutes ago sunlight had been streaming through the long windows, falling on the patterned carpet and the polished wooden floor. Now the sun had disappeared behind a wall of clouds and the rain had started again, the wind lashing the drops against the windows.

Najwa smiled for a moment, remembering the local joke, "Don't worry if you don't like the weather, it will change in twenty minutes." But that was not enough to damp down her growing feeling of unease. She, Rafnhildur, and Ingilin, a petite blond in her late twenties, were the only reporters at Bessastadir. They had been promised brief, but exclusive, interviews with all three presidents and the SG about the Sustainability Summit. The topic was not very exciting, but her New York editors had been very enthusiastic about Freshwater and Kermanzade appearing together. Najwa knew she was guaranteed airtime. But where were they? Presidents were almost always late but there was something not quite right here. She watched Harald Ingmarsson stare at his watch again, his face creased with worry.

Najwa walked over to the array of framed pictures on

the wooden sideboard and picked up a photograph showing President Gunnarsdottir on top of a mountain, with her arm around a blond woman of a similar age. Both wore matching all-in-one ski suits and hiking boots.

"Who's this?" she asked.

Rafnhildur looked up from her smartphone. "Eva. Olga's partner."

"A gay president. Very progressive."

"Is it?" said Rafnhildur. "It's quite normal here. Nobody cares who you sleep with."

"And everyone calls her Olga?"

"That's her name. What else would we call her?"

"Madam President? President Gunnarsdottir?"

Harald laughed. "We are not very big on formality."

"Wait," said Najwa. "Can you hear that?"

Rafnhildur tilted her head to one side. "It sounds like people moving around outside. Must be the security teams."

Najwa shook her head. "Not that. There's something else. Popping sounds."

Yael looked through the car window to where Michal lay on the ground, her cuffed hands clutching her leg.

It took a second for Eli to realize that the first bullet had passed through the shattered windshield and he had not been shot.

He lunged at Yael.

She instantly raised the gun in her right hand and used the stock as a club, swinging it against the side of his head as he moved toward her. Delivered hard and fast enough, it was a blow that could kill, but at the last second she pulled the blow. Eli dodged away and the gun stock only glanced against his head. Still, he slumped down against the car seat, his eyes rolling, panting erratically.

Yael lowered the gun in her left hand, about to check him, when Eli's hand shot out for the pistol, yanking it from her hand.

They sat facing each other, each of them pointing a gun.

Eli smiled, breathing regularly now, his manner calm and focused. "Fooled you. You always were too soft, Motek."

Yael stared at him for a moment, her mind racing. Eli was right about her being too soft. But not today. She softened her face, and her voice. "Were you serious?"

"About what?"

She put her pistol down on the car seat. "Having children," she said, sliding closer.

Eli glanced at the weapon, and his hard face relaxed for a moment. "Yes. Especially after last Friday." His gun moved, barely perceptibly, but downward. "Come home with me."

Yael instantly grabbed the grip in one hand, the muzzle with other, and twisted the weapon sideways. With the gun now free of Eli's hand she rammed the weapon upward into his jaw. He slumped backward.

She opened the car door and pushed Eli out. He crumpled on the ground near Michal. She retrieved the second plastic cuff from her boot and jumped out after him. She bound his hands together, laid him on his side, and bent over Michal. The Israeli woman was shivering, her face contorted in pain.

The bullet had clipped her thigh and passed through the flesh, as Yael had intended. The wound was seeping blood but no artery had been severed. Michal's bag lay nearby, a small black nylon rucksack, which Yael knew would include a medical kit. She looked inside and found a field dressing and a bandage. She stood over Michal, holding the dressing. "I remember you."

"And me you." Michal's eyes radiated hatred. "The golden girl. The magician."

"That's me. And you, the late entrant, a few years older than the rest of us. Determined to show that you could keep up. Do you want this?"

Michal nodded, her face rigid with pain.

"Phone," said Yael.

"It's gone. It must have fallen out in the car. Look for it there."

Yael said nothing and turned on her heel. A black handset lay on the road, and she picked it up. It was narrow and heavy, a special model she knew was made by an Israeli manufacturer. Protected by a biometric lock, it could only be opened with a combination of a fingertip and an alphanumeric password.

She glanced at Eli, who was still semiconscious. She rifled through his clothes until she found her iPhone and his telephone, an identical model to Michal's. Then she stood up and walked back to Michal, whose face was pale and covered with sweat. Yael handed Michal her phone.

"Unlock it," Yael ordered.

"Do it yourself."

Yael showed Michal the field dressing in the palm of her hand, turned, and started to walk away.

"OK, OK," shouted Michal.

Michal placed her right index finger over a pad on the front of the phone and tapped out a six-digit code. The handset lit up. She gave it to Yael.

Yael dialed 112. "I wish to report a shooting. One person wounded, another unconscious. Where are we? Hold on, I can give you the exact GPS coordinates." She read a series of numbers from the screen. "Thank you. We need an ambulance, urgently. Please hurry."

She put the phone under the car's right front wheel and kneeled down by Michal. Yael pressed the dressing against the wound, bound it tight in place with a bandage.

"Played for a fool for a decade," said Michal, her face contorted with pain. "How does that feel?"

Yael smiled. Beyond Michal's agony and fury there was something else in her eyes. "Not as bad as unrequited love. Sharing extreme danger, hotels, bathrooms, meals, almost everything a couple does, except one thing. The thing you wanted most of all."

"Fuck you."

"Yes," said Yael. "He did. And very well."

Yael stood up. She placed Eli's phone under the left front wheel and got into the driver's seat. She looked in the side mirror. Eli was stirring, but there was no need to run him over. Just a quick back and forth across his feet, and Michal's, would ensure that they would not be able to come after her for a long time.

Assuming that the car still worked. The vehicle had slowed right down by the time it hit the tree. The front bumper was bent inward but seemed to have absorbed most of the impact.

Yael turned the ignition key. Nothing happened. She tried several times more and eventually the engine started. She slipped the car into gear. It jumped forward and there was a crunching noise. She felt the wheels jolt as they crushed the phones. She saw Eli again in the mirror. He was definitely waking up now, puzzled as to why he could not move properly. The crunching noise continued. Yael swallowed, took a deep breath, and put the car into reverse. As she touched her foot to the accelerator, the car flew backward. She stared at Eli in the mirror and the look of disbelief on his face as the car raced towards him. A couple of yards from Eli's legs she touched the brakes, yanked the steering wheel and skidded around him. She rammed the gearshift into first, spun the steering round again, and drove away as fast as she could.

The crunching noise was getting louder. She glanced in the rearview mirror to see smoke trailing from the exhaust pipe. She switched the radio on. A male voice was reading what sounded like the news. She could not understand the sentences but could hear the words "Freshwater," "Kermanzade," "Fareed Hussein," and "Bessastadir." Then she heard her own name, several times. A siren wailed in the distance.

33

The popping stopped. Najwa looked through the window and instantly stepped away and to the side. Four bodies lay prone, crimson streaks mixing with the rainwater trickling off their ponchos. A heavyset man wearing a dark blue suit walked slowly up to each one. He carried a pistol with a silencer attached, and quickly fired it once into each of their backs. One by one, the bodies twitched and lay still.

Najwa felt sick with fear. Fear and guilt. Forewarned of a potential murder on Friday, she had said nothing. The sniper had almost claimed another victim, she had another exclusive. She was playing with people's lives for the sake of her career. And now, it seemed, it was payback time.

Harald turned toward her, about to speak, when the door opened. Kent Maxwell stepped inside, his gun in his hand, his suit jacket and trousers dark with rain.

"What's happening?" Harald jumped up and strode toward him, his eyes wide.

Maxwell raised his gun. "This."

That sound again, louder now. The back of Harald's

head exploded. He flew backward, hitting the wall by the door, sliding to the floor as bone fragments, blood, and gray jelly oozed down the wall behind him.

Najwa froze for a second, beat back the urge to vomit. She had been under fire, in Iraq, Lebanon, Gaza; seen bodies freshly killed or stinking and bloated in the heat, ravaged by torture, hands tied behind their backs, buried in shallow graves. But they were dead before she got there. She had never witnessed executions a few yards from where she was standing, then another in front of her. And witnesses were not usually allowed to live. She thought of her sister, Fatima, for a moment. It was night now in Jeddah, she would be fast asleep in her luxurious home. She was a prisoner in all but name. But she would be alive in the morning.

Najwa's hands were clenched so tightly her nails almost drew blood. She forced herself to breathe. Ingilin sat rigid with terror. Rafnhildur bent double, coughing and spitting, her half-digested breakfast hanging from her mouth as the sour smell of vomit wafted across the room.

Maxwell lowered his gun. He glanced at the three journalists one by one, as if checking they were still there. He needed something from them. Something that, for now at least, would keep them alive. He gestured with the pistol at Najwa. "You are on screen. OK?"

Najwa nodded.

He turned to Ingilin. Her eyes were blank. "You good to film?"

Ingilin did not reply.

Maxwell jabbed her leg with the pistol. "I asked you something. Or do I need to find someone else?"

Her head bobbed up and down like a children's toy woodpecker. "Good. I'm good."

Finally, he pointed the gun at Rafnhildur. The Icelandic journalist wiped her mouth as she stared at Ingmarsson's body. She swallowed hard, her shoulders shaking, tears trickling down her face. Najwa instantly understood: Harald had been her lover.

"You produce," said Maxwell. Rafnhildur did not answer. He fired twice into the ceiling. The noise was much louder as the bullets hit the ceiling, spraying the room with chips of plaster. The Icelandic journalist flinched.

Maxwell pointed his gun again at Rafnhildur. "Are you with us? Because if you aren't you can join your friend over there," he said, gesturing at Harald's body.

"Sure. I'm here," said Rafnhildur, nodding and shaking.

Maxwell walked toward the door. He pushed Harald's corpse aside with his foot. "Now *get moving*. You are live in five minutes."

Yael drove Eli's car as fast as she could on the long straight road toward Bessastadir. The tundra was empty on either side, the stubby grass rippling in the wind. Rain gusted inside the car, spattering the dashboard, her clothes and face. The crunching noise faded in and out, but was definitely getting louder. She kept one hand on the steering wheel as she tried calling Joe-Don again. Nothing. Not even a message in Icelandic saying that the call had failed. No reception bars showed on the screen. And then she remembered: her iPhone was protected by a ten-digit alphanumeric PIN. After three wrong attempts the handset locked. Eli must have tried to get in.

Thunder boomed, rolling across the flatlands like distant artillery. The sky turned nearly black as the clouds opened. Scattered raindrops became an instant deluge, the road sodden before the water could run off the sides and into the squishy mud. The car almost skidded, and Yael's face was drenched as the wind hurled the water through the broken windshield. She could barely see fifty yards in front.

She slowed down to twenty miles an hour, steering with the sides of her knees, and entered the iPhone's PIN plus a six-digit correction code. It lit up, and she was about to try Joe-Don when she saw a new welcome screen with a text message:

Hello, Motek.

The iPhone was useless, hacked by Eli. She dropped it on the passenger seat. But at least she still had the Nokia. Putting one hand back on the steering wheel, Yael reached around to her calf and pulled away the adhesive tape. The dark blue candy bar phone felt tiny in her hand after her iPhone, but at least it was switched on and had five bars of reception. There was only one number programmed in: Joe-Don's. She pressed CALL. Nothing happened. She pressed the call button again.

"Come *on*," she hissed aloud with frustration. She held the phone away from her ear and stared at the screen. The car swerved slightly and she quickly righted it. A ringing noise began. Yael exhaled with relief and she clamped the phone back to her left ear. The ringing stopped. Eli's voice said:

"Hello, Motek."

Yael slammed the Nokia onto the dashboard so hard it cracked, threw it onto the backseat, and checked the car's GPS. She was approaching Álftanesvegur, the main road along the peninsula, which eventually turned sharp right onto Bessastadavegur. That was the only access route to the presidential residence. There would certainly be a police checkpoint there. They would hold and detain her, at first for her own safety, for much longer when they found Eli and Michal. She would have no chance of getting into Bessastadir.

She checked in the rearview and side mirrors. There was a single car on the road behind her, a light blue Lada Niva four-wheel drive. It had been behind her for some time, always keeping a steady distance. There was nowhere to turn off. A threat, or a contact? She slowed down, put on the hazard flashers, and parked on the side of the road. Then, checking that one pistol was safe in her jacket pocket and the other tucked into her rear waistband, resting against the small of her back, she got out of the car, stepped into the road and flagged down the Lada.

It slowed, pulled over to the side of the road, then stopped. Even at a distance the driver looked familiar.

"Please get in, ma'am," said Michael Ortega. "I'm here to help."

Yael stared at him in disbelief. What was her doorman doing here? And who was he working for? She looked inside the Lada and hesitated for a moment as she considered her options. Her car was very obviously damaged in a crash and about to die. Her name was being mentioned in news broadcasts. The police would soon be after her, probably already were. Eli doubtless had a backup team somewhere nearby. The Lada Niva was bland and unremarkable, the sort of car that locals took off-road on the weekends. Ortega was an army veteran. If he wanted to shoot her, he would have done already. He was alone in the vehicle, had neither brandished a weapon nor asked for hers. She climbed in, sat in the front seat. Ortega glanced at her for a moment, said nothing as the car pulled away.

Yael watched the bare landscape go by for a minute or so, the rain pattering against the windows, her right hand holding the Jericho in her pocket. If nothing else, it was a pleasure to sit in a car with an intact windshield. The radio was on, tuned to a local news channel, she guessed. A GPS mounted near the rearview mirror showed their location on Altnesvegur.

Yael took out the Jericho and pointed it at him. "Explain."

Ortega glanced at her, kept his hands on the steering wheel. "No need for that, ma'am. You're safe now."

"Drop the *ma'am*. Who sent you, why are you here, and what do you want?"

She stared at him, focused but calm. Michael Ortega. Last seen on Friday evening on the corner of West Eighty-First and Riverside Drive, hailing a taxi for Yael and her mother to take them to the KZX reception. Three days later, here he was on Altnesvegur. A memory flashed through her mind: she had sensed a strange current between Ortega and Barbara, a glance, the subtlest of nods. At the time she had thought no more of it. Now he had the soldier's look: wired, ready for action, but under control. The pieces began to fall into place.

Ortega said, "I was told to keep an eye on you, make sure you are safe."

"You've been following me? Since when?"

Ortega smiled. "Since I was told to watch your back."

Yael pushed Jericho's muzzle against Ortega's temple. "How long is that?"

Ortega winced. "Around a month. As I said, I'm here to help. Really."

Yael did a rapid mental calculation. A month ago Michael Ortega had been living under the Soldiers' and Sailors' Monument on Riverside Drive, a couple of blocks from her apartment. She looked in the rearview mirror, the passenger side mirror, then ahead. The road behind them was deserted, the road ahead also empty, wet tundra leading away on both sides, the wind gusting over the stubby grass.

She kept the gun against Ortega's temple. "Who. Sent. You?" she asked again, although she already had a good idea what the answer was.

Ortega started to reply when the radio announcer suddenly broke off midsentence. A second of silence followed, a burst of Icelandic, the words "Al-Jazeera" and "Bessastadir." The broadcast switched to English.

A male voice said, "Najwa, this is Faisal at Al-Jazeera in Washington. You are live, broadcasting on television and simultaneously on the Internet. Najwa, where are you and what is happening?"

Yael listened hard. Najwa. Whatever this was, it was not good. She glanced at Ortega's face. It was remarkably calm, considering there was a gun pointed at his head. He was not a threat, she decided. For the next the few minutes at least, which was enough. Yael put the gun back in her pocket and turned up the volume.

"Thank you," said Ortega.

Najwa said, "I am here at Bessastadir, the residence of the president of Iceland. The presidents of Iceland, the United States, and Iran have been taken hostage, together with Fareed Hussein, the secretary-general of the United Nations. We are in the front reception room of the residence, in the same room as the hostages and the captors. I can confirm that all four are alive and are unharmed. However, at least three members of President Freshwater's security detail have been killed, together with Harald Ingmarsson, President Gunnarsdottir's press secretary."

A male American voice interrupted her. "No location or security details."

Yael recognized him immediately: Kent Maxwell. Maxwell was a traitor, doubtless bought off. But Maxwell was a foot soldier, not a general. Who was running the operation? She had to get to Bessastadir immediately. Hostages. Dead bodies. A war in the making. This was her world. She felt the dark hunger, familiar, almost exhilarating, course through her. But first she needed to see herself what was happening. She turned to Ortega. "You have a smartphone?"

He reached inside the door compartment, handed Yael an iPhone. Yael quickly went online and found Al-Jazeera's website. The station was running the same live feed from Bessastadir as the Icelandic radio station. Najwa was speaking to camera from Bessastadir. There was no sign of Fareed or the presidents. Yael switched off the radio and turned up the volume on the iPhone.

Najwa's voice could be heard. "OK. Understood."

Faisal asked, "Najwa, are you safe and well?"

"I am fine, but I am also being held hostage, together with my Icelandic colleagues Rafnhildur Eriksdottir and Ingilin Sigisdottir."

"Najwa, can you tell us who has captured you and what do they want?"

"Yes, Faisal. Jaysh al-Arbaeen, the Army of Forty, the same group which claimed responsibility for the car bomb found last week in Washington, DC. We don't yet know what they want. I am not in a position to speculate."

Maxwell's voice said, "Stop talking. Camera—right corner."

Yael stared at the phone screen as the camera moved across the room. The three presidents and Fareed Hussein were gagged and plasti-cuffed to gilt chairs, Freshwater back-to-back with Kermanzade and Hussein with Gunnarsdottir. The chairs had been tied together. A block of plastic explosive was in Fareed Hussein's lap. The attached timer showed 19 minutes and 53 seconds, counting down steadily. Hussein trembled, his face pale. Dave Reardon sat a few feet away, blood seeping down the side of his neck from a gash on his forehead. His arms were wrapped around his legs, his wrists plasti-cuffed to his ankles.

"Fuck," said Yael.

Ortega looked at her. "How bad is it?"

"As bad as it gets. They are tied together. Fareed is wired. There's a timer. Nineteen minutes. How far out are we?"

Ortega glanced at the GPS. "Five miles or so."

"Speed up."

Ortega put his foot down. The Lada was built for clambering up dirt tracks, not racing down wet motorways. The wind buffeted the vehicle as it hit eighty miles an hour, then nudged ninety.

Yael looked back at the iPhone screen.

"Najwa, our thoughts are very much with you," Faisal said. "What do the terro—Jaysh al-Arbaeen actually want?"

"They have not issued any demands. However, our captors have made it clear that any attempt to storm the residence or free the hostages will result in the bomb being detonated. As will any helicopter overflights or the appearance of any vehicles within one kilometer. They say they have the residence completely surrounded. There are . . ."

Maxwell raised his hand. "Enough. I told you, no details."

The screen split, one half showing the scene at Bessastadir, the other the Al-Jazeera studio in Washington, DC.

Now Yael understood. Eli and Michal were a diversion, tasked with getting Yael out of the way and taking her back to Israel. There was no Kidon team here, and there did not need to be. The threat was already inside the residence. It always had been. Kent Maxwell, taking care of the Americans. The silver-haired Iranian and his team were not Kermanzade's security detail, either. They were the threat. For a moment she was back at Patsy's Pizzeria on Second Avenue, with Joe-Don.

Yael stares closer at the photograph of the Iranian man. She points at the side of his right eyebrow where an inch or so of skin was ridged and puckered. "What's that?"

Joe-Don looks down. "A scar, from the Iran-Iraq war. He was a commando. Three of his brothers were killed. He is the last one of his family. Apart from his son."

The plump, silver-haired man she had seen at the Hotel Borg meeting was not really plump, nor did he have silver hair. He was Salim Massoud.

Ortega glanced at Yael. "What now?"

Yael said, "How many phones have you got?"

"Three. One iPhone, two burners."

Yael held out her hand. "Give me a burner, please." A plan was forming in her mind. She called Joe-Don, his number memorized, and this time it went through. He answered, and she sagged with relief as she spoke.

"Tell me you are not here," he said. "Tell me you just got back to the hotel with some new additions to your shoe collection."

Yael looked at her Timberland boots, caked with mud and bird shit. "That's next. Meanwhile, I'm heading your way."

"Don't do that. *Turn around*. There is a major terrorist incident here."

"I know. I just saw Najwa on the net. She looked pretty calm, considering."

"It's the scoop of a lifetime. If she lives to tell it. Fareed is wired. If he goes, they all die."

"I saw. Where are you?"

"Go back to the hotel."

"You know I won't. And you really don't want me blundering around the site of a major terrorist incident without your help."

"Hotel. You are not needed. They are mustering the Marines from the embassy. And what's left of Freshwater's Secret Service detail. The Viking Squad are giving them a chopper."

"What use is that? They'll blow the hostages to bits as soon as they hear it."

"Hotel." Joe-Don sounded less convinced each time he said the word.

"Either I find you or I force you to come shoe-shopping with me."

"This is it. The last time."

Yael smiled. "You and me. Promise."

"The road to Bessastadir is blocked by two Icelandic police cars. I'm sitting in one next to Magnus."

"On my way," said Yael, and hung up.

Next she needed a phone number. She tapped out a text message, added the prefix +90 697 before the number and pressed send. The Lada slowed down and she looked up to see that their car was approaching a roundabout. The turn-off on the right, to Bessastadir, was blocked by a line of police cars, their blue lights flashing under the darkening sky. Yael grabbed the GPS and expanded the digital map. The road ahead and to the left both led to housing estates.

They were almost at the roundabout when Ortega asked, "Where to?"

Now she had a chauffeur, it seemed. "Left at the crossroads." Ortega may not be a threat, but she still needed to understand what was happening here.

Ortega did as he was instructed, and they drove for two minutes.

"Left again," said Yael.

Ortega turned onto a side road leading to a housing estate. There were no other moving vehicles or people around.

"Pull over, please," said Yael.

He parked by the side of the building. The phone beeped. She checked the message. The number started with +90 697. The text was two letters, SM, followed by a series of numbers. The phone beeped again. A photograph this time. She opened the picture file: Istanbul's shoreline sparkled in the summer sunshine.

She smiled, for a moment thought of Yusuf, the way his black hair fell over his forehead. Soon, told herself. She forced herself to focus, and put the phone in her pocket. Her fingers curled around the Jericho. In an instant the barrel was pushing against the side of Ortega's head.

He winced, his face twisted in pain. "There's really no need—"

"I'll decide that. Was it you?" she asked. "In my apartment, the tell on the coffee table?"

"Yes."

"Who sent you?"

"Clairborne."

"Why?"

"To bug your place."

"So why didn't you?"

"Because someone else told me not to. Someone even scarier."

"Who?"

"I think you know that."

"I like you, Michael. Something tells me I can even trust you. That's why I got you the job as a doorman. And that's why you are still alive." Yael pushed the gun barrel harder against Ortega's head. "But don't get cute. *Who*?"

This time he did not flinch. "Your father."

34

Kent Maxwell ripped the duct tape from President Freshwater's mouth and held a sheet of paper in front of her.

"What is this?" she demanded. A trickle of blood seeped from her upper lip.

"Our demands. You are going to read them on television."

Freshwater stared at him, her black eyes pulsing with fury, her body straining against her bonds. "You are a traitor. You will be taken alive. You will be put on trial. You will spend the rest of your life in a super-max prison with no visitors and the lights on in your bare, concrete ten feet by seven feet cell twenty-four hours a day."

Maxwell smiled. "Read them, Madam President. Practice the sentences. Know the words, so you don't stumble when the world is watching."

She spat on the paper. Saliva and blood trickled down onto Maxwell's shoe.

Maxwell turned slightly. He pointed his gun at Dave

Reardon and pulled the trigger. Reardon slammed backward, his face contorting in agony, his ankle shattered.

Freshwater turned pale. "Bastard," she said, her voice shaking.

Maxwell smiled. "The choice is yours. Read and we will get a medic to treat his foot. Refuse and I will shoot the other one. Then his knees."

"Give me the paper," she said.

Maxwell put the sheet on her lap. He gestured at Najwa and Ingilin. "Camerawoman, over here please. We are back on air."

Ortega's news was no great revelation to Yael. She had sensed her father's presence recently: in her apartment, perhaps in Central Park, on the roof of the bazaar in Istanbul. Her father, she was sure, had shot the gun out of Eli's hand while he was chasing her. Nor was it a coincidence that her mother had reappeared in her life. "Is he here, in Iceland?" she asked.

"I don't know," replied Ortega. Yael pushed the gun back against his head. His eyes widened in alarm. "Really. I don't know. Probably. He is a ghost. He appears, disappears, reappears. Can you put that down, please?"

A ghost. It was as good a description of her father as any. Yael glanced in the rearview mirror. There were no other cars passing by or entering the housing estate. If Ortega wanted to kill her he would have done it by now. He couldn't kidnap her on his own. Clairborne would have sent a team, in multiple vehicles. Who else would have sent him but her father? She lowered the Jericho. Ortega exhaled with relief.

Yael stared across the road. A white split-level villa stood surrounded by a well-maintained garden. The walls were freshly painted, the windows shining. She could see inside the kitchen, a packet of breakfast cereal still on the table. Two cars were parked in the drive, and a children's bicycle lay on its side on the path. Normality. Meals eaten in company. Holidays. Trips to the beach. What did her father want? And why was he back now?

Yael picked up Ortega's phone, glanced again at the number on the screen. "I need to get into Bessastadir."

"It's sealed off. They have boats patrolling the coast, police on every road. How are you going to do that?"

"Through the front door," said Yael, as she dialed a number.

Salim Massoud watched the Iranian agent with hooded eyes skillfully apply a dressing to Reardon's foot, tie it in place with a fresh bandage, and give him a morphine shot. The American sat on the floor, leaning back against the wall. His forehead was still beaded with sweat but he had stopped shaking. He would die soon, like all of them, but not from his wound.

Massoud then looked at the three journalists. All were as composed as could be expected. Forcing them to broadcast from inside the residence kept them busy, focused their minds and stopped their imaginations from running wild. He looked at the clock on the bomb strapped to Fareed Hussein's chest. Fourteen minutes and seven seconds.

Maxwell turned to Ingilin. "Freshwater." She nodded and moved the camera toward the president. He looked at Rafnhildur. "Are we good to go?" Rafnhildur nodded. "Live in ten."

Massoud nodded at Maxwell. The demands were irrelevant, a diversion. The point was to have Freshwater calmly looking at the camera when it happened, live on global television. She would read them every five minutes. At least the end would be instantaneous. Unlike the Sunni barbarians and their beheadings.

Maxwell was tense, sweating, kept glancing at the clock on the bomb, Massoud saw. He had believed Massoud's promise of a negotiated passage, of a speedboat to a waiting freighter and five million dollars in a numbered account in the Cayman Islands. There was no speedboat and no freighter. This was a one-way trip. The money was real, however, but it would soon be returned to its source, a subaccount of Nuristan Holdings. War would be inevitable, and with it, the toppling of Kermanzade's government. Massoud was proud to be a martyr for his faith. His family traced its lineage back to the battle of Karbala. He had no fear of joining his ancestors. His only regrets were that he was leaving his son behind, and that he would not see the new Islamic order arise again in his homeland.

Rafnhildur had begun the countdown when Massoud's phone rang.

Massoud frowned. Nobody had this number except Clairborne and a handful of people in Tehran, all of whom knew not to call in the middle of an ongoing operation. He looked at the screen. *Unknown number.*

He took the call. "Yes?"

"Salim Massoud?"

"Who is this? How did you get this number?"

"I think you want to talk to me."

Massoud's tone changed as he recognized Yael's voice. "About what?"

"Farzad."

"No," said Joe-Don. "No, no, and no."

Yael watched the emotions play out: anger, exasperation, flashes of something much softer. She was sitting in the rear passenger seat of the police car next to him, with Magnus in front. The vehicle was one of two parked across the black stone road in a V-shape, the edges of their front bumpers touching, the blue lights on the roof slowly turning.

She looked out of the window for a moment. The sky was still almost black, the rain hurling against the windshield, thin tendrils of water draining down the glass. She handed Ortega's iPhone to Joe-Don. Its screen showed Al-Jazeera's news feed, and the channel was now broadcasting nonstop from the residence. The camera showed the four hostages sideways on, still sitting in their chairs, bound together. Fareed Hussein sat staring, as though oblivious of the bomb on his lap. The timer showed 12:57, the seconds ticking down. Freshwater remained straight-backed. Kermanzade and Gunnarsdottir stared ahead, as though determined to show no emotion.

Yael took Joe-Don's hand in hers, his skin rough and callused against hers. "You knew what was coming. That sooner or later we would need to use the tape of Farzad. That's why you hacked it from Clairborne's computer and gave it to me. He is our only chance. I'll be in and out in an hour. Then we can all go home."

"And I am responsible for your safety," he responded. "Which is why you are not stepping out of this car and are staying at least five hundred yards from the residence." Joe-Don reached between the seats and pressed the central locking button. The locks thunked.

She leaned forward and pressed the same button. The doors unlocked. "Magnus?" she said.

The Icelander held a detailed map of Bessastadir over the steering wheel, his knuckles white. "This is a catastrophe. Three of mine and five American Secret Service agents dead. Half of them killed by their Iranian counterparts and the rest by Kent Maxwell. Three presidents and the secretary-general of the United Nations held hostage. At Bessastadir. Live on the Internet. All on my watch."

"If I don't go in, what other options are there?" asked Yael.

"Not many, I am afraid," Olafsson replied. "Karin is the nearest, but she is two hundred and fifty yards away and cannot do anything on her own. There is a fifty-yard stretch of no-man's-land before the terrorists' perimeter around the house. They have lookouts checking the roads, the beaches, and the shore. All armed. We have boats patrolling, but cannot land nearby. The residence has a clear view for miles around, which means a clear field of fire out as well as in. We cannot come in by helicopter. The terrorists are on a suicide mission. So is anyone who walks into that place."

They all knew that Yael's plan was the only option. And that time was rapidly running out.

Yael checked herself in the rearview mirror. Eyes clear. No makeup. Skin still wet from the rain. Pale, but not sickly. She looked at Joe-Don, a half smile playing on her lips, the adrenalin flowing. "Farzad is our only chance. You know it. I know it."

"So does Massoud," said Joe-Don. "What if it's a trap?"

She shrugged. "They've got what they want. Four high-value targets. The whole world is watching. I don't add very much. And he wants to talk. He wants his son back. The sooner I am in, sooner we are done."

The wind sent a fresh flurry of rain against the car windows. Yael took out both her pistols and her phone and handed them to Joe-Don.

"Ankle holster?" he asked. "Ceramic knife?"

"Nothing. You know how thoroughly they will frisk me. And send the sound file to Ortega's phone."

Joe-Don nodded, leaned toward her, suddenly uncertain. Yael hugged him, briefly.

Olaffson grimaced and shook his head. "I will radio to Karin."

"Thanks," Yael said, as she opened the car door.

Yael stepped out of the police car and began walking. The sky was dark with dense gray clouds. The wind howled and groaned across the empty grassland, thick with salt and the smell of the sea, buffeting her from side to side so hard she could barely walk. The black stone road was slick with rain, its tiny cobbles glistening. She could see Karin standing by the side of the road wearing a green parka.

Karin watched Yael approach, and quickly hugged her when she arrived. "*Fara med Gudi*, go with God," she whispered in Yael's ear.

Yael continued walking until the first Iranian security guard came into view. He was tall, at least six feet, with a long, curved nose. He wore a black rain cape, the Glock pistol in his hand tracking Yael as she came toward him. Her senses were turbocharged, her skin prickling from the rain, the adrenalin burning away her fear as the shrieks and caws of the seabirds carried on the wind. Bessastadir loomed ahead, first the steeple of the small church and then the pristine white wall and red-tiled roof of the presidential residence, ringed by more men in black rain capes.

The man with the Glock gestured to her that she should follow him. She counted six bodies lying on the ground outside the house, two Icelanders and four Americans. Two more Iranians in capes stood by the front door, but they stepped aside as the tall man escorted Yael forward. She stepped into the residence, and he gestured for her to take her coat off. He frisked her briskly, thoroughly, professionally: armpits, small of the back, ankles, even behind her ears. A few seconds later the door at the end of the corridor opened.

"Hello, Ms. Azoulay," said Salim Massoud. "Come with me, please."

35

The Iranian guard made to follow Yael, but Massoud shook his head and waved him off. She walked after Massoud alone, through the house to the lounge in President Gunnarsdottir's private quarters. He sat down at the head of the long wooden table, Yael at a right angle next to him. They sat in silence for several seconds as the grandfather clock ticked loudly and steadily.

His silver hair, his cheek implants, had gone. Here was the man whose face Yael knew well from photographs. Intelligent, calculating brown eyes; well barbered, with a salt-and-pepper beard; skin the color of cappuccino; generous, almost sensual lips.

She said, "We don't have much time. I will be brief, and direct, if I may."

Massoud inclined his head.

Yael started speaking: "Your demands are absurd. A verbal commitment from the president, vice president, and Senate majority leader to the withdrawal of all American forces and military advisers from Iraq. The removal of Hezbollah from the list of terrorist organizations. The cancellation of all military aid to Israel and the ending of all intelligence cooperation. Shall I go on?"

A flicker of a smile crossed Massoud's lips. "No need. There is no expectation that they will be met. They do not need to be, for now. But they are out there, being discussed on Twitter, talk shows, blogs, and in the newspaper comment sections. And once Iran and the United States go to war, they will become part of America's conversation. Soon the body bags will start coming home, and the American people will ask why their sons and daughters are dying, and for what? Each pillar of American foreign policy will crack. Then they will collapse. There is nothing to discuss."

Yael slid her chair back and started to stand up. "You will guarantee me safe passage back to the police line?"

"Wait."

"For what?" asked Yael. She stood behind the chair but did not move.

Massoud said, "You did not come empty-handed."

Yael pressed a button on Ortega's iPhone and then passed it to Massoud. A video window showed a thin young man pacing back and forth in a gray concrete cell. His face was blank but he scratched ceaselessly at his back, his shoulders, his neck, his limbs twitching. Yael glanced at Massoud. The assassin had vanished, replaced by a father. She watched the emotions flow across Massoud's face: the anguish of a parent who is watching his child suffer; the fury that he, as a parent, cannot prevent it; the pure, animal lust for revenge against whoever had done this.

Massoud's fingers were locked solid as he gripped the phone. "How long has he been there?"

"Five years. Since the Americans picked him up. He is in reasonable health, considering."

"Where is he?"

"Utah. In a private prison run by a black ops division of the US government known as the Department of Deniable, or DoD. One hundred miles from the nearest human settlement."

"Who put him there?"

Yael gestured for the phone, and Massoud handed it back. She called up a sound file and played it.

"Now you make sure to do a real good job with that photograph," said Clarence Clairborne. *"We want him looking just right for his daddy's birthday card."*

Yael glanced at her watch, careful not to reveal her tension. It was 6:21. By her calculation, they had six minutes. "The guards, security and catering services are all provided by the Prometheus Group. Clarence Clairborne personally oversaw the tender for the work, the negotiations, and the fine detail of the contract."

Massoud asked, "You can get him out?"

Yael nodded.

Massoud said, "What do we do now?"

A wave of relief coursed through her as Massoud spoke, although she did not let it show on her face. "We" was the smallest but most important word of any negotiation. It showed that the two opposing parties now shared a common agenda. In Massoud's mind, he and Yael were working together. She just had to guide him further down her path. "You stop this. Order your men to stand down. Will they do that?"

"Of course. Then what? How will you get Farzad released?"

"That's the easy part, Salim. The United States is a land of many, and competing, law enforcement and intelligence agencies. The DoD is not popular. It is especially unpopular with the Federal Bureau of Investigation, whose agents have long been waiting to take it down as soon as the right political conditions arise. They raid the prison. Farzad will be freed immediately. He has committed no crimes."

"When will this raid take place?"

Yael said nothing, but gave him a pointed look and then glanced at her watch.

"I need a guarantee," Massoud insisted.

"I give you my word."

Massoud stared at her. "Your word. OK. And Claiborne?"

"He will be taken care of."

Yael and Massoud walked into the front reception room, Massoud with his pistol in his hand. The air was fetid, thick with the smell of blood, fear, and vomit. Everyone stared at them: Kermanzade, Gunnarsdottir, and the Icelandic journalists with a glimmer of hope, and Freshwater, Hussein, and Najwa with amazement. Yael smiled back, as reassuringly as she could, and looked at the clock on the bomb between the four chairs. The timer showed three minutes and fourteen seconds.

Massoud gestured to Ingilin. "Turn off the camera."

She pressed a button and nodded. "It's off."

Kent Maxwell turned to Massoud. "What's she doing

here? And it's time I left. Like now. That was part of the deal."

"You may leave. In fact, I will speed you on your way." Massoud raised his gun and shot the American in the chest.

Maxwell stumbled backward, slid to the floor, blood bubbling in his mouth. Massoud then turned to the journalists. Najwa watched him, wondering if she could grab the gun and somehow turn it on him. The Iranian smiled, as if reading her mind. "You may go. All three of you." He glanced at the timer. "If you run fast enough you will make it to safety."

Najwa and the two Icelandic journalists glanced at each other, a current of understanding passing between all of them.

"No. We'll leave when this is over," Najwa said.

"As you wish," replied Massoud. "But the camera stays off."

"Absolutely." Najwa resisted a powerful urge to touch her lapel, check the thin wire that led to the mobile telephone in the inside pocket of her jacket.

Massoud turned to Freshwater. "Madam President. I will be brief. Even if I were to cut all of your bonds, and those of your colleagues, by then it would too late to reach a safe distance. But, I can defuse the bomb in time."

"What do you want?" asked Freshwater.

"Three things. One: my son is released from your DoD prison. Two: my team is allowed to leave."

"Your son, OK. But your people here, no. Absolutely not. They killed American citizens."

Massoud shrugged. "Casualties of war."

Freshwater refused to meet his eyes, stared ahead, duty struggling with self-preservation—and the lives of her fellow hostages. "No."

Massoud turned on his heel, toward the door.

Kermanzade squeezed her eyes closed.

Hussein said, "Renee . . . please."

Freshwater looked up, swallowed hard, exhaled. "OK. Anything else?" Massoud spoke softly into her ear, and she nodded. "That part would be a pleasure. And now, if you would please . . ."

Massoud walked around to the bomb. The timer showed fifty-eight seconds. He bent over the small keyboard and started entering a series of numbers.

A loud pop. The Iranian tumbled forward, red seeping from his chest.

Najwa instantly turned to Ingilin. "Get this!"

Ingilin swung the camera around.

Maxwell smiled, then suddenly shook as more blood poured from his chest. He jammed his gun under his chin and pulled the trigger. A thunderous boom, and he slumped forward.

The timer showed forty-nine seconds.

Yael crouched down next to Massoud. "The code, Salim, tell me the code."

"Farzad . . ."

"We will free him, I gave you my word, so did President Freshwater. Tell me the code."

"Farzad. . . ." Massoud grimaced. "My son's . . ."

Yael gently shook Massoud. "The code. Please."

"Birth . . ." said Massoud. He shuddered and went limp.

Yael wheeled around. The clock showed thirty-six seconds. Farzad's birthday. But when was it? She knew, she realized. Her mind flashed back to her breakfast with Joe-Don in La Caridad.

Every year his father gets a birthday card from him. Same as yours—August twenty-first," said Joe-Don.

"How old is he?"

"Twenty-six. So he was born when?"

Born when? She had the day, the month, but what year? She couldn't remember. She looked at the clock on the bomb. Thirty seconds.

Focus.

It was now May 2014. If someone was born in August and was twenty-six then they were born in . . . she punched in 2181986.

The countdown continued.

She inhaled hard, entered 218198 when her finger slipped.

The clock showed twenty-five seconds. She heard the sound of her own breathing, murmured prayers in English and Icelandic. Hussein was silent, sitting slumped.

Najwa looked at Ingilin, then at Yael crouched over the bomb, checking that they were getting the footage.

Yael wiped her right hand on her jeans, running the numbers through her head again. If he was twenty-six now, he was born in 1987. August 21, 1987. That was it. She tapped in 2181987. The clock continued ticking down.

Fareed Hussein closed his eyes.

The clock showed twenty seconds.

What was wrong? She had the math now, she was sure.

She tapped in 2181987 again, glanced at the clock.

Fifteen seconds.

Format.

Yael tapped in 1987218.

Ten seconds.

She entered 1987821.

Five seconds.

She tapped in 8211987.

The clock stopped.

36

Yael watched with amusement as Fareed Hussein brushed aside the attentions of the paramedic. The tremulous hostage with a bomb in his lap was gone, replaced by the world's most important diplomat, one with a mission to accomplish. The SG briskly waved away an intravenous drip, his arm still tangled in the gray rubber tubes that led to the blood pressure monitor, sat up on the gurney, pulled out his phone, called Roxana, and started to dictate a statement for a press conference that evening.

The ambulance was making steady progress on Altnesvegur, heading back across the flatlands to downtown Reykjavik. The wide road was almost empty and they were still some way from the outskirts of the city. The sky darkened, layered with thick gray clouds, and rain spattered the windshield. There were five of them inside: Fareed, the paramedic, and the driver, while Yael and Joe-Don perched on passenger seats at the rear next to a gray steel oxygen tank. Yael glanced behind her: a police car followed ten yards or so behind, while another led the way in front.

She leaned against the rear door, feeling the engine's vibration against her back. She had never felt so exhausted, as though every reserve of her energy had been burned through, then further stocks she had not known existed. Every few minutes she shivered from the aftershocks of the adrenalin as it slowly seeped from her system. All she wanted was to get back to her room at the Hotel Borg, lie in a long, hot bath, eat something, and sleep. She watched through the windshield as the gray blur in the distance slowly turned sharper. The outskirts of Reykjavik came into focus, a now familiar vista of a tangle of highways and low-rise apartment blocks.

The driver's baseball cap was pulled so low over his head she was surprised he could see where they were going. The rain flurries were hitting harder now and the light was fading. There was no need for his wraparound mirrored sunglasses, but that was his business. Yael looked at the paramedic. He was dark for an Icelander, and strikingly good-looking, with black hair, ice-blue eyes, and high cheekbones. Something about his appearance seemed almost familiar, but she could not place him.

Hussein finished his call to Roxana and put his phone down. The paramedic untangled the blood pressure monitor cables, removed the sensor pad from Hussein's arm.

"One hundred and thirty-five over eighty. Very good, considering what you have just been through," he said, as he carefully packed away the monitor.

Hussein nodded his thanks, a curious look on his face as he came to the end of his conversation with Roxana. Yael looked again at the paramedic. He had an accent, and it was not Icelandic. He smiled at her. And then she remembered. The Belgrade Hyatt. Waiting for David.

Three more women emerge from the Jeep, followed by six children and two teenage boys. One catches Yael staring at him. He is tall, older than she first thought, perhaps eighteen or nineteen. He has high Slavic cheekbones and striking ice-blue eyes. He smiles, shyly.

He looked much older, wearier, but it was definitely him. What was he doing here posing as a paramedic?

The connections crackled in her mind. Suddenly she was back on the concrete bench at the KZX reception at Columbia University, pushing Bonnet aside, diving to the floor as the brick fragments exploded around her. She remembered his name, and its later appearance in reports from the UN and various intelligence agencies. The special, deadly skill set that he had developed.

Yael glanced at her bodyguard, her eyes flicking to the paramedic then back at Joe-Don. Joe-Don was also staring at him, an unreadable expression on his face. Yael's unease deepened, but she needed first to understand what was happening here.

Yael watched as Hussein ended his phone call and turned to gaze at the paramedic. The two men knew each other, that was obvious. There was tension on the SG's face, but no fear. Then suddenly, Yael knew what he was going to say.

Hussein smiled. "Hello, Armin."

The paramedic turned to Yael. "Miss Azoulay, you are in no danger at all. I am in your family's debt. Your brother saved my life. You and your bodyguard are free to leave."

"Thanks. But I'll stay," Yael said.

"As you wish." Kapitanovic reached inside his pocket,

took out a blue UN laissez-passer, and handed it to Hussein. "Your atonement is finished."

Hussein took the booklet, flicked through the pages. "I don't think so. But I hope yours is."

Yael watched closely, remembering now more detail of both what she had read and the accompanying rumors that swirled around the UN building. Armin Kapitanovic, a young Bosnian man, had escaped from Srebrenica to Belgrade with her brother David's help. A few months later, he crossed the front lines and returned to the besieged enclave. He became a legendary sniper and led raiding parties out of the enclave behind the Serb lines. Kapitanovic survived the fall of the town, but lost his family. His father and brother had taken refuge on the UN base but were forced out by Frank Akerman and the Dutch officers, taken away, and killed by the Bosnian Serbs. His mother hanged herself soon afterward. Then Armin Kapitanovic disappeared.

Sometime in the late 1990s, a few years after the Bosnian war was over, a man called Rifaat al-Bosni had joined the United Nations. He worked with refugees in Kosovo, Chechnya, Iraq, and Afghanistan. In each place that he had been posted, the most brutal militia leaders had been found murdered, often killed with a single shot from a long distance. That much was known. The identity of the sniper was not. Each death triggered a flurry of gossip and speculation. Some said that al-Bosni was the killer. There were even whispers that al-Bosni was really Armin Kapitanovic, the legendary sniper of Srebrenica. Many wondered how al-Bosni had found employment at the UN, but the questions faded away once it was made clear that he had high-level protection on the thirty-eighth floor. Soon after the Syrian war started, al-Bosni disappeared.

Over the years Yael had often wondered what happened to Kapitanovic, even made a few inquiries. But they led nowhere. Now she knew.

She turned to the Bosnian. "The UN forced your family out of the Dutch base at Srebrenica. They all died. Then you went to work for *Fareed*?"

Kapitanovic said, "I wanted to save lives. He gave me the means and the opportunity."

In her exhaustion, Yael struggled to process what she was seeing and hearing. Kapitanovic was al-Bosni, OK. But had Kapitanovic/al-Bosni also been the sniper, the killer of warlords? "The means and the opportunity to do what?"

"To remove bad men."

The SG weighed the laissez-passer in his hand. "It was off-the-books. Nobody knew about it, and there was nothing in writing. It was highly effective. Our humanitarian programs' efficiency always soared after a visit from Armin. Local warlords suddenly became so much more cooperative. Aid convoys passed easily through checkpoints. Many more lives were saved. Rough justice is sometimes the best we can do."

"Exactly," said Kapitanovic as he swiftly reached underneath the gurney and held a Browning pistol to Hussein's head. "Now it's my family's turn."

Joe-Don looked at Yael. His shoulders were tensed, his mouth locked tight. Armin Kapitanovic was al-Bosni. She blinked three times, code for *wait*. Joe-Don inclined his head, almost imperceptibly. Yael knew Joe-Don was unhappy, but he trusted her and would not intervene. And he still had his Glock in the holster against the small of his back.

Hussein glanced sideways at the muzzle of the gun. "Before you pull the trigger, Armin, at least let me say my piece."

The Bosnian nodded.

"Yes, we made another mistake. Another bargain that went wrong. Srebrenica was an irritant, a tiny island of government territory in a Bosnian Serb sea. Everyone knew the war was over. America was pressing us, Britain, France, Germany. Tidy it up. Let Srebrenica go. Give it to the Serbs. Then we can sign the peace deal, the fighting will stop and the refugees can go home. That's why Akerman was toasting the Bosnian Serbs. Not because he liked them. He didn't. Because we all thought it was the end of the war."

Kapitanovic pushed the muzzle against the SG's head. "The prisoners? The eight thousand men and boys. My father. My brother."

Hussein grimaced as he spoke. "There was a deal. It went wrong. They were supposed to be held for a few days, then released."

Kapitanovic's voice rose in anger. "It took days to kill them all. Days when you sat in your office, drinking coffee, sending memos. Why didn't you *do* something?"

Yael judged the distance between her hand and the gun. She caught Joe-Don's eye. He was also taking the measure. They both knew it would be a very risky move to go for a grab. Kapitanovic's finger was on the trigger. The safety catch was off. But more than that, she wanted to hear what Hussein had to say. Kapitanovic was asking the same questions that she had stored up over the years. Hussein had always dodged answering, fobbed her off with platitudes. But now he could not.

The SG continued talking. "Armin, I am truly sorry for your loss. But I work for the UN. We don't have an air force. We try and keep the peace. We do our best. We kept Srebrenica alive through three years of siege. But sometimes we fail. We don't fight wars. You must ask that question in Washington, Paris, London. We didn't know what was happening. Dutchbat had pulled out. So had the military observers. Ask the P5. They knew what was happening, much better than we did. We found out later that there was a satellite feed, to the CIA station in Vienna. They were watching in real time. Men standing, waiting. Men, dead, on the ground. Diggers. Bulldozers. Raised earth. Ask the Americans. They knew. And they did nothing."

Yael saw the pressure of the gun against Hussein's head ease slightly before Kapitanovic spoke. "You have could screamed, shouted, held a press conference, demanded a meeting with the White House, an emergency session of the Security Council. Done something. Anything."

"Yes. I could have. But I didn't. And I will live with that for the rest of my life."

Yael looked at Kapitanovic. His face was fixed, determined, but the Browning was trembling. She slowly reached for the pistol.

Kapitanovic knocked her hand away with the muzzle of the gun. "I told you, Miss Azoulay. You are in no danger here. But please don't interfere."

Yael ignored the pain in her hand, slowly moved it back

toward the gun, her right palm turned upward. She glanced through the front and rear windshields. The police cars were still bracketing the ambulance. No other vehicles were in sight. Armin was operating alone. She shot a look at the driver. He seemed completely unperturbed, kept a steady pace. *Something about him* . . .

Joe-Don's voice broke the silence. "That was a nice shot in Kandahar, Armin. A moving target at what, seven hundred yards?"

Kapitanovic started with surprise. "Eight."

Yael looked from one man to the other, momentarily puzzled. Then she understood. *Sharif.*

Yael gazed at Kapitanovic, kept her eyes on his. "You took a life to save many lives then, Armin. But there has been enough killing today. Give me the gun."

Kapitanovic's hand trembled. He started to speak but no words came.

Yael reached for the muzzle, guided it away. This time the Bosnian did not resist. Kapitanovic handed the Browning to Yael. She passed it to Joe-Don. He immediately slid the magazine out of the stock, checked under the gurney for more concealed weapons. There were none.

Fareed looked at Yael, thanking her with his eyes. He turned to Kapitanovic. "There was nothing you could have done. Akerman was determined to clear the peacekeepers' base."

"On whose orders?"

"Nobody's. Nobody was giving orders. It was complete chaos. Akerman seized control. Everything happened so fast. All our systems collapsed."

"But you didn't stop him."

"No," said Hussein. "I did not."

Kapitanovic turned away, tears flowing down his face.

The driver turned around at the sound. "I hate to interrupt your reunion, but we are almost there."

Yael's stomach flipped over. She got up and walked through the back of the ambulance to the driver's seat. He turned around to look at her. She lifted off his baseball cap and then removed his sunglasses, barely managing to control her quivering fingers.

The driver's eyes were startling. One blue and one brown.

"Hello, *Aba*," said Yael.

Sami sat at the table in Kaldi, his laptop open in front of him. The place was jammed, the hum and buzz of excited conversations so loud he could barely concentrate. A television had been set up on the bar, showing Najwa standing outside the Harpa concert center, surrounded by other journalists who were shouting questions at her. She looked pale, extremely fatigued, and modestly triumphant.

He glanced at his story, which was already up on the *New York Times* website.

ELEVEN DIE IN ICELAND TERROR ATTACK

President Freshwater, Icelandic and Iranian counterparts, UN Secretary-General taken hostage, freed unharmed

---

By SAMI BOUSTANI

REYKJAVIK—At least eleven people were killed today after Iranian terrorists took the presidents of the United States, Iran, and Iceland hostage along with Fareed Hussein, the secretary-general of the United Nations. Six American Secret Service agents died, along with three Icelandic security agents, the president of Iceland's spokesman and Salim Massoud, a senior Iranian official. Kent Maxwell, one of the Americans who was killed, appeared to be working with the Iranians.

The crisis ended when senior UN official Yael Azoulay managed to defuse a bomb that had been placed in the residence with just seconds to spare. The terrorist attack was broadcast live over the Internet by Najwa al-Sameera, the United Nations correspondent for Al-Jazeera, and two Icelandic journalists, Rafnhildur Eriksdottir and Ingilin Sjonsdottir, in part via a concealed microphone after the terrorists ordered the camera feed to be closed down.

Sami's editors were demanding more of everything: more details, more color, more analysis. It was the story of the decade, if not a lifetime. And if he had not been inside the residence, at least he was here in Reykjavik. The concealed microphone he had given Najwa had worked perfectly. He had been able to listen in real time to everything that was happening. And Quentin Braithwaite, who had arrived in Reykjavik a few hours ago, was also proving most communicative about what had happened inside Bessastadir and what would likely happen next at the UN.

Sami was halfway through updating his story when he felt a presence behind him. He did not need to turn to know who it was. He knew her smell, the way the air vibrated around her, the sheer presence of her. The hum of conversation in the bar lessened as the revelers began to notice who had just walked in. Scattered applause sounded, swelling to a rolling crescendo.

Sami stood up, pulled Najwa toward him and held her tight. "Mabrouk," he said. "You made it."

She laughed, gently freed herself, grasped Sami's hands. "So it seems."

Someone thrust a bottle of champagne into his hand. He stared at her: her tousled hair, her crumpled clothes, her scuffed boots. Her brown eyes held his. The bar was completely silent now, with every eye in the room on the two reporters.

Sami had been dreaming about his next move for some time, but he had not anticipated an audience. After today, however, it didn't matter.

The air turned thick between them.

He put the champagne down, pulled Najwa toward him.

She smiled, said, "But what about Y—"

Sami did not reply, only held her closer, felt her breasts crush against his chest, her hair in his hands, breathing in her musky smell, as her mouth opened to his.

37

A couple of hours later, Yael walked into the presidential suite of the Hilton Reykjavik Nordica. Roxana stood up as soon as she saw Yael and walked toward her, radiating enthusiasm.

"Yael, I'm so pleased to see you, it was amazing, incredible what you did today," she exclaimed, air-kissing Yael on each cheek. "Well done."

"Thanks," said Yael, swiftly dodging an oncoming hug as she stepped away and scanned the room.

Roxana ignored Yael's distancing, stepped closer and took her arm as she continued talking. "You saved Fareed's life."

"She did more than that," said Hussein. He was seated at the end of the brown sofa at the far end of the suite. He smiled, stood up, and started to walk toward the two women.

"I know," said Roxana. "We are all so proud of her. She is a hero." Roxana lowered her voice conspiratorially. "Have you heard, there is a rumor that the White House wants to give a dinner in your honor? President Freshwater wants to say thanks. That's twice you have saved her life."

The SG's press secretary was back on form, noted Yael. Her body language was confident and expansive, her hair sleek, her makeup lightly and skillfully applied, her Prada jacket and skirt pressed and spotless. Zest had gone, noted Yael, replaced by something much heavier and richer.

"No," said Yael. "I hadn't. But that's not really my kind of thing. I don't like being in the public eye."

Roxana laid her hand on Yael's arm as she spoke. Her blue-gray eyes were wide open, trusting, entreating—and hoping. "I *completely* understand."

Yael smiled inside. Roxana was so predictable. First the empathy, then the attempt at manipulation. They both knew that after this afternoon Yael was untouchable, at least for the near future. Roxana would instantly be calculating the potential benefits for her career—which were considerable, if she played her cards right and could engineer, if not an alliance, at least a rapprochement with Yael. She and Yael worked for the same boss. All the good press and media coverage generated by Yael's skill and heroism would boost the UN and the SG's image, and so add to Roxana's stature and prestige.

Roxana continued talking. "The last thing you want at the moment is to be the center of attention. But it would be *such* amazing publicity for the UN, and all the good work we do. At least think about it."

"I will, when the invitation arrives. Meanwhile, I need to talk to Fareed."

Roxana's smile faded slightly as the SG stood in front of the two women. She looked puzzled for a moment. "Yael, I don't remember, did we agree to meet here?"

"No," said Yael. "*We* didn't."

Hussein said, "Roxana, leave Yael for now. She has just saved the world. The White House can wait. So can everyone else. We have things to talk about."

Yael stepped back and looked at the SG. He was still paler than usual, but was no longer gray. He smiled at Yael, a genuine smile, full of warmth, as if to say, "I wondered when you would get here."

Once she returned to the Hotel Borg Yael had taken a very long shower and ordered a large, medium-rare hamburger with a small bucket of french fries, which she ate with gusto. After that she had tried to rest for a while, but it was impossible. The questions that she had filed away for years—about Rwanda, about David, about why she continued to work at the UN—were spinning through her head, demanding answers. Tonight, she knew, she would get them. She got up, changed into clean jeans, a T-shirt, and a black turtleneck sweater and made her way to the Hilton.

Roxana watched warily, a half frown on her face, aware of the powerful emotional currents passing between Yael and the SG and wondering how to respond.

For a moment Yael was back on the thirty-eighth floor, the previous Friday morning. Was it really only three days ago that Roxana had, in effect, ordered her out of the SG's offices and Fareed had acquiesced? Yes, it was, give or take a time zone or two. But they all knew that now Yael was the SG's confidant, and Roxana the outsider.

Roxana, however, was not about to cede so easily. She gave Yael her best UN press officer smile, which showcased her white teeth and did not reach her eyes. "Yael, it's fantastic to see you. But Fareed and I are in the middle of planning the press conference," she glanced at her Patek Philippe watch, "in just over an hour, at ten o'clock tonight. How can I help?"

Yael glanced at Fareed. It was a clumsy gambit, and had no chance of success. The SG nodded, almost imperceptibly. She had not made any arrangement to see him but they both knew that their next conversation had been a very long while in the making. Roxana was right, Fareed owed Yael his life. The debt was about to be paid.

Yael said, "You can leave."

Roxana looked confused, then indignant. She began to speak, her voice rising, "Yael, I don't think you understand—"

"I understand perfectly. You asked how you can help. I just told you."

Roxana looked at Hussein, expecting him to come to the rescue.

"Thank you Roxana," said Hussein. "I will call you later."

Roxana stepped back, her mouth open in amazement before she replied. "But Fareed, we have to—"

The SG smiled as he replied, but his voice was cold. "I said, later."

Yael walked over to the floor to ceiling window that looked out over the harbor, feeling the weight of her iPhone in her jeans pocket. Reykjavik sparkled in the night, the apartment block windows a honeycomb of white and yellow, car headlights sweeping along the black tarmac roads, the harbor lights a rainbow of colors shimmering on the water. Mount Esja loomed in the darkness, a great brooding presence. She watched a fishing boat chug into port, its port and aft lights blinking.

Yael turned around to see Hussein watching her. She could feel the emotions running through him: affection, comfort in her presence, guilt. He asked, "Would you like something to drink, to eat?"

"Tea, please."

"Tea for two. Coming right up," he replied as he walked the length of the suite to the kitchen area.

Yael strolled around, taking the measure of the place while Hussein made the drinks. Yael had stayed in hotels around the world, often in very comfortable conditions. But this was probably the largest and most luxurious hotel room she had ever stepped inside. It was certainly the whitest. She stepped inside the bathroom. A large Jacuzzi sat in the center. She quickly checked the shelves: one toothbrush, no women's cosmetics on display.

She walked out, sat back on the sofa. Now, at last, it was just her and the SG. President Freshwater had gone straight to Keflavik airport and would be halfway to Washington, DC, by now. Kermanzade was on her way back to Tehran. Eli was under arrest. Michal was in the hospital under armed guard. After the death of Salim Massoud, the remaining Iranians had surrendered and were in custody. As for Sami and Najwa, well, yes, Sami and Najwa. An Icelandic journalist had already tweeted a photograph of the two journalists embracing and kissing in the Kaldi café, which had instantly gone viral. Yael felt a twinge of jealousy, sure, perhaps of both of them, to her slight surprise. But overall, she was pleased. Najwa was a better prospect for Sami than she ever would be, especially now that she was a journalistic superstar. And lately, someone else was much on Yael's mind.

The SG reappeared with a tray. She watched him pour the drinks, glancing at her uncertainly. She took her tea, then handed him her iPhone. A text message was displayed on the screen.

He read the message, leaned back, exhaled loudly, closed his eyes for several seconds. "Who sent you this?"

"That doesn't matter. Is it true? Did you let my brother die?"

Hussein looked at Yael, started to speak, stopped, looked away. He picked up his teacup and saucer. The white china rattled. A trickle of liquid slopped over the side. He put the cup and saucer back down, not just his hand but his whole body trembling slightly.

Yael sipped her drink and waited.

Hussein sat up. "I don't know whose idea it was. Maybe it was Bonnet's, maybe the French foreign ministry, maybe it was mine. It just seemed to appear out of the discussions, the telegrams and the confidential cables and then suddenly it was part of the consensus, the solution, the thing that we all needed to do. The . . . the . . . *plan* . . ."

"Which was what, exactly?" asked Yael. She put her drink down, pulled her legs up underneath her and leaned back on the sofa. She felt oddly calm and composed.

Hussein closed his eyes, swallowed and started talking. The words poured out.

"David"—he looked again at Yael, guilt and shame written on his face—"and the other eight were supposed to be taken hostage by the Tutsis. Then there would be a rescue mission by French troops. That was Bonnet's responsibility. He was the liaison with the French Ministry of Defense."

"I know that," said Yael. "Bonnet told me. But what came next? What was the point of it?"

Hussein paused, looked at the ceiling for a moment, continued talking. "Once the French rescued the nine UN staff, they would have boots on the ground. There would be some fighting, enough to justify more French troops, a full-scale intervention to back the Hutus. The Hutus were Francophones, the Tutsis favored Britain. Britain had Uganda, so France got Rwanda. That was the deal. The P5 agreed. That's why nobody intervened to save David and the others. They were only supposed to be held for a day or two, then released. But the Hutus had their own ideas. They killed them. They had always planned to. Rwanda turned into a bloodbath, just as they wanted. Then everyone backed away."

Yael's stomach turned to ice. For a second she could not breathe. "So my brother, and the other eight UN workers, died because you, or someone, had a bright idea to gamble with their lives, then another eight hundred thousand innocent people were killed because the P5 were carving up Africa like a turkey at Christmas?"

Hussein looked away, his voice a hoarse whisper. "Yes."

Yael fought to bring her emotions under control. Hussein was telling the truth, that much she knew. But not yet the whole truth. Her voice was level as she continued speaking. "You said this *plan* appeared and then somehow became part of the consensus. But that's not entirely true, is it? You knew all along why David died. All these years. Every time I asked you, you dodged the question, changed the subject. But you knew, all along. Because it was you. It was your idea."

Hussein could not look at her. "I . . . it was . . ."

"Fareed, please. Tell me the truth. The *truth*."

"Yes. *Yes*." Hussein was almost shouting now. "It was *my* idea. I drafted the secret memos. I persuaded the P5 and the other Security Council members." He put his hands on his face, let out a cry of anguish. "Yael, I am so, so sorry."

Yael wiped her eyes with the back of her hand. "So am I."

Hussein swallowed before he answered. "If it had worked . . ."

Yael picked up the tea tray, stood up, and hurled it against the picture window as hard as she could. The crockery exploded, shattering into jagged white fragments as the hot liquid spattered across the glass.

A pounding sounded on the door. Hussein jumped up, suddenly nimble, and walked quickly across the room. He opened the door. "It's fine, we're OK, really, just an accident, we'll clear it up," Yael heard him say.

Hussein turned around and returned to the sofa. He sat down and reached for her hand. She knocked it way, and sat at the other end of the sofa, tears coursing down her face. She picked up a napkin, blew her nose, sat for a few moments breathing deeply and slowly.

Hussein waited for several moments. "I'm so sorry. We gambled with their lives. And we all lost."

Yael blew her nose before she replied. "Why didn't you do something, shout and scream at the P5 to rescue them?"

"I did. I made call after call. I held emergency meetings with diplomats from every one of the countries on the Security Council. They all promised to contact their capitals, push for action, do everything they could."

"Which was?"

"In the end, nothing."

He stared at the window, a faraway look in his eyes as the tea slowly slid down the glass and dripped onto the floor. "After that, and Srebrenica, I realized that I couldn't do these kind of deals. I don't have the skills, or the stomach for it. But someone has to do this work."

Hussein looked at Yael, paused for several seconds, continued speaking. "It took awhile, a decade or so, but eventually, I found someone. Who could operate behind the scenes. Who was much better at dealing with warlords and killers than I ever could be. Someone who could be trained, someone with enough steel to do the cold mathematics, the cost-benefit analyses: justice or peace? Arrest the killers or appoint them to run a government? And someone who reminded me, every day, of the human cost of the mistakes that I had made."

Yael closed her eyes for a moment before she spoke, tried to put her emotions aside and think logically. She had come with a mission: to find out the truth about David's death. So what had she learned? Of course the Rwanda plan for the UN staff had been Hussein's idea. Nobody else would have the contacts and inside information to try and construct such an arrangement. She sensed from the first day she went to work for him that he was involved. Did she believe his claim, that he had met with all the Security Council ambassadors to try and rescue David and the other eight UN workers? There was no way of knowing. In the end there were no blacks or whites, just a sliding palette of shades of gray, of compromise and ambiguity.

And she knew all about that. When Hussein had chosen her to do the P5's most secret work, the behind-the-scenes deals that kept superpower diplomacy rolling and the global corporations in business, she had readily accepted. She had loved it, relished every moment. Warlords were transformed into statesmen. The inconvenient were sacrificed, victims went unavenged, all for the greater good. Because in the end, she could, she told herself, rationalize what she did. But some things could never be rationalized. She picked up her iPhone, called up a sound file, and pressed the play button.

FRENCH MAN: We need at least five hundred. That will have maximum impact.

HUSSEIN: No, no, that is unnecessary. It's far too much. A couple of hundred at most would be sufficient for our purposes. Less would suffice. Even a few dozen.

She expected him to look shocked, or angry. Instead Hussein shrugged, recovering some of his confidence. "My dear Yael, talk is cheap. Did the war happen?"

"No."

"Who stopped it?"

"Me, I guess."

"Who do you think sent you the sound file?"

Hussein placed his palm on her hand. Yael looked down.

One part of her wanted to slap his hand away, walk out of the room, and never see Fareed Hussein or anyone from the UN again. Another part wanted his reassurance.

"You did?"

Hussein nodded. "Yes, I did."

"But you sacked me."

"Only for a while. I had to let you run, on your own. And you did very well. You stopped a war. But that is all in the past now. I am resigning. Quentin Braithwaite will take over as acting SG until the P5 and the General Assembly agree on my successor. I will announce this at the press conference tonight. That is, if Roxana is still organizing it for me. Maybe she will resign as well."

Yael smiled, despite herself. "Roxana? She isn't going anywhere."

"No. I think not. Your job will remain, no matter who replaces me. You will be promoted to undersecretary-general. You can continue in your present role or carve out a new one. You can do whatever you want. If you stay."

"I'm thinking about that. Meanwhile, I would like you to do something for me. Something very much in your interest."

"Which is?"

"You release the Rwanda and Srebrenica documents."

The SG sat back. "How is that in my interest? They will destroy my reputation and any chance of a legacy."

"I don't think so. It was twenty years ago. Another world. You were just a civil servant, implementing policy, not making it." Her voice was barbed. "You can blame the P5. Again."

Hussein blushed, looked away.

Yael said, "Roxana can spin it for you—you will be a pioneer of transparency, facing up to the UN's greatest failures."

Hussein half-frowned, pondering this idea. "And I get?"

"Something you want more than anything."

A pang of guilt shot through Yael. How well the SG had taught her. She watched, first comprehension, then the emotional hunger on his face.

Hussein asked, "Something or someone?"

"Someone. Do we have a deal?"

The SG nodded.

Yael said nothing, looked down at her iPhone, and pressed a button.

A few seconds later the suite's phone rang. Hussein picked up the handset, listened for a few seconds.

"Reception," he mouthed at Yael. "Thank you, but I am not receiving any visitors now. Please direct them to Grace Olewanda, my secretary, or Roxana Voiculescu if they are media interview requests. No, no visitors at all."

He frowned, stopped speaking for a moment, blinked several times in surprise. "She says she is my *what*?" Hussein stared at the phone for several seconds, as if it was the first time he had seen such a device, a look of wonder spreading across his face. "OK. Tell the security detail and send her up."

38

Yael lay back in the thermal lake and closed her eyes, breathing in the sulfurous tang of the mineral-rich water. The night air was cool but the Blue Lagoon was the temperature of a warm bath. She could feel her muscles relaxing, the tension draining away. She checked the clock mounted on the outside wall of the lake's glass-walled café: it was well after ten. He would be here any minute. She waved at Joe-Don, who was sitting by the door, nursing a Diet Coke and watching her carefully.

Yael and her bodyguard had gone straight to the Blue Lagoon from the Hilton. The thirty-mile journey usually took around forty minutes by road. The helicopter that brought them both, and her security escorts, had made it in less than half that time. Two members of the Viking Squad stood on the wooden walkway that ran around the lake, one on Yael's right and the other on her left, machine pistols across their chest. A third stood on an arched bridge, ten yards away, that connected the wooden jetties jutting out into the lagoon. The crackle of their radios drifted through the night.

The water was a milky indigo and thick wisps of white

steam floated above the surface. The lamps around the edge were a soft golden color in the dark. Islands of black, jagged lava jutted out from the water, their bases ringed by white mineral deposits. Shadowed mountains soared in the distance.

Yael had the place to herself. The Blue Lagoon had been cleared for her arrival. She closed her eyes for a few moments, rerunning her conversation with the SG in her head. She too had played a game with someone's life, exploiting and manipulating a lonely young woman. But nobody had died, and a father and a daughter were now talking to each other again. And Rina Hussein was not the only daughter seeking a reckoning with her father.

Yael felt his presence nearby before she saw him, naked apart from a pair of swimming trunks, walking along the wooden bridge towards the Viking Squad policeman. The policeman held his arm out for a second, looked at the new arrival, then stepped aside.

Yael watched Menachem Stein walk to the end of the bridge, onto to the nearby jetty. He placed a small black bag on the wooden walkway and made his way down the steps. She felt her body stiffen as he slid into the water.

"Hello, Yael," he said.

She stared ahead, did not reply.

"Mazel Tov, congratulations. That was good work today."

"You're late," she replied, sliding away.

"*Slichah*, sorry. You only had to wait a few minutes."

"Much more than that," she said, half to herself.

She looked up at the sky. A passenger jet slowly descended to Keflavik airport, its wing lights blinking in the dark. "Still, I suppose I should thank you."

"For what?"

"Istanbul. Shooting Eli's gun out of his hand, when he was chasing me across the roof."

"It was a tricky shot. I didn't want to kill him."

"Maybe you should have. It would have saved me a lot of time and trouble."

Stein leaned back and stretched in the water. A seagull flew low, cawing loudly, wheeled sharply to the right, then soared away.

He cupped some water, let it drain over his head. "I like this place. It reminds me of the Dead Sea. But I never liked Eli. Even less when I saw him threaten you."

"Was that you in New York? The photographs in Joe-Don's mailbox?"

"Of course. A father needs to keep an eye on his daughter. Even if she won't talk to him."

Part of her was pleased by the news, but she would never admit it. "Michael Ortega?"

"Ortega was originally recruited by Clairborne. Then I turned him, to keep an eye on Clairborne. And then to watch you. Thanks for getting him the job as a doorman. That made my life easier."

"How long has this been going on? Your paternal surveillance operation?" Yael asked as she stared at Stein. This was the first time she had seen or spoken to her father in eight years. His hair was grayer, the crows'-feet around his eyes deeper, his features more worn, sharper. He looked calm, but Yael sensed the emotions spinning underneath, his hunger to reconnect, flowing like a charge through the water. *Not yet, Aba, you are going to have to work much harder.*

"Long enough."

Yael asked, "Who else is working for you?"

Stein looked at his daughter, amusement glinting in his eyes. "Guess."

An idea flashed into Yael's mind, one so outlandish it seemed too ridiculous to even vocalize the name. She did so, anyway. "Roxana?"

"From day one. We told her what she needed to know to advance her career. She told us what we were interested in."

"Which was?"

"You, mainly."

Yael stretched her arms and legs out, let them float on the water. "That explains it."

"Explains what?"

"Roxana gave a dinner for some of the UN press corps. All she wanted to talk about was me, or so I heard."

"How else am I supposed to find out how my daughter is?"

Yael looked down, determined not to smile. "And Fareed?"

Stein laughed. "Fareed works for Fareed. But he is always ready to trade."

"Did you kill Schneidermann, so Roxana could be promoted and get you more inside information?

Stein stopped smiling. "Of course not. That was the Iranians. Who do you think I am?"

"I know who you are. I don't know what you are."

Yael lay back and stared at the sky. Stars glittered, thin points of light on a black velvet backdrop. The warm water was soothing. The exhaustion was rolling over her in waves. Part of her, a large part, just wanted to close her eyes and drift off to sleep. But she had so many more questions. "Eli said Mossad placed me in the UN. That they had dirt on Fareed and blackmailed him to give me a job and promote me. That's why they wanted me to come home. So they could debrief me. I've been working for them for years without even knowing it. Is that true?"

"It's part of the truth. One version."

"Tell me yours."

Stein turned towards Yael as he spoke. "We had copies of the Rwanda and Srebrenica documents. We let Fareed know and also that we would be happy if your UN career progressed. He agreed with us. But what you did, what you achieved, you did on your own. Tel Aviv would not be happier if you landed at Ben Gurion and told them everything you knew. But they weren't about to kidnap you. Nobody is going to kidnap you while I am around. Eli set up a rogue operation to bring you back. Nice work, by the way. Ortega was supposed to catch up with you much earlier. But you did very well on your own."

Yael turned to him, then looked away, damping down the emotions bubbling inside her. First she needed to understand, then she could shout, scream, cry, or do whatever it was she felt like doing.

"Who is this 'we' and 'us'?" she asked.

"We have a lot to talk about. I'll get to that."

Stein moved closer. Yael pushed him away, feeling him flinch. "No. We don't. I read the classified files about you. Everywhere where there is violence, conflict, every squalid little war, you are there, providing advice, arms, intelligence, and other 'services.'" Her voice rose with her emotions. "Profiting from all the death and destruction. Kosovo. Darfur. Congo. Syria."

Stein remained calm. "Is that why you wouldn't talk to me for so long?"

"Is that why Mom left you?"

"In part. But when she eventually agreed to hear what I have to say, she started thinking about coming back. At least she and I are talking now."

Yael felt her father's eyes on her, brought her feelings under control. She needed answers. Getting emotional would not bring them. "Who. Is. We?"

Stein dipped his head under the water for a moment, floated on his back before he answered. "*We* is a small group of current and former politicians, industrialists, business people, diplomats, and others who know that sometimes you need to take shortcuts."

"What kind of shortcuts?"

"Necessary ones. To sidestep the system. To get the job done." He turned to Yael. "You know about that, I think."

"Tell me some names. Who?"

Stein slowly shook his head. "I cannot do that."

Suddenly Yael was back in her childhood bedroom in their New York apartment, listening to a babel of languages. "The ones who visited Aleph. You and Mom told me they were clients. But they were your backers."

Stein nodded. "They were both. Aleph started as a research outfit, then we realized that we could act with the information that we had. But we needed a new operation.

We couldn't just launch ourselves like white knights, ready to save the world."

"Which was Efrat Global Solutions?"

"Exactly."

"So Efrat, which had its long and bloody fingers in almost every war zone in the world, was really a force for good, working behind the scenes to save lives."

Stein smiled. "Yes."

"Mom tried to tell me the same thing, when I saw her in New York. Do you really expect me to believe that?"

"It's a lot to process, I understand."

Yael did not answer, swam out into the lake. Stein remained at the side. The water was very buoyant and she floated on her back for a while, staring at the sky, picking out the constellations, listening to the seabirds squawk. A torrent of questions tumbled through her mind. She sorted them into a list.

Her father was leaning against the wooden jetty, his body floating in the water, watching her as she swam back.

Yael positioned herself a couple of yards away and began to speak.

"Kosovo in 1998. You supplied military advisers and intelligence to the Serbs."

"We had people on the ground, yes. They fed us back information. It was passed to NATO. The NATO bombing started, the ethnic cleansing ended. Hundreds of thousands of people went home. Alive. Kosovo is now an independent state."

"Iraq. You worked with Saddam Hussein, through a front company."

"Same story. We only operated in Kurdistan. We gathered information, supplied disinformation to Saddam. Kurdistan is now a de facto independent state. The only success story of that war."

"Darfur. Your operatives liaised with the Janjaweed, the regime's militia."

"We were tasked by the Pentagon with intelligence gathering. We could get in where they could not. At that time, eight or nine years ago, there was serious planning going on for western intervention. But it didn't happen."

"Either way, Efrat made plenty of money. It profited from the wars and the killing and the destruction."

Stein rested his hand on Yael's shoulder. She flinched for a second. Stein said, "Yes, it did. That is the world in which we live."

Yael brushed Stein's hand off. "Congo—KZX and the Bonnet Group? The coltan plot? You were distributing weapons."

"They were duds."

"What?"

"Old, rusty AK-47s. They didn't work. Was there a genocide in Congo?"

"No."

"Why not? Because you were alerted."

"By Fareed."

"And who instructed him to do that?"

Yael closed her eyes for a moment, slid back under the water. The wind had picked up now, was blowing hard and cold. Her father had told Fareed to leak the sound file about the planned attack on the Tutsi refugee camp so she could stop it? It was too much to think about. "Let's say, for argument's sake, that I am prepared to believe something of what you claim. Why didn't you tell me this before?"

"I tried. You wouldn't take my calls. You didn't reply to my e-mails or letters."

"You brought Kapitanovic here so he could kill Akerman."

"I did, yes."

"You facilitated a murder."

Stein stared out over the water. Small waves were breaking the surface. "Akerman had facilitated many more. He was a dead man walking. Kapitanovic had been waiting a long time. It was much worse than you know. Akerman was on the Bosnian Serbs' payroll. He had been since the start of the siege. He used to tip the Serbs off when the Muslim soldiers' raiding parties broke out. He had blood on his hands. He's no loss."

"And Bonnet?"

Stein's face darkened. "Charles Bonnet, more than anyone else, is responsible for the death of David. I don't know what he told you. He was in operational command. Sure, Fareed dreamed it up, a cock-eyed scheme. But Bonnet was tasked with making it happen. Every step of the way. He was working for the DGSE, the French intelligence service, and they knew better than anyone the kind of slaughter that was planned."

"Who was on the roof in New York?"

"Me and Kapitanovic. I was the spotter. He took the shot."

"He missed."

"Only thanks to you."

"Why didn't he fire again? Bonnet was still in range, lying on the ground. Kapitanovic had a laser scope. He couldn't miss."

"There still was a risk."

"Of what?"

"Hitting my daughter."

"The car bomb in DC. The police got a tip-off. Was that you?"

Stein tipped more water over his head, did not reply.

Yael leaned back and exhaled slowly, watching the steam float. "How does Mom know Reinhardt Daintner?"

Stein started with surprise. "What?"

"I saw them at the Columbia reception. He had his hand on her arm. They looked very comfortable in each other's company."

"KZX was a client of ours, once. Barbara handled their account."

"A client or one of your backers?"

"Does it matter?"

Yael waited before she replied. She was no longer sure that she knew the answer. "What do you want, Aba?"

Stein stretched out his arm and picked up the black waterproof bag from the wooden walkway. He took out a thin brass nameplate. "Remember this?"

Yael nodded, suddenly back in her parents' office, when her family was whole.

Stein handed the nameplate to her. "It's time to come home."

39

Clarence Clairborne flipped between the news channels. A day after the terrorist attack, coverage from Reykjavik was still rolling 24/7. He switched to CNN. A male reporter in his forties stood against a familiar, bleak landscape ringed with guard posts and razor wire. His voice faded in and out as helicopters roared overhead, each with the letters *FBI* painted on the side. A SWAT team ran across open ground toward the perimeter fence.

Clairborne's expression did not change. He poured himself a generous measure of bourbon, and took a long swallow, then opened the second drawer in his desk and took out a Colt .45 revolver. He checked the cylinder: six bullets in place. A commotion suddenly erupted in his office anteroom: raised voices, male and female. His office door started to splinter.

He picked up the gun, placed the photographs of his son and daughter in the center of his desk, and raised the barrel to his head.

Yael felt a soft touch on her shoulder, felt the change in the engines' vibrations as the airplane slowly banked. She opened her eyes. The dream was still with her.

She is seven years old, sitting on her brother's shoulders as he strides across Central Park, pretending to be a giant, walking between the trees. Her mother prepares the picnic, her father is play wrestling with Noa. Her little sister is shouting with delight. The sun is shining, the air is warm, and it smells of summer.

The voluptuous brunette flight attendant smiled kindly. "Please lift your seat back up, madame, we are preparing for landing."

Yael nodded, pressed the button on the side of the seat, felt its back spring into place. She dropped her hands to her legs. She could still feel her brother's shoulder muscles under her thighs as the familiar yearning swelled inside her.

She swallowed and wiped her eyes, reached inside her purse, and took out the brass nameplate that her father had given her.

Yael smiled as she ran her fingers over the indented letters: "Yael Azoulay: Office Manager."

She turned the nameplate over in her hands. She had not seen it for more than twenty years. The metal had been polished to a golden shine. She would think about her future and her father's offer. But not today, and probably not tomorrow.

She yawned softly, stretched her legs, looked out the window. The Bosporus shone in the summer sunshine, Istanbul spread along the coastline, beckoning.

THE END

AUTHOR'S NOTE

My interest in the United Nations began in the early 1990s, when I covered the Yugoslav wars as a journalist. That experience led to my nonfiction book *Complicity with Evil: The United Nations in the Age of Modern Genocide*, which examines the UN's failures in Bosnia, Rwanda, and Darfur. I welcome feedback from readers and reply to every e-mail. Contact me at aleborwork@gmail.com or follow me on Facebook or Twitter: @adamlebor.

ACKNOWLEDGMENTS

Like Yael, I was captivated by Iceland. I am especially grateful to Eliza Reid and Erica Jacobs Green, the cofounders of the Iceland Writers Retreat, for bringing me to Reykjavik in spring 2014. Paul and Marigrace O'Friel were warm and gracious hosts during my stay and took me on a memorable hike up the Búrfell volcano. Stefán Eiríksson, formerly of the Reykjavik Metropolitan Police, gave me an informative briefing about crime and law enforcement in Iceland. Lára Aðalsteinsdóttir, Project Manager at Reykjavik UNESCO City of Literature, was an excellent ambassador for Iceland's rich cultural and literary heritage.

As always, a big thank-you goes to my agents, Elizabeth Sheinkman, and Suzanne Gluck. Hannah Wood at HarperCollins in New York was, once again, an outstanding editor, seamlessly zooming out to fix structural problems and zooming in on telling details. Thanks also to Claire Wachtel for launching the Yael Azoulay series, Bill Warhop for his sharp-eyed copyediting, and Katherine Beitner and Amanda Ainsworth for their diligent publicity work.

In London my thanks go to the team at Head of Zeus, especially Anthony Cheetham and Madeleine O'Shea for her thoughtful editing and incisive suggestions. As always, "Z," was a most useful guide to the dark world where American corporate interests meet power politics. Thanks also to my friends and hosts in New York: Peter Green, Bob Green, and Babette Audant, Josh Freeman, and Matt and Emmanuelle Welch. Otto Penzler at the excellent Mysterious Bookshop in Manhattan kindly hosted launch events for both *The Geneva Option* and *The Washington Stratagem*. Thanks also to Jewish Book Week in London for inviting me to chair two events where I could talk about the Yael Azoulay series and to Dan Friedman at the *Forward* newspaper.

Special thanks to Lawrence Lever, of Citywire, who encouraged me to develop a course on storytelling, then made it available to his colleagues. Special Agent Anne C. Beagan of the New York Field Office of the Federal Bureau of Investigation and Lt. Joseph Leal of the UN Department of Safety and Security provided valuable insight. I am grateful to several other UN officials who asked to remain anonymous and to Carne Ross, of Independent Diplomat.

Justin Leighton, Roger Boyes, Clive Rumbold, Andrew Haslam-Jones, Mekella Broomberg at JW3, and Annika Savill were always supportive, as were my fellow writers Alan Furst and Matthew Dunn. Thanks most of all, of course, to my family for their love, patience, and pride in my books.

ABOUT THE AUTHOR

ADAM LEBOR writes for *The Economist*, *Newsweek*, *Monocle*, the *New York Times*, *Literary Review*, and numerous other publications. He is the author of *The Geneva Option* and *The Washington Stratagem*, also featuring Yael Azoulay, and *The Budapest Protocol*. His nonfiction books include *Tower of Basel*, the first investigative history of the Bank for International Settlements; the groundbreaking work *Hitler's Secret Bankers* (short-listed for the Orwell Prize), which revealed the extent of Swiss complicity with the Third Reich; *City of Oranges*, a history of several Arab and Jewish families in Jaffa (short-listed for the Jewish Quarterly Wingate Prize); and *Complicity with Evil*, an investigation into the United Nations' failure to stop genocide. He lives in Budapest.

www.adamlebor.com

@adamlebor